At Plains University, [......]
But when they ent[......]y
become something m[......]

SHELBY is **MORGAN**,
a sagittarius, expert with bow and arrow.

INGRID is **FEL**,
a miles—a sword-wielding gladiator.

CARL is **BABIECA**,
a trovador, skilled at music—and theft.

ANDREW was once **ROLDAN**,
an auditor who specialized in combat magic.

At the university, their lives are dull and predictable. In the city of Anfractus, they use their wits, their skills, and their imaginations to live other exciting and sometimes dangerous lives.

And now that danger has followed them home. . . .

o

PRAISE FOR

PILE OF BONES

"An absorbing tale of role-playing, magic, and the danger that can ensue when the boundaries between the real and the make-believe disappear . . . Intelligent . . . [A] fascinating read."
                                                                —*RT Book Reviews*

Ace Books by Bailey Cunningham

PILE OF BONES
PATH OF SMOKE

PATH OF SMOKE

BAILEY CUNNINGHAM

ACE BOOKS, NEW YORK

THE BERKLEY PUBLISHING GROUP
Published by the Penguin Group
Penguin Group (USA) LLC
375 Hudson Street, New York, New York 10014

USA • Canada • UK • Ireland • Australia • New Zealand • India • South Africa • China

penguin.com

A Penguin Random House Company

PATH OF SMOKE

An Ace Book / published by arrangement with the author

Ace Books are published by The Berkley Publishing Group.
ACE and the "A" design are trademarks of Penguin Group (USA) LLC.

For information, address: The Berkley Publishing Group,
a division of Penguin Group (USA) LLC,
375 Hudson Street, New York, New York 10014.

ISBN: 978-0-425-26107-1

PUBLISHING HISTORY
Ace mass-market edition / August 2014

PRINTED IN THE UNITED STATES OF AMERICA

10 9 8 7 6 5 4 3 2 1

Cover art by Gene Mollica.
Cover design by Lesley Worrell.
Interior text design by Kelly Lipovich.

For my father.
You gave me Walt Whitman, Annie Dillard,
Madeleine L'Engle, Leonard Cohen.
You offered me stories about brave rabbits
and drew me a secret map to a numbered island.
You bound my first book and read my raw stories.
You carved me a frog with my name on it.
There will never be enough coffees and drives
down the hill. I remember the day you let
go of the bike, and I flew, for the first time.
Thank you.

Acknowledgments

I'd like to thank the usual suspects for making this book possible. Mom, Dad, and Lee, thanks for your continual support. Medrie and Mark, thank you for your conversation and warm hospitality. Rowan, thanks for fixing my pumpkin. Bea and Danielle, thanks for the blue room. Marty and Jamie, thanks for the Christmas-light tour and for always being my compass points. Ken, thanks for wandering through the stacks with me (and for introducing me to dark elves). Melanie, thanks for the great conversations about writing and for inspiring me with your own work. Kathleen, thank you for the advice you've given me about teaching. I love how you see the world. Alexis, thanks for reminding me how cool the eighteenth century was (even with its nose problems). I'd also like to thank my students for getting me to think about *Beowulf* and other influential texts while I was writing this. And a final thank-you to the Green Spot Café in Regina, where I worked on the manuscript while slowly becoming addicted to their steamed bun and sour soup. On what felt like the coldest day of winter, the owner traced a heart on my coffee to warm me up.

Sometimes, it's the little things that give you the energy to keep going.

PRONUNCIATION

Most of the terminology in the book comes from ancient Latin. We have scant knowledge about how people in first-century Rome may have actually sounded, but classical linguists have done their best to reconstruct this. I base my own pronunciation on the recordings of Wakefield Foster and Stephen G. Daitz, which can be streamed here: www .rhapsodes.fll.vt.edu/Latin.htm.

The vowels *a* and *o* are generally long, while the short vowel *i* sounds like *EE*. The consonants *c* and *g* are always hard, as in *cat* or *gold*. The modern-day term *Sagittarius* would sound more like *sag-ee-TARR-ee-us*. The consonant *r* is rolled slightly when singular, and more strongly when doubled, like the Spanish or French *r*. The word *Anfractus* has a slight growl to it: *an-FRRAC-tus*. The *um* ending is nasal, resembling the French *u*. French would elide the final syllable, but in Latin, it's voiced. The consonant *j* more closely resembles *y*, so *Julia* becomes *Yulia*. The consonant *v* is never pronounced as a hard *v*, but rather as *w* or *iu*, which means that *impluvium* would sound like *im-PLOO-wee-um*. The only exception is *trovador*, which comes from Occitan rather than Latin.

I've tried to obey rules of grammatical gender and plurality, except in the case of *nemones*, an invented plural form of *nemo*.

PART ONE

TROVADOR

1

HE SAT IN THE WINDOW OF THE BLACK BASIA, watching the Subura below. It was a hive of drunken people, sweating and belching and singing as they clogged the narrow streets. They were on the hunt for something that could only be found in this quarter. Nobody came here for the food. The alleys were a city of their own, full of treasures and bleak endings. A familiar alley might turn into a trap before your eyes. Anfractus never stayed the same for long, and the Subura was its dark heart. People came here in search of solace, odd miracles, and luck. The furs waited for them, clinging like moss to the stone walls. Their charms and delicate hooks could snag a purse in seconds. Babieca pulled his knees up to his chest. He could smell the fish sauce from the caupona across the street. The sky was beginning to darken.

He was only two stories up, but the fall would still break something. He loosened his grip on the sill. A trovador had once told me that you could sing yourself a staircase. Not a real staircase. More like one of the stone skyways that criss-crossed the horizon. If you sang the proper song, you could make the air thicken, just enough to support your weight. He swore that he'd seen someone do it. But he was a drunken senex, with very few teeth, and Babieca didn't trust what he said. A song like that would be something rare and dangerous. The notes would play you without mercy, and when it was done, you'd be someone else. Someone who knew how to walk on air.

"If you fall," a voice said, "someone will have to settle your bill."

Babieca climbed down and replaced the shutter. The street noise was muffled, but he could still hear it. He reached for the cup of wine that he'd left by the bed. It was made of cheap blue glass, although it bore a slight resemblance to a more expensive design. He drained the cup, then refilled it.

"You're the father of this house. Can't you forgive my debt?"

Felix paused in the act of fastening his sandals. "I suppose I could. It would make more sense to auction off your possessions, though. Your lute might be worth something."

"It's got a crack."

"Most things do." He slipped on his tunica, dyed saffron and covered with rich panels of embroidery. "What about your cloak? That's worth something."

Babieca shook his head. "I stole it. I liked the tigers dancing along the edges. They think they're real."

"That wine is going to your head."

"I know. That's the point."

"Don't drink too much more. Aren't you supposed to be at the domina's party?"

"There's time."

Felix sat on the edge of the bed. His mask was silver, and carved with things that Babieca couldn't quite make out. Wings, or olive branches, maybe.

"I've never seen you without that," he said.

Felix looked at him curiously. "Of course you haven't. It's a part of me."

"Maybe the only real part."

"Watch yourself. I could have you barred from this house."

"You wouldn't do that."

"Care to try me?"

He approached the bed and took Felix's hand. His thumb traced the amethyst ring, carved to resemble Fortuna's wheel. "You wouldn't throw me to the furs."

The meretrix looked at him for a moment. Then he took his hand away. "This won't happen again."

"You've said that before."

"I mean it this time." Felix rose. "We have to stop."

"Why?" Babieca drew closer. "What's the harm?"

"It's pointless."

"It was fairly pointed a moment ago. Or have you forgotten?"

Felix adjusted his tunica. "It was a bad choice."

"One that you keep making."

"Babieca—"

He touched Felix's hair. It was slightly damp. "I think we fit."

The mask regarded him. "Not with each other."

Babieca's hand dropped. He was stung, but smiling. "I guess it's true what they say about meretrices being fickle."

"You know it's not that."

He sat on the bed, which still smelled like both of them. "Don't let me keep you. I'm sure you have several more cocks to fall on."

"More like balancing the ledger."

"How much for another hour?"

His eyes darkened. "Keep your coin."

"No, truly—how much?"

Felix looked at him for a long moment. Then he left the room.

Babieca lay down. The sheets were patterned with small, indeterminate animals, leaping over thickets. Maybe they were foxes. Nothing seemed real, save for the odor of sweat, smoke, and grilled cabbage from the caupona below. He touched the pillow. It was unraveling in the corner. He didn't know what made him push Felix. Something about the mask, and the way it changed his eyes. The mask was naked—it was the rest of his body that remained hidden. Everyone knew this about meretrices, of course. Spadones were the only gens who were more accomplished at hiding their emotions. He imagined them playing Hazard, the eunuchs and the wolves, caught in a perpetual stalemate. Nobody blinking. The unwrinkled surface of their faces like blank papyrus.

What had brought them together? The first time seemed hazy around the edges, like a furtive moment stolen in the baths. It had been hot—that much he remembered. The paving stones had become coals, burning unprotected toes whenever someone slipped. Laughter, imprecations, the sour stink of wine. He'd run into Felix while heading toward a cell downstairs, the coin in his hand. He'd wanted a mouth to devour him, bones and all, spitting him out like an owl-pellet after it was done. Felix had appeared in the narrow door, hair slick with sweat, digging a rock out of his sandal. They were both wilting from the heat. Babieca had looked up at him, at his mask, glowing like metal from the forge. What was said? He could only remember a few scattered words. *Once.* That haunted him. *Once.* A promise and a threat. Felix had broken his word. Perhaps he'd intended to.

Babieca sipped the wine. Once, he had nearly fit someone else. He remembered a tongue like a lock-pick in his mouth, a charm to release the exhausted mechanism. There'd been a stone bed, a fox, a little death. Fortuna's mark on smooth skin. He looked down at his own thigh, smudged with dirt and sweat, but unmarked. No daub of paint. Had the river washed it away? He thought of the face, pale as boxwood. The expression of relief as every angle softened. Maybe all he'd ever wanted was silence. Babieca took another drink, but forgot that he was supine, and spilled some. Red droplets flushed to life against the fabric. They blurred the lines of the possible-fox, until it resembled a tinted shadow.

He was almost a meretrix himself. They shared a spoke on Fortuna's wheel. The irony was that meretrices—not the desperate pretenders who fucked unmasked in tiny cells, but those who belonged to a legitimate basia—were infinitely more respectable than him. A trovador was only as good as his next song, and he had no courtly connections to exploit. He was supposed to perform at Domina Pendelia's tonight, but only in the background. A trained monkey could do it. He got dressed, then hunted for his instrument. Sometimes, Felix would ask him to play. *Once.* A smile playing at the edge of his mask. He found the lute under the bed, next to its case. His thumb found the crack, the way a tongue would find a loose tooth. He traced the groove in the lacquered wood.

How did it happen?

The auditor loved to ask. Dozens of times, he'd asked, thinking that this time it would work. Babieca would smile slightly and look away.

I'll tell you when we're older.

The hardest thing hadn't been watching him drown. That happened too swiftly. He'd barely had time to wipe the blood from his eyes, and then he was surfacing. No. The hardest thing had been the ride back, their bodies lashed together by a belt. The feel of him, still slightly warm, but empty. His doll's head bobbing gently against Babieca's shoulder. And he wanted to hold the auditor in that safe little crook forever, but he wasn't holding anything. Just a lukewarm vessel whose contents had already begun to settle. He'd held on to the hand, regardless. The knuckle with its funny islet of bone, protruding slightly. Like the crack in the lute. He closed the case and swung it over his shoulder.

Maybe Felix and Drauca visited each room, making the beds together. They were called father and mother, after all. Some of their chores should be ordinary. He rubbed at the wine on the sheets but only succeeded in making it worse. Fortuna stared down at him from the mural above the bed. She was dancing with a silenus, who grasped at her silks. Babieca couldn't imagine a time when the silenoi had danced with anyone. He'd heard rumors that some of the basia were willing to service them, but that must have been a dangerous transaction. Sex with a homicidal goat. It would take an experienced mask to pull that off.

He slipped on his sandals, then grabbed the cup for good measure. The wine was too sweet, but he'd stopped discriminating a few cups ago. It occurred to him that he'd never seen Felix drinking at the basia. Nothing but water. He supposed it was safer to keep your wits about you. Still, there was something disconcerting about it. Like a host who remained forever lucid while his guests tore the walls down. He left through the narrow door. A man was passed out in the hallway, drooling thin ribbons of wine. Babieca saw a shadow in the corner. A fur, most likely. The shadow hesitated. They seemed to face each other for a moment, although he couldn't tell precisely what he was looking at.

Trovador and fur—different spokes, but irresistibly related to each other. The Fur Queen ruled the undercity from her hidden tower, its roots clutching the wreckage of Old Anfractus. The rest of the towers scraped the sky, but the Fur Queen's tower was sheathed to the hilt underground, hidden from view. A tree growing in reverse. Babieca started to say something, but the shadow was already gone.

At least they had a queen. Trovadores had nothing but a circle of pretenders, all claiming to be the "arch-bard" or some other ridiculous title. They lacked organization, connections, respectability. Their tower was an endless drunken song. Or so he'd heard. The gens wouldn't accept itinerant players. Only those with a reputation were allowed in, and Babieca was a nemo, an unknown. *Snap a string,* they'd say, whenever he tried knocking on the door. Now, at least, Morgan was in the same boat. The Gens of Sagittarii had repudiated her. They could be outcasts together, enjoying their shared marginality. Morgan, though, wasn't quite as serene about her exile. The spicy life of a jongleur was one thing— everyone talked about how exciting it must be—but there were no satisfying stories about homeless archers. Morgan had been the only die-carrying member of their false company. The most respectable among them. Now she was without a gens, and they were without an auditor.

He made his way down the corridor. It was getting dark, so he unhooked one of the bronze lamps and took it with him. It was shaped like a dwarf riding a giant cock. His expression, obscured by wear and drops of oil, was hard to read. Babieca thought that he would probably be more nervous to mount a giant phallus. Where would it take him? How would he steer? The dwarf's expression was placid, though, as if this sort of thing happened all the time.

Babieca descended a short flight of stairs, and then the corridor widened. He set down the lamp and walked toward a new source of light, until he found himself in the atrium of the black basia. The floor was covered in a mosaic of blue, green, and white tesserae. It depicted Fortuna as the mother-meretrix, spinning her wheel, as various couples danced beneath. The mosaic was tamer than the friezes, in which every possible act of love (and a few impossible ones) were displayed in vibrant colors. Even the lares were pictured, although nobody was quite sure how they mated. Salamanders joined tails, while undinae gathered in an underwater embrace, their ragged hair filled with shells and seaweed. Gnomoi kissed beneath the earth, like blind moles in love. Only a few people had ever seen a gnomo, so the depiction was a bit fanciful. They resembled pale children with long fingers, each ending in a claw that could scrape rock and sift through precious minerals.

The fourth family of lares—the caela—hovered in the borders. The artist had used dark tesserae, rendering them as clouds or scraps of mist. Nobody had seen one in centuries. They'd been included purely for the sake of continuity. Their eyes were voids. Babieca found it difficult to look at those pinpricks of plaster, holes in the world that threatened to devour him. Those eyes saw him for what he was, and for a moment they held him, pinioned to Fortuna's spinning wheel. He blinked and looked away. They weren't coming back anytime soon. They'd been gone when Anfractus was still a primitive settlement—a warren of huts, caves, and cook-fires.

The atrium was full of revelers, all wreathed and spilling wine on each other. He fit right in. A few of the more cautious ones stood against the pillars, nursing a glass of sweet hippocrene while they watched the festivities. He noticed more than a few women on the edges, carefully considering what they might want. Some were veiled, while others had trimmed their hair short, in the style of the female barbers who worked beneath the aqueduct. The women didn't drink nearly as much. They needed to remain on guard, even in a space as removed from the city as this. A delicate transaction always had the chance of turning deadly, and it was better to be armed. The meretrices carried numerous weapons— Felix had pointed a few of them out to him—and Babieca was amazed at how a comb, a necklace, or a ring could be transformed into a killing device. His own stubby gladius, barely a blade at all, seemed paltry in comparison. Poor old thing. He'd been meaning to replace it, but money was tight.

A spado passed him, wearing a mint-green tunica and an embroidered cap. His heart seized for a moment. But it wasn't Mardian. Just a smooth, round man with wispy blond hair, scanning the room with a practiced eye. His chin was bare, save for a few pale whiskers. Mardian was more solidly built. This one was a palace eunuch, perhaps one of Eumachia's retinue. Babieca imagined him tucking in the daughter of the basilissa, wishing her sweet dreams as he snuffed out the lamp by her bedside. Or maybe he sang to her in his sweet, trilling voice. A song about the Anfractus of memory, where salamanders danced in the streets and the fountains poured wine. There was no curfew, no hurried running for cover at sunset. The silenoi remained in the forest, lacking the temerity to approach the gates. Like bears or mountain lions, they were an abstract part of nature, safely removed from everyday life. A city whose streets weren't perilous by night. That would have been something to see, if it had ever existed.

The musicians sat in their alcoves, playing languidly on the cistrum. Their tempo was a slow burn, filled with the gentle clinking of bronze rings, the slap of bare feet on marble. Babieca looked down at his own feet, dirty in mended sandals. The nearest block of marble had been carved with a cheerful phallus, beneath which was the message: *Here resides pleasure.* This one didn't have wings, or a dwarf riding sidesaddle. Its crudity suggested that it was older than the rest of the atrium. There were similar paving stones throughout the city, meant to provoke laughter and guide people toward the Subura. Occasionally, the meretrices would pass out loaves of bread and sweetmeats that were shaped like sex organs. Tonight, the only fare was roasted chestnuts—the kind sold at the Hippodrome—and he'd already eaten too many.

He heard someone murmur, and looked up from the cock near his toe. A woman was making her way slowly into the atrium. She leaned on an ivory cane, and her left foot dragged behind her, its delicate sandal grinding across the marble. Her left arm trembled as she moved, and the fingers of her hand clenched and unclenched, as if the hand possessed its own agenda. Her head lolled a bit to one side, and her face was narrowed in concentration as she took one step, then another, gripping the cane for support. Babieca was struck by her beauty. Unlike the fashionable dominae, whose hair was forever being teased into a tower of pins and golden thread, she wore a delicate braid that fell across one shoulder, tied with a scarlet ribbon. Her stola was made of cream-colored silk, with a hint of purple in the embroidery. Her ivory mask was carved with images that Babieca couldn't quite make out. Like Felix's mask, it seemed to shift in the lamplight, unsettled and full of possibilities.

The musicians played more softly. People continued to talk, but they were all watching her. They didn't even try to conceal their interest. Suddenly, Babieca was happy to be a nemo, an unknown. He couldn't endure the weight of their stares, the bite of their curiosity. He watched them whispering to each other, clucking slightly or exchanging knowing glances, while she focused on each step. Their looks and murmurs couldn't quite reach her. They stopped at her mask. She looked up, and Babieca saw that her green eyes were sharp. They betrayed nothing.

She scanned the crowd and then gestured slightly with her right hand. A small crook of the finger. Although she wasn't looking at him, Babieca felt that she could see him clearly, in spite of his nobodyness. He shifted. Felix was one matter, but this was Drauca, the house mother. You didn't simply approach her. Not unless you wanted everyone to notice you, and that was the last thing that he needed right now.

A boy emerged from the crowd. He was beautiful and unmasked, which marked him as an apprentice. He was clad in the tunica praetexta of a high-placed adolescent, with its red stripe signifying his youth. Drauca smiled at him. Then she made a strange gesture with her right hand. It was hard to discern the shape that she traced, but it reminded him of the sign language used by merchants in the Exchange. Different hand shapes corresponded to different numbers, and the merchants were able to have polite conversations with their clientele, while their hands clashed and bartered ruthlessly. These hand shapes were more complex, and he couldn't tell what was being said. The boy responded in kind, even more swiftly than Drauca. She smiled with a hint of pride. Then she made one last hand shape, and the boy dissolved into peals of laughter.

Now the whole atrium was staring. His laughter was high-pitched, almost braying. There was something sweet about it, but also a little odd. Then Babieca realized that he was deaf. He didn't respond even slightly to the music, or the whispers. Instead, he concentrated entirely on the weft of Drauca's hands. His own movements were steady and fluid, while hers wavered, on account of her trembling fingers. Perhaps it constituted an accent. She smiled and touched his smooth cheek with her hand. Then he disappeared into the crowd.

Babieca felt a hand on his shoulder. He turned and saw Fel. Usually she worked outside the basia. It was rare for her to venture inside. The fading light from the impluvium sparkled against her scale lorica. She reminded him of a frieze. *Frozen miles.* One hand rested on the chipped hilt of her sword.

"There's a drunk passed out in the hallway," he said. "Don't you normally deal with that sort of thing?"

"Right now, I'm more concerned with the drunk in the atrium."

He scowled. "I'm perfectly lucid."

"Touch your toes, then."

"Fuck off."

"We have to go. The party will be starting soon."

"Nobody's going to miss a nemo trovador. Here." He started to remove his lute case. "You can give this to one of the servants from the undercroft. They'll strum just as uselessly in the background, I promise."

"She asked for you."

"That's because she likes to see me suffer. It's one of her pastimes."

He tried to catch Drauca's gaze, but she was already shuffling out of the atrium. Her cane tapped a soft cipher against the ground. Everyone had returned to the business of drinking and sizing each other up. He sighed.

"What's your interest with the house mother?"

"She's beautiful."

"Stay away from her, trovador."

"Why? I've charmed one meretrix, already."

"You're as charming as a fart in the frigidarium."

He blinked at her. "You're full of crotchety wisdom tonight."

"When you stand in one place for hours on end, you learn to study people. I understand them, and I understand you."

"What do you understand about me?"

"That you're a kitten who likes to annoy great cats. Eventually, though, one of them is going to take a swipe at you."

"At least you've offered me an adorable metaphor."

"Let's go."

He frowned at her. "It's not like we live in different worlds. Aren't we all just climbing the same ladder?"

"If that's true," she said, guiding him by the arm, "then you're on the bottom rung, and she's near the top. Your chances of being shit on are remarkably high, but you won't accomplish much of anything else."

"I'm a good climber."

"You can barely walk in a straight line."

"Fine." He allowed himself to be led toward the door. "I'm a competent stumbler."

"Let's fill that cup with water."

"No. It's too late for that. If I sober up now, I won't be able to play."

"That's sad."

"You just don't understand music."

They made their way through the crowd and exited the basia. The sky above them was the color of the boy's tunica, a brilliant red stripe. As the sun set, people quickened their pace, in search of egress or entertainment. The basiorum were protected—mostly—which made them a preferred destination. A pack of silenoi weren't going to break down the door. They wanted a proper hunt, and there was no sport in killing those who couldn't at least run or put up a fight. The baths and cauponae were safe for that same reason. The alleys behind them were a different story, as were the skyways above. The silenoi thought of them as a network of stone branches, part of a giant tree that shaded the city, and they liked to climb.

Anfractus was a very different place after dark. You rolled with your life every time you ventured down a blind alley, but it was a city of alleys. Unless you were willing to explore them, you'd spend all of your time gambling, eating, or stretched out in ecstasy. Not a bad existence, but it cost money. Fear had turned many into furs. Once you ran out of coins, either you learned how to steal or you fled.

They walked down Aditus Papallona, which cut across the entertainment district. A few people looked suspiciously at Fel but said nothing. The sight of armor made them nervous. The commerce of the Subura wasn't exactly beyond the pale, but it carried an element of risk. Nobody wanted to run afoul of the miles, who patrolled this area in force. They didn't realize that Fel was barely a miles. The gens accepted her, but to them, she'd always be a sentry who guarded a brothel. Her contacts were unreliable. It was for that very reason that she escaped notice.

"Why does she need another party?" Babieca asked. "Her fucking life is a party."

"Just be thankful that she never turned us in."

"Is that our measure of an ally? People who don't try to have us killed?"

She steered him away from a caupona. "There aren't many safe spaces left for us. The basia is protected, and my gens doesn't give a cracked die about me, so I can still roam the city. But you and Morgan have to stay hidden."

"Nobody knows me."

"People saw you." She lowered her voice. "The basilissa's daughter. Mardian. Those miles that we attacked."

"Felix."

"He's protecting you."

"I'm not sure I'd call it that."

"I don't know what game you're playing with him, but you'd best stop. You aren't the only person who needs his help. If he decided to turn his back on us, the entire company would be exposed."

"We're not a company."

Babieca watched an auditor pass. He wore a patched tunica and was talking to something invisible that seemed to be following him. A salamander, most likely. The trotting shadow must have said something funny, because the auditor snorted, then kept walking.

Everything has a chaos, he'd said. Salamanders lived in fire. Gnomoi lived beneath the ground, breathing basalt. Air was the chaos of humans. They'd stolen it from the caela, the lares of wind and smoke. Nobody remembered precisely how such a theft had taken place, but people were here, and the caela were gone. Did they lose a bet? Was it simply a bad spin of the wheel? Fortuna did like to keep things interesting.

A few months ago, they had sneaked into the Arx of Violets and committed treason against Basilissa Latona. They'd climbed up through the toilets and crept, reeking and scared, to the patio of lions. That was where they'd heard Latona say that Anfractus wasn't enough. She wanted Egressus, and she was willing to kill Basilissa Pulcheria in order to take the city. Saving Pulcheria had been their first quest. But now they were three instead of four, and Latona wanted them dead. If there was something worse than dead, she wanted that too. He'd felt a flicker of hope while Narses, the high chamberlain, was leading them. But he was gone.

Now there was only Mardian, his twisted apprentice, shadowing them at every turn.

Of course, Babieca thought, *if someone had burned my face off, I'd probably be looking for a bit of revenge too.*

They turned onto Via Rumor, the busiest street in the city. Most people were heading for their own alleys. They lacked the experience or the connections to remain after dark. That was where he should have been going, but Domina Pendelia offered them a certain degree of protection. There wasn't likely to be bloodshed at her house. A lot of drinking, a few stolen kisses in the garden, but that was it. Even Morgan was safe there, so long as nobody figured out who she actually was.

Her domus was in an old and fashionable vici, a bit removed from the clamor and foot traffic of Via Rumor. Glowing braziers flanked either side of the blue door. Fel knocked lightly. A member of the house staff appeared.

"Do you have an invitation?"

Babieca patted his lute case. "I'm the entertainment. She's the muscle."

He looked dubiously at Babieca. "You're drunk."

"Merely lubricated. Now let us in. Unless you want to explain to your domina that one of her instruments has gone missing."

"Fine. Don't talk to the guests."

They walked through a dim corridor. The only light came from the lararium, where someone had lit candles and left a few scraps of oil-soaked bread. Flies buzzed around the crumbs, and tears of wax obscured the image of the lares. All he could make out were eyes and claws, indistinct against a peeling background. It was good luck to leave a coin, but he couldn't spare anything. He stopped, briefly, to rearrange the bread crumbs. Fel looked at him strangely but said nothing. Then they kept walking until they reached the atrium.

Every lamp in the domus had been lit, and even with the fresh air coming through the skylight, the room was hot. People lounged on triclinia, drinking, sucking oysters, and dipping crusty bread into bowls of fish sauce. The smell of the food was overpowering. Trestle tables had been set up throughout the room, and they were covered with delicacies: roasted boar, spiced quail eggs, and dormice rolled in honey. There were delicate mushrooms, and cow udders that had been stuffed with something that he'd rather not know about. He put a few mice into his tunica, before Fel could notice. Something nudged his foot. He looked down and saw a tiny frog machina, its gears whirring as it brushed against his toe.

"Sorry. He got away."

Julia emerged from the crowd. She was wearing a head scarf, but a few strands of red hair had escaped, and they fell across her eyes. Brushing them away, she knelt down and retrieved the mechanical frog. It trembled in her hands.

"So I'm not the only entertainment," Babieca said.

"What can I say? Drunken idiots go wild for things that hop."

"I thought you didn't like playing with toys."

"I like the feeling of a full purse." Julia looked up at Fel. "It's nice to see you both. I suppose it's been a while."

"More than a month," Babieca said. "Not that we're counting."

"I meant to send you a tablet."

"It's fine," Fel replied. "We aren't—" She searched for the right word. "You know what I mean. There's nothing that binds us together."

"Not anymore." Babieca examined the frog. "It may be a toy, but it's still a bit of genius. Did you make it?"

She looked a little embarrassed. "I had help. But yes."

"Well done. Now, all you have to do is equip them with poison darts, and we'll have a truly interesting party."

"That's actually not a half-bad idea," Fel observed. "You could make a fortune if you partnered with the Gens of Sicarii."

"I've got enough problems without involving assassins in my life." Julia looked down at the metal amphibian, which strained against her hand. She was awkwardly silent for a moment. Then she smiled at Babieca. "Well, I should look for the rest of them, before they crawl under the domina's bed. May Fortuna smile on your music."

"It's not mine," he said. "But thanks."

Julia disappeared into the crowd. Babieca felt a strange sadness as he watched her go. An artifex would make four. Not quite the same, but still, they'd be a company once more. There'd been a moment, after the grim business at the harbor, when he'd thought that Julia might join them. But she wouldn't step into the shadow of the auditor. Babieca didn't blame her. They were under the wheel now, their faces pressed into the mud. Joining them would have been folly. Better to hang on, even if it meant chasing frogs.

"I'm going to patrol the undercroft," Fel said.

"All you'll find are people fucking in the hypocaust."

"Well, it's a living. Are you going to be fine?"

"Yes." He unpacked his lute. "I suppose I will be."

Fel descended the stairs that led to the domina's dusty undercroft. He'd worked there once, stoking the hypocaust. It seemed like a lifetime ago, but really, it hadn't been so long. Breaking his back for hours so that the domina could enjoy a heated bath. Until the day that a lean shadow had wandered in.

You'll get more heat if you leave some roasted pumpkin seeds in the corner. That's where the salamander sleeps.

He took his place among the musicians, who had arranged themselves near the impluvium. Orchids danced in the water as they played. Babieca's fingers knew the melodies, and his concentration wandered. He watched the lovely, rich people seated on couches before him, exchanging gossip. They picked their teeth, cleaned their ears with tiny silver spoons, and pressed forward with their ragged alliances. Beneath the uncertain lamplight, he saw a flash of bracelets, a tall wig on fire with opals, naked feet and blurred mouths, like the lares gently disappearing on their shrine. All the duplicity and beauty in the city of Anfractus seemed to be gathered here, a storm whose perfection could destroy him.

At one point, a spado joined them. He sat on the edge of the impluvium, framed by orchid shadows, and sang. His voice was ermine. High and aching, it was beyond anything that Babieca's poor instrument could produce. It filled him with a strange sense of grief, although he couldn't say exactly what was sad about it. The song was in a language that he didn't understand. The speech of the founders, perhaps, or something from beyond the forest. He caught one word, a word that seemed oddly familiar. But before he could remember where he'd heard it, the people were clapping, the spado politely inclined his head, and the word vanished.

He saw Domina Pendelia, heading toward them. Most likely, she had some demand. She wanted them to wash plates or clean up someone's puke in the fountain. Babieca had no desire to become a good investment, so he ducked through the peristyle and into the garden. Two women lingered by the statuary. One said something soft beneath her breath. The other laughed. He stepped behind the fountain and unlatched the hidden gate, which led to the narrow alley behind the domus. The shadows were cool against the stone walls, and moss tickled his fingers as he leaned against one, adjusting his sandal. He was beginning to feel sober, which was terrible. He'd need to launch an attack on the domina's undercroft, where she kept the wine. If he could distract Fel, he'd probably be able to steal a small amphora. She'd never miss it.

Babieca heard footsteps. He started to reach for his sword but then remembered that he hadn't brought it. Only miles were allowed to bear arms at the domina's party. There was a throwing knife, tucked into the hollowed-out sole of his right sandal. He wasn't much good at throwing it, but in the dark, it might pass for a bigger weapon. Aside from brandishing his cock, it was the only option. He bent over to retrieve it but slipped on a paving stone and fell to his knees. Cursing, he tugged on the knife, but it was stuck.

"Preemptive falling. That's a good strategy. They might think you're asleep."

He sighed. "Just help me up."

Morgan offered her hand. She helped him to rise, then brushed off his tunica.

"You look a fright." She wore a green stola. Her hair was caught up in a series of ivory pins, and Babieca stared at them, as if they were something unreal. He'd never seen Morgan in anything but a rust-colored cloak and a suit of leather armor.

"Your shoes," he said, marveling at them. "Are those cork heels?"

"I don't want to talk about it."

"Really? I've got nowhere to go, and I'm certain there's a story behind this."

"I'm supposed to blend in, remember? There's a bounty on my head, but everyone's looking for a sagittarius. Nobody will notice another girl in a dress."

"You're not another girl in a dress," he said.

"Well—" She looked away, suddenly embarrassed. "Don't get any ideas. I can kill you with these shoes."

"I've no doubt."

They both leaned against the wall. Babieca heard faint strains of laughter from the garden, and more distantly, the hum of Via Rumor. The nocturnal citizens of Anfractus were moving from party to party, hunting for diversion. They assumed that their lamps and knives and connections would keep them safe as they darted between houses, avoiding the shadows. Most of them were right. But before the night was over, a few of them would disappear.

"You played nicely," Morgan said.

"I strummed my fingers bloody, and all I have to show for it is a pocket full of dormice." He reached into his tunica. "Want one? They're still warm."

"No thanks."

"Shit. I must have dropped them." He closed his eyes. "All they're going to remember is the spado's voice."

"It's hard to forget."

"The worst part is that I'm sober."

"Here." She handed him a wineskin.

"Where did you steal this?"

"It's better that you don't know."

He took a sip, then passed it back to Morgan. "This is usually the moment when you lecture me on public drunkenness."

"I don't have the strength." She took a sip, then put the wineskin away. "Is this what we've become? Entertainment for that woman?"

"I'm the entertainment. Fel's the muscle. And you—" He blinked. "Why are you here, exactly? To make us look bad?"

"I'm her eyes and ears."

"A spy." He smiled. "A bit like your previous post on the battlements, only you get to wear much nicer shoes."

"I have a dagger, although I'm not telling you where I put it."

"Good. Let me imagine."

"I'd prefer that you didn't."

Babieca felt the moss tickling his hair. "I saw Julia."

"Everyone loves her frogs."

"Do you think she'd ever—" He shrugged. "I mean, we could use an artifex."

"It's not safe for her to be seen with us."

"Because we're so terrifying."

"Babieca, she still has a chance. The Gens of Artifices will support her."

"Who's going to support us?"

She chuckled. "At least we're still getting work."

"Until Domina Pendelia decides to throw us under the wheel."

"If that was her plan, she'd have done it a long time ago."

"You aren't normally this trusting."

"What choice do I have?"

"You could roll again. Shoot another arrow." He smiled. "Maybe if you rolled high enough, you could hit the basilissa from here."

"Don't be stupid."

"It was a hell of a shot, though."

She looked at her hands. "It was."

"You'd need another stone arrow. We could ask the gnomo who lives in Pendelia's garden. Do you think he's still there?"

"I have no idea."

"Maybe if we listened hard enough, we could hear him."

Morgan looked at Babieca. Then she touched his hand, lightly. She was about to say something, but stopped. They both heard the sound of footsteps. Quickly, Morgan pulled him into the shadows. They crouched in the corner of the alley. He felt better, knowing that Morgan was here. Not much better, but a little.

Two figures stepped into the alley. One was slender and wore a white cloak with the hood pulled down. The other was large and wearing some kind of dark mantle. He seemed out of proportion, somehow. When he walked, he took halting, delicate steps. *Click. Click. Click.* His sandals brushed against the stones.

The figure in white carried a lantern. As they drew closer and the light fell upon the one in the dark mantle, Babieca had to stifle a gasp. It wasn't a mantle. His body was covered in coarse fur, and his cloven feet struck the ground as he walked. *Click. Click. Click.* His horns were covered in delicate striations. Babieca prayed to Fortuna that those burning green eyes couldn't see him. Morgan was squeezing his hand so tightly, he thought she might break it.

They stopped a few feet from the mouth of the alley. Babieca was certain that the silenus would be able to smell them, but he seemed distracted. His eyes were on the figure in white.

"There isn't much time." His voice was low, and accented.

It was the first time he'd heard a silenus use human speech. The words chilled him. It was like hearing a bear suddenly call you by name.

The figure in white lowered her hood, and Babieca felt himself begin to shake. He'd never wanted to run so badly in his life. Basilissa Latona held up the lantern.

"Does it hurt? The light?"

"No. But it is distracting."

"You prefer the dark."

"We always have."

"Let's make this quick, then. I have something that you want."

"Yes. It belongs to us."

"Of course. And it's doing me no good, collecting dust in the arx. I'm prepared to return it to your people. But I'll need something in return."

"It belongs to us," the silenus repeated. There was a growl in his voice.

"Yes. I heard you the first time." Latona's expression didn't waver. "You'll have it. But first, I need to speak with your master."

"He will not enter the city. He despises it."

"No bother. I'll come to him."

"Your kind is not allowed in his court."

Her voice grew cold. "If you wish to continue your hunt—in my city—then you will grant me an audience. I promise that I won't darken his doorstep for long. I have but a single matter to discuss with him."

"You wish to talk. That is all?"

"Yes." She smiled. "Talking never hurt anyone."

"Bring what we seek. Then you can talk."

"I'm afraid it has to be the other way around. First, I'm going to talk with your master. If we reach an agreement, then I'll return your heirloom."

"Talk." The silenus spat on the ground. "Always talk with you people."

"Don't you have your own talk? Your own stories?"

"We hunt."

"So do we. The only difference is that we tend to drink a lot, and tell ridiculous stories while we're doing it."

"That is why you never catch anything."

There was a sound at the mouth of the alley. The basilissa lowered her hood and extinguished the lantern.

"The necropolis," she murmured. "Tomorrow. Return with your master's decision, and we'll see where this story goes."

The basilissa and the silenus hurried out of the alley. For a moment, Babieca heard the *click click click* of hooves, receding toward Via Rumor. Then there was silence.

He looked at Morgan. She was pale and hadn't let go of his hand.

"We have to find Fel," she whispered. "After that, we're getting the hell out of Anfractus, before that thing smells us."

2

SOMEONE WAS IN HIS BEDROOM.

He could hear them screaming. Or clanging. Was it more like clanging? It came from all directions, an impossible howl that seemed to encompass multiple registers of abrasive sound. Four banshees standing in the corners of the room, screaming for his murky little soul. Carl was afraid to open his eyes, but there was no other choice. The first thing that he noticed was a yellow Post-it stuck to his pillow. *Do not go back to sleep,* it said. The noise was actually a series of four alarms that he'd rigged up the previous night. His bedside clock, his phone, his laptop, and an old watch with a broken band, all screeching in unison.

It sounded like the end of the world. And it was, nearly.

"First day of term," he muttered.

He shut off the phone and the clock. The watch and the laptop were on the opposite side of the room, balanced against a crest of dirty laundry. He knew himself too well. The laptop alarm was programmed to get louder with each passing moment, like a hysterical child in a grocery store. The watch, having nothing to lose, would beep itself to death. He crossed the room in his underwear and shut them both off. Where had he even found that watch? It was an old Casio, with a cracked face and only half a strap, but it could still scream. He held it for a moment. Owning a watch seemed outdated now, like owning a pince-nez. He replaced it gently on the pile of laundry.

The first day of term was an exercise in chaos. Every professor in the department would be frantically proofreading syllabi. Even those with eagle-eyed precision would make a scheduling mistake, which nobody would notice for months. You couldn't even get near the bookstore, the lines were so long, and the cafeteria resembled some nightmarish scenario from a high school movie. Someone was always in tears at the parking office, pleading for another spot. *Please, anywhere but Z-lot.* Everyone seemed slightly drunk as they walked into each other, attempting to study printouts while texting at the same time. The only quiet place was the library, since nobody would even think of going there until the week of midterms. For now, it was a holy oasis. The librarians murmured peacefully to each other, like monks taking the air in a silent courtyard. They hadn't yet been asked, *Where are the books?* or, *Is this a computer lab?*

He couldn't remember what his first day of classes had been like. It was only five years ago, but when he tried to recall it, there was nothing but a smooth blank. Grad school had replaced everything with its deep roots. His life before—making popcorn at a video store, getting drunk in basements, endlessly driving in search of some imprecise event—seemed like a foreign film without subtitles. He could recall doing all of those things, over and over again, but the voices and colors had faded.

Suddenly he wanted to call his mother and ask her what he'd done as a teenager. That boring, burning stretch of adolescence. Mothers were archives. If he asked, she would be able to tell him who he'd been, what he'd wanted. She'd been on guard, trying to protect him from the sharp corners. He could see her as she was then, wearing a green skirt and smelling faintly of smoke, as she read him snippets of

Góngora. She'd always loved *Solitudes*. There was something about pastoral poetry that moved her. Perhaps it was the comfort of a golden age that had never really happened, or the rough desire of shepherds, hurling their love-plaints across the dark expanse of fields. Góngora, Lope, Virgil— she could spend hours reading their descriptions of a clearing, or a blind cow, moved to tears.

Carl almost called her. Then he realized that he didn't know where she was. She'd been at a conference on poetics in Valencia, and there'd been talk about some writer's retreat in Mexico City, but he wasn't sure of her precise location. She was a particle floating between countries. He imagined her in the air, craving a cigarette as she edited her newest sheaf of poems. His mother was one of the most productive people that he'd ever known. She would vanish for a month or two, only to reappear with a new chapbook, or some edited volume that she'd collaborated on. Her work was internationally respected, and she always seemed to be in transit, on her way to an awards ceremony or a symposium.

Every time she arrived at a new hotel, she would send him a photo of the drapes. He wasn't sure why, but they seemed to inspire her. As a result, he had a whole folder of garish patterns on his computer, textures that resembled carpeting from an old Boston Pizza.

He got dressed and crammed his bag full of textbooks. This was the first time that he'd serve as a teaching assistant for a second-year course. History 200: The Middle Ages to the Eighteenth Century. The professor, Tim Darby, reminded him of a disheveled actor who'd once starred in films about surfing.

When he was six, his grandmother had bought him a set of *Encyclopedia Britannica*. He adored the leather binding, black and oxblood, with golden leaf on the pages. They were the heaviest books that he'd ever seen. He read them from cover to cover. It took a long time, but he didn't leave the house much, so that helped. Years later, obscure bits of information were still floating around in his head, like dust from those gilt pages. It was a useful exercise. While other kids were out riding three-wheelers and trading Transformers, he was sifting through details, figuring out what was needed and what could be left behind. His mother would hand him a sandwich and shake her head. *Why can't you just read comics?*

History appealed to him, because it was a contradiction. You had the debris, which was real, but voiceless. Then you had the stuffing around the debris, the social text, which historians fluffed into patterns. It was the debris that he adored. The objects, lifted from a matrix of dirt, cooed over, labeled, and loved by archivists with delicate horsehair brushes. Even as a kid, he'd dreamed of having an apartment with objects on display. *Oh, those are my artifacts,* he'd say.

Now, his apartment had bare walls. The balcony faced Broad Street, and he could hear the murmur of traffic from below. They'd be here soon. He grabbed two granola bars and put them in his pocket. He didn't feel ready for the outside world. He wanted to strip back down to his underwear, get mildly stoned, and watch *Party Down*. But he'd run out of summer.

Now the real test would begin. It was easy to keep the lie going when they weren't distracted. They'd had time to organize, to make plans. Today, that luxury was over. They'd have to lose sleep if they were going to keep this up. All it took was the tiniest slip. At first, he'd thought that Shelby would crack. She spent more time with him, and he knew her moods. But lately, Carl was beginning to fear that he'd be the one to say something. He could feel the words like a weight on his chest. Sometimes, he'd say them silently in front of the mirror.

You died.

He went downstairs. They were waiting for him on the street.

"First day of term," he said with a fake smile. "Who's pumped?"

Shelby handed him a coffee. "I'm not ready. My hair's fucked, this sweater smells like fries, and I can't remember what room I'm teaching in."

"RC 111," Andrew said. "It's in the Innovation Centre."

"Is it a smart room? I'm intimidated by them."

"Yes. It's full of buttons and has very little seating."

"Perfect."

Carl gave him a granola bar. "Put this in your bag for later."

Andrew took it without quite looking at him. Lack of eye contact was nothing new with him, but this seemed different. Still, he smiled slightly as he took the bar.

"Kashi Crisp. Thanks."

"They have the least amount of sugar," Carl said. "And taste, I think. But on the plus side: ancient grains."

"Fitting that a historian would like his grains ancient."

"I prefer the ones loaded with sugar. But these are heart-smart."

"According to your mother?" Shelby asked.

"She's looking out for all of us."

"Does she still think that you're dating Tammy?"

"Hey." Carl took a long pull of coffee. "Don't knock imaginary Tammy. She's gotten me out of many conversations that I'd rather not field."

"Why not just admit that you're a complete rake? Your mom's a poet. I don't think she's going to judge you."

"Poets can be surprisingly focused on grandchildren."

"I think you'd be a good father," Andrew said.

Carl blinked and looked at him. "Why?"

"Well, you're kind of obsessed with Lego. You like to barbecue, you call every dog 'buddy,' and in nearly every picture of you that I've seen, you're holding a baby."

"I've got a lot of cousins."

"I don't know. It seems like you're halfway there."

"It took four alarms to get me out of bed. I don't think I'm cut out for fatherhood at this point in my life."

"Let's focus on not getting kicked out of the MA program," Shelby said. "Then we can talk about crazy hypotheticals."

They walked from Broad up to Albert Street. The wind licked at their jackets. By the end of the month, they'd be wearing gloves and hats with earflaps. For now, the weather seemed to balance on a knife's edge. Scraps of summer remained, but everyone could feel that winter was due to arrive. You could feel a collective sigh in the city of Regina, at the moment of the first snowfall. The time for shoes was over. The boots would have to come out, and with them, a pile of layers to fend off the cold.

He'd squandered four months of buggy, dry heat, and now the snow was on its way. He wasn't ready for anything— teaching, toques, an honest conversation with his mother. Carl wanted to run back home, but they were already crossing the park, and it was too late. In a few hours, he'd be in front of a classroom once again, explaining the finer points of a history syllabus. Five hundred years of blood, sex, and politics, condensed into a dark espresso. Most of them would be half asleep, distracted by their phones, or slowly coming to the realization that they were in the wrong class. But a few would be listening, and it was for their benefit that he made jokes, paced the room, and showed images of crumbling Roman via. Someday, they might be in his exact position, and he could think of no finer revenge.

They crossed Wascana Park. Geese wandered along the pathways, hissing at joggers. The lake was clear, reflecting the parliament building in all of its rippling, neo-Victorian majesty. The original building had been destroyed by a cyclone. Papers and desks and people flew out the windows as the foundations cleaved apart. Now it was a copy, but a brilliant one. Carl loved the different kinds of marble inside. Once, he'd gotten so turned on by the architecture that it had made him light-headed. The brutalist design of Plains University didn't have quite the same effect. The only space on campus that excited him was the room with fur on the walls. It had once been used for LSD experiments. He also liked the Pit, which resembled a dry, carpeted hot tub in the middle of the Administration-Humanities building. Students gathered there to study, and it always smelled faintly of Cheetos and ripe socks.

The park didn't talk during the day. It was mostly sedate. At night, it awoke, opened its mouth, and sang. You knew that you'd be swallowed if you listened to the song, but you couldn't help it. You'd never heard anything so enchanting, so frightening. Carl looked at Andrew, now immune to the park's pull. He looked fragile, in frayed jeans and an oversized *Community* T-shirt with Abed Nadir on it. *Cool cool cool,* the caption said. This was the outfit that he'd chosen for the first day of term.

Carl remembered the first night that he'd discovered the real park. He'd been wandering back home from Athena's, the campus pub, where he'd consumed entirely too much tequila. His tongue felt pickled, and as he walked past a rusted ventilation duct—placed inexplicably next to the pub—he thought briefly about prying off the grate and climbing down. As a kid, he'd dreamed of doing just this, in the hopes that he'd find the Teenage Mutant Ninja Turtles. Donatello would teach him how to build a siege engine, all MacGyver-like, and then Splinter could show him how to meditate and achieve satori. Which must have been harder for a rat, but he certainly made it look easy in the comics. Distracted by the thought, he'd nearly run into a weathered sculpture, which looked almost exactly like the ventilation duct. He'd stared at them both in confusion, trying to see the art, to figure out what made one of them an installation, while the other was merely a rusted-out conduit. Unable to figure it out, he'd kept walking.

This was long before he'd met Shelby or Andrew. He was still an undergrad, writing forgettable essays on the Thirty Years' War, *glasnost*, and Renaissance optics. He should have been gearing up for grad school, but already he felt himself growing disillusioned. He no longer had that roller-coaster feeling in his stomach when he read about buried artifacts. Only a few years ago, he would have wet himself at the chance to join an archaeological dig, to roam through haunted foundations in search of the past. Now he selected courses based on how many credits they offered, what time they'd been scheduled (morning classes interfered with his hangovers), and, sometimes, how close the room was to a vending machine. He seemed to receive the same mark on all of his papers, accompanied by the same comments. The handwriting was different, but the faint praise (*thoughtful discussion; good use of outside sources*) didn't change. He didn't feel as if he were being groomed for an illustrious career as an academic. Instead, he felt as if he were being managed, like an unexceptional child in a Montessori classroom.

That night, wrapped in his tequila blanket, he'd stumbled through Wascana Park. The geese shadowed him, their glowing eyes winking in the dark. Faint shapes moved on the margins of his fuzzy awareness. He heard skitterings, the crunch of gravel, the curious presence of animals watching him like something on display. The moon was full and slightly jaundiced. *Plenilunada,* he thought. His mother used to whisper that in his ear when he was little, pointing to the full moon. He'd thought, at the time, that she could control it, make it wax and wane on command. His mother, who held his small hand while offering him names for everything, first in Spanish, then in English. While he was thinking about this, he'd walked between two trees. There was nothing distinctive about them. He'd felt suddenly light-headed. The world lurched violently. He fell to his knees, retching salt, lime, and undigested nachos.

Only after his stomach was terribly empty, after he'd opened his eyes and wiped a string of bile from his lips, did he realize that it was daylight, and he was no longer in the park. He was in the city of Anfractus, the city of infinite alleys, with the sun beating down on him. Smoke stung his eyes. The heat was suffocating. For some reason, he was naked, and all of his memories felt as if they'd been scattered about. He couldn't think of where he'd come from. All he knew for certain was his name.

Babieca.

The campus was a warren of demihysterical students, clutching their phones and their oversized textbooks as they ran from lineup to lineup. Academics wandered among them, trying to prepare for lectures as they walked. They mechanically sipped coffee, their eyes glued to books with titles like *Powers of Horror* and *Of Grammatology.* Some were dressed fashionably, while others wore rumpled clothing and looked as if they'd just woken up. Carl recalled his favorite philosophy teacher, who'd worn the same outfit to every class: a pair of gray sweatpants and a *Looney Tunes* T-shirt with a hole in the middle of Bugs Bunny's face. He'd never met anyone more brilliant or fascinating than this man, bleary and unshaven, too busy thinking about Immanuel Kant and the sweet sting of causality to wash his clothes. He'd observed over the years that male academics could get away with a lot. As long as they were interesting, they could show up to class in a pair of overalls, sporting a facial tattoo, and nobody would comment.

They went to the bookstore to cash in their TA vouchers, which would allow them to afford the pile of books they'd soon have to interpret. There was no such voucher for their graduate seminars, each of which boasted a long reading list. Sometimes you could cobble together the readings on your own—if you got to the library quick enough—but often, there was an overpriced custom courseware package to buy. It amounted to a binder full of photocopies, most of them askew, whose very presence seemed to offend the corporation known as CanCopy. A steaming envelope of freshly pressed articles, chosen for their difficulty. He wasn't sure he had any room left in his brain to memorize those dizzying arguments, produced by academics who had once lined up at a bookstore counter, just like him, clutching the same voucher and wondering how they were going to pay the power bill.

Andrew headed off to find his books. Carl started to follow him past the shelves of branded merchandise, but Shelby grabbed him by the arm. He almost yelped but managed to bite down on the exclamation. She dragged him into a corner filled with Plains University socks, sweaters, and bunnyhugs.

"What's the plan for tonight?"

"No parking," he said automatically. That was the phrase uttered whenever one of them spoke about "park business" on the wrong side of Wascana. Companies were supposed to remain discreet. Not that they were a real company. Not anymore. But if one of Mardian's people happened to hear them—or worse, one of the basilissa's—their lives would take an unpleasant turn. After what they'd done, it was important to stay off the radar.

She sighed. "Things must have gone well and truly pear-shaped if you're the one advising me about parking."

"Hey. I can be discreet. I've done a pretty good job this summer."

"With a few slips."

"What do you expect? We're with him all the time, and he likes to ask questions. In case you've forgotten, that's sort of his thing."

"It might help if you didn't look so shifty."

"I keep telling you—that's just my face."

Shelby peered over the racks full of clothing. Andrew had vanished into the crowd of students who were trying to find their textbooks.

"Maybe we could fit him with a silent alarm," he suggested. "Something that makes our phones buzz whenever he gets within ten feet."

"Don't be a dick."

"I'm halfway serious. We're running out of options. Do you think he really believes that story we told him about the battle in the library?"

A few months ago, they'd fought for their lives next to the circulation desk. Carl could still remember the sweat running between his hockey pads—their poor excuse for garniture. A salamander had nearly set fire to the stacks. And they'd told Andrew that it was a live-action role-playing game that had gotten out of hand. The smoke alarm, the shattered glass, they'd managed to explain all of it somehow. They'd blamed it on his medication, on stress, on a prank involving the sprinklers. But nobody knew if he actually believed them.

"He hasn't exactly mentioned it," she said.

"He's in therapy. Some hack is forcing him to draw how he feels about life, and all we give him in return are terrible excuses."

"They're not so bad. I really could be attending an art class."

"Every other night?"

"I told him it was a compressed summer class."

"And summer's gone. What's your next excuse?"

"At least mine's plausible."

He frowned. "I could really be playing in a rec league."

"Uh-huh."

"I used to play hockey all the time."

"Pee-wee? Or Atom?"

"Shut it." He absently picked up a pair of socks. They were branded with a coyote, of all things. "Fine. What should we tell him?"

"That's the thing. I don't know." She folded her arms across her chest. "I thought you'd be the one to crack first. Are we supposed to lie to him forever?"

"Maybe not forever." He felt something heavy in the pit of his stomach. "Maybe—I mean—he could find his way back."

"We don't even know if that's possible."

"If we tell him, it's all over. That much we do know."

"It's stupid," Shelby muttered. "Stupid and cruel."

"Pottery."

She blinked. "What?"

"You can tell him that you've moved on to pottery class."

Shelby laughed helplessly. "Right. Instead of studying and preparing for my tutorials, I've decided to make a vase."

"Tell him it's an amphora. That sounds more interesting, at least."

"And what about you? What if he wants to see one of your hockey games?"

Carl shuddered at the thought. "I guess I really could join a rec league. Something a bit cheaper, like roller hockey."

"I think miniature golf is closer to your speed."

"What about the bas—"

Andrew materialized, clutching a pile of books. He must have used his elbows. Maybe he was the one more suited to playing hockey. The thought made Carl grin.

"What bass?"

"Pardon?" Shelby was stalling.

"What bass?" Andrew repeated. "I interrupted Carl. He was saying something about—"

"Bass fishing." Carl tried to make it sound perfectly logical. "My cousin wants to take me bass fishing. Mom was telling me the other night. Isn't that weird?"

"It really is," Shelby murmured.

"Which cousin?"

"Mauri."

"Isn't he a vegetarian?"

Fuck. He could see Mauri in his mind's eye, skinny and smiling, as he ordered a lentil burger with extra chard. Suddenly, Carl hated him for being so healthy.

"We're not going to eat the bass," he said haltingly. "It's a catch-and-release thing. Probably, we'll just drink a lot of beer and ignore the fish."

"When is this happening?"

Shelby knocked over a rack full of bunnyhugs. "Oh *crap*. Why did I do that?"

Andrew helped her replace the rack. She gave special attention to each hanger, ensuring that the clothes were arranged by size.

"Can I see your books?" Carl asked. The key to distracting Andrew was to relentlessly change the subject. If you kept it up long enough, he'd usually abandon whatever question he'd been about to ask. Books were like catnip.

As he rattled off details about the publishers and individual editions, Carl smiled. His insides felt like a car crash. Soon the lies would feel true. On that day, he'd be able to look Andrew in the eyes, to smile at him, without a quiver of regret. Like an advisor, he'd be able to say—without blinking—that the job market was looking up, that a bachelor of arts had never been so valuable, that you couldn't put a price on critical thinking. He'd sweeten the knife before plunging it in. They'd both believe in a tremendous future, unscrolling across the sky.

A memory came to him, jagged around the edges, as if someone had abruptly tuned his mind to a halfway point between stations. He felt stone beneath his back. He saw a decaying tapestry. Fortuna was a ruined face. Her eyes had faded, but they still saw him, sweating, full of fire. Kissing the shadow. The rhythm that drove them, older than any-thing. The shadow moved, and Babieca felt something rising within him, a sweet, scalding incandescence that would burn everything to ashes if he let it loose. And he did. The mouth closed over his own. Ashes covered his body, a dream of collapsing staircases and blind alleys. The spark moved through him, leaving nothing behind, as the tongue sifted through his remains. He was shuddering and crying, but his body had flattened out to silk. There was only the cry, the beautiful breakdown.

But they hadn't kissed. Not in this world. Babieca—his other—had shared a furtive, happy moment with Roldan. The auditor, gone. The shadow. But why did Carl remember? Who had been the real shadow? Was Babieca just a character in a dream, or was he an extension of Carl, some nested memory that would never leave him? Babieca's particular skill set would have been useful in grad school. He'd never have to pay for another book, and being a musician had a certain mystique. It was a lot sexier than collecting Lego and back issues of the *Byzantine Historical Annual*. All those buttons and forgotten fibulae. Perhaps they really would save him, as he'd believed when he was young. Their lovely endurance. If a fine silver toothpick could survive the collapse of an empire, then—maybe—he could survive this.

Andrew was distracted by the color inset of his Broad-view anthology and nearly walked into a group of students as they were leaving the bookstore. Shelby steered him, gently, around the four girls, who were trying to puzzle out their letters of admission. The acceptance letters were so stylized that it was often difficult to figure out where you'd been admitted, or what courses you were required to take. Carl had showed up to the Department of Kinesiology on his first day, a little bewildered by the fact that everyone was wearing jogging shorts and gleaming with a sense of healthy purpose that was completely unfamiliar to him. At first he'd thought they were on some kind of party drug, but they were simply conscious and in a good mood.

They were about to split up. The Department of History was in another building (for now, at least—the offices were always being shuffled around). Andrew and Shelby were both heading for the Department of Literature and Cultural Studies, with its life-size posters of theorists and famous authors blown up to unnerving proportions. He was concerned that they hadn't decided anything in their sotto voce conversation about fake art classes and hockey practices. Would Andrew continue to believe their lies? They seemed like something delicate and confectionary, a gingerbread castle without a drawbridge. There'd be no escape for them once the towers began to crumble. So far, he'd gamely put up with their behavior. He hadn't asked why Carl and Shelby were spending more time together, or why they often stopped talking in midsentence when he approached them. Andrew could be oblivious to certain things—hipster irony, forced smiles, the fact that not everyone wanted to talk about intrusion versus portal fantasies in literature—but he'd surely realized that something peculiar was going on.

They crossed the science building, which was floored in polished granite. It had six levels, all encased in a smooth web of concrete and dazzling glass. The elevator intoned each floor, and a bank of large-screen televisions played a loop of experiments. Many of them involved sparks, fizzing beakers, and balloons. At the end of the loop, the screen would black out, displaying a single word: *Science!* Curiously, the sound was turned off, so you couldn't actually learn how the experiments were being performed. Carl was certain that he'd blow himself up, were he to attempt any of them.

Shelby paused in front of the lab café, which sold pastries and trough-sized noodle bowls. You could feel the collective anger in the lineup as everyone attempted to pay for small coffees with their debit card. This was where they had to part ways.

"I've got lecture until ten fifteen," she said. "Then I'm

done with my tutorial at eleven forty-five. Shall we meet back here around noon?"

That was a lie. She'd shown Carl her schedule, and her Monday tutorial was finished at eleven fifteen. If they met back here shortly after, they'd have some precious time to work on their excuses before Andrew showed up at noon. Carl glanced at Andrew. He wasn't looking at either of them. His concentration seemed to be wandering.

"Sounds good," Andrew said, after a moment. "Happy teaching, Carl."

This time he was looking at Carl. Looking directly at him, which was unusual. He didn't blink. His face was placid, but the look had a kind of challenge to it. Carl shifted nervously. Then he smiled, and nodded.

"You too, buddy. See you soon."

Shelby also gave him a look. *Do not crack,* she was saying.

They parted.

Carl cut across campus, enjoying the morning chill. The weather was playing with them. For the moment, he could enjoy it, the way you'd flirt with something kind of beautiful that might kill you later. He unzipped his jacket and let the wind have its way. Students were smoking and searching through their bags, while cars endlessly circled the parking lot. Pigeons were nesting in the International Languages building, and they crooned at him as he walked by. As the cold light suffused him, he felt, for a moment, that he might be a functional adult. He had a bank account, a long-distance plan, even an RRSP (which he tried not to burglarize at the end of each month, when he could barely afford rent). His wallet was full of discount cards, whose punched holes and delicious icons—muffins, burgers, steaming cups— reminded him that he had options, that he only had to spend twenty more dollars to receive a free artisanal cupcake.

Andrew and Shelby were lucky. They had each other. Their neuroses intersected at several significant angles. He was part of their dyad, but at a slight remove, unable to lock on to their specific frequency.

"Hello."

At first, he thought that Shelby had followed him. Did she want to compare notes right now, under some false pretense of going to the bathroom? He turned, about to congratulate her on the daring move, but it was Ingrid standing before him.

"Hey. How goes it?"

She wore cargo pants and a blue sweater frayed in the shoulders. Her bag was held together by an ingenious system of safety pins. Carl wasn't nervous around her, precisely. He wasn't nervous around anyone—not in the traditional sense of the word. His mother had always called him shameless. But Ingrid's shadow was a miles, and he worried that someday he'd find himself looking down the edge of her blade.

"I've seen better mornings. Neil screamed like Janet Leigh in *Psycho* when I dropped him off at day care. He told me that my hug was *unappealing*. Luckily, they managed to distract him with some game involving Popsicle sticks."

"I take it you didn't get much sleep."

"I don't really sleep. It's more like a series of unplanned naps. I managed to get about half of the reading done"—her face fell—"but I may have read the wrong chapter. Everything got a bit surreal just before dawn."

"Don't worry about it. Tutorials are mostly bullshit in the first week. Half of the students are in the wrong class."

"Explaining the plagiarism policy should kill some time."

"Oh, for sure. I do it in a series of different voices. Always gets a laugh."

She smiled. Not because he was being funny, but because she was kind. He realized, not for the first time, that the park was the only thing he had in common with her. How must he look to this studious person, who paid a mortgage and designed crafts for her son? He was a kid with a beard, untouched by the life-altering responsibility of parenthood. He had nobody to keep him accountable, except for his mother, a voice stretched over a long-distance connection. There was nothing to stop him from self-destructing, no small, serious boy to grab his face and order him to watch *Dinosaur Train*. He recalled Andrew's words, and for a moment, something flared in him, a hot and secret wish to be needed that way.

"Are we meeting up as usual tonight?" Ingrid asked. "I might be late. Paul's going out for a few drinks. He almost never goes out, and I feel like—"

"It's fine," Carl said. "We'll wait for you."

The two of us, he meant.

"Carl—" She trailed off.

"Yeah?"

"Is it—working? You know. Is it going okay?"

He knew. And it wasn't. Everything was collapsing. Everything was on fire, and he didn't know what to do. He had no survival instinct. He just stood there, watching the drapes melt, wondering if the foundation would somehow survive. He wasn't sleeping well. Every night, he saw the shadow's face, pale as boxwood, floating. He dove into the water, but it turned to stone every time, filling his mouth with blood. All he could do was leap. And sometimes he'd wake up on the floor, astonished. Sleep-diving.

"It's a day-by-day thing," he said. "It might work."

"I'm sorry that it's come to this."

"Has this sort of thing happened to you before?"

"Not exactly. But I do know a lot about lying."

"Right. Of course. And you've got two people to manage. That's got to be hard."

"Sometimes it is." Her expression darkened. "But sometimes—it's almost too easy. That's when I get scared."

"Of being trapped in the lie?"

"Something like that."

Nothing made sense. The lies least of all. But this was what they had, now. If they were going to survive, they had to become a real company. Morgan was wrong. They couldn't leave Julia alone. They needed her.

"We'll wait for you," he repeated. "In the clearing."

"I'll see you then. Happy teaching."

"Thanks. You too."

She shouldered her knapsack and walked toward the Education building. Carl rummaged through his bag for the history textbook. The granola bar was sitting on top of it. He ate it in two bites and crossed the campus green. History needed all of the help that it could get. Even a bearded kid who lied through his teeth. Maybe Paul would show him how to play hockey. It was always good to sprinkle in a little truth.

3

BABIECA LEANED AGAINST THE WALL OF HIS
alley, sweating. It was always hot in Anfractus. The city
seemed untouched by winter or any other season. The heat
settled over his body as he pulled the familiar stones from
the wall. He unwrapped the cloth bundle inside and placed
his instrument carefully on the ground. He was always worried that the long nights would do damage to its surface, but
it slept like a baby in that dark space. The miracle of the
alleys. He looked down and sighed. Transitions always left
him hard.

He counted the coins in his purse. It cost money to roll
with a warm body. He'd have to sing, and that usually left
him spent in a different way. Babieca slipped on his sandals,
feeling taut and irritable. Desire shouldn't be so complicated. He was sure that Morgan didn't have these debates
with herself. Maybe hitting things with arrows brought some
kind of physical satisfaction. He'd have to ask her, the next
time that she was drunk and willing to indulge him.

Babieca knew that the alleys held some kind of secret.
Every visitor to the city received their own alley. It became

a part of their body, a secret corner that no one could violate. If he screamed, or stabbed himself, or climbed the walls, it would make no difference. As long as he stayed within his alley, he remained invisible, unborn. The safety was temporary, though. No matter how scared and disoriented you felt, you always walked. The breath of the city, the rush of its reckless heartbeat, was inescapable.

On that first day, he'd knelt in a puddle of his own ichor, feeling like he'd forgotten how to breathe. Who was he? How had he gotten here, to this place that reeked of warm bodies, soot, and bursting fruit? Naked, defenseless, ill-named. He'd tasted a word on his tongue, but it refused to materialize completely. Leaving this protected space seemed like the worst kind of folly. But it was equally impossible to stay. He could hear possibilities revolving just beyond the mouth of the alley. He could feel the presence of objects, coins rustling in purses, fabric dragging across pockmarked stone, dirks and gladii asleep in their leather beds. The metallic whiff of cosmetics and the sweat beneath. Laughter and cursing. How could he resist that dangerous symphony? Here he was safe. But outside he could be something. He could steal a life that mattered.

It might have been easier had he simply become a fur. Then he'd have brothers and sisters, along with the support of the Fur Queen. They'd dine on leftovers in the rusty silence of the underground tower, as she looked on, perhaps with a maternal smile. Thieving and music were so close to each other, as someone used to remind him. All he had to do was shimmy up his spoke on Fortuna's wheel, and he'd find himself on the other side. He already knew how to pick an easy lock. He was probably halfway there. All that separated him from a fur's life was the cracked lute, banging against his side.

In the hands of a real trovador, it was an exquisite weapon, capable of destroying realms. For him, it was little more than a source of income. When had he last felt the kiss of true music? It must have been that night, in the Tower of Sagittarii, when he'd played the ancient lullaby. It had felt as if he might put the whole city to bed, leaving it blind and ready to be plundered. He could have passed through any door, silent as a breeze, and walked away with a small fortune. But the song had earned him nothing, in the end. A curious look from Morgan. The grudging praise of a small mechanical fox. Could that have been his only chance? Fortuna sometimes dropped a small blessing at your feet, and if you ignored it, she turned away from you forever. That was what it felt like. A blessing that he'd crushed beneath his sandal, like a pale, unseen flower.

He met Morgan and Fel at the giant clepsydra. Its ancient mechanism, driven by water wheels and whispering tanks, chimed the hour for everyone to hear. Fortuna's wheel moved with every shudder of the hidden gears. Her six daylight faces were twinned by the shadow aspects, claimed by the night gens. Babieca wasn't sure anymore if there was a tangible difference between them. Fortuna was in all of them, the drowned and the saved. By day, she healed alongside the dutiful medicus and watched over the spado as he copied out vital documents. By twilight, she sang inspiration to the trovador, matching her drink for drink. And by night, she crept behind the furs and the sicarii, grindstone to their blades. With a light touch, she guided them forward, as you would guide a sleepy child up the stairs to bed. If only she hadn't been so fond of games. You couldn't trust a patroness who might bet against you at any moment, kissing the die before she let it fall.

Morgan looked impatient. She kept playing with the worn fibula that held her cloak together, as if it were a toy. Fel watched people as they passed by the roaring clepsydra, sometimes pausing to stare at the wheel. She saw Babieca but didn't acknowledge him. The trovador had come to think of this as her natural style of greeting. *I see you. And what of it?*

"You're late," Morgan observed.

"Hardly. I came as soon as my head cleared."

"We've been waiting."

"Transitions vary," Morgan said, without taking her eyes from the crowd. "His alley could be a few minutes behind."

"That would certainly be convenient for him."

"Why are you shitting on me already?" Babieca asked. "We just woke up. I couldn't possibly have done something to offend you." He sniffed himself. "Granted, this tunica has seen better days, but the spray from the clepsydra is already improving things."

"It's not you," Morgan said. "I'm just worried."

"You think Julia's going to say no."

"It's not a question of yes or no. Even if she agrees—and she'd have to be profoundly stupid to join us—what are we supposed to do? We're no longer welcome in the Arx of Violets. We don't have access to any information, and there's still a bounty on our heads."

"Quite a generous one too." Babieca smiled. "I was happy to see that I fetched such a fair price. It's good for my sense of worth."

"We're supposed to be running away from this kind of trouble. If we continue on this path, we'll be walking directly into a storm."

"That's nothing new for us."

She frowned. "You're the one who nearly pissed himself when that silenus appeared. Now you're suddenly excited at the prospect of getting killed?"

"How sweetly you exaggerate. If I remember, you were the one who held my hand so tightly that you nearly broke it in several places."

"We can debate how terrified you both were at a later time," Fel said. "If you want to catch the artifex, it's best to go now, when the towers are busy with patrons and sup-plicants. We'll have a better chance of blending in with the general throng."

"That's a funny word," Babieca said. "*Throng.* Vaguely obscene."

"You sound like—" Morgan abruptly stopped herself.

Babieca saw a flash of remorse in her eyes. Then she looked away. Neither of them said anything. He knew that she'd been about to say the auditor's name.

"Let's go," Fel said. "The only benefit I can see in your plan is that it might be stupid enough to work."

"It's *our* plan," Morgan reminded the miles. "You agreed to it."

"Only because we could use an artifex."

"Strictly speaking," Babieca said, "she's an apprentice artifex."

Fel looked coolly at them. "So this is what we have to work with. A horny singer, a disgraced archer, a miles with no connections, and a tinker."

"She's pretty. If that helps."

Fel almost smiled. "It doesn't hurt."

"I object to the term *disgraced*—" Morgan began.

But Fel was already leading them up Via Dolores. It was strange to think that only a short while ago, Morgan had been their leader. Now her dangerous profile meant that she had to avoid too much attention. Fel pulled them along, a bunch of dazed goslings. Babieca didn't take offense to being called a horny singer. He was happy to be somewhere in the middle of their almost-company. The one in the middle rarely got attacked first.

They followed Aditus Papallona to the edge of the Subura, where the Tower of Artifices was located. As usual, builders crowded the stairs, testing out new machines. Babieca nearly tripped over a barking lapdog made of whirring cogs and shining brass plates. The dog cocked its head, and one of its ears swiveled toward him, but there was no spark of life in its eyes. The foxes—Propertius and Sulpicia—were the only living machinae that he'd encountered in the city, and whatever had forged them was lost to antiquity. Now, as Julia often reminded them, artifices were mostly cheap entertainers. They dreamed up new party favors, singing fountains, and thrilling naumachia to please the basilissa and her court. Frogs, toy boats, and bored doves who piped the hour. Julia's mother, Naucrate, had been a true artifex. She'd crafted a bee that had nearly brought down the city of Egressus.

They kept to the rose-tinted shadows as they climbed the stairs. None of the builders were paying attention to them. The tower might have been on fire, and the artifices would have kept working, oblivious to impending doom. They squinted at tablets and old fragments of papyrus, tightening bolts or simply observing their creations, like stern dancing-masters.

"Builders," Fel said beneath her breath. "They always smell faintly of piss and last night's meal. Don't they ever wash?"

"You're not exactly a flower beneath that armor," Babieca said.

"At least I haven't spilled wine on it."

"Do you even drink?"

"When it's appropriate."

"You and Morgan would make a lovely couple. Sober and awkward."

Morgan gave him a cold look but said nothing. To his surprise, Fel reddened and looked away. He'd never realized that she could blush.

"Forgive me," Babieca murmured. "That was a thoughtless comment."

"This is why I prefer guard duty," Fel replied. "The quiet."

"Honestly, though—"

"I don't care what you think of me, trovador." She looked straight ahead, negotiating the pile of parts, some moving, that covered the stairs.

Babieca didn't reply. It seemed wise to drop the matter, and Morgan was already glaring a hole in the back of his head.

At the top of the tower, they found a group of artifices milling around Fortuna. They'd built a miniature version of the clepsydra, whose wheel revolved slowly, singing with each pass. Her expression was impassive. Rather than throwing coins into the pool at her feet, the builders tossed old parts: exhausted gears, stripped bolts, springs that no longer endured tension. A few glass eyes floated in the embrasure, queer without the context of a face. Artifices clustered beneath the high red-glass windows, trading gossip and tools. Julia was not among them. Babieca searched for her red hair, but she was nowhere to be seen.

"Odd," he said to Morgan. "I was certain that she'd be paying her respects."

"Perhaps her faith is wavering. Or she simply wants to avoid the crowds."

"We can try the Brass Gear. She might be working on a commission."

"A tavern," Fel said. "At least you'll be in your element."

Babieca shrugged. "We all have our chaos. Mine happens to be wine."

"We could also make a bit of coin," Morgan said.

"Not at the Gear. It would be like playing to a room full of statues." He gestured to the artifices, who were currently ignoring them. "I could start playing right now, and they wouldn't even look up from their tablets."

Wanting to test his theory, Babieca removed the lute from its case.

"What are you doing?" Morgan hissed.

"Just watch. I'll demonstrate."

He sat on the edge of the pool, tuning his instrument. He could sense Fortuna's gaze like moonlight on his hair. Once the strings were warm, he began to play something simple. It was one of his own compositions. He'd written it a few nights ago. Felix had unexpectedly fallen asleep, and rather than waking the house father, he'd strummed by the window instead. It was a pleasure to get lost in the music, to feel the sweet sting in his fingers once again. The notes reminded him of lazy flies, hovering unsteadily before they left through the open window. The reeking summer wind had carried them beyond the Subura, a flake shaved from the sweating ice of his memory. Some blue day from long ago, when things had been less opaque.

This time, as he played the tune, he could feel a subtle difference. The vaulted ceilings offered an unexpected thunder to the music. The little staff of notes grew more profound, until they seemed to be coming from all directions. The tower hummed with his song. The music was doing what it wanted, what it needed, and he was little more than a conduit. The builders had ceased their conversation. Morgan was trying to signal him, but he couldn't stop.

Once, while he'd been practicing, Roldan had placed a twist of dried fruit in his mouth. Unable to focus on anything but the song, Babieca had let the fruit crumble down his chin. He could hear Roldan's laughter, and he played that as well. The notes were summer, strong wine, baking bread. He knew that if he just kept playing, if he never stopped, then the world would slow down and finally let him catch up. The hot drag of grief and bitter joy, so close that they might have been the same note, would lie down and reconcile, if only he could play them right.

When he stopped, everyone was looking at him. The builders had put away their tablets and were staring with a mixture of curiosity and suspicion. Babieca felt a presence at his feet. He looked down, and his stomach nearly flipped. All of the machinae were gathered around him, a tight circle of rapt spectators. There were mice with tails of coiled wire, spiders that trembled on articulated legs, and small lizards clinging to the edge of the pool. A mechanical sparrow had settled on his foot. There must have been a hundred creatures, a wild menagerie of moving parts, all gathered before him like expectant children. They whistled, preened, and gently scratched the ground, waiting for him to continue. For the first time, Babieca felt as if they were more than clever toys. In their dark, patient eyes, he could see something like a coal-glimmer of life, more than reflex, and it made him profoundly nervous.

"We have to go," Morgan whispered. "Now."

They hurried back down the stairs. The artifices watched them go but didn't say anything. Babieca turned and saw that the machinae were still in a circle. They didn't follow him, but neither did they return to their builders. They seemed to be locked in a silent exchange, a language of turns and bright flashes that he couldn't decode.

When they left the tower, Babieca was momentarily blinded by the sun. He felt slightly feverish and tried to steady himself. Before he could move, Fel grabbed him by the arm, dragging him into the cool shadows of a nearby alley.

She nearly slammed him against the wall. He could feel

the moss on his back, the sharp stones digging into his bare skin.

"What *was* that?"

He shook his head. "I don't know."

"Have you lost your mind? That was one of the last places where we could move unseen. Nobody knew us. Now, they're going to remember the idiot trovador who charmed all of their machines, like Fortuna herself was playing through him."

"I don't know," he repeated, lamely. "I didn't think that would happen."

"You've well and truly fucked us."

"Fel—" Morgan tried to interpose herself between the two of them. "I don't think he knew what he was doing."

"He never does. That's exactly the problem."

"No. He has a gift."

He blinked at this. He'd always thought that, like most people, Morgan saw him as a poor nemo with no talent to speak of. His songs had been a means to an end, a way to generate quick coin. Nobody had ever used the word *gift* to describe his abilities. He looked at her, a bit strangely, as if she were just now coming into focus.

"Do you really think so?"

Morgan sighed. "You're shit at controlling it, but every once in a while, I can hear something in your music. Something that moves me."

They were silent for a few moments. Babieca stared at the walls of the alley. He knew that Anfractus was trying to tell him something, but the words lay just out of reach. His fingers were beginning to smart. As he felt the pain, he knew that the dream was over. Like Felix, the music was done with him. Somewhere in his gut, Babieca felt an animal clawing to get out. He pushed it down, and it screamed. But it wasn't strong enough to resist. He swallowed. The song had left him bloodless, yet he was still alive. That made everything worse.

Unexpectedly, Fel placed a hand on his shoulder. "I'm sorry."

Had she seen his expression? Had she felt the hoarse pain, struggling to escape? Babieca simply nodded.

"It's fine. You were right. I've fucked us again."

"Well"—her mouth betrayed a smile—"some of us could use it."

He laughed in spite of himself. "Dear miles. I never knew."

"For now, you'd do best to shut up, and keep that lute in its case."

"I solemnly swear."

"We can make use of your other talents," Morgan said, leading him into the sunlight. "The less dangerous ones."

"Like what?"

"Being a shameless strumpet."

"I can do that with one hand tied."

They walked to the Brass Gear, which had one foot in the entertainment district while the other balanced on more respectable ground. Artifices had once occupied some of the highest positions within the city, a select few advising the basilissa herself. Now they practically shared a spoke with trovadores and meretrices. They were entertainment. Still, the gens cleaved to their academic image. Along with the spadones, they archived and protected knowledge. Babieca remembered wandering through their undercroft with Julia, gazing at the parts and sleeping machinae that no longer functioned. Sulpicia had emerged delicately from the hoard of gears and broken charms, and her presence had startled them both. He wondered what she was doing at the moment. Probably keeping an eye on Eumachia, the daughter of the basilissa. How strange, to be a mechanical fox with the spark of life, wandering through the Arx of Violets on swift feet.

The common room of the Brass Gear was sparsely populated. At this hour, most of the builders were still paying their respects at the tower. It would be imprudent to remain here for too long, since many of the builders who had witnessed his musical event were probably on their way to the caupona. He squinted. Great brass discs were positioned in the corners of the room, and they reflected the lamplight in a way that dazzled him, for a moment. When the spots cleared from his eyes, he saw that only a few of the tables were occupied. An older woman in a patterned stola was working on a mechanical dove. Beside her, a boy was scowling at a tablet. The scattering of parts before him suggested that the design wasn't going too well. The ale-wife moved behind the counter, serving drinks from a cracked amphora.

"I'm going to ask her about Julia," Babieca said. "Give me some money."

"Absolutely not," Morgan replied.

"I need something to bargain with."

"Just use your body, like any decent person would."

"Fine. If she wants a bribe, I'll show her the cobwebs in my purse."

Morgan rolled her eyes. "Just lift up your tunica and be done with it."

"What sort of crass world are you living in? Do archers simply grunt and lift their tunicae whenever they meet each other on the battlements?"

She gave him a light shove. "Just go. Be creative in the face of adversity."

He smoothed his hair and approached the L-shaped counter. The ale-wife was pouring hot chickpeas into a clay vat.

"Let me help you with that," he offered.

"You'd only smash your fingers." She smoothly replaced the vat, which fit into a round opening in the counter. "What's your pleasure?"

"I could name several."

She gave him a flat look. "What do you want to drink? We've got spiced wine, hippocrene, and barley beer so thick you could balance a knife in it."

"I'm actually looking for some information."

Her expression didn't change. "I don't know what cheap scrolls you've been reading, but I run a caupona. I'm too busy to fuck about with intrigue. Go to court if you're looking for that."

"I can respect that you're busy—"

"Drink something, or go away, nemo."

The insult stung him, but only slightly. "Fine. I'll have—"

She'd already poured him some wine from the amphora. "One maravedi."

Babieca reached into his purse. This investigation was growing more expensive by the moment, and the whole point had been to avoid spending anything. He handed over the coin, and the ale-wife snatched it quickly, as a bird might snatch a seed from your hand.

"Enjoy," she said, and started to walk away.

"Wait. Please."

She turned, now looking annoyed. "Fortuna preserve us, boy, is this your first drink? Just drain the cup, and I'll get you another. It's not so difficult."

He cleared his throat. "As I was saying before, it isn't intrigue that I'm looking for. It's a young artifex. A woman, about my age, with red hair."

"I see a lot of women. She doesn't sound familiar."

"She's Naucrate's daughter."

Her eyes narrowed. "That's a significant name, boy. Don't throw it around unless you can prove what you claim."

"Did you hear about the bee that nearly killed Basilissa Pulcheria?"

"That's old news."

"Well, the bee was Naucrate's design. She gave it to her daughter, and then a fat spado took it from her. Is this starting to sound more plausible?"

"Not really."

"We need to talk to her. I've seen her in this tavern, building birds."

"You've just described half of our patrons."

He touched her hand, lightly. "Let's talk about this upstairs."

The ale-wife looked at him curiously for a moment. Then she burst into laughter, sliding her hand away. "This was your plan? To seduce me?"

Babieca struggled to maintain his composure. "I assure you, it was no jest."

"And I assure you, fuckwit, that your tiny cock holds no interest for me."

"Really? You haven't even seen what it can do."

She shook her head and returned to pouring drinks. "I've no interest in whatever games you've taught the little brain to play. I chase the velvet, not the fur."

"But I'm not a—" He bit down on the word *fur* as realization dawned. "Oh. You're in search of a different type of refreshment altogether."

For a moment, she looked at Fel, who was standing by the door. Babieca knew that look very well. Then she returned to her task. "No time, anyhow," she said. "Someone's puked in the necessary, and after I clean that up—"

"Leave that to me," Babieca said smoothly. "If you give me one moment to speak with my friend, it's possible that we can work something out."

Before she could reply, he grabbed his drink and walked back to the entrance. Morgan gave him an expectant look.

"Well? What did she say?"

"She knows who Julia is, but she's not quite willing to tell us. Not yet."

"What does she want?"

"Fel."

The miles stared at him. "What?"

"Do I need to draw you a picture? She wants to peel off your lorica."

Fel reddened, staring at the floor. "Out of the question."

"Just go and flirt with her for a while."

"That was supposed to be your job."

Fel's voice had a strangled quality to it that Babieca hadn't heard before. He tried very hard not to smile. "I have to clean up a pile of puke. I assure you that your task will be far sweeter. Now go. Make us proud."

"This is ridiculous," Fel muttered.

"Once we're a company, we won't have to resort to these sordid activities." He could no longer keep himself from smiling. "For now, we've got to—how did Morgan put it— be creative in the face of adversity?"

"I'm sorry," Morgan whispered.

"I despise both of you right now," Fel said. "I hope you understand that."

Cleaning out the necessary was no joyful task, and by the time Babieca finished, he was covered in sweat and unsightly stains. He'd also torn a hole in his tunica, which would do nothing to improve his appearance. When he emerged, Fel was still talking with the ale-wife. She saw him, disentangled herself politely, and walked back to the entrance of the caupona.

"You stink," she said.

"What a triumph of logic. Did you find out where she is?"

Fel looked embarrassed. "Yes."

"Well done! You must have really—"

"Finish that sentence, trovador, and I'll carve out your guts."

"Understood."

"It was very sweet," Morgan said beneath her breath, as they followed the miles. "She definitely has a soft side."

"That threat goes for both of you," Fel said, without turning around.

They circled the edge of the Subura, until they came to Aditus Claustrum. The street was packed with squat, three-story insulae. Laundry hung from lines suspended over the alleys. The vici wasn't precisely disheveled, but it was a far cry from the northern part of the city. This was where people with shaky prospects tended to settle. The ground floor of each insula was rented out by various shopkeepers. Babieca saw mercers, silk merchants, and scent-peddlers. The dyers had to work at the edge of the city, on account of their stink. Urine was used to fix most dyes. A concession was made, though, in the form of bottles placed outside the shops. Occasionally, a passerby would stop, piss into one of the bottles, and then continue on his way. At the end of the day, the shop owners would deliver the bottles to the outskirts of the city and collect a few coins for their malodorous gift to the dyers.

Fel stopped outside a small workshop fronting one of the insulae. A tablet affixed to the wall proclaimed that the builder could fix anything. A shattered organ leaned against the wall of the workshop, attesting to the fact that the sign wasn't completely accurate.

"She must have earned herself an apprenticeship," Morgan said. Her expression betrayed a flash of remorse. "Maybe we should just leave her alone."

"I don't think so." Babieca squared his shoulders. "You know that she's a part of this. No amount of hiding will save her, in the end."

"Do we really need to rush the inevitable?"

"What we need," Fel said, "is a fourth. An artifex could be very useful."

"You don't know her very well," Babieca said. "She isn't the most agreeable builder in the city. She's got a bit of a temper."

"Perfect. So do I." Fel opened the door.

The bottegha was lined with shelves. Devices and debris were everywhere, sometimes indistinguishable from each other. Babieca saw rings and charms, broken sundials, music boxes, dolls with articulated limbs, and divining rods. A bin was overflowing with mechanical frogs. Julia stood behind the counter, frowning at a tablet. Behind her, a tattered curtain separated the shop from what must have been the sleeping quarters beyond. He smelled smoke from a brazier, and the aroma of grilled mushrooms.

Julia looked up. The polite smile vanished from her face when she recognized him.

"What are you doing here?"

"We wanted to see your new workshop." He nodded in appreciation. "It's very compact. Lots of frogs."

"You have to leave. The master will be back any moment."

"I thought you had no use for masters."

Her eyes darkened. "In case you haven't noticed, I don't have a lot of options."

"I thought you were studying at the tower."

She kept her eyes on the door. "After the incident at the Arx of Violets, none of them were willing to teach me. They look down on me, just as they looked down on my mother. Do you know what they used to call her? Queen of the Cloaca. Fucking halfwits. They had no idea how much work it took to keep the sewer running, or what a marvel the design was."

Morgan approached the counter. "Julia, I know you aren't exactly on friendly terms with us, but we're somewhat entangled."

The young artifex laughed bitterly. "What an excellent description. I suppose we are. You need to leave, though." Her face betrayed a flash of desperation. "I have a trade here, a real mystery. It's actually working out. I can't jeopardize that."

"We need your help," Fel said.

She glanced at the miles. "I thought you'd managed to escape this bizarre company."

"It's not a company. *We're* not. Yet. But you could change that."

Julia backed away but only managed to get tangled in the curtain. "The wheel would have to crack before I agreed to join you."

Babieca leaned over the counter. "We understand your hesitation. But something happened a few nights ago."

Julia frowned. "At Domina Pendelia's? I was there. Aside from an orgy and some character assassination, I saw nothing out of the ordinary."

"The real action was in the alleys."

"I don't want any part of this, whatever it is."

"That's the problem. You're already a part of it." Babieca smiled sadly. "I know that you want to live your life in peace. But is that really what Naucrate would have wanted?"

Julia's face went white. Before he could react, she grabbed a handful of his tunica. With surprising ease, she hauled him over the counter, like a sack of root vegetables. He landed facedown on the floor, and she knelt beside him.

"Say her name again," Julia murmured, "and I'll break every bone in your body, starting with the one you love most."

He coughed. "I'm not sure why this keeps happening to me today."

"Julia." Morgan carefully walked around the counter. "This involves the silenoi. That's why we need your help."

"You couldn't pay me enough to go near them again."

"We think that—" Morgan also kept her eyes on the door. She lowered her voice. "Latona is going to make some sort of deal with them. She has something that they want. An 'heirloom,' she called it."

"What does this have to do with me?"

"We know where she's meeting them," Fel said. "If something goes wrong, that mechanical bee of yours is the only thing that can stop them in their tracks."

"*If* something goes wrong?" Julia's laugh turned into a kind of sputter. "You've all gone soft in the head. What's your plan? To follow the basilissa to her secret assignation?"

"Nobody else knows of this," Morgan pressed. "You understand, as well as we do, what Latona is capable of. Anfractus isn't enough for her. If this transaction is successful, it could bloom into an alliance that will destroy us all. The silenoi could hunt the streets during the day, picking us off like stunned cattle."

"That couldn't happen," Julia said. But she didn't sound convinced.

Slowly, Babieca rose from the ground. "We need you," he said. "Roldan is gone. If you join us, we'll be a company once more."

"I'm no auditor," she said, uncertainly.

"Companies change. You may not be able to speak with lares, but you're a builder. Your mother was a true artifex, and she passed that on to you. Her talent is in your blood."

Her face fell. "I like this job."

"If that were so, you wouldn't still be listening to me."

Julia looked forlornly at the bin of frogs. "I just got the hang of making those," she said. "They're all the rage."

"We're going to the necropolis," Morgan replied. "Just before sundown. Can you meet us there?"

"I don't know."

"Think it over. We'll wait for you."

"I can't promise anything. I need to think."

"In the meantime," Babieca said, "remember that hopping frogs may be the rage, but that bee of yours is part of something much larger. Perhaps we all are."

"I suppose you can be charming," Julia replied. "Mostly when you're silent, though."

"That's what I keep saying," Fel agreed.

"We really do need you." Babieca gave her a curious look. "You're the only one who's mad enough to help us."

"I definitely get that from my mother." She sniffed the air suddenly. "The mushrooms are burning, and the master will return soon. You have to leave now."

"Hopefully we'll see you among the graves," Babieca said. "Once you get past the swampy smell, the marsh lights can actually be romantic."

"Just get out of here," Julia said, trying to conceal her smile. Then she disappeared behind the curtain. Fire was a constant threat in this neighborhood, and even a skewer of mushrooms was capable of burning down the insula.

Once they were outside, Babieca let himself relax a little. "I think we made an impression," he said. "It might actually work."

"Mentioning her mother was a wild throw," Morgan said. "It could have ruined everything. How did you know that it would work?"

"I didn't. I only knew that it would make her angry."

"You're not allowed to talk for a while," Fel said.

"That hardly seems fair."

"You can still sing. We need money, after all. Just no talking."

"I'm not sure that I like where this new company is going."

"I'm certain you'll grow to appreciate it," Morgan said sweetly. "Companies change, after all. You said it yourself."

Babieca didn't reply. Perhaps Fel was right. He'd talked himself into enough blind corners for one day.

4

CARL DIDN'T REMEMBER FALLING ASLEEP, BUT he woke up on the couch with a slow, spreading ache in his left shoulder. They'd returned before dawn, and the transition had left him feeling shaky and wired at the same time, like an ancient fuse about to burst. The glass on the coffee table still had some dregs left: an unpleasant mixture of rye and Coke with a few ashes floating on the surface. He washed it out, then stood in the small, bright kitchen for what felt like several minutes, trying to spark some neural activity.

His mind felt oxidized. If he'd been teaching today, it would have been the perfect time for group work. Then he could watch them blearily from the front of the room as they highlighted, flipped through the textbook, or acknowledged without shame that they'd read nothing. He could turn them loose on each other, allowing the talkative ones to seize control, while the introverts made notes and refused to engage. Carl's teaching strategy could best be classified as mellow. Sometimes he was full of energy, but most of the time he sat back and let them come to their own conclusions. As long as they occasionally wrote things down and didn't make any offensive comments, he felt that the tutorial was going well. A teaching assistant was a kind of liaison between student and professor. His job was to translate Dr. Darby's lectures, in the same way that a foreign language was broken down with flash cards.

Students would usually avoid the professor's office, with its accumulation of books, art prints, and moldering exams stuffed into corners. They felt more comfortable visiting the shared TA office, with its bare walls and slowly dying ficus beneath the window. Often, graduate students were only a few years older than their undergraduate charges, and the power differential wasn't quite as obvious. In the first six months of his MA, Carl had been yelled at, cried on, touched inappropriately, and given cookies with a heart-shaped note (from a shy computer science student, who'd booked weekly meetings purely to talk about Minecraft). One of Shelby's students always seemed to be coming from the gym and would show up to their meeting in a tank top and shorts that reminded her of Bob Benson from *Mad Men*.

He'd just keep stretching, she'd told Carl, *all casual, like any moment this was going to turn into a hot yoga session.*

Luckily, this was an off day. No tutorials. He should be studying for something. He couldn't remember what, but there was always something. The life test that he would someday fail miserably. Shelby might want to organize a reading party. His apartment was the only one with a balcony, which meant that he'd probably be hosting. Carl surveyed the living room. It was sort of clean, if you squinted and wore shoes. He spied only a few dust bunnies, receipts, and loose change hiding in the corners. He had a kind of fondness for dust bunnies. They reminded him of tumbleweeds. When they got big enough, he liked to pretend that he was in a spaghetti western, and his apartment was the back lot of MGM. *Prairie Showdown.* Something that allowed him to wear a black hat.

The barrel-sized container of coffee from Bulk Barn was empty. That would be a problem. Aside from an old Celestial Seasonings sampler—which he'd inherited with the apartment—there was nothing left to keep him awake. Carl removed a take-out box from the fridge and shoveled cold fries into his mouth. He found an old tin of mixed nuts in the cupboard. The cashews had been picked over, but a few walnuts remained, lying in a bed of salt. A trip to Safeway might be in order. Both the fridge and the cupboards were turning into a kind of burial ground for meals past.

When he was living in Toronto, he'd shared an apartment with two girls. It was a small place, and the girls had slept in a bunk bed. He could remember coming home to the smell of polenta and roast vegetables, or chicken that was delightfully charred. They would split a pack of cider and watch *The Wire*, pausing to replay half of the conversations when none of them could figure out what was going on. His dinner contribution always amounted to picking up giant burritos from Kensington Market. Still, he'd felt as if he were adding fuel to the fire, helping to power their crazy, idealistic machine. A year ago, he'd run into one of the girls—Haley— at the Regina Folk Festival. She'd looked beautiful and healthy. She was almost finished with her thesis on animal consciousness in literature. Carl had wanted to ask her if he was still the same, if she could see the flush of anger and confusion beneath his smile. Instead, he'd split a piece of coconut pie with her, and they'd talked about Detective McNulty's greatest moments.

Making friends in a graduate program wasn't too difficult. Everyone shared a trauma bond with each other, and there was always a party or clothes swap or study session at someone's tiny apartment (freezing in winter, tropical in the summer). The issue was avoiding the cloud of hysteria that seemed to fall whenever more than three grad students were in a room. The conversation always turned to essays, exams, and the bleak horizon of jobs. If someone received funding, they were celebrated in public but immolated privately. It was a game of *Survivor* that you played with your close friends. He was lucky to have found Shelby and Andrew, but their friendship also had an edge of logic to it. None of them were in competition for the same grants. Their radical differences made them less threatening to each other.

His phone buzzed. Shelby must have been reading his mind.

Downstairs, the text said.

Carl pressed the buzzer. The speaker delivered only static, but you could still open the door. This was a gamble. His apartment was located above a sex shop, and many people assumed that the top floor was a massage parlor. More than once, he'd been woken up by middle-aged businessmen pounding on his front door in search of a happy ending. One of these days, he'd open the door and name his price. A bit of extra money wouldn't hurt. And it wasn't as if the act were so foreign. He gave himself handjobs all the time.

He threw on a shirt and a pair of shorts. Weather in Saskatchewan turned on a dime. But if the sun was out, you dressed for summer. That was the rule. Even if you ended up shivering in a patch of cold light, at least you'd exposed your skin to some fresh air. Once winter came, no part of your body could be left uncovered. Sometimes when the wind was cutting through his jacket, he felt like a raw potato covered in tinfoil, completely vulnerable to the horror of the seasons. He opened the patio door, just a crack, and stuck one toe into the breach. The air was surprisingly warm. He chose to trust it, in the dumb way that you trust an ex who tells you that nothing has changed, not really.

He heard the door swing open.

"There's no coffee," he called from the bedroom, looking for a pair of socks. "I do have gin and walnuts, if that's what you're looking for."

Carl stepped out of the bedroom. He expected to see Shelby, but there was nobody there. He looked around. The patio door was open a bit wider. That was unlike her. Usually, she made a point of washing his dishes, because she couldn't abide the thought of them creating new life in his dirty sink. He squeezed through the opening that led to the patio. The door always got stuck on its runners, and pushing it only made things worse.

There was nobody on the patio. Carl felt a prickling in his stomach. Had he even looked at the number that was texting him? It could have been anyone. Mardian. Or someone else hired by the basilissa to hunt him down. Nobody was following the rules anymore, and the division between city and park made no difference. It wouldn't take much to figure out his address. Ingrid had found him easily enough. Carl tried to listen, but the noise from the street below filled his ears. He reached into his pocket, realizing as he did so that his phone was on the kitchen table. Slowly, he picked up a the pair of barbecue tongs. They were the closest thing to a weapon that he could find. They were grimy and didn't feel reassuring in his hand.

"Your toilet's running."

Heart pounding, he turned, holding the tongs like a knife.

Andrew blinked at him. "Are we patio-fighting? Is that a thing now?"

"*Fuck.* You scared me."

"Sorry. I had to go the bathroom. I noticed that your toilet was running. Sometimes it helps if you put a brick in the tank."

Carl lowered the barbecue tongs. "I thought you were a burglar."

"You let me in."

"I know. Sorry. I had a weird sleep."

"How was practice?"

"What?"

"Hockey practice."

"Oh. Right." Carl stepped back into the living room. Most of the time, Shelby was here to temper his lies. He wasn't used to spinning them without her. "It sucked. I'm out of shape, and I can't stick-handle for shit."

"It seems kind of late—eleven thirty at night. Is that normal?"

"I don't know. It's the only time that we can reserve the rink, I guess."

"Between your hockey practice and those art classes that Shelby's taking, it feels like we almost never see each other in the evening."

Carl felt a stab of guilt. "Yeah. I'm sorry. It won't be forever."

That was probably a lie, but he couldn't think of anything else to say.

"How's therapy?" Carl winced even as he said the word.

"Fine." Andrew looked away for a second. "Also, I'm catching up on my DVD sets. Did you realize that you can watch *Game of Thrones* in both Urdu and Brazilian Portuguese?"

Carl supposed that they wouldn't be talking about the sessions. He could hardly blame Andrew for avoiding the topic. Maybe each session was just forty-five minutes of silence.

"That sounds like a sweet time. The language settings, I mean."

"I've already learned how to say *Winterfell* in six languages. In Spanish, it's *Invernalia*."

He thought of Andrew, fiddling with the menu on his DVD, while his friends were in another world. He'd been there once, by their side, whispering to salamanders and bribing gnomoi with delicious marble. Now he was like a child whose parents had separated. Everyone wanted what was best for him, but nobody would tell him the truth. Carl realized that magic was cruel. There was no other way to describe it. How could you offer someone a life full of endless wonder, then snatch it away? It seemed like an awful payment for the sacrifice that he'd made. He didn't understand the rules, or why they were so bloody important. He didn't understand why death was a boundary that you couldn't cross, even in a place like Anfractus, where the stones had arguments while mechanical spiders brushed your feet. What was the point of power, with its wings dipped in blood and all of its many-colored fires, if it couldn't cheat death?

The poet Catullus had been right. *Nox est perpetua una dormienda.* Death was the perfect, dreamless night. Even in Anfractus, it was a permanent shift in state. Years from now, decades even, Andrew might find his way back to the city of infinite alleys. But he wouldn't be the same person. Roldan would sleep forever, with no stone or blue hen's egg to mark where he'd fallen. In the meantime, Andrew had no shadow. Carl could see the effect that its loss was having on his friend. He smiled less. His eyes no longer held that sweet anticipation, which was always visible just before they transitioned. The small thrill of knowing that change was possible, that he could step into the skin of another. It seemed that every last trace of memory had vanished. Carl wondered if Roldan's alley still existed, if it waited for him, or if it was gone. His belongings were buried underneath the house by the wall. The patched tunica, the sandals and smallclothes, and the dagger that Felix had given him.

Carl sat down on the couch. A second later, he wanted to stand up. He wasn't sure what he was doing. Why was Andrew here? Had they made plans? He was a terrible host. Shelby was much better at organizing things. Carl felt like an alien who'd suddenly been thrust into a complex social situation. He knew how to make small talk, to put people at ease, but this was different. He couldn't lie all of the time. Even the lies of omission were getting to him, chewing up his insides, like fiberglass.

"*Pues, nada*—" Carl blinked. "Sorry. Force of habit from talking to my mother on the phone. I mean—so—how are things?"

"You're acting strangely."

"What do you mean?"

"You seem nervous."

"I'm just hungover. I need a coffee."

"Did you go out for drinks with the team?"

He stood up. The action seemed to negate the lie that was building. "I need a coffee," he repeated. "Let's go to the Dodger."

"Sure. We can get a prairie scone."

"I can't believe they're called that. As if scones were somehow different in a flat province." He put on his shoes. There was a pebble stuck in the sole. He shook it out, then slipped his foot back in. The pebble was still there. "Fuck!" Carl smacked the shoe against the ground, again and again, until the pebble flew out.

"Maybe you need a green tea."

"No. Sorry. I don't know what's wrong with me today." He checked his phone. No messages from Shelby. "Did we have plans? Are we meeting at the library, or something? I feel like I'm forgetting something."

"Shelby's in Moose Jaw, visiting her aunt."

That was what he'd forgotten. Shelby was occupied for the day. There would be no monitor to ensure that he kept the lie turning on smooth wheels.

"Right. She must be going crazy."

"I've heard that Moose Jaw has a pretty good arts scene."

"They've certainly got a large moose statue. That's something."

"You're right, though. We didn't make specific plans. I came over because I forgot my copy of *Beowulf* in your knapsack."

"Oh—yeah, I thought it was heavier than usual."

It seemed like a thin excuse. And it wasn't like Andrew to simply show up without texting first. He liked to plan things in advance.

"Normally I wouldn't need it," Andrew continued, "but I made some notes—"

"Not a problem. The knapsack's in my room. You can fish it out, if you're willing to brave the mess."

"It's nothing I haven't seen before."

Andrew disappeared into his bedroom. Carl walked into the kitchen and opened the humidor that was sitting on the table. He rolled a joint. The resin stuck to his fingers, but he liked the tacky feeling that it left behind. Just a trace of skunk. He slipped the joint into his pocket, along with a lighter, and closed the fragrant box.

"Who's Julia?"

Andrew was standing in the entrance to the kitchen. For a moment, Carl had forgotten that he was even there. The question made no sense at first. Then his stomach did a flip as he realized what Andrew had just said.

"Who?" He tried to keep his tone neutral.

"Julia." He was holding his copy of *Beowulf.* "There was a letter from SaskTel in your bag. It was still sealed, but you'd written *find Julia* on the envelope."

"Oh. Right." Shit. He must have been doodling on the

envelope. The lecture had stalled a bit, and Darby was talking about the religious wars. His mind had wandered. *Find Julia*. Was his subconscious trying to completely screw him over?

"Who's Julia?" Andrew repeated.

An engineering student named Sam, who moonlights as an artifex.

The truth had a peculiar simplicity. If only it didn't sound crazy.

"She's—a student. I have to find her e-mail, so I can give her the syllabus."

"It's not available online?"

"No . . . Darby's a weird traditionalist. He hates posting course materials on WebCT. If it were up to him, we'd be mimeographing all of the assignments by hand."

"That seems really inconvenient."

"Just one of the many joys of working for an aging hipster."

"Soon we'll be the aging hipsters."

"I'd prefer not to think that far ahead." He filled a Nalgene flask with water. "Ready? We should probably get there early, before they start playing dubstep."

"When did every café become a performance venue?"

"We live in the age of multitasking. I think it all happened while we were in college. The world suddenly accrued this new layer of irony."

"Don't say that in front of your students. They'll eat you alive."

"It already belongs to them." Carl shook his head. "Isn't that odd? It was ours, but we missed it. Like a flash."

"You really do need coffee. You're starting to sound like Jennifer Egan."

Andrew seemed to have forgotten about the Julia thing. Carl was relieved. That was a rookie mistake, and if Andrew had pressed, he wasn't sure how far he could take the lie. The truth sounded impossible. Julia was a character, a shadow, whose life and memories belonged to an engineering grad student named Sam. Julia was an artifex who specialized in bees and frogs. Her mother, Naucrate, had maintained the fountains and the great cloaca of Anfractus. In this world, she was a glimmer in the mirror, a spot on the corner of Sam's vision. But on the other side of the park, she was a person with her own guarded intentions, her own patchwork of nagging fears and anxieties. Possibly, she had inherited the spark of life from her mother, the ability to forge a true machina with a soul—if that was what the spark was.

Carl paused in the act of locking the door. For a moment, he stood in the hallway, which smelled like old wood and cigarettes. He could hear music coming from the sex shop below. For some reason that he couldn't fathom, Love Selection insisted on providing a soundtrack. You'd expect them to play cheesy movies, but instead, the radio was tuned to soft jazz or classical music.

"Did you forget something?" Andrew asked.

He nearly replied in the affirmative. *Yes. I forgot to tell you that we're heroes, or maybe the next closest thing. I forgot to tell you that Wascana Park is some kind of spell that leads us to another world. Maybe it's all just a dream, but the memories are real. I forgot to say that we kissed once, even if it feels like years ago. We were naked with each other, and I don't know if that will ever happen again, but I still think about it. The way you grinned before climbing on top of me, the same grin that flashed out of you just before midnight, when the park turned. I forgot to tell you that we were lashed together by a lover's belt, and that I held your cooling hand as we rode away from the harbor. Behind us, I knew that the undinae whispered our doom, even if I couldn't hear them. He forgot to tell you so much, Roldan. That he loved to fix your sleeves. That he was writing a song for you. That someday, when you were both older, he really would tell you the story of the cracked lute.*

"No," Carl said. "Just lost my train of thought, for a second. Let's go."

They walked down the narrow flight of stairs, avoiding the mildewed step that would always try to steal your shoe. Broad Street was brilliant and humming with traffic noise.

A Greyhound bus thundered toward the depot. Orange rings of construction had appeared on every corner, and parts of the street were laid bare. He could smell braised pork from the nearby Vietnamese restaurant. Broad and Albert streets were the main arteries of Regina. Broad felt more exposed, and many of its façades were crumbling. Albert eventually became a series of strip malls, before giving itself up to the Ring Road, which encircled the city. Living on Broad meant sharing space with galleries, community centers, and parking lots that stretched like bald spots over the urban landscape. There was a constant cycle of demolition and construction, which reminded him of a body shedding its cells.

A woman walked by, wearing a sundress and yelling into her phone. Carl didn't recognize the language, but there was something beautiful and liquid about it. Even though she was clearly agitated, the syllables felt strangely calm, as if they knew better. He realized that her dress was covered in pineapples and toucans. He couldn't imagine being angry while wearing fruit.

They walked down Eleventh Street, where the construction had raised a cloud of yellow dust and grit. Carl saw an exhausted construction worker smoking in a trailer. His curly hair was matted with sweat, and his eyes were distant as he inhaled. He was skinny, and his steel-toed boots looked almost clownish. *Muster Point*, the sign next to him read. It sounded almost fun, like the rumpus in *Where the Wild Things Are*. Men mustering in a hot, smoke-filled trailer, carefully avoiding eye contact as they allowed themselves to unravel in the sunlight. He'd never learned how to muster, not properly. He couldn't fake that affability, that ease with which some men related to each other, as if they'd always been friends. He felt more at home with the slightly damaged. Men whose neuroses burned brightly, who could be as fragile as dandelions, their emotional flotsam always close to the surface.

Maybe the young guy was exactly like that. Maybe he was lost in thought, trying to figure out if he should apply to art school or wondering if someone would eventually recognize his talents as a DJ. When Carl had worked at a grocery store, arranging produce and throwing rancid cardboard flats into the compactor, nobody had asked him about grad school. Customers had assumed that he was a burnout, or that he lacked the evolutionary skills to become something useful, like a certified accountant. Wreathed by smoke, caught unawares, the kid in the trailer might have easily been him. Another wild thing under the sun. The traffic noise died down as they continued a few blocks away from Broad. The streetlights in this neighborhood were painted red, and the signs were in Mandarin as well as English. They walked past the old firehouse, with its peeling orange roof and clock tower. Now it was a heritage museum, but Carl could imagine it as was it nearly a century ago, klaxons ringing, on perpetual alert. Fires and tornadoes had always been a part of Regina's history. They crossed at Osler Street and made their way to the Artful Dodger. It was quiet at this time of day. A few burned-out hipsters sat on the couches near the front door, listening to oversized headphones. Posters for Funk Friday and the Cubanéate Latin Dance Party decorated the walls. The parquet floors had recently been sanded, and there was a faint tickle of sawdust in the air. The raised seating in the performance area was empty and covered by a scattering of pillows. It reminded Carl of an empty Hippodrome, although he couldn't say this aloud.

Two staff members leaned against the counter, enthusiastically debating the merits of different game consoles. "No," one of them was saying, "what makes it totally superior is that you can play Alex Kidd in Miracle World. And normally, you can't even *get* that title, but I found a copy when I was in Toronto."

"Here." Andrew gave him some cash. "I trust you to order my sandwich."

"I'm honored."

"I'm going to look at the art."

Carl ordered their lunch, along with two coffees. When the sandwiches came, he saw that Andrew's had a thick slice of tomato. Quickly he unwrapped the sandwich and popped the tomato into his mouth. Better to dispose of it than to watch Andrew make a face while he tried to remove the tomato without touching it, like a kid playing Operation. He swallowed it whole and then took a long pull of coffee, which made him nauseated. Andrew emerged from the gallery just as Carl was uncapping the Nalgene, trying to add another liquid to the mix.

"Let's go to the park," Carl said. "I feel like they're about to play Vampire Weekend."

"You're all about the diss today," Andrew observed. "I really don't see what separates us from them."

"For one thing, I'm no longer twenty. I don't hang out in raw spaces."

"You sound like a PSA for getting older."

"Fine. We share a spoke. Have it your way."

"You share a what?"

Carl blinked. The words had come so easily. *We share a spoke on Fortuna's wheel.* If Shelby were here, she'd yell, "Parking!" But he was on his own, and apparently he couldn't keep his worlds separate from each other.

"Never mind," he said. "The sawdust is getting to me. Let's go."

They crossed to the micropark on the other side of the street. Decades ago, a building had burned to the ground on this spot, and the green corner was a kind of memorial. There was a mysterious sculpture involving rocks in a metal grid, and tiled benches, surrounded by blooming purple echinacea. The park had fallen into disrepair, but there was something appropriate about the encroaching weeds. The whole area had been left to its own devices, and parts were allowed to decay while others thrived. The chokecherry trees cast their shadows against a nearby wall whose white paint was falling away, revealing a layer of metallic blue. Carl leaned against the crumbling brick. Sunlight filtered through the bowed trees, moving across the sculpture whose significance was a mystery. Something to do with caged nature, or maybe it was about nature taking control. To him, it resembled a necropolis, with its orderly plots in the shape of dice.

He set the coffees and sandwiches on the ground. Then he lit the joint, shielding it from the light wind. The weeds nodded in silent agreement. Carl took a long drag. He held it in his lungs until it was a sweet, persistent burn, filling him up. Then he exhaled a current of smoke and slid down the wall. His muscles relaxed. He sat on the ground and listened to the generous silence of the little park. Andrew took the joint from him. Carl watched him inhale, then cough. He had virgin lungs. Unlike Carl or Shelby, he'd never picked up smoking. There was something miraculous about it, as if he'd grown up in a convent.

Andrew coughed again. Carl rubbed his back. It was an unconscious gesture. Andrew said nothing and handed the joint back. Carl took another drag. Then he stubbed it out and put the roach in his pocket.

"This is a strange park," Andrew said.

"The Romans had parks like this," he replied. "Little green spaces, in the middle of Rome's dirty sprawl. You can really only have a park in a city. Otherwise, it would just be a clearing. The two are symbiotic."

"The park needs the city."

"It's a love affair."

"I think someone broke up with this park. It's seen better days."

"I like the breakdown. It's comforting."

"Spider."

"What?"

"Giant spider. Right behind you."

Carl turned around. A four-foot spider reared up, its legs flashing in the sun. Its mouth was an enormous black hole. He shouted. Andrew stared to laugh.

"It's only a garbage can," he said. "Look."

Carl approached the creature. His heart was still in his throat. Upon closer examination, he realized that it was a stylized garbage can. Its eyes were colored glass.

Andrew continued to laugh. "Your face was amazing."

A flash of memory returned to him. They were at the insula in Vici Arces. They hadn't yet met Felix. He'd been about to steal some grapes when he'd heard Roldan scream. He was standing before a painted dog, baring its teeth. *Beware of dog*, read the caption below the painting. A primitive security measure. Roldan was pale but laughing. How quickly fear could effervesce, when you were in the right company.

"Fuck," Carl murmured. "I thought it was a spider demon."

"It's just art." He unwrapped his sandwich and tossed the plastic into the spider's mouth. "See. It wants our garbage, and our compassion."

"You didn't see it bearing down on you."

Andrew took his hand. "Don't worry. I'll protect you from Shelob's daughter. Or granddaughter. As spider-demons go, it's a bit of a runt."

Carl could feel himself traveling back to that night in the hidden room. The sad tapestry, the sharp edge of the stone pallet. These were Babieca's memories, diffuse and shadowed in places, like stained glass. They danced before him, and he couldn't be certain where he was standing, or what remained unseen. But he'd known that something was different. Some door—previously closed—had been left ajar. It was something between an invitation and a dare.

This was different. The door wasn't open, but for the first time, he could see a ribbon of light underneath it. He felt the bone islet on Andrew's knuckle. He was afraid to hold on too tightly, afraid to move at all.

"You're going to protect me?" Carl repeated. The question was lame, but he couldn't think of anything else to say.

"Why not?" Andrew stared at the eight-legged trash can. "There's a lot of stuff out there. We can't always see it, but it's there, like dark matter."

"What sort of stuff?"

"Violence. Heartbreak. Senseless pain."

"You can't protect me from that. You can't protect yourself, either."

Andrew shrugged. "Sometimes it feels like the horrors outweigh the blessings in this world. But there's also the great stuff. Baby universes that are just learning to walk.

Raspberry ginger ale. The sloth sanctuary in Costa Rica. The smell just before it rains. Getting a whole bus to yourself. Parks that rise out of the ashes, like this one."

Carl took in the ragged edges of the park. It tugged lightly at him. It was the same thing he'd felt in Wascana Park, just before a transition. The sensation was weaker—not that irresistible drag toward another world—but he could still sense it. A pressure as light as Andrew's hand in his own. Carl wondered, for the first time, if all parks had a kind of magic. If this little piece of greenery had its own current, then maybe it was connected to Wascana Park, somehow. Maybe they were all connected.

"We'll have to look out for each other," Carl said. "I'll take first watch."

"You'd sleep through an attack."

"You don't know that."

"Didn't it take four alarms to get you out of bed?"

"If ogres or dragons were involved, I know I could stay awake."

"The problem," Andrew said, "is that we don't have rearview mirrors. We never see the bad stuff coming. It always hits us from behind."

"That might be a good invention. A metaphysical rear view."

Andrew smiled. "Monsters in mirror are closer than they appear."

"We could take this to Dragon's Den. They'd be all over it."

"What if we could see it coming? Not just the bad stuff, but the good stuff, as well?" Andrew looked at him oddly. "What would you do? Brace for impact? Or try to swerve?"

"I'm not sure how to drive this metaphor."

"I mean it, though. Aren't we obligated to say something? To prevent the crash before it happens?"

"I'm not sure that's possible."

"It must be. It's so easy to predict where someone else is headed. We never see our own blind spot, but with other people, it's like the GPS voice is screaming, *wrong turn*."

"I don't see any crashes in your future," Carl said softly. "Maybe a flat tire, but that's easy enough to fix."

Andrew was silent for a moment. Then he said: "Something's following me."

"What?"

"A shadow. I dream about it. Sometimes, I see it when I'm not looking at anything in particular. I catch a glimpse of its tail, or a flash of its eyes."

"You're dreaming about cats?"

"Salamanders."

Carl went cold. "Are you sure that's what they are?"

"Pretty sure."

"Maybe—" He searched for an innocuous response. "Maybe it's just a stress dream. Some people dream about their teeth falling out, but you dream about newts."

"I don't know what they want. Sometimes I think they're trying to warn me."

Carl squeezed his hand. "You're going to be fine. It's just a dream."

"Sometimes," he said, "this feels like the dream."

They sat for a while, in silence. The chokecherry shadows moved across the wall. A prairie dog emerged from the leafy depths of the sculpture. His nostrils twitched. Then he disappeared back into the undergrowth. A semitruck roared in the distance. They finished their sandwiches and left the park. Andrew said very little as they walked down Broad Street. Carl knew that he was thinking about the salamander dreams. He knew that it was probably a bad sign.

But selfishly, he was glad.

It meant that some part of the shadow had survived.

PART TWO

MILES

FEL WATCHED THE ENTRANCE OF THE NECROP-
olis. Aside from a few sad wolves who were working the
marsh, the area remained deserted. Coming here for a quick
turn must have been a last resort. Maybe if you lived in
the attic of a crowded insula, with only the pigeons for
company—maybe then, you'd find yourself following one of
the wolves in this place. It took a certain lack of self-reflection
to spend yourself on someone's grave. Only sweepers and
water-bearers couldn't afford to visit the basia. Fel supposed
that she shouldn't judge. All of the insulae were subleased,
which encouraged the worst type of competition among the
poor. Not everyone had the luxury of joining a company or
working in a rich domus. Many of the people in Anfractus
took odd jobs, and all they could afford was an attic room,
without any space for a cookstove. They ate greasy food from
the cauponae and drank from the fountains. Only the most
expensive homes were connected to the aqueduct.

She'd thought about that sort of life. After leaving
Domina Pendelia's service, she could have purchased a room
in one of the insulae. Her stipend from the black basia was

enough to afford a stove on wheels and a peg to hang her cloak on. If she'd saved her money, she might have one day been able to hire a painter. She imagined one wall of her room painted with geometric designs, or Fortuna dueling with the first miles. A skilled painter could use tricks of perspective to make the room seem bigger. Her life might have been a series of heated arguments with the landlord, payments to the water-bearers, endless trips up and down the stairs. If she'd chosen to save money by living on the top floor, she'd have to climb a ladder. Strange to think that she'd come so close. It would have been a simple decision to turn her back on that other world, with its shadowed anxieties, its obsession with technology and performance.

But then she'd discovered that she was with child. Although he'd been conceived in this world, she knew that he belonged to the other. He was safer on the other side. Her Clavus. The bright nail that she'd carried inside her, through all of the infinite alleys. He had another name, but to Fel, he would always be Clavus.

She watched a boy slip into the necropolis. He wore the red-striped *tunica praetexta*, the uniform of adolescence. Faint moonlight struck the silver bula that he wore around his neck, which, along with the tunica, signified his childhood. The amulet was hollow and could be filled with precious things: little charms, gemstones, phalloi for good luck, a lock of his mother's hair. For a moment, she thought of scolding him. What was a citizen's child doing in the necropolis, just before sundown? If he was coming to pay his respects, he wouldn't be alone. He might have been seeking physical gratification, but why not visit the basia? It was obvious that his family had money to spare.

Before she could say anything or cross over to the entrance, he vanished into the necropolis. No matter. It would have been imprudent to address him. The last thing she needed was for a young, nervous citizen to remember seeing her tonight. She only hoped that he was gone before the silenus arrived. Sometimes they preferred children. With shorter legs, the prey could still run, but not for very long.

Fel didn't really know what she was doing here. They were supposed to be hiding from the basilissa, not observing her movements. If they wanted to survive, their best bet was to avoid the court altogether. But Morgan and Babieca couldn't forget what they'd seen in the alley. If their suspicions were right—if Latona was about to make a deal with the silenoi—then the ripples would spread throughout the city. Fel couldn't quite believe that she was willing to endanger her own people, simply to gain a political foothold. But she remembered the conversation that she'd heard, on the patio of lions. The basilissa was no longer content with holding one city alone. She wanted Egressus as well. Perhaps she wanted everything. An end to the current, decentralized model of city-states. A return to the empire of the builders, which had been dismantled centuries before, and only survived in the form of its inventions: the cloaca, the great via, the faith in Fortuna that united them all.

From what she knew, people had suffered beneath the empire. The silenoi had been a constant threat, and the basilissae—rather than acting as diplomats—had murdered and schemed in order to secure their place in court. She wasn't sure that things were all that better now, but at least it was possible to survive during the day. If the silenoi were allowed to hunt beneath the sun again, everything would change. Not even Babieca was willing to let the dice fall, and trovadores weren't supposed to care about anything, except for their music. If he was worried, then something might actually be on the horizon.

Her scale lorica was chafing, even with the padded tunica underneath. Fel touched the die around her neck. It promised power, but the last time she'd tried to use it, she hadn't been fast enough. Maybe if she'd rolled more quickly, the battle would have gone differently. She could still see the miles, burning from Roldan's charm. And the boy that she'd cut. He'd been dressed like a man, in an ill-fitting lorica, gripping his gladius with both hands, but he was little more than a boy in armor. Dimly, she remembered a conversation between their shadows. The memory saddened her. The details were obscure, but she knew—with a sick feeling—that she had destroyed some part of him. All because she'd hesitated.

Morgan and Babieca stepped out of the rushes, their sandals squelching in the mud. Babieca swatted at the flies buzzing around his head. This was one of the oldest parts of the city, abandoned to the elements. It still resembled the primitive camp that Anfractus had once been, long before the coming of the builders. While the rich mingled on the hill of Vici Arces, the poorest of nemones gathered here, stealing grave goods to sell on the street or striking deals with starving wolves. They were denied the luxury of sleep. Instead, they shuffled along the grave plots, baring sad angles, hiding rotten teeth, pretending to peddle rags and bits of glass. Did Felix and Drauca think about these children of the necropolis? Did they bring them food, or a needle and thread? Fel doubted it. Their labor was what allowed the black basia to exist, with its posh client registry. Without the wolves, the masked ones would have no respectability.

"She's not coming," Morgan said. "I knew it."

"Give her a few moments." Babieca scratched at a bug bite. "She's scared, just like us. That makes her smart."

"She's no fighter."

"Nor am I. But for some reason, I seem to be here."

"This was practically your idea."

He scowled. "Don't pin this on me. I only said what we were all thinking. Without Julia, we're not a company."

"We're barely a company with her," Fel said. "What does she bring to the table? An annoying bee that will fly around our heads? If we're lucky, it will distract one of the silenoi, while the rest of the pack eats us alive."

"You're very inspirational tonight," Babieca observed.

Fel shook her head. "I'm sorry. I'm distracted."

"By what? We need your concentration."

"Even distracted, I'm still the only person who can fight in close quarters. Don't worry about where my mind is at. Worry about not falling on that stubby sword of yours."

"I'm not useless in close quarters," Morgan said. "A sagittarius—"

"Yes, you're both exquisitely trained, we know." Babieca turned back to Fel. "What's distracting you?"

The miles looked at the full moon. "My son."

"He's safe on the other side."

"He's never completely safe, unless he's with me."

Morgan smiled kindly and touched her shoulder. "You've been at this for longer than us. You must know more about the other side. Can't you feel that he's protected?"

"The basilissa no longer respects the boundary. She could send someone—"

"If something had happened, you would know. Isn't that what mothers always say?"

Fel sighed. "Yes."

They heard footsteps. Julia emerged from the reeds. Her expression was one of profound annoyance. Fel saw that she had lost a sandal. Her foot was caked in mud.

"You've a bare foot," Babieca ventured. "Starting a new trend? I could see it becoming all the rage, if the dominae start walking around half shod."

"I don't wish to talk about it," Julia said. "Suffice it to say that a bat flew into my hair, and now I want to go home."

"Back to that stifling workshop?" Babieca shook his head. "This is much better. You've got the stars above you. Night-fliers to keep you company."

"Stop talking."

"Here." Fel reached into a bag slung over one shoulder and removed a pair of sandals. "You can borrow mine."

"Do you always carry an extra pair?"

"No. I've got these." Fel lifted her right foot. She wore a leather boot with a row of spikes on the sole. "Caligae. Standard issue, for managing poor terrain."

"I want a pair of those," Babieca said. "Morgan, the next time you're in the arx, can you steal some for me?"

"When have you ever had to manage poor terrain?"

"You've clearly never been to the men's necessary in the Seven Sages."

"Enough." Fel turned to Julia. "Did you bring that— device?"

"The bee?" She looked slightly embarrassed. "To be honest, I wasn't sure if I'd be able to control it. Sometimes it has a mind of its own. I brought something else, though." She gestured to a pouch hanging from her belt. "It's not as impressive, but it could help."

Babieca reached for the pouch. "It's a frog, isn't it?"

She smacked his hand. "Get away."

"Am I right?"

"The less you know, the better. Hopefully I won't need to use it."

"We'd better go inside," Fel said. "She'll be here soon, and we need to find a place where we won't be seen."

They filed into the necropolis. The air smelled richly of earth, and beneath that, decay. The grave flowers masked the odor slightly, as well as the smoke from a few scattered lamps, but death was still everywhere. The plots were arranged into patterns that resembled dice. The tombs were the pips, dark and solitary, with their bronze plaques and scattering of dried petals. Many of the plaques had greened with age. Though the names were barely legible, the sigils above them represented every spoke on the wheel. She even saw a tomb that belonged to a sicarius. How strange, to honor a killer with grave goods and a funerary plaque. Fel tried to read the words, but they had slipped away. Perhaps the sicarius had also been a devoted wife or an impassioned scholar. Killing was a vocation, but it didn't have to be a life. Wasn't she more than her gladius? The question should have been easier to answer.

The graves of children saddened her the most, with their blue hen's eggs, some cracked, others yet whole. She couldn't imagine her bright nail sleeping in a place like this, next to the grave of a forgotten killer. He should feel the sky above him, the shadows of trees and careful, questing footprints of animals. Or he should live forever, among the stars, like the basilissae who were carried off by Fortuna when they died. He should drink cups of sunlight at her table, and sleep to the lulling creak of her wheel as it turned, ceaselessly, making music all night.

They stepped over pottery shards, mysterious cloth bundles (better to leave them undisturbed), and the leavings of animals. Even in this place where the world held its breath, life gathered, with scratching claws and small bright eyes. No doubt there was also a fur or two in the shadows, waiting for them to drop something valuable. Some of them lived in the necropolis, eating the sweet bread that families left on the graves. Perhaps they shared it with the wolves, along with a bit of stolen oil. A funerary feast.

"Why would she choose the necropolis?" Julia asked. "Her ancestors are buried beneath the arx, in a private undercroft. If she wanted to be surrounded by the dead, why not simply go down there? It would be safer."

"She doesn't want to involve the court," Fel said. "They call this place the silent city. It's as far from the palace as you can get."

Morgan held up a hand for silence. In the distance, they heard something. It might have been the boy she'd seen earlier, drunk after his conquest. But as Fel listened more closely, she could hear two distinct sets of footfalls.

"Wolves?" Babieca murmured.

Morgan shook her head. "Wolves make no noise. They know the terrain too well. This has to be them."

Fel signaled them to follow. She led the group into a corner that was thick with decaying flowers. A flickering oil lamp hung above the collection of tombs. Fel snuffed out the lamp and picked up a handful of the desiccated petals.

"Here," she whispered, handing them to Morgan. "Put these in your hair. They'll cover our scent. I hope."

They crushed the flowers in great handfuls. Fel had the impression that she was seasoning herself with a dry rub of spices. Then she gestured for them to stand against the wall. The ancient bricks were covered in grime and spider-silk.

"From now on," she whispered, "don't move, or breathe. If we're lucky, the silenus will be distracted and won't notice us. But his sense of smell is very keen. If he looks even once in our direction, you'd best run."

"I hope you've got a weapon in that pouch," Babieca told Julia. "Something that you can throw in his face while we're fleeing."

"I wouldn't precisely call it that."

"Fortuna help us, if all you brought is a pile of—"

"Shut up," Fel hissed. "They're coming."

A small light moved toward them. At first, it resembled a collection of fireflies. It was actually a lamp, which the basilissa held before her as she made her way between the tombs. She drew closer, and Fel saw that the lamp was carved in the likeness of Fortuna. She held the wheel in her hand, and flame sprung from the ivory matrix where the spokes met. The flame trembled in the stale air, casting shadow wheels against the ground. The silenus walked next to the basilissa, either as a sign of social parity or because she was unwilling to expose her back. From the waist up, he resembled a muscular man whose chest was covered in scars. Below the waist, he was an animal with cloven feet, leaving half-moon footprints in the dust. He had long, curly hair, and his eyes were the color of iridescent moss. Fel tried not to look at him. The silenoi were hunters, and they knew when a fox or a rabbit was watching them.

The wrongness of the situation was almost too much. The miles and the sagittarii had been created, in part, to fight the silenoi. Over the centuries, a tentative pact had emerged. The hunters were allowed to roam the cities after dark, picking off the drunk, the stupid, the helpless. In exchange, they made themselves scarce during the day, allowing the cities to function. They no longer killed indiscriminately, but they still devoured Latona's people. The necropolis swelled, in part, because of their attacks. They had put more than one defenseless child underground. Now, to see Latona meeting with one of them—as if they were diplomatic allies—filled her with a terrible sense of unease. Nothing good would come of this.

The basilissa paused. "I like this corner," she said. "How do you find it?"

"All of these graves look alike." His accent had an unmistakable growl.

"You ought to be more discriminating." She surveyed

the orderly plots. "I'm sure that you've done your part to contribute to the death toll."

"We are not here to discuss the hunt."

"But we are. The hunt is part of it, at least." To Fel's surprise, she sat down on the floor of packed earth. "Join me."

The silenus betrayed an expression of distaste. "It is undignified."

"Nonsense. We shall be on the same level." Latona smiled. "You still tower over me, even from a sitting position. I promise you won't lose your sense of superiority."

Awkwardly, the silenus joined her on the floor. He knelt on his haunches, rather than sitting completely. It was probably difficult for him to cross his legs in such a fashion. Latona knew that and chose to exploit it, beneath the guise of maintaining their equality. She was already playing with him. Fel supposed that was what she knew best. Of all the games that Fortuna had devised, the games of court were the most dangerous. She was always playing. The game could have no winner. At the moment of her death, another piece would take her place, and the match would simply continue. It must feel strange, knowing that you would live and die on a board whose edges you could scarcely comprehend. The same board upon which your ancestors had played, offering their brief and forgotten strategies, like graffiti on a basia's wall.

"Where is it?"

Latona smiled slightly. "To what are you referring?"

"You know."

"Ah. The heirloom."

"You promised to bring it."

She looked contrite. "Well, as it turns out, the treasury is a vast and confusing place. So many precious things, dusty and uncataloged. I've had a bit of trouble locating the item in question. My spadones tell me that it could be hiding under a mountain of rubies and rusted armor. It's a small thing, you see. History tends to lose track of small things."

"He will not be pleased."

"Your master has no cause for concern. We shall find it anon. The treasury always gives up its secrets."

The silenus clenched his fist. "You have nothing."

"Far from it." She withdrew a small bag from her wine-dark stola. "I've brought some entertainment with me."

His expression was wary. "Entertainment." It wasn't a question, but there was a slight edge of curiosity in his voice.

Latona emptied the contents of the bag. A pile of black and white stones fell to the ground. She shook the bag slightly, and two remaining blue stones fell out.

"Those ones like to hide," she said. "But we need them most of all."

"What is this?"

"Latrinculi. A game. Sometimes it's called 'bandits.' Do you know it?"

"We have our own version," the silenus replied. "Instead of pebbles, we use finger bones."

"How practical." Latona drew a small knife from her belt. The silenus growled. She handed the knife to him. "Inspect it, if you like. Or cut my throat. I have no guards with me, and you're much stronger. You know I couldn't do any damage with this, even if I wanted to."

He sniffed the blade. "Why did you bring it?"

"To draw the board." She began cutting lines into the dirt. "A blade is a tool, like any other. Do you know why the old empire was so successful in their military campaigns?"

"They had no honor."

She laughed softly. "That was only part of it. They won because of the gladius—the short sword that every miles carries. The weapon is swift and efficient. It goes in"—she carved a long line, dividing the board in two—"then out again, in the blink of an eye. A clean strike. No fancy hilt getting in the way, no fuss. Death in a single stroke. Of course, it requires a sort of intimacy. Like the sting of love. So swift, you barely feel it."

"We hunt with spears, not swords."

"Exactly. Spears are perfect for the hunt. But when you're

fighting for your life in a cramped alley, or on the topmost floor of a burning insula, you want a sword."

"City fighting." He spat on the ground—a respectable distance from the board that she was drawing. "The hunt wasn't made for cities."

"Oh? You seem to have no problem finding prey on my streets."

"The territory belongs to us. We lived here long before your cities were built. They're simply in our way."

Latona put the knife away. "Perhaps it's time to modify that arrangement."

"How?"

"Black or white?"

He looked annoyed. "Answer the question."

"It's too abstract. Mine is simple. Black or white?"

The silenus sighed. Or perhaps it was a growl. It was hard to tell. "White."

"Interesting."

"What's interesting about it?"

"Nothing at all." She handed him the white stones, along with a blue one. "This piece represents the basilissa. Once it's surrounded, the game is over."

He laughed harshly. "You are a pawn in your own game."

"A piece is not the same as a pawn. And games are impossible to predict. Even the most skilled player can fall to a neophyte with a bold strategy. That is one of Fortuna's most difficult lessons to grasp. The wheel never stops."

"We do not worship Fortuna. We worship Bromios."

"Unless I'm mistaken, they're related."

"Distantly," he muttered.

"So. You know the rules, but there's one piece of knowledge that I lack. Your name."

He blinked. "Why?"

"Because you already know mine. It creates an inequality."

"Septimus."

"Very well, Septimus. *Plegona li joc*."

His eyes widened. "You know our language?"

"I know that phrase, and what it means."

He stared at the pile of white stones. Anger flashed across his face. "The challenger names the terms. You have tricked me."

"No. I simply obscured my motive. That isn't quite the same thing."

"You deceive like a citizen."

She smiled. "I shall take that as a compliment."

"Name your terms, then."

Latona regarded the small blue stone in her hand—her simulacrum. "Should I win, your master shall meet me in a place of my choosing."

"And should you lose?"

"Then I shall meet him anywhere." She began counting her stones. "Up a tree. On a bed of hot coals. In the jaws of a giant bear, if it pleases him. I shall come alone, and unarmed."

"I cannot promise that he will agree."

"Of course not. But as his ensign, you can suggest it to him. A change of scenery."

He closed his hand around the blue stone. "Very well."

"Good. Let us play."

The basilissa placed one of her black stones on a makeshift square. Septimus thought for a moment, then followed with one of his white stones. She allowed her opponent to gain ground, only to strike at him from an unexpected direction. She began on the defensive, but halfway through, she switched to a more aggressive strategy. Fel had played latrinculi with Drauca, who was quite good. Latona was in a different class entirely. It seemed as if she'd been playing bandits forever. And the more that Fel thought about it, the more she realized that the basilissa had probably grown up with the game. She was a part of the game, after all. That small blue piece represented her, all of her dreams and fears, winking in the dark.

For a while, it looked as if Septimus might win. But Latona was only biding her time. In the blink of an eye, his dearest piece was surrounded on three sides.

Septimus glared at her. "You chose this game on purpose."

"I do have a fondness for it." She placed a finger lightly on one of her pieces. "Do you have a countermove? There is one, in fact, that can get you out of this situation. Very tricky to execute, but perhaps you've been concealing your true strategy." Latona smiled at him. "Those eyes of yours conceal so much."

He studied the board for a moment. Then he moved one of his black pieces. It was nowhere close to the right move. Fel had no idea if Latona was even telling the truth about that counter, though. As far as she could see, there was no escape. The basilissa paused for a moment, as if she were considering her response. Then she cornered him.

"The game is yours." He scattered his white pieces.

"So it would appear." Unexpectedly, Latona reached out her hand. "It was never my intention to trick you. I hope you can forgive me."

Septimus looked uncertainly at her outstretched fingers. His eyes narrowed. Then, slowly, he took her hand in his own. The basilissa looked into his eyes, her glance unwavering. Then she delicately withdrew her hand.

"The order of things is about to change," she said. "Your master knows this, as well as I. Together, we can shape what's to come."

"Do you think that you can predict it?"

"I have my intimations. I'm certain that we've noticed the same signs."

"They remain unclear. Every night, we burn a pyre in offering to Bromios, and the wisest among us read the smoke."

"What have they seen?"

"I cannot say. I lack that particular gift."

"You've heard nothing? Not even a whisper?"

Septimus studied her for a moment, as if deciding how far to trust her. Having been played only moments before, he would have been justified in saying nothing. But they were both in the game. He had to make a move.

"They say that the walls are thinning. Shadows are coming through."

"The oculi have seen the same thing." Latona gathered up the black and white stones, placing them back in the pouch. "The seal is breaking."

"That shouldn't be possible."

"All magic—even the deepest magic—eventually fails. That's the price of power. The wheel never stops."

"Didn't your goddess create the seal? Why would she make something that would eventually fall apart?"

"Nobody knows who made it, or why. All we know is that it's dying."

"Without the walls—"

"It's a different game entirely." She picked up one of the gleaming blue stones, turning it in her hand. "The unknown. That's what my mother was afraid of, and my grandmother. They cleaved to the safe spaces, and died in their corners. I want something better for my daughter. The board needs to expand."

"If that is your wish," Septimus said, "I believe that we—"

Something clattered to the ground. Septimus turned, growling. Fel saw a flash in the opposite corner. The lamplight flared, and she recognized a familiar amulet. The bula. Only, as she looked more closely, she realized that it wasn't a boy's talisman. It was delicate, almost heart-shaped. A girl's bula.

"Eumachia?" Latona stood up. "Is that you?"

The shape darted. It was hard to see from the shadows, but Fel realized that it was the basilissa's daughter. She'd cut her hair short and dressed in a boy's tunica, but her face was unmistakable. Septimus snarled, ready to leap forward.

"No!" There was real fear in Latona's voice. "She's my daughter!"

"*Julia,*" Fel hissed. "If you've a distraction, now is the time!"

Eumachia's sandals echoed as she ran. Septimus was growling, but he still hesitated. The hunter in him warred against the politician, who knew that running down the basilissa's daughter would cause problems. But his eyes gleamed. The hunter was winning.

"Julia—"

Latona heard her. The basilissa looked in their direction. "Who's there?"

The artifex reached into her pouch. "Look away!"

She threw something on the ground. Fel heard a soft click. Then the necropolis was ablaze with light.

Morgan grabbed her hand. "Come on!"

And they ran. The cloud of light burned behind them, and Fel could hear Septimus, cursing in his own liquid language. Latona shouted something, but she couldn't make out the words. All she could feel was Morgan's hand, pulling her away from the crash of impossible sunlight that exposed every grave. The silent city trembled in protest. As they passed the grave of the sicarius, the light was still so intense that she could almost read the forgotten name. Before the letters aligned, they were already outside.

"Where are the horses?" Julia asked. "We don't have much time."

"There are no horses," Babieca said.

She stared at him. "What do you mean there are no fucking horses? Have you any idea how fast a silenus can run?"

"Shut up and follow me," Fel hissed.

The miles led them to a pile of reeds. Quickly, she brushed them away. Three stinking, mildewed cloaks were beneath them. She handed the ragged bundles of cloth to Morgan, Julia, and Babieca.

"Put these on. Make sure your faces are covered."

Babieca made a face. "We'll look like—"

"That's the point. Now put them on."

"What about you?"

"It won't conceal my armor. Besides. One of us has to look like a customer. Morgan could be recognized, but my face is unknown."

"I could be the customer," Babieca murmured.

Fel silenced him with a look.

They pulled on the rotting cloaks. As Felix had promised, the hoods were voluminous and covered most of their faces.

"Where did you find these?" Julia asked.

"There's no time to explain." She heard a sound near the entrance to the necropolis. "Just—try to look tired. And don't say anything. Morgan—"

The sagittarius looked at her curiously. "Yes?"

"I'm sorry."

"For what?"

Latona and Septimus emerged from the necropolis. The basilissa held the lamp before her. Light skittered at their feet. The silenus looked at her, and his eyes were lanterns of their own, burning green in the darkness. Fel tensed. Her heart was pounding, but she knew that this would work. It had to.

When they were a few paces away, she leaned forward and kissed Morgan.

Her breath was startled, but she didn't move or cry out. Her lips were soft. They opened beneath Fel's kiss, and she felt her blood catch fire. Morgan pressed against her. Beneath the stained cloak, she was warm and smelled like grave flowers. Fel touched her hair. As her fingers brushed the dark curls, she realized that she had always wanted to do this. From the moment that she'd first seen Morgan, a part of her had always been reaching out, then pulling back. Now there was no hesitation left. She held the archer in her arms, knowing that this was a beautiful mistake. In a few seconds, it would haunt her. It wasn't real. But she had one breath left, one heartbeat, and if she wanted to, she could draw it out until the end of days.

Fel stepped back, just as Latona and Septimus approached. Morgan was blushing furiously beneath her hood. She stared at the ground, astonished, smiling.

"What is this?" Latona demanded. "A midnight orgy?"

Septimus said nothing. Fel realized that he was holding his tongue. Perhaps he didn't want them to realize that he could speak.

She lowered her head. "Pardon, Your Grace. I only came here for a bit of comfort."

Latona examined the rest of them. "You can afford three? I wasn't aware that a miles earned such a generous salary."

"Beg pardon, Your Grace, but"—Fel chose her words carefully—"I've gambled some tonight. Hazard, mostly. I know it's not right, but I've—well, it's been a good night, Your Grace, and I don't have many of those. I wanted to celebrate."

"The wolves must be hungry."

"We are, Your Grace," Babieca said. His voice was a defeated whisper.

She shook her head. "Fine. I shall keep your secret, miles. Tell me—did you see a boy come running out of the silent city? A—girlish sort of a boy?"

"Yes, Your Grace." Fel pointed to the line of reeds. "I think he ran that way."

Septimus glared at her. Did he know that she was lying?

Latona sighed. "If I'd known that I was going to chase a boy through the marsh, I would have worn something more appropriate." She gestured to Fel's caligae. "Something like those. What a lovely invention. Shoes with spikes."

"You can have them, Your Grace."

"No. You keep them." Her eyes lingered on the three "wolves." For a moment, Fel thought that she could see through the dirty cloaks. But she simply smiled. "Enjoy your fortunate night, miles. And forget that you saw us here."

"Of course, Your Grace."

Latona and Septimus walked farther into the marsh. Septimus didn't look back, although Fel could almost sense that he wanted to. He must have smelled the flowers on them. The real wolves who prowled the necropolis would smell the same. But had he detected the acrid smell of her fear, the wine on Babieca's breath, or the scent of Morgan's hair? She had an awful feeling that they'd only escaped punishment for a night. The basilissa would remember that she'd encountered a lucky miles who had seen her in the company of a silenus. The cloaks had been Felix's idea. She'd come to him because she couldn't think of anything else to do. And the ruse had worked, but now her face was known.

"I can't believe that worked," Babieca murmured. "You really sold it, with the kiss."

"Yes." Morgan couldn't look at her. "That was unexpected."

"I did apologize," Fel said.

"Yes. You did." Morgan's voice held all sorts of things. Fel wanted to sound out each one of them, but there was no time.

"The kiss needed to be"—Fel searched for the right word—"credible."

"Credible."

She felt her own cheeks redden slightly. "If it had been—"

"I understand." Morgan smiled thinly. "And it was."

"What?"

"Credible."

Fel also smiled.

"Can we get out of here?" Babieca asked. "Before that thing smells how close I came to pissing myself?"

"We can leave the cloaks in the house by the wall," Fel said. "We may need them again."

"Smelling awful has become a sad theme in my life," he observed.

"What about Eumachia?" Morgan asked.

"She's the wild throw in all of this." Fel gestured for them to follow her. "A lot depends on how little she trusts her mother."

"I've talked with her before," Morgan said. "She's ambivalent, but not outright suspicious."

"And after tonight?"

"It could work in our favor."

They walked toward the city. Morgan stayed close to her. A few times, they nearly touched. But both maintained a slight distance.

"I stole that dazzler from the workshop," Julia said. "If my master finds out, he's going to murder me."

"Not if the basilissa gets to you first," Babieca replied.

Fel looked at Morgan. She almost said: *You're safe with me.* The words rattled inside, like dice, but didn't escape.

2

SHE WAS NAKED AND SHIVERING IN THE PARK.
A gray slice of light had just begun to outline the trees, and
a few curious geese were approaching. Ingrid pulled her
duffel bag from beneath a pile of leaves. Normally she put
more thought into hiding her clothes, but she'd been dis
tracted the night before. She was proud, at least, that she'd
been able to remember this location. The house by the wall
demanded a clear memory. Otherwise, it would spit you out
in some random place. Felix had warned her about the
house. If you relied too much on it, you would eventually
forget your own alley. The house wasn't a safe space—
anyone could use it. And if your alley vanished, what was
the result? Did you feel it, like losing a limb? She thought
of the auditor's lost alley, dissolving into smoke, or simply
being devoured by the brick maze of Anfractus. His dagger
and old tunica were safe, but that corner   his only mark on
the skin of the city—was gone.

"Why couldn't you just beam us back to your house?"
Carl asked, struggling to pull on his pants while balancing

against a tree. "I could be drinking hot chocolate right now, instead of freezing my balls off."

Ingrid winced. "If you're going to mention hot chocolate and your balls in the same sentence, please stay out of my pantry."

"It was just a metaphor. I swear."

"Anyways, you know that I couldn't take us directly to the house. All of our stuff is here, and Paul could be asleep on the couch. Imagine if you woke up to find four naked people in your living room, including your sister."

"Speaking of four people—" Sam poked her head out from behind a tree. "Maybe you've all forgotten, but this is not where I hid my clothes. Can someone please lend me something to wear, right the fuck now?"

"Sorry—we get caught up in the post-transition banter sometimes." Shelby gave her an oversized shirt and a pair of sweat pants. "Here you are."

Sam looked critically at the Moosehead T-shirt. "Where did you get this . . . ensemble?"

"It belongs to Carl, actually."

"That explains a lot."

Carl glared at Shelby. "I was looking for those."

"Really. You were looking for the worst outfit in history."

"If it's so terrible, why didn't you give it back?"

"I don't like this line of questioning."

Sam emerged from behind the tree. "I feel like I've just come from a Riders game."

"Where did you stash your clothes?" Shelby asked.

"On the other side of the park."

"That's okay. I can drive you over there."

She looked relieved. "Thanks. Not that I don't appreciate this, but"—she looked down at her bare feet—"I'd prefer not to step on a beer bottle."

"I've got flip-flops," Ingrid said. "Give me one second."

"Are those mine too?" Carl demanded.

She ignored the question and handed the flip-flops to

Sam. "These should do until you get to the car. Shall we meet back at my place, in a few hours?"

"What are you going to tell Paul?" Shelby asked.

"Study meeting. He rarely asks questions anymore."

"Can we go back to the issue of how everyone is stealing my clothes?" Carl gestured emphatically to the flip-flops. "This seems like—"

"We'll see you in a bit." Shelby cut him off smoothly. "Thanks for lending us your living room."

"We're going to have to start calling it the war room," Ingrid said. "And Sam—will you be coming, as well?"

"I can pick you up," Shelby added. "That is—if you're comfortable talking strategy with us. Ingrid has a variety of international creamers at her place, if that sweetens the deal."

Sam looked torn. "I mean—I've never been part of a company before."

"Parking," Carl said. "Oh wait. Is it parking if we're in the park?"

"No pressure." Ingrid wrote down her address on an old receipt and gave it to Sam. "If you show up, I can promise cold cuts. But I understand if you're wary."

"It's not that. I'm just not sure how to do this. Or even what 'this' is." Sam looked at the ground. "I've always sort of done my own thing. I'm an only child. I guess that shows."

"You don't have to decide right now. Just show up if you feel like it. If my son's in the proper humor, we might even go to the park."

"I didn't know you had a son." Sam looked at all of them. "I guess I don't know much about any of you. Which is odd, considering the fact that I'm wearing your clothes."

"My clothes," Carl said. "If you want to be specific."

"Ignore him," Shelby said. "Let's find my truck. Ingrid, should we bring something? Coffee, or something sweet?"

"All offerings are welcome," Ingrid replied. "I may even get to sleep for a few hours. The very thought of being unconscious makes me happy. What does that say?"

"That you're a mom." Shelby waved. "See you in a bit."

Ingrid crossed to the parking lot. The little sedan was waiting for her, with its cracked window and arm-strong steering. Paul called it the Angry Smurf. The interior smelled faintly of juice, and the backseat was an explosion of Neil's artwork. She sat on something sharp. It was a pine-cone covered in glitter-glue. Nobody had explained that her house, her car, and even her office would one day resemble the inside of Michael's. Neil was mad about crafts.

She drove home with the windows open, fighting sleep. The radio played a country song whose lyrics were drowned out by static. The chorus was something-something-*fearless*, or maybe it was something-something-*feelings*. By the time she arrived home, she was nodding faintly to the indecipher-able song.

Ingrid slipped into the house, being careful to shut the door softly. The living room was gauzy with gray light. She could hear the fridge humming, and Paul's snoring, both rhythmic and soothing in their way. She took off her jacket and walked down the hallway. Neil and Paul were asleep in the master bedroom. Paul was on his back, while Neil slept diagonally, taking up an astonishing amount of space on the bed. His feet were practically touching Paul's chin. She could use Paul's room, downstairs, but he probably hadn't washed the sheets. Ingrid mostly left that part of the house to him and didn't like to intrude on his space. He kept it reasonably clean, save for the bathroom, which was a bit of a cave.

Instead, she went into Neil's room. The walls were cov-ered in various posters: the solar system, the human body, the process of erosion. For a time, he'd been wild about cells, then the digestive system, then the desert. His intensities were everywhere, spreading across the house in the form of books, foldout diagrams, and toys. A small shelf held his prized volumes. There was *Knuffle Bunny*, *The Magic School Bus*, and *Why Oh Why Are Deserts Dry?* Currently, he was dividing his attention between books and screens. Ingrid sensed that this was a pivotal moment, and she'd been trying to champion the fun of reading, but the screen was incredibly seductive. He already knew how to work the TV,

DVD player, and game console, and he could search for videos on YouTube. More than once, she'd asked him how to use the remote.

Ingrid curled up on his small bed. The pillow smelled like his shampoo. That was the last thing that she remembered.

When she opened her eyes, the light had changed. She checked her phone. Nine A.M. Why hadn't Neil woken her up? She'd expected to hear his voice in her ear, asking if she wanted a bonus kiss. Her body felt strange. Not rested, exactly, but more alert than usual. It was amazing what three consecutive hours of sleep could do. Ingrid couldn't hear any of the usual noises coming from the kitchen. She walked down the hallway. Neil's artwork decorated the walls. Each picture was surreal. The family receiving a baby bat for Thanksgiving. Paul on his hands and knees, searching for tape, with two black squares looming over him (were they windows?). The Negativitron from LittleBigPlanet, whose heart was surrounded by vortices of color. King Pig sitting on a hoard of golden eggs, with a slice of stolen birthday cake next to him.

She continued into the kitchen. Paul had primed the coffeemaker and left a note:

> Took Neil shopping. Didn't want to wake you. Blintzes in the fridge.

Ingrid loved her brother intensely in that moment. She pressed the magic button on the coffeemaker and threw a cherry blintz in the microwave. She could picture Neil running up to the counter at Canadian Tire, wanting to pay for something. His wallet was full of plastic gemstones and cutout pictures of dinosaurs. Or he would be forging ahead with the list in hand, telling the entire store that they needed extra toilet paper.

Ingrid had never been especially shy, but after Neil came into the world, she found herself talking to strangers a lot more. She had learned to improvise. Children spoke their own language, and small acts of translation were often necessary. Even when Neil wasn't cheerfully addressing people, they would strike up random conversations with him. Ingrid hadn't realized, prior to becoming a mother, that kids were such incredible lightning rods for attention. People would ask her questions about him, or they would offer unsolicited parenting advice. Sometimes it felt like he was a tiny celebrity, and everyone wanted to interview her about his curious habits. Ingrid couldn't remember the last time that someone had asked her about her thesis, but just yesterday, she'd engaged in a five-minute conversation about Neil's favorite brand of string cheese.

The microwave chimed. She ate the blintz in three bites and poured herself some coffee. It wasn't often that she had the house to herself. The realization brought with it a curious mixture of excitement and regret. She missed Neil when he was gone, but at the same time, it was thrilling to be left to her own devices. Mornings were usually a storm of activity. Eating breakfast alone made her feel as if she'd suddenly become a different person. A writer, maybe—someone who could finish whole sentences, who rolled out of bed whenever she felt like it. Someone whose bathtub wasn't full of Angry Birds.

Ingrid turned on Radio Canada. The sound of French in the background was comforting. She fought the urge to gulp down her coffee. It wasn't imperative that she remain conscious. Nobody was demanding her attention. Lying down on the couch, she stretched out her arms and legs in a snow-angel pattern. It was all hers. The cushions weren't scattered on the ground or being used as part of a fort. She wanted to do everything imaginable: drink wine, jump up and down, smoke a cigarette, set her computer on fire, start a band, organize all of her books, clean the gutters, have a thirty-minute shower, and fly over the city, watching the park unscroll beneath her in long strands of green and silver.

Instead, she topped up her coffee, ate another blintz, and played games for an hour.

As her character—a paladin—leveled up in experience, Ingrid couldn't help but think about the other, more danger-ous game that she was playing. She'd thought that a history of mastering computer games would give her some sort of advantage, but the streets of Anfractus were unlike the realms that she'd explored as a teenager: the scattered settlements of Lost Guardia, Serpent Isle, even the retro-text mazes of Zork. Nothing could have prepared her for the crush of Via Rumor, with its alleyways that offered everything from mercy to violence. At first, she'd thought: *Is this a game?* The similarities were unmistakable—there were companies, and quests, and monsters. The gens resembled medieval guilds, manipulating everything from the great height of their towers. It felt, for a little while, as if she could recapture her childhood.

The first time that Fel had spied a corpse, decaying near the mouth of an alley, she'd realized that the stakes were much higher. The wrong move could kill you. *Save and reload* was not an option. Andrew had been lucky. If he'd met a dagger in an alley, rather than nearly drowning, he wouldn't have come back.

She should stop. Ingrid knew that. She had Neil to think about, and it wasn't safe. She rolled with her life every time she crossed over. The dull ache below her knee was a constant reminder that the game could be cruel. But how could she choose between two kinds of magic? How could she separate the shock of her everyday life, with all of its comedy and grief and sharp edges, from the wonder of the park and what lay beyond? It reminded her of the single philosophy class that she'd taken as an undergrad, before breaking up with the discipline (literature had seemed like the more stable romantic choice). Her professor had been talking about Plato's *Symposium*, and how it was a heartless text. Alcibiades, the Athenian party animal, was a typical college student who wanted to drink and fuck and expand his horizons. But Socrates said no, you mustn't drink (he was drunk), and you mustn't fuck (the sex look in his eyes), and love should be celestial and spherical and stop that, my ass is off-limits.

But the choice was impossible. She wanted all of the magic. She wanted to play both sides, the gladius and the lullaby, though she knew that they would tear her apart. The old scar was acting up. She popped a pill. It would go away, if she didn't think about it. Sometimes, in the dead of night, she actually wanted the pain. She'd wake up with her leg stiff, a fire in her nerves, but she didn't reach for the bottle. The ache reminded her of that other world. If she was willing to endure it, the memories would come rushing back. Sunlight on her blade, the screams of the Hippodrome, the sand burning her feet. The clarity hurt, as if it didn't belong here, but she dragged it to the surface. Ingrid refused to limit herself. Perhaps that was the one thing that she shared with the basilissa.

The doorbell chimed. Setting down her coffee, she crossed the living room. Habit made her stare through the peephole. It was Sam. Her body was distended into a teardrop shape by the curved glass. Ingrid opened the door with a smile.

"You came."

Sam looked slightly nervous. "Yeah. I guess I'm dumber than I thought."

"There's safety in numbers."

"I think that only applies when you're in a crowd."

"If it makes you feel better, we can put tinfoil on the windows."

Sam chuckled. "I guess I am being paranoid."

"Not at all." Ingrid gestured for her to come in. "We're absolutely in danger. But I've got cherry blintzes."

"You don't seem too bothered by the situation."

"I have a four-year-old. I'm used to dealing with minor apocalypses."

Sam stepped into the living room. Ingrid closed and locked the door behind her. Putting tinfoil on the windows might not have been the worst idea. Or maybe some kind of tinting. Could you tint an entire house? It seemed like a question that only Beyoncé could answer.

"Coffee?" Ingrid asked.

The trip to the kitchen would buy her some time. Sam was a complete cipher, and she didn't have the faintest idea of what they might talk about. Everything was parking, although at this point, it didn't matter. Her life had become a parking lot, and she would endlessly wander through it, like that episode of *Seinfeld*. Funny, how *park* had antithetical meanings. A square of protected land in the middle of an urban sprawl. A hateful verb, expressed through clenched teeth. An accident site where civilization crashed into nature, leaving behind a spray of safety glass.

"No thanks," Sam replied. "I think I'm already vibrating at a high frequency."

"Ah. Okay. Well, let me know." Ingrid sat down. "I've also got luncheon meat."

"I'm fine. Thank you."

They both stared off into space for a moment. Ingrid's mind wandered back to last night. She couldn't believe that Fel had kissed Morgan. It was unlike her—unlike both of them. She tried to remember the kiss in detail, but it rippled, indistinct, as if she were watching it transpire on a hot day. They were both sweating beneath their armor. Slowly, the sun went down, and the marsh fire surrounded them. She was a yew bow, awash in moonlight and curving beneath impossible pressure. Fel opened her mouth to admit Morgan's tongue, and an arrow pierced her side. It was the gnomo's arrow, with its obsidian head. She cried out.

"Did you say something?" Sam asked.

Ingrid blinked. "No. Sorry."

"Okay."

This was painful. Why had Sam come so early? What was keeping Shelby and Carl? Ingrid wanted to check her phone, but it seemed rude. Sam had her hands folded politely in her lap, as if she were visiting an older relative. Ingrid suppressed a sigh. Had she really become this boring? Sam wasn't that much younger. There must be some point of commonality between them. Didn't they spend most of their time in the same library, scouring articles, searching for some detail that would validate whatever they were doing?

"What are you working on?" Ingrid asked. It was a safe question, a mechanical one. A conversational entrée for people who didn't know how to talk about sports or the news.

"Wind."

"I'm not sure I follow."

"My thesis analyzes the effects of high-velocity wind on bridges throughout the province. So I guess I study tension and anxiety."

"There's a metaphor in there somewhere."

"Yeah. Probably. What about you?"

"Gender and sexuality in the young-adult canon."

"Huh." Sam tapped her knee lightly. "The canon. That sounds explosive."

"It's not like—"

"I get it."

"Oh. Right."

Sam got up and examined a row of framed drawings. "Did your son do these?"

"Yes. He calls them his museum of captivity."

"Why?"

"No idea."

"They're fun." Sam pointed to one picture. "Is that a dinosaur?"

"It's an archaeopteryx."

"Oh." She sounded faintly impressed but also a bit confused. "I don't remember being into dinosaurs when I was little."

"I suppose we all go through that phase, but none of us remember it." Ingrid smiled. "When Neil first started talking about dinosaurs, I tried to recall how I'd felt about them. But it was so long ago. It's odd, to think that we all used to be little paleontologists, rattling off statistics about prehistoric fauna. If those childhood intensities lasted, the earth would be teeming with archaeologists and firefighters and astronomers. Doesn't sound so bad."

"I had a lot of sticker books," Sam said. "I remember that much. Is there a future in collecting stickers?"

"Anything's possible."

"He seems really smart and creative. Your parents must be proud."

Ingrid stared uncomfortably out the window. "They don't see him very often."

"Oh." Sam looked embarrassed. "I'm sorry. I didn't mean—"

"It's fine. They live in Alberta. I moved out here for my degree, and my brother, Paul, came with me."

"Alberta. That's so close."

"Distances can be deceiving."

There was a knock at the door. Ingrid offered a silent prayer of thanks to whoever might be listening. She didn't need to be having this conversation right now. There was no delicate way to explain that your foster parents had gradually lost interest in you, like an outdated toy. Neil was still a baby when she'd last spoken with her foster mother. The connection had been full of static and untenable silences. "Diapers are expensive," April had said. "I'm glad we didn't have to go through that. It was hard enough raising the two of you."

How difficult we must have been, she thought. *Shell-shocked kids who barely spoke, trying to make ourselves as small as possible.*

Ingrid opened the door. Shelby looked out of breath, as if she'd just run across the driveway. Her expression was peculiar.

"What's up?" Ingrid asked. "Where's Carl?"

"In the car. We brought veggies and dip and Andrew."

She said "Andrew" like he was also included with the veggie tray. It took Ingrid a moment to process what she'd meant.

"He's here?"

"He called, and—I'm sorry, but I couldn't think of an excuse. I already feel like shit. All we do is exclude him."

Ingrid peered over her shoulder. Andrew was getting out of the car. He waved to her, shyly. He was carrying a two-liter bottle of cream soda.

She waved back. "You couldn't think of anything to throw him off the scent?"

"He knows that we study together. What other reason could we possibly have for meeting in the middle of the day?"

"We need to discuss strategy. How are we going to manage that?"

"I don't know. We can talk in code, or something."

"Is everything okay?" Sam asked from the living room.

"It's all good." Ingrid kept her voice low. "No cause for alarm. I'm just going to quietly set myself on fire, but once that's done, I'll put more coffee on."

Lying was nothing new to her. Ingrid understood the intimate contours of the lie, the way to put a proper spin on it, with just the right amount of detail. She'd been lying to Paul and Neil for years. With Paul, it had become a depressing reflex. She spun lies without even thinking about it, not even entirely original lies, but Paul trusted her. It was actually harder to deflect Neil's questions. When they were lying in bed, in that softly textured moment between waking and sleep, and he asked her where she'd gone . . . her heart fluttered, and she wanted to tell him everything.

Darling, you wouldn't believe it. There are stone skyways, and a clock shaped like a giant wheel, and little mechanical spiders that skitter at your feet, and invisible things that lap up the oil from crumbling shrines. And your mother knows how to use a sword.

And she half expected him to say: *I knew that, already, Mummy.*

But he slept on richly in her arms, his feet making small patterns, like a cat kneading the blanket. So she didn't have to say anything. But she suspected that he was dreaming of her other life, dreaming of the miles with one greave and a chipped sword. Perhaps even dreaming of that alley, just off Aditus Papallona—smelling of incense and garbage—where she'd first felt him move inside her belly.

Ingrid made coffee. Sometimes she felt like this was her greatest skill—the ability to produce coffee in any situation, even in her sleep (once, according to Paul, she had primed the coffeemaker while sleepwalking). She could recall her foster aunt's funeral, where she'd made coffee for everyone.

She'd been barely twelve, but even April said that she made the best coffee. It felt good to dole out the small cups. Everyone thanked her with weak smiles. And it was useful. She felt no grief. She'd barely known the woman. This, at least, was something that she could do. Her response to death: a cup wobbling on its saucer.

Shelby unwrapped the veggie tray. "It looked bigger in the store," she apologized.

"It's fine," Ingrid said.

They crunched carrots and played with their cups. Nobody was willing to speak. Andrew was watching Sam. Not in a dramatic way, but every once in a while, in short glances. Why were they studying with an engineering student? It was a good question. He'd met Sam during the library battle, and Shelby had explained that she was a member of the failed LARP. Sometimes the lies curved back on each other, like a Moebius strip. That was a dangerous moment. When the helices crossed, there was always the chance that everything could dissolve.

She could sympathize with his confusion. Only a few months ago, he'd been part of a closed triad with Shelby and Carl. Now there were these two extra people, and he couldn't remember how or why they'd been admitted to the group. It was like being told, as a child, that you would be spending time with a previously unknown relative. You were expected to be polite, to express a love that you were told must exist, although you'd never felt it. Andrew took their sudden friendship at face value, but a part of him didn't quite trust it. She worried that Paul might feel the same way. But if that was true, then he hid it well.

"So—" Andrew spoke, and everyone looked up. He wasn't expecting the attention. His eyes scraped the ground. "What's everyone working on?"

"Well," Ingrid replied, "I have to hammer out my prospectus. It's overdue."

"It sounds like you're forging a weapon," Andrew said.

"Sometimes it feels that way."

"I'm writing an abstract," Shelby said. "The Canadian

Society for Eighteenth-Century Studies is having their conference in London this year. Something about parallel enlightenments. I'm not totally sure what that means."

"Are the enlightenments dueling?" Carl asked. "Like some kind of UFC match?"

"Possibly."

"Cool."

Andrew looked at him. "What about you?"

"Me?"

He frowned slightly. "What are you working on?"

"I—"

Carl trailed off. They all looked at him. Ingrid wondered if this would be the moment. He was close to breaking. She prepared herself to make more coffee. A condolence beverage. Nothing said *Sorry for lying to you about our portal fantasy* like a cup of dark roast.

"I . . . have an idea." Carl stood. "Ingrid, is it okay if I use your printer?"

"Ah—okay. That's fine. The office is down the hallway."

"Thanks." He disappeared.

"Was that odd?" Andrew asked.

"He didn't get much sleep last night," Shelby said. "I think he was at—"

"Hockey practice?"

"Right."

Sam chuckled.

Andrew looked at her. "What is it?"

"Nothing." She couldn't quite meet his gaze. "It's just— the thought of him stick-handling is kind of funny. I don't know why. I'll stop talking now."

Ingrid glanced at the doorway. This would be the perfect moment for them to come home. Neil would distract everyone. What was taking them so long? She looked around the room and realized that nobody had brought any books. This was becoming the worst farce in history. No wonder Andrew was confused. They were all acting like Martians.

"So—Ingrid—" Shelby was gesturing with a carrot.

"You know that person who was just hired in your department? I think her name is—Lapona? Patty Lapona?"

Ingrid gave her a long look. "Patty Lapona."

"I didn't know that the ed department was hiring," Andrew said. "What's her specialty?"

She struggled to maintain a neutral expression. "Urban education," she said slowly. "I think that's what Patty Lapona specializes in."

Sam was beginning to catch on. Her mouth opened slightly, as if she were watching a train derail itself in slow motion.

"So," Shelby persisted, "I hear that—Patty—is gunning for the chair's position. She's even met with the dean."

"I didn't realize that," Ingrid said flatly.

"A person like that can be hard to deal with. You need to protect your . . . department. Otherwise, she'll run amok."

"Does she have any weaknesses?" Sam asked. "I mean, academically?"

"She's arrogant," Ingrid replied. "She doesn't respect the traditional alliances. That sort of thing could blow up in her face."

"You all seem to know a lot about this Patty," Andrew said. "Are you sure that she'd make such a terrible chair?"

"She'll destroy the city," Shelby murmured.

"What?"

"I mean—the campus. She'll destroy it with—" Shelby was losing it. "Prairie dogs."

Andrew blinked. "Prairie dogs?"

"Yeah. She's got this plan—"

Carl emerged from the hallway, carrying a stack of papers. "Okay, everyone. I know we came here to work, but I thought we could try this new game, just for a bit. You know—to get our creative mojo flowing."

He handed out papers to each of them. Ingrid glanced at hers, and saw that it was a character sheet. *Fel the Fighter.* Her stomach tightened. This wasn't parking—not precisely. But it was dangerously close. It felt like a terrible idea.

"Hey—" Shelby looked up. "Why does my ranger only have *four* charisma?"

"I thought that would be obvious," Carl replied.

She glared at him.

"Let's sit on the floor," Carl said. "We don't need a board, since this is paper-based. I've got avatars for everyone."

He reached into his pocket and withdrew a small tin.

"Are those my sewing supplies?" Ingrid asked.

"Formerly. I left them on the desk." He opened the tin and withdrew three small objects: a thimble, a toy brontosaurus, and one of Neil's plastic gemstones. "These pieces will represent our company of heroes."

"A thimble?" Ingrid asked.

"You can have that one. It's your sewing kit, after all."

"Thanks. I think."

"Andrew, you get the gemstone, because your magic user has . . . elemental powers. Sam gets the brontosaurus."

"And why is that?" Sam asked. "What does a dinosaur have to do with my"—she glanced at her character sheet—"*tinker*? Really?"

"Consider it an homage to Robert Jordan." He placed a twenty-sided die on the floor. "I hope none of you mind that I took the liberty of pregenerating your characters. I thought it would speed things along."

"So we're playing an RPG," Andrew said. "I thought we were going to study. Carl, were you carrying that die in your pocket the whole time?"

"That's not important." He smiled. "This isn't your average tabletop adventure. It's a beta version of a new tabletop game, called Path of Smoke. It's set in a pseudo-Roman world."

That piqued Andrew's interest. "Republican, or imperial?"

"Imperial. Think Nero's Rome, when everything was going pear-shaped."

"Hmm." Andrew looked at his character sheet again. "A magic user in ancient Rome. This could really take off."

It was working. Ingrid stared at Carl, trying to convey just how dangerous this was. But he was already shuffling through papers.

"Our first quest," he said, "involves a political conspiracy. The corrupt Augusta wants to take over a neighboring city." He glanced at his notes. "She's made some sort of deal with the army of satyrs."

Andrew looked up. "The satyrs have formed an army?"

"Oh, yeah. They don't fool around."

"I thought satyrs mostly got drunk and had sex with nymphs."

"Well, these ones are a bit more goal-oriented. If the Augusta has her way, they'll destroy the Imperial City. Our company has been hired by the Augusta's advisor to find an ancient weapon, which can destroy the satyrs."

"Satyrn."

"What?"

"*Satyrn* is the plural of *satyr*. From the Greek."

"Of course it is." Carl set down his notes. "Is everyone ready? Pull up a pillow, and let's get started. We begin our quest in a smoky tavern, in the disreputable part of town."

They all sat down. Ingrid's mouth was dry. Andrew looked fascinated. He had no idea that his life was on the line. She had the inescapable feeling that Fortuna was listening to them. She would be the judge of this hazardous game. If Carl revealed too much—if Andrew saw through this, to the truth that lay buried beneath—the park would be closed to him forever. That was how the wheel turned. They could bend Fortuna's rules, but they couldn't cheat.

"You emerge from the tavern," Carl said. "The air smells of smoke and perfume. In the shadows of the street, you noticed a small shape. It's hard to make out."

"Let's have a closer look," Shelby said.

"Is that the will of the company?"

They all nodded slowly.

"You draw closer to the shape. It's a young girl, and she's beckoning you forward. You realize that it's the daughter of the Augusta. She wants to speak with you." This time, he looked directly at Ingrid. "Do you follow her?"

She heard the door open. Neil burst into the room, with Paul close behind.

"Mummy! We bought soil for the plants! And an owl light, and even a shovel!"

Ingrid hugged him. "That's wonderful. It sounds like Uncle Paul is planting."

Paul waved to everyone. "Hey. What's going on? Have you all joined a cult?"

"We're playing a game," Ingrid said.

"Man." He shook his head. "Your geekery knows no bounds. Well, if people want to stay for supper, I'm making enchiladas."

Neil leaned in close. He smelled like sunscreen. "Oh! That is one of mine gemstones!"

"Is it okay if Andrew borrows it for a while?"

He nodded. "Yes. It offers excellent petection."

"That's good," Andrew said. "My magic user only has two hit points, so I need all the petection that I can get."

"What kind of game is it?" Neil asked, examining their pieces.

"It's an imagination game, sweetheart. We imagine that we're going on an adventure."

"Like Candy Land?"

"Sort of."

"Let's play, Mummy. We can win."

"Well, we need to work together, love. It requires good sharing skills."

He nodded. "I'm ready, Mummy. I will play with you."

"All right." Ingrid kissed his cheek. "Perhaps you will be our secret weapon."

"Like a pig machine!"

"Exactly."

Carl smiled slightly. "The girl beckons you into the shadows. What is the company's will? Do you follow her?"

Ingrid turned to Neil. "What do you think? Should we trust the little girl?"

Neil glanced at Sam's piece. "Trust the brontosaurus. She is a herbivore."

"That's a good point." Ingrid looked at Sam. "You're the

newest member of the company. It should be your decision. Shall we follow her?"

Sam held the toy dinosaur in the palm of her hand. "Why not?"

3

THE CLEPSYDRA THUNDERED ABOVE HER.
Looking up, Fel watched the faces grow closer. All of Fortuna's guises were represented. She was sweet apothecary, death on swift feet, a gladius cleaving scale armor, an artifex struck by inspiration. Was it all a game to her? The charming little lives, rolling like knucklebone dice on the streets of her city? Perhaps that was all they were. Tallies on a celestial sheet. An army of pawns, moving across a dust-choked board.

But what was the point of the game? When would it end? Fel had never been particularly religious. Like everyone, she kept Fortuna in her thoughts and offered a few crumbs for the hungry lares who crowded the shrines. But she'd never studied the mysteries. Once, her shadow had seen a set of paw prints appear out of nowhere. There'd been a flash of fire, then screaming. But the memory was distant. Had it truly been a salamander? It was strangely comforting to think that magic was alive in the world. There had to be something other than the silenoi, a balance of some kind. Otherwise, they were all just prey.

She knew what they had to do next, but it seemed only

slightly less ridiculous than their original plan to hide in the necropolis. Their fates hinged on the caprice of a girl who had no reason to help them. Eumachia was the basilissa's daughter, and ultimately she would remain loyal to her mother. But why had she been skulking around the necropolis, dressed as a boy? If she'd lost faith in Latona, then they might have a chance. Unless she decided to turn them in. Fel imagined herself rotting beneath the Arx of Violets, a plucked stem, surrounded by others that had turned to sickly sweet powder. They would never see the light of day—not after what they'd done. Latona would ensure that their punishments were inspired and lasting.

Morgan and Babieca emerged from the crowd on Via Rumor. They joined her beneath the fountain, whose spray lightly touched them all. Babieca stuck out his tongue to catch some of the cool mist. Fel wanted to scold him, but the words died in her throat. What was the point? It was like telling a child not to jump in a puddle. The point of a trovador, she supposed, was to remind them of their simplest desires. How did that old song go? Something about the small rain, and love in your arms again. What we all longed for: wine, a warm bed, some kindness now and then, like small rain.

She looked at Morgan. The sagittarius looked back and smiled wanly. Her dark hair curled in the mist. The rust-colored cloak fluttered around her ankles. Fel wanted to take her hand, but she was afraid of leaving a smudge, a fingerprint, on that smooth surface. Perhaps their first kiss had also been their last. Morgan hadn't spoken of it. Fel could read those signs easily enough. But there was something vaguely promising in her smile. Not an invitation, exactly, but more of a neutral gesture. It wasn't a closed door. Fel knew next to nothing about the contours of her desire. Babieca, however—he would know more. If she got him sufficiently drunk, he might even tell her something.

"Where is Julia?" Fel asked.

"Working," Morgan replied. "She'll be at the bottegha for most of the day."

"Building the perfect frog weapon." Babieca scratched

his head. "Have we fully considered that angle? Instead of this wild gambit, we could hire ourselves a mechanical army. They'd be terrifying, if our enemies were barefoot."

"You could charm them again," Morgan suggested. "I'm sure they'd follow you around the streets of Anfractus, if you played the right tune."

He looked away. "I'm not even sure how that happened."

"Try to remember. It's the first useful thing that you've done."

"Excuse me? Have you forgotten how I put those archers to sleep—"

"Honestly," Fel hissed, "would it be possible to have a civil conversation without you two clawing at each other's eyes?"

"She truly loves me," Babieca said. "She just can't admit it."

"I've got an arrow with your name on it, if that's what you mean."

Fel stared at them for a long moment.

Babieca started to say something but wisely decided to keep silent.

"Sorry," Morgan said. "We're listening."

"Good." Fel drew closer to the wheel, whose roar would mask their words. "This all depends on how well each of us can exploit our influence. Morgan, you've spoken with the daughter before. She seems to have a soft spot for you."

"I wouldn't call us sisters," Morgan said, "but she tolerates my presence. She trusted me enough to introduce me to her fox."

"That's a start. It won't be easy to meet with her, though. We can't walk into the Arx of Violets and request an audience. But I think I know a way."

"This sounds like a back-alley plan," Babieca said.

"Is there any other kind?"

"In this city? I suppose not."

"First, we'll need to meet with Felix. That's where you come in."

Babieca looked at her in surprise. "The last time I saw

the house father, he looked as if he wanted my balls in a chafing dish."

"And I'm sure you didn't provoke him."

"I don't like where this conversation is going."

"You don't have to say anything. He'll be meeting with me. I just need you there as a distraction, to throw him off guard."

"It's more likely that he'll throw me out of his tabularium."

Fel shook her head. "I know him better than you do. He's well trained, and he knows how to conceal his thoughts. But he has his weaknesses."

Babieca stared at the fountains. "Whatever you think I may have meant to him—you're exaggerating my worth. I was never the one who made him weak."

Of course not, Fel thought. *You were only the shadow, the substitute.*

"He won't be expecting to see you," she replied. "That's enough."

"Can he really secure us an audience? I thought he'd been forced to distance himself from the court—after what happened."

"He can set us on the right path," Fel said. "As long as you don't speak."

"What if I think of—"

"*Don't* speak. You're strictly ornamental. Understand?"

He exhaled. "Certainly. Bind the silver tongue. What could go wrong?"

"Don't answer that," Morgan said. "He's a master of sullen rhetoric."

Fel turned to her. "While we're at the basia, I'll need you to keep watch. I've no doubt that we're being followed, at this point. It would be easy to plant someone in that crowd, and you have the best eyes."

"I can patrol the atrium, but the conditions aren't exactly ideal for a fight. If something does happen, what we'll need is your gladius."

"I trust you to protect us."

Morgan chuckled. "I suppose all of my training has led to this moment: target practice in the black basia."

"Your arm is swift and deadly. If you pick the right spot, you can do more damage with your bow than I could hope—"

"Yes, you're both great at killing things," Babieca cut in. "Close up, from a distance, with one hand tied—I trust that you'll achieve maximum carnage. Now, can we please head to the Subura? If I keep sweating, my ornamental status is going to fade."

They walked toward the entertainment district. A wall of cheap marble—not the yellow and green varieties that graced the finer homes—divided the Subura from the uphill neighborhoods. Fires were frequent in this area, and the wall was meant to protect the property of the wealthier citizens. A tired miles leaned against the marble, sweating beneath his armor. Fel nodded politely at him but kept moving, before he had the chance to register her face. Via Rumor sloped downward, and the city's ordure flowed with the contours of the street. Decorative drains were installed at the crossroads, shaped like silenoi with gaping mouths. Fel imagined that they didn't appreciate the artistic likeness. A wagon rumbled by, and they paused at the pedestrian stone, waiting for it to pass. Various people stood next to them, shifting impatiently, checking their portable sundials. Everyone was in a hurry. This was the hour for business lunches, meetings beneath the aqueduct, the renewal of social obligations. Roast snails, olives, and flatbread would be followed by a visit to the Hippodrome, to watch the chariot races or to exult as the sands were bloodied.

The street popinae were buzzing. Fel wanted to stop for a plate of figs, but if they went in, they'd never convince Babieca to leave. Behind the L-shaped marble counter, a wooden shelf held amphorae of various quality—from the cheap wine that made your stomach curdle to the sweet summer vintages preferred by more discriminating customers. A rickety staircase led to a loft on the second floor, separated by a curtain. Fel could just barely hear a rhythmic *thump thump thump* issuing from the loft, accompanied by flakes of laughter. It seemed that many things were on offer, including some of the staff. If the customers heard the noise, they ignored it, concentrating on their plates. A server was updating the menu, scrawled on the wall facing the bar. They'd run out of chickpeas.

Morgan stayed close to her as they walked. Babieca lagged behind, taking in the local color. It felt strange to be leading this company, if that was what they were. Morgan had been their unofficial leader until a few months ago. Now she deferred to Fel, in spite of the fact that they'd never spoken of this. No official transfer of power had taken place. Morgan had simply allowed herself to fade into the background. On a practical level, she needed to remain unobtrusive. Her face was known to the court. But it seemed to go deeper than that.

A twinge of pain brought her back to reality. That old wound. An oil massage would take the sting away, but there was no time for a trip to the baths. Fel imagined the heat of the caldarium, which made the coffered ceiling resemble a shimmering conch shell. The pleasant murmur of conversation, while people reclined on long benches, cooking in their towels. How inviting it would be, with Morgan beside her. Dipping their toes in the hot water. Laughing at the nobles, who tried to conduct business while sweat gleamed on their bellies.

"Fel?"

She stopped. "What?"

Morgan was staring at her. "You almost walked into that pedestrian stone."

"Sorry. I was preoccupied for a moment."

"What were you thinking about?"

Pulling you into the frigidarium. Kissing you beneath the cold water. Never coming up for air, not even when we heard shouting from the crowd.

"Nothing in particular," she said.

A litter passed them. The embroidered curtains were drawn, but Fel caught a glimpse of a slender hand. The flash of sunlight on silver bracelets. The domina, the artisan, the poor aquarius baking to death in his attic cell—they all shared similar desires, which could only be satisfied in this part of town. Rumor had it that Driope, the basilissa's mother, had visited the basia after nightfall. A woman that powerful could have her pleasures delivered, if she so wished. Certain needs were highly specific, Fel supposed. The merest hint of them could not be allowed to darken the threshold of the Arx of Violets.

They approached the black basia, the largest of the wolf dens. Customers had added more graffiti to the walls. Meretrices stood on the balconies. Most of them were immersed in conversation with each other. The sunlight made their masks glow, like newly fired steel. They drank, laughed, and made jokes in various languages. At times, they spoke with their hands, in the manner that Drauca often employed. Felix was not among them. He would be in his office, reviewing scrolls with a barely suppressed sigh. He had told her once that Drauca was the mistress of accounts. The house mother had a brilliant understanding of numbers. He was more of a social liaison, and being stuck in a tabularium made him want to scream.

The atrium was full of clients who mingled with staff or simply studied them from afar. The masked and the unmasked crossed the marble floor, dancing cautiously with each other. Sandals, caligae, cork-heeled shoes, and even a few bare feet, all shuffled across Fortuna's mosaic. Promises were exchanged. Offers were extended. The meretrices were under no obligation to perform. They gave only what they chose, and no amount of money or sweet begging would convince them otherwise. Fel noticed two women sitting on a stone bench. One was clearly a domina, her hair swept up in a towering wig. The meretrix who joined her was short and slightly plump, with a mask studded in opals. They sipped from their silver mugs, exchanging pleasantries, while their sandals touched. Unlike the men, some of whom were already pawing at each other's tunicae, the women on the bench seemed to have all the time in the world.

"I'll stay here," Morgan said. "I can find a spot on the second floor. That balcony has fairly good visibility."

"Be careful," Fel replied. "There are miles about, and they don't take kindly to having an arrow pointed at them."

"I'll stick to the shadows." She chuckled. "Standard practice when I visit a basia."

"Fortuna save me," Babieca muttered. "Don't play the shy flower. Plenty of people would love to take a turn with you."

"I wasn't digging for a compliment."

"You might even catch a break, if you don't wound anyone too seriously."

"There's the sting I was waiting for."

"Trovadores always tell the truth."

She frowned. "I don't remember hearing that anywhere. In fact, you're the most accomplished liar among us."

"I'm not a liar. I'm a storyteller."

"Call it what you want, lyre-boy."

"I told you to stop calling me that."

Morgan turned to Fel. "I'll be upstairs, if you need me."

"Good. This shouldn't take long."

The sagittarius vanished into the crowd. Fel watched her ascend a spiral staircase. Her hand lingered on the polished railing. The cloak concealed her weapons. To the casual observer, she was just another client. Another person scrabbling for position on the wheel. Aside from the Hippodrome, this was the only spot in Anfractus where every spoke was represented. A spado was eating lemon sharbah. Beside him, a medicus clutched his bag of instruments, talking nervously to a masked man. A fur was making a deal. His dirty feet tapped against the floor, preoccupied, as he counted out coins. Fel looked for the two women, but their bench was empty. Perhaps they'd had less time than she'd imagined.

The rustle of the cistrum followed them as they left the atrium. The hall that led to the tabularium was quiet and lit by hanging lamps. There was a fresco on the wall, depicting two men engaged in a precarious act of desire. One reclined on the bed, while the other squatted on top, using a leather strap for balance. In the background, someone was spying on them. Clients had written messages beneath the fresco, many of them libelous and misspelled. They excoriated or praised various members of the house. *Fok well, fare well.* That was her favorite graffito, which she'd seen on the wall outside. There was something cordial about it.

They stepped into Felix's office. Shelves on the far wall held scroll cases and bound account books. The scrolls were stacked diagonally, like oranges in the market. There were also piles of wax tablets, their faces sweating beneath the lamplight. Felix sat behind a table made of olive-colored marble. Its legs were shaped like a lion's paws. He was gently holding a bound book with pumiced covers. When he heard them approach, he looked up and let go of the book. It spilled out its pages, a long, lettered tongue that struck the ground beneath the desk.

"Was I expecting you?" he asked wearily.

"No," Fel said. "We were hoping to talk with you for a moment, though."

He waved her toward the chair. In spite of the cushion, it was uncomfortable. The taut leather strap dug into her back, and there was nowhere to put her arms. The tabularium only had two chairs, so Babieca remained standing. He didn't look particularly happy about it.

"Will you be working tonight?" Felix asked. He didn't look at Babieca. His concentration was divided between her and the book, which he was trying to fix. He resembled a weaver, spinning the pages back into place.

"Actually, no. My night is free. Unless you require—"

"Of course not. You should enjoy the evening. There are plenty of distractions in the atrium, if you're feeling inclined."

She tried to conceal her discomfort at the idea. "We're actually here to discuss something specific. A favor, really."

He looked up. "A favor."

"Just a small one," Babieca said. "Nothing you couldn't easily accommodate."

The miles gave him a long look, which she hoped would remind him that he wasn't supposed to talk. Babieca ignored her.

The house father set down the book. "You've served the basia well. I'm happy to grant you a favor, within reason."

"There are two of us here," Babieca muttered. "*We're* asking a favor."

"I see you," Felix said, without looking at him.

"I'm not sure you understand what that word means."

He turned back to the miles. "What do you need? Our coffers are a bit stretched, but I could offer you a modest increase in your wages."

"Thank you, but no. That's not what this is about."

"She'll take the raise, though," Babieca said. "Effective immediately."

She resisted the urge to strike him. "By the wheel— trovador, what part of holding your tongue is so difficult? Shall I do it for you?"

"I think I saw that on a fresco."

Felix finally smiled. "He's right. You deserve the increase. I'll make a note of it in the account books. Now, what do you actually need?"

She shifted in the chair. "To arrange a meeting of sorts."

"This is a house of pleasant assignation. Meet whomever you choose—you don't need an introduction from me."

"It's not that kind of meeting."

"This is taking forever," Babieca said. "Let's cut through the courtly shit and simply pretend that we've all been extraordinarily gracious. We need to arrange an audience with the basilissa's daughter. It stands to reason that Latona can't know about this."

The house father stared at him. "I think you've overestimated my influence in court. I can't simply send a tablet to Eumachia, requesting that she have lunch with two strangers."

"We've already met. She and Morgan are practically sisters."

"From what I hear, she hasn't even left the arx in two days. Latona is keeping a close eye on her, for whatever reason."

"We know why," Fel said. "We saw them both at the necropolis. Eumachia was dressed like a boy, and hiding. She came to spy on her mother."

His eyes narrowed. "What were you doing there?"

"That's a bit of a long story."

He pushed away the account books. "I suddenly have time. This sounds more interesting than the ledgers."

She stared at the mosaic on the floor. It was tame compared to some of the frescoes, but a few of the positions still strained her imagination. "I'm not sure where to begin, or how much to actually tell you."

"Are you in danger?"

"No more than usual," Babieca cut in. "But now the threat is— What's the word—"

"Diffuse?"

"I was going to say *hairy*. But that works."

Felix was about to say something. Then his eyes widened.

"He's catching on," Babieca murmured.

"Is this— I mean—" Felix swallowed. "You're referring to the hunters?"

"They're cozying up to the basilissa, from what we can tell. She's poised to make some kind of agreement with them, and it doesn't smell good. If she has her way, those fucking goats could be hunting us during the day."

"That's impossible."

"You really had to be there to see how possible it is. They played latrinculi and everything. It was like a picnic among the gravestones."

Felix drummed the tabletop with his fingers. "What does Eumachia have to do with this?"

"Like we said—she was there, spying on Mama. She saw everything. Then she ran off, with Latona and—what was the hairy bastard's name, again?"

"Septimus," the miles said.

Felix turned to her. "She was meeting with the princep's brother?"

"So it would seem."

He shook his head. "What the hell is she up to?"

"That's what we're hoping to find out."

"If you pursue this, you risk exposure."

Babieca leaned across the table. "If we do nothing, we could end up on a menu, before we know it. Whatever this is, it affects all of us."

"Even wolves?" His expression was even.

"I wasn't going to say that."

"But you were thinking it."

Babieca took a step back. "We need your help," he said simply. "Whatever you may think of me, right now—let it go. We have to work together."

"You were the one who—" Fel bit down on his reply. "It matters not. Why do you want to meet with Eumachia?"

The miles stood up. Her legs were falling asleep from the chair. "Latona is meeting with the chieftain. She took great pains to ensure that he would come to the arx."

"What is your presence going to accomplish?"

"Would you rather we got drunk in a caupona, while Latona sells us out?" Babieca gestured to the shelf full of scrolls. "You can't hide in your office and pretend that it isn't happening. All of this will go up in flames, if we don't do something."

"I'm not hiding," he said coldly.

"Oh? What would you call it then? A sudden desire to balance your accounts, to stay neutral and unsullied, while the rest of us actually do something?"

"Stop spitting at each other," Fel said. "You're like two toms. All of this tail-flicking accomplishes nothing."

The house father sighed. "You really think that Eumachia can help?"

"She's got the foxes. They're highly resourceful. And if she already mistrusts Latona—perhaps we can work that to our advantage."

Felix considered it for a moment. Then he rang a bell on his desk. They heard sandals shuffling along the hallway, and a young man stepped into the tabularium. It was the same meretrix that they'd seen speaking with Drauca. He inclined his head. Felix made a gesture with his hand, too quick to discern. The miles only knew a few words in that language, anyhow, and Felix was obviously adept. The young man nodded. Then he left the room.

"Come with me," Felix said. "We're going to the undercroft."

"What's there?" Babieca asked.

"Gold, mostly. Wine. Clothes. The walls are thick. We should be able to talk there without being molested."

"I didn't even know that the basia had an undercroft."

The house father smiled slightly. "Every building in Anfractus has an undercroft. It's where we keep our secrets."

"I thought your office was secure," Fel said.

"It is. For the most part. But underground, we'll be absolutely safe."

"I'm beginning to doubt that anywhere is safe."

"You must have suspected that before now."

She shrugged. "I hoped that I was wrong."

"Trust your instincts. This place is many things, but it's never safe. The wrong alley can lead you to a grim ending. Not the happy one that you were expecting. Although—" He rose from the desk. "If you were really expecting that, it's a surprise that you've lasted."

"I'm not that naïve. But still—" She looked at him carefully. "Anfractus hasn't been entirely cruel. It's given us surprising gifts."

"That it has."

His eyes met hers. There was kindness in them, but also an old pain.

Babieca stared at them both curiously for a moment but said nothing.

Felix pushed a tapestry aside, revealing a narrow door. There appeared to be no lock—just a shallow, square recess in the middle of the door. He reached beneath his tunica, withdrawing a polished obsidian die attached to a leather thong.

"Die lock," he said. "Only the housekeepers can open it."

He inserted his die into the recess, and it turned it to the right. There was a low, grinding sound, deep within the wall. Felix unhooked the lantern from its chain and pushed the door open. They followed him down a long flight of steps, worn by countless footfalls. The air was cool and smelled of packed earth. Spiders shied away from the light, gleaming like latrinculi stones in their gossamer webs. The walls were very close, and the ceiling dripped. Babieca looked nervous as he made his way down, step by step. If something came at them from the opposite direction, there'd be little room to fight. All Felix had to do was put out the lantern. He seemed unaffected by the darkness, the thick air, the tortuous steps. He had obviously come this way often and knew every turn with a casual intimacy.

They descended the last step, and the chamber opened up. The undercroft had high, barrel-vaulted ceilings, and the walls were treated with lime, which gave them an eerie glow beneath the lamplight. Felix attached the lantern to a chain. Its light flickered across gold, silk, and giant amphorae. Masks of every color and texture gleamed on stone shelves. Faces of ivory, onyx, carnelian, and graven ash, looking out through gaping eyes. Beautiful stolae hung on bronze rods, moving slightly with the breeze that they'd stirred up. There were crimson-dyed tunicae, and row upon row of shoes with cork heels. There was even a leather chlamys, studded with emeralds, in homage to the basilissa's ceremonial vestment. Perhaps more than one client wished to fulfill their desires with the city's matriarch. A masked version was the next best thing.

There were stacks of finery, which burned beneath the lamplight. Bracelets in the shape of serpents and lions, with sparkling eyes. Rings large and small, their amethyst hearts depicting scenes from mythology or famous battles. Hundreds of pins and fibulae, carved with geometric shapes, or decorated with winking tesserae. Next to them, wigs of every color formed a riotous tower that threatened to cover the entire wall. Some were teased by gold pins or pearl nets.

Others had been fashioned into miraculous shapes: high honeycombs, sundials, ships with swan-headed prows, mountains of hair dyed red, azure, and gold.

Babieca removed a kohl-black wig and put it on.

"How do I look?"

"Put that back," Fel hissed. "It probably costs more than everything you own."

"Actually," a voice said, "it suits you."

Drauca emerged from a wall of giant amphorae, stacked behind her like battlements. The house mother was dressed in a green stola, embroidered with nightingales. Her foot dragged slightly as she walked, leaning on the ivory cane.

"Where did she come from?" Babieca asked.

"There's more than one entrance to an undercroft," Felix said.

Drauca smiled. "In this neighborhood . . . especially." She spoke with a faint slur. Her voice was soft but confident and held a note of dry humor.

"Thank you for joining us," Felix said.

"It must be dire . . . if we're meeting in this . . . stale armpit."

Felix gave her a sidelong look. "Don't pretend you haven't come here to try on clothes or to escape from the novitiates."

She turned to Babieca. "F-Felix is jealous . . . because the wig looks better on you . . . than it ever did on him."

He replaced the wig. "Sorry, house mother. I couldn't resist."

"What's your name?"

"Babieca."

"I once . . . knew a horse named Babieca."

Before he could reply, Felix gestured to the miles. "The two of you already know each other. I believe you've played bandits and acedrex."

"On . . . slow evenings." Drauca smiled. "Hello . . . F-Fel." She inclined her head. "Mother."

"I suppose there's no sense in being coy." He turned to Fel. "Why don't you tell Drauca what you just told me? Leave nothing out."

Drauca looked at her expectantly. The words froze in her mouth. The house mother had a presence that made her nervous. There was tremendous strength in her eyes. The slight tremor in her hand did nothing to belie this. Around her neck, a die made of rock crystal hung from a slender chain. There was something inside it, but the light was too dim. Like a frosted window, the die concealed its heart.

Fel told her about what they'd seen at the necropolis. When she reached the part about Eumachia dressed in boy's clothing, Drauca raised an eyebrow. Fel kept talking. She stopped short of describing the kiss. That probably wasn't relevant.

Drauca considered her words for a moment. Then she shook her head slightly. "The girl has lost faith." Her eyes seemed to darken beneath the mask. "There is nothing worse . . . then being b-betrayed by one's own . . . mother."

"What do you think of their plan?" Felix asked.

"Foolish and . . . sh-short-sighted. They are defenseless. Not even . . . a company."

"Actually," Fel said, "we are."

For the first time, she actually believed it.

"You . . . are but two."

"There's an archer in your atrium," Babieca said, "and an artifex who's building us an army of toys. That makes four."

Drauca looked at him closely. Recognition sparked within her eyes. "I . . . have seen you before. At the black basia. You were with . . . another." She frowned, turning to Felix. "He was slight . . . his eyes danced. What was his name?"

The house father said nothing. It was as if he couldn't quite pronounce the word.

"Roldan," Babieca said, after a moment.

"Yes. An auditor. Was he not . . . of your company?"

"He passed beyond the wheel," Felix said.

Drauca looked first at Felix, then at Babieca. She nodded slowly. "The wheel must turn. Sometimes we are above . . . sometimes, below. It never stops. But one day . . . all of our sh-shadows may come back to us."

"Perhaps," Babieca murmured.

Unexpectedly, Drauca touched the trovador's face. "Even y-yours," she said.

He reddened slightly but said nothing. Her hand lingered on his cheek. Then she withdrew it and turned back to Felix. "They want an audience with . . . E-Eumachia?"

"That is their hope," he replied. "Of course, it will be difficult to escape Latona's gaze."

"Difficult . . . but not impossible."

"Can you do it?" Babieca asked. "I don't understand how."

"Simple." She smiled. "The girl may have lost f-faith in her mother . . . but she still trusts her aunt."

4

INGRID LANDED IN A PATCH OF BLACKBERRIES.
A few of the ripe ones burst, and the smell reminded her of
summer. Instinctively, she put one of the berries in her
mouth. Its silken hairs teased her tongue as she bit down.
Sweet. She could almost forget the dull ache in her limbs
and the pain behind her eyes. To live in a blackberry bush,
under the stars. That would be her fairy tale of choice. Sleeping among the darkest of the hillside thickets, with the taste
of summer in her mouth, like goblin wine.

She could barely make out the shapes beside her. One of
them swore. That was Carl. Next to him, Shelby was dusting
herself off. There were thorns in her hair.

"Rough transition," she said. "Kind of like being spit out."

"Maybe we're using the—thing—too much," Ingrid
replied. She was a bit groggy, as if she'd just woken up.

"What thing?"

"The—" Ingrid searched for the word. "You know what
I mean." Her brain felt like it was smothered in wet cotton.
"Placey-place. With the smudge."

"Do you mean the house by the wall?" Carl asked.

"That's it."

She felt a hand on her shoulder. Not Shelby's hand—Carl's. Had he ever touched her before? It was so strange that she almost laughed. He was still naked, after all. They all looked as if they were in the middle of a postmodern porno. As her eyes adjusted to the dim light, she saw that he was frowning at her.

"Everything okay in there?"

"There's no brain damage, if that's what you're getting at."

"Sorry. Just checking."

She leaned against a tree. "Does anyone else feel incredibly hungover?"

"Well—" Shelby grimaced. "My head is a bit wonky. Carl? What about—"

He was throwing up behind a bush. Once that was over, he wiped his mouth with his sleeve, then turned to Shelby.

"What was the question?"

"How are you?"

"Oh. Well—a bit better, now." He examined the bush and made a face. "I guess you really can't bring anything from Anfractus. Not even dinner."

"Gross."

"I'm just stating facts."

"Could it be the house?" Shelby asked. "Felix did warn us not to use it too much, right? Maybe it's messing with our equilibrium."

"I think we left too early," Ingrid said. "The transition is supposed to occur with the rhythms of the sun. But we were only on the other side for a few hours. Our bodies were still adjusting. When we leave unexpectedly—it's kind of like jumping out of a moving car."

"It feels worse this time. I've never seen Carl purge before."

"I put some leaves over it," he said guiltily.

Ingrid reached for her duffel bag, which was hidden in the tree. "Let's just get dressed. I think better when I'm clothed."

"Really? I'm the opposite." Carl pulled on his boxers. "If it were up to me, I'd only wear shoes. And—maybe some kind of fanny pack, to hold my cards."

"That image is going to stay with me," Shelby muttered.

"I like my body."

"Yeah. You like it too much. That's the problem."

"Excuse me for having self-esteem."

"I think she's stuck on the fanny pack," Ingrid said. "I have to admit, that's creeping me out, as well."

"Then where will I put my change?"

"I can think of one place."

"Okay, even if I had the square footage—and I'm not saying that I do—"

"Be quiet," Ingrid whispered. "Both of you. Listen."

Something was moving, beyond the trees. Ingrid looked around. Several pairs of glowing eyes looked back at her. The ducks were listening, as well. They knew that something was wrong. Could ducks sense evil? Was that a thing?

"What is it?" Carl asked softly.

Ingrid put a finger to her lips. All she could hear was the wind. Then a plane moaned overhead. It was so loud, she nearly screamed. When the sound of the engines had receded, they all looked at each other. Shelby tried to stifle a laugh.

"I really did hear something," Ingrid said.

"Yeah," Carl replied. "It's called a 747."

"There was something else. I swear it."

"We could ask the ducks. They seem pretty chill."

Ingrid threw the duffel bag over her shoulder. "Fine. Let's just go. I need some tea and a hot shower."

"That sounds great."

"You can use your own shower."

"It has shitty pressure. Yours looks—"

She glared at him. "Have you been staking out my shower?"

"You've got a great bathroom," he said. "Is dreaming a crime?"

"No. But it's profoundly unsettling."

They walked past the gazebo, whose peeling gray floor

was outlined by the park lights. The nearby wastebasket was overflowing with cigarette butts. In the distance, Ingrid could hear the occasional car as it crossed the Albert Street bridge, with its stern façade of Queen Victoria looking down on motorists. A wind was blowing the sulfur smell of Wascana Lake toward them, and it burned her throat. Who knew what was living down there, in the radioactive depths of the constructed underdark? This whole place had once been a windswept ossuary. Human and buffalo bones together, asleep beneath the surface. Ingrid imagined them in their silence, turning to yellow glass over the course of nearly two centuries.

In the 1930s, the government had hired workers to dam the lake. They would have been desperate for any kind of job. Did they realize that someday the resulting park would be a green shadow within Regina, a strange mirror image of a royal wood? Aside from the occasional coyote, there wasn't a great deal of wildlife. Rollerbladers had replaced the fauna. The grasslands of Saskatchewan were gradually being parceled off to developers, with little thought for how this might impact provincial ecology. Paul had told her once that the grasslands were some of the quietest places on earth. He liked to go bird watching, although his teammates ribbed him about it, mercilessly. Sometimes they'd steal his Audubon guides and replace them with *Maxim*.

Ingrid was happy to see her dented gray car waiting for her across the parking lot. She wasn't sure how Sam was getting home. Maybe she'd call a cab. She thought about leaving some kind of note for her—*Text me when you get back, and I'll pick you up*—but Sam's duffel bag was back in the clearing. She didn't have the strength to turn around. The comfort of the couch was too close. She could already smell the vanilla air freshener in her hallway, and lingering over that, an echo of whatever Paul had cooked for dinner. There would be leftovers wrapped in neat tinfoil packets. If she was quiet enough, she could make herself a plate in the semidarkness of the kitchen, without waking them up.

Neil could sleep through anything. She'd brushed his

teeth while he was unconscious, and he'd simply sighed, trembling beneath some rich dream. But Paul was a light sleeper. Often he heard her struggling with the screen door. He'd come stumbling down the hallway in his pajamas, rubbing his eyes and asking if she wanted him to throw something in the microwave. Her sweet brother, who could fix any problem with the correct seasoning.

Ingrid herself was a survivalist cook. She ate what was required to avoid fainting, but she'd never moved past the one-pot meal. Paul made his own pasta and seemed genuinely happy when he was deboning a chicken. It hardly mattered if his fingers were slick with blood or bread crumbs. His natural state was to be covered in something. Ingrid wasn't sure where he'd learned to cook—certainly not from their parents—but she was grateful. If not for him, she would have subsisted on hash browns, guacamole, and tofu crumbled up into a bowl of instant noodles.

"It's not too late," Carl said. "Would anyone else vote for waffles at Humpty's?"

"It's two thirty in the morning," Shelby clarified. "Do you really want to deal with the clientele at this hour?"

"Drunks can be funny. They have such bad reflexes."

"I'll pass."

"Ingrid? Can I interest you in a vinyl booth?"

She laughed. "That has to be the strangest proposition I've ever received."

"I call it brunch after midnight. I think it's going to catch on with the academic set."

Ingrid turned to him. "Carl, why don't you want to go home?"

His crooked smile faded. Then his eyes clouded, and he shrugged, in the way that you do when you're holding something back. "I live on the second floor. My apartment is like a toaster oven, and the sex shop below me is open all night. It's hard to sleep when there's a dildo-related dispute going on right outside your window."

"The clubs are still open. Why not go out?"

"I'm not in the mood for rejection tonight."

"Oh, come on. You must clean up."

"He has a weakness for the unattainable," Shelby said, putting an arm around his shoulder. "That's a taste that we both share, I'm afraid."

"I'm better with a wingman. Or wing-lady." He frowned. "Scratch that. *Wing-lady* sounds like a demented superhero. Let's just go with *copilot*."

"Tell you what," Shelby said. "Come back to my place, and I'll have one drink with you. It's going to be a gin and Coke, because that's all I've got."

He brightened. "You're on."

"Just one. I'm tired, and I don't want you dragging me anywhere."

"I swear it, on my honor as a grad student."

"That oath is worth nothing."

"Well, it's all we've got."

Shelby turned to Ingrid. "You could get in on this action, if you wanted. I've also got some pretty flat cream soda in the fridge."

For a moment, her laconic expression changed to one that was hopeful. Ingrid knew what she was really asking. Her stomach did a bit of a flip. It was late. She already felt bad for leaving Paul and Neil. Part of her wanted nothing more than to sink into clean sheets, to forget entirely about the basilissa and what she might do to them. It wouldn't take long. The hot shower would speed her toward a sweet oblivion. But at the same time, she wanted to know what just one drink would lead to, after Carl went home. The possibilities multiplied within her mind. It had been a long time. Maybe she'd forgotten it all. She would need to consult an instructional website before getting into bed with another human being.

"I'm not sure," Ingrid hedged. "Hard alcohol does a number on my stomach. It's been years since I had tequila, and I still remember—"

Shelby was staring at her. At first, Ingrid thought that she was trying to look disapproving. But her eyes were too wide for that. She seemed horrified.

"Okay, I know my gastro issues aren't exactly the

classiest topic of conversation, but Carl once threatened to put his—"

Then she realized that Shelby wasn't looking at her. Instead, she was looking at something over her shoulder. Ingrid didn't want to turn. She really didn't. A part of her knew, already, what Shelby had seen. There was no sense in denying it. The hairs on the back of her neck and arms were already standing at attention. But for a moment, she clung to the bliss of ignorance, as if it were a blanket that she could pull over her face. *Let me keep dreaming,* she almost said. *Don't force me to wake up.* It was no use. Time to open her eyes, and face the horror.

Ingrid turned. Shelby stood very still beside her, saying nothing. Carl had moved into an odd position, sort of adjacent to the two of them. It was as if he wanted to step forward, to interpose himself between them and whatever was coming, but his body refused to cooperate. He stood at a curious angle, fused to the pavement. More statue than savior. Ingrid could feel the adrenaline setting fire to her heart and lungs. Her hands trembled. *We're rabbits,* she thought. *This is how a small thing feels, before the teeth, before everything goes dark.*

A silenus was making her way across the parking lot. At first Ingrid thought that she carried a spear. But then she realized that the wood was grayish and peeling. She must have torn it from the floor of the gazebo. Not that she needed a weapon. The contours of muscle were visible, even beneath her dark pelt. She could pull off their limbs, one by one, as a bored child might pluck daisies. Her eyes reminded Ingrid of the park lights, sodium-yellow and flickering with excited vapor. She moved with slow assurance. Her hooves lifted sparks from the uneven pavement, as if buried power lines were somehow responding. It wasn't the *clip-clop* of a prancing horse. It was a hammer, breaking through stone. Ingrid half expected to see glowing hoofprints, like something out of a Washington Irving tale, but there were only spiral cracks in the ground. The world was her windshield, and she was a collision, a nightmare of velocity and hunger that would kill them in a moment of exquisite calculus.

Ingrid could feel an older part of her brain, something prehistoric, slowly taking control. This was a mammoth, and she was a bug caught in its shadow. Running wasn't an option—they were in the middle of an empty parking lot. It might as well be a concrete safari. The silenus would overtake them in a moment. She needed a weapon. All she had in her pockets was a phone, a ring of keys, and some loose change. In the old Celtic stories, magical things were afraid of iron. She could pummel the creature with toonies. But this wasn't a storybook monster. This was Grendel's mother, a homicidal satyr with nothing to lose. Nothing short of a grenade would slow her down.

Then Ingrid realized that she did have a weapon.

"Everyone in the car!"

Instinctively, she grabbed their hands. For a moment, it felt like she was running through the park with Neil. *We are stars, Mummy,* he would squeal in delight. *Look at mine feet—they aren't even touching the ground!* But they weren't sailing over puddles, or letting the tall grass whip against their bare ankles. They were stumbling across a deserted parking lot. The silenus didn't break into a run. She kept her pace indifferent. After all, there was nowhere for them to go. She could close the distance between them in a moment.

Ingrid reached the car. She pulled out the keys, but her hands were shaking. The key ring dropped to the ground.

She sank to her knees. In that moment, she was every final girl in a horror film, losing her keys, pounding on the wrong door, hurtling down a sinister alley. Maybe Fortuna was shouting at her from the sky. *Not that way, idiot! What are you thinking?* She reached for the fob, but her body was electric with fear. She couldn't get her fingers to work.

You are not going to die on your knees in Wascana Park. You are a miles. The parking lot is your Hippodrome. The pavement is nothing but sand. Pick up the bloody keys.

Ingrid grabbed the key ring. She unlocked the doors.

"Get in!"

Carl slid into the backseat, slamming the door behind

him. Shelby sat beside her. Ingrid started the engine and checked the rearview mirror. The silenus was about twenty feet away. Or were monsters in the mirror closer than they appeared? It didn't matter. She slammed the car into reverse and stepped on the gas. The tires squealed. Her little car slammed into the silenus. They collided at an angle. Carl, who wasn't wearing a seat belt, lurched forward with the impact. Shelby braced her hands against the dashboard.

Ingrid felt the collision rattle through her body, like a sudden current. She shifted into first. Suddenly, she could hear Paul's voice, shouting at her—*clutch, fucking clutch, you're going to kill the transmission*—but she ignored the startled cry of the engine. As the car began to tremble, she finally shifted into second, turning in a wide arc that left an acrid trail of rubber on the pavement. She could smell it. Beneath that, she could smell her own sweat. There was bile in her mouth. Heroes weren't supposed to throw up during a car chase, but she was certain that she might. The silenus was standing in the middle of the parking lot. She didn't even look winded. Her eyes were two amber slits.

"How strong are they?" Carl demanded from the back-seat.

"I'm not sure," Shelby replied.

"You should know—you've killed two of them."

"That was Morgan, not me! And I had a bow."

"Dear Fortuna," Carl began. "Bless this hatchback—"

"What is she even doing here?" Ingrid stared at the hunter, immobile as a lamp in the middle of the pavement. "They can't cross the boundary."

"Remember those coyote sightings, from a while back?" Shelby's voice was low. "I guess we were right. They weren't coyotes."

"Since when can they cross over?"

"It's a brave new fucking world, who cares? Just step on the gas!"

Ingrid hesitated. "I don't want to kill her."

"You'd need a tank."

"There's a human under that fur . . . right?"

"I—" Shelby looked at her helplessly. "I don't know. Maybe."

Ingrid gripped the steering wheel. She closed her eyes and slammed her foot against the gas pedal. The silenus didn't move. For a second, Ingrid thought that she might swerve, that she couldn't hit a living thing head-on. Surely not a living thing with intelligent eyes, regarding her as if she were a suicidal prairie dog. But she didn't swerve.

The impact tore through her. Every nerve caught fire, and she felt it in her teeth, behind her eyes, in the soles of her feet. The hood crumpled. She heard shearing metal. The glass of the windshield cratered, spiraling out in long, claw-like patterns. The silenus flew backward. She rolled across the ground, struck a concrete divider, and then was still.

Smoke was pouring from the hood. Ingrid could smell something chemical, something that she knew was danger-ous. The superheated metal of the car made a *tick-tick-tick* sound. The headlights cast a mosaic of broken yellow, illu-minating the ground in pieces. Nobody spoke. She could hear Shelby's ragged breathing. Carl was staring out the back window, like a kid trapped on a nightmarish road trip, hands pressed against the glass.

The silenus didn't move.

"Is she dead?" Shelby whispered.

Ingrid couldn't let go of the wheel. "I don't know." She looked in the rearview mirror. The silenus was completely still. A light wind played with her fur. If you squinted, it might have been a deer. She didn't see any blood. Why wasn't there any blood?

"We should go," Shelby said. "Right? Before she wakes up?"

"What if she doesn't wake up?" Ingrid asked.

"Look—" Carl began. "I'm all for silenus equal rights. Satyr pride, you can't judge a monster by its hooves, and all that. I get it. But this isn't Mr. Fucking Tumnus, okay? Shel-by's right. We have to go, before that thing eviscerates us."

"She's human." Ingrid closed her eyes for a moment. "I don't know how she crossed over in this form. I didn't even think that was possible. But it's happened before. The coyote attacks—you said it yourself. They're all human. Part of the time."

"You have no proof of that," Carl said. "They're a wild gens. We don't even know if they were human to begin with, or if they've always lived on the other side."

Ingrid turned to look at him. "Maybe you're right. But what if the sun rises and that monster turns into someone like us? She must have internal injuries—I mean, God, I hit her *twice* with a car. She could be dying."

"She wants to eat us!"

"I don't think they actually eat their prey."

"Oh, right. They just carve out our hearts and sacrifice us to their crazy forest god. That's so much more humane."

"I don't see how their forest god is any less—"

Shelby grabbed her shoulder. "Ingrid. *Look.*"

She craned her neck to see through the rear window. The body of the silenus was gone. There was only a smooth patch of concrete. Not a drop of blood.

Her heart was pounding. She could taste acid. She wanted to run, but she was strapped into the seat. Ingrid tried to look through the cracked windshield. Nothing but shadows and dancing lights. *Tick tick tick.* The wounded groans of the car, whose front end was a wreck. The wind was starting to pick up. There was a knife edge of cold to it as it swept across Wascana Lake. A goose approached the car. He seemed quite unafraid. For a moment, that made Ingrid feel better. Then he hissed, eyes flashing in the headlights.

Ingrid checked the rear view. She saw a shadow, then—
"Carl, get down!"

The glass of the rear window exploded. Carl dove forward, just as a wooden plank tore through the opening. Her makeshift spear. It buried itself in the bottom of the car, whose insides gave a shuddering cry. They'd been harpooned, like a white whale. Carl was pressed against the passenger-side window, knees drawn up to his chest. His hair was covered in glass, and he looked more dazed than frightened. Ingrid saw blood on his forehead. She realized, through her own haze of fear, that Shelby was right. The silenus might be human, but not at the moment. She would take apart the vehicle, one bolt at a time if necessary, until there was nowhere left to hide. They were already running out of windows.

Ingrid floored the gas pedal. She felt Carl slam against the back of her seat. The car was making every terrible sound that she'd ever heard before, all at once. Wind sang through the broken window, as chips of safety glass danced around them. But the check engine light hadn't yet come on. That was oddly reassuring. As long as the light stayed off, it meant that the car wasn't quite dead. Just mostly dead, in the words of Miracle Max.

They tore down the footpath, which followed the Albert Street bridge. The park lights flared as they passed, making rainbows on the cratered windshield. It was hard to see through all the cracks, but Ingrid had walked this way hundreds of times. It was how she relaxed after long days of studying. She'd breathe in the night air, letting the silence relax her. She remembered every shadow, every curve of the path. This wasn't so different, save for the fact that they were going a lot faster, and her legs were covered in bits of glass, like snow.

Shelby twisted around in her seat. "Carl, are you okay?"

"Yeah," he said weakly. "Although I may need that shower after all. I've got a feeling that these pants have been compromised."

"You're bleeding."

"Really?" He sounded surprised. "Huh."

"How bad is the cut?" Ingrid asked. "I can't see."

"I'm not sure. His hair's a mess."

"Try getting Moby-Dicked in the back of a car," he shot back. "Then we'll see what your precious curls look like."

"Actually, it was Ahab—"

"Turn," Ingrid yelled. "Grab onto something!"

She swerved to avoid the reservoir, next to the bridge. For a moment, she saw a buffalo's face in terra-cotta, looking at her curiously. The wheel was like a rock. But she wrestled it with both hands, and the car gave a horrible shudder as it turned, kicking up dust and gravel. They drove over one of the park lights, which had been artfully arranged by the edge of the lake. She heard a *pop* as the tires crushed it.

The city would have to bill her, if they survived. What was the protocol for that? Should she leave a note?

Dear Regina—I owe you one decorative light, regrettably destroyed in a satyr chase. Please accept this money order.

"Can you see anything back there?" Ingrid demanded. "Is she following us?"

"Yes!" Carl screamed. "Very much *yes*! Drive faster!"

She glanced at the rear view. In the distance, she could barely make out a dark form, keeping pace with them. She was running on all fours now. Ingrid tried to swallow around the lump in her throat. The engine screamed. The tachometer was redlining, and she could feel the gearshift trembling violently beneath her hand. In a few moments, the transmission might drop out of the car. This wasn't a James Bond movie, after all. Her little gray four-banger couldn't handle this kind of pressure. Most likely, it was a write-off. How was she going to afford a new car? How would she get Neil to day care? It was amazing that her mind kept distracting itself with these questions, even as her stomach churned and she feared that she might throw up.

They tore past the educational signs, which told the history of Wascana Park in helpful infographics. Light cast golden sparks upon the lake. A few ducks swam in the dark, unruffled by their passage. No doubt, they'd seen worse. Luckily, the paths were empty at this time of night. Up ahead, she saw the dome of the parliament building, ringed by lights.

"Hold on again," she said.

"Again?" Carl asked. "I've got a death grip on the holy-shit handle."

"Good thinking."

She drove over a concrete divider and down the pathway that led through the gardens. Neat plots of flowers whipped by them in explosions of color. There was the occasional palm tree, which struck Ingrid as an impossibility in Saskatchewan. How did they survive the winter? Maybe it was just the park's magic in action. She tried to keep the car steady without crushing too much of the local flora. She could smell their scent on the wind. It reminded her of incense. For a moment, she felt relaxed. She forget that they were driving down a pedestrian path, murdering the greenery. Then she saw the shadow in the rearview mirror. It was closer.

They passed the statue of Elizabeth II astride a horse. The queen regarded them coolly, her features lit from below. *If this were a fantasy novel,* Ingrid thought, *the statue would come alive, and fight for us. Elizabeth in all of her martial glory, protecting the colony.*

But the horse didn't move. Like the park itself, the statue was ornamental. A pattern laid atop stolen land, meant to distract everyone. A lake diverted, so that citizens could walk along its edge, holding waffle cones and smartphones. What chased them was older than the park, older than anything within the city limits. Perhaps she belonged to the land itself. She remembered the feel of red clay beneath her hooves, the wind, the endless skies. The silenus was a force of nature, like the cyclone that had destroyed the original parliament building. There was no escape. They might as well try reasoning with a storm.

The car was slowing down. Ingrid pumped the gas. The engine was barely hanging on, but it was only a matter of time. Behind them, the shadow was closing the distance. She drove to the foot of the golden edifice, with its neo-Victorian façade. Rows of pitiless windows stared down at her. The seat of provincial government, as big as a castle. It remembered everything, from the first unions to the current Sask

Party. It would protect them. Surely, there was some place in that massive building for them to hide. Some marble statue that they could use as cover while they waited for the sun to rise. If push came to shove, they could topple some of the busts and use them as weapons.

"Why are we stopping?" Shelby asked.

"The car's about to die, and we've got nowhere else to go." Ingrid gestured toward the parliament building. "If we can get inside, we should be able to wait it out."

"Wait it out?" Carl leaned forward in the backseat. "And what if your theory is wrong? What if she doesn't turn back? She'll be eating us by sunrise."

"I told you, they don't eat—"

Shelby flung open the door. "If we're going to make it, we have to go now!"

They abandoned the car and ran up the marble steps. Ingrid took them two at a time. She couldn't look behind her. She could feel the shadow approaching. Oscana's avenging angel, or whatever else she might be. She was hunger. That was all that mattered. Shelby was dragging Carl behind her. The windows bore no expression. They would admit nothing.

They reached the entrance. Panting, Ingrid looked around her for something, anything that could break the glass. Why hadn't she taken the makeshift spear? Or a rock? Her brain seemed to be on a permanent delay. The adrenaline was still spiking through her, making her knees shake. The bile was rising in her throat. Carl and Shelby stood next to her, holding each other up. She could hear them breathing.

The shadow moved below them. Walking upright now, and in no hurry. All that separated them was a flight of stairs. Ingrid could see her eyes, the color of yellow traffic lights. They were looking directly at her.

She placed one hoof on the first step. *Click.* Ingrid swallowed.

Then she heard the roaring engine.

At first, she thought it was her car, about to explode. But it was much louder. The silenus turned, but there was no time to move. Even she wasn't fast enough. The truck slammed into her with a sound that was indescribable. The silenus flew. Ingrid watched her, a dark star falling. She landed ten feet away, in a bed of purple crocuses.

Sam stuck her head out the driver's-side window.

"What are you waiting for? Get in, before she wakes up!"

PART THREE

SAGITTARIUS

1

SHELBY WOKE UP AT AN ANGLE. THE ARM OF the couch was digging into her neck, and the living room swam before her, a goldfish bowl of unfamiliar shapes. When she squinted, she could make out shelves hanging from eyebolts screwed into the ceiling. They rocked slightly in the breeze coming through the open window. She tried to read the books' titles, but even when she could make them out, their meaning eluded her. They were all about vectors, shearing forces, and torsion. A shiny laptop sat beneath them, displaying a vintage screen saver. Toasters with wings. She hadn't seen that one in ages. It made her think of simpler times, before DVD-ROM drives and high-speed Internet, when you still had to sweat over an AUTOEXEC.BAT file to make your game work properly. It felt like you were searching for buried treasure, as you tried to anticipate the number of file pathways to open. Would twenty be enough? Fifty?

Waking up in a strange place reminded her of sleepovers. The disorientation that you felt in the middle of the night, trying to find your friend's bathroom. The fear of encountering her parents in the hallway, slightly disheveled and all

too real in their bathrobes. All those dark kitchens and rumpus rooms that were not her own, suggesting alternate lives
on familiar cul-de-sacs, yet somehow sinister as well.
Because if their lives were simply mutations of her own, the
difference of a few throw pillows and a larger television,
what did that make her? How could she be special, when
Donna Green's parents had the same carpeting, the same
terminal microwave whose glass dish also chafed in secret?
All those staircases that were mirror images, as if she'd
fallen into a suburban Escher painting.

But the uncanny houses weren't the only thing that made
her uneasy. There was also the long night, the hours spent
with her eyes open, while Donna slept soundly next to her.
Trying to be comforted by her friend's breathing, while the
acid climbed up her throat. Now and again, their elbows
would touch. Shelby knew that if she rolled over, Donna
would embrace her, still dreaming of Toby Fleischman and
his aviator sunglasses. She would not think of Donna's small
breasts beneath her Our Lady Peace T-shirt, or the faint blond
hairs on her arms. Or kissing the freckles on her back, which
formed a constellation that Shelby had already named.

It must be strange, she remembered thinking, to be a boy
in the same predicament. If you touched your best friend, he
might kill you. The barest suggestion of intimacy was forbid-
den. Desire never went away, but fear held it in abeyance.
Girls weren't as brutal in their retribution, but they had a way
of closing ranks against you. She was already baffled by the
politics of being a girl in a small town. The rules and signs
were oddly foreign to her, as if she'd missed some crucial
orientation about how to communicate. Most of the time, she
was faking it. The last thing she needed was a murder of
rumors flying around school, and all because, in the gauzy
predawn light of Donna's bedroom, she'd forgotten her mask.

Carl wasn't in this memory. But he emerged from the
hallway regardless, yawning and scratching his belly. He
was wearing a pair of Sonic the Hedgehog boxers. Carl
wasn't her type. Too much hair and bravura. Plus, he'd make
an awful boyfriend. She couldn't imagine him pulling her

hair back while she threw up, or answering the phone when she was avoiding her mother. He was more likely to forget to pick her up, losing track of time within a skunk cloud while he played games on his vintage Sega Genesis. In spite of all that, he had a certain dark charm, like a tom with fleas who eventually wore you down. She could almost see why Andrew had liked him, once. He did have nice legs.

Carl stretched and farted. Then he saw her on the couch and grinned.

"Sorry. Thought you were still asleep."

"You're really the whole package, aren't you?"

"Come on. We nearly died last night. Car chases make me gassy."

"Let me see your cut."

"It's okay."

"Don't argue."

He sighed and knelt by the couch. Shelby gently lifted the bandage on his forehead, which was spotted with blood. The edges of the wound had crusted over, but it looked clean.

"You probably needed a stitch."

"Going to the hospital didn't seem like the best option."

"I know. It should be fine. Just don't aggravate it."

"What do you think I'm going to do—stick my head in a barrel of rats?"

"I've seen your apartment. I wouldn't trust any of those surfaces."

"Don't worry about my surfaces. They're fine."

"Just—"

He frowned. "What?"

Shelby looked at him again. He was so vulnerable, smiling uncertainly as he knelt before her, like a squire in his underwear. She was suddenly filled with love for this man, this little boy, who kept her secrets and walked with her every day to school. This endearing shipwreck who never knew what he wanted but always carried an extra granola bar, in case Andrew's blood sugar decided to bottom out. She hugged him. At first, he was surprised. But then he pulled her close and said nothing. Shelby realized that she was shaking.

"It's going to be okay," he whispered.

"Really?"

"Trust me."

She pulled away. "I'd trust you more if you cleaned your bathtub."

"I told you, the sliding door makes it hard to really get in there."

He knew what she was actually saying. They both understood each other, caught in the silence of that unfamiliar living room. There was no sense in asking the real questions. *Are you taking care of yourself? Flossing and eating oranges? Guarding against loneliness, the way that Foucault recommends?*

Carl disappeared into the bathroom to get changed. Shelby pulled on her shirt and began hunting for a missing sock, which she found beneath the table. Carl returned, still sporting bed-head. He handed her some gum, which she took gratefully. Both of them chewed in silence. Then they heard footsteps, and Sam emerged from the hallway. For a moment, she looked terrified, as if she'd stumbled onto a pair of incompetent burglars.

"Shit. I forgot that you were here."

"Thanks for letting us stay the night," Shelby replied.

"At this point, it's probably best that we stick together. Like a team, or whatever." Sam yawned. She was wearing a Wesley Crushers T-shirt and faded pajama pants. "I actually had a great sleep. Must have been the adrenaline. Does anyone want coffee?"

"That's not really a question," Carl said.

"Good point. I'll go prime Majel."

"Who?"

"Majel Barrett. She's my Keurig."

"I can't tell if that's disrespectful or highly appropriate."

"Well, I'm sketchy that way." Sam disappeared into the kitchen. "Did either of you hear from Ingrid? I thought she was supposed to text in the morning."

Shelby checked her phone. "I've got nothing. Maybe she's still asleep."

"Doubtful," Carl said. "Neil wakes her up at six thirty, like clockwork."

"It must be difficult—lying to more than one person, I mean."

"The other day, I told Neil that bales of hay wrapped in black plastic were burnt marshmallows. Lying to a four-year-old isn't tough."

"But Paul must suspect something."

"I'm sure he's got his own shit to distract him. People tend to believe that things are going fine, until entropy bites them in the ass."

"Entropy is the heat death of the universe," Sam called from the kitchen. "If anything, it would freeze your ass, rather than biting it."

"Way to be comforting," Carl replied.

As it turned out, Sam had only two mugs. Shelby drank her coffee out of a Moosehead tumbler without complaining. Carl nosed through her bookshelf.

"Hey." He pulled out a slim volume with *Ediciones Catedra* stamped on it. "What are you doing with *La Celestina*?"

"It's one of my favorite plays."

"Seriously?"

"What—science students can't enjoy Late Medieval theater?"

"It's just not really that common. In Regina, I mean."

"I haven't always lived in Regina. Plus, I've got a weakness for sketchy midwives."

"You speak Spanish?"

"Yo entiendo mas que yo puedo hablar."

"How would you feel about talking to my mother on the phone? We'd have to change your name to Tammy, but it could still work."

"Excuse me?"

"Never mind. It was just a thought."

"Tammy is his imaginary girlfriend," Shelby clarified. "He made her up, so that his mom wouldn't find out that he's a pansexual slut."

"Oh, look who's talking. Last night, you were trying to convince a single mom to have drinks with you."

"I wasn't trying to convince anyone of anything."

"Wait." Sam turned to Shelby. "You're into Ingrid?"

"Not *into* her. That suggests real focus. I'm just sort of passively—"

"Stalking her?" Carl suggested.

Sam ignored him. "I thought—I mean, when your shadows kissed, I assumed it was just supposed to be a distraction. I didn't realize that there was actual chemistry happening."

"It's not that simple." Shelby didn't believe her own words, but if she kept talking, they might start to make sense. "Our shadows do things that we can't control. Morgan has her own inner life that's separate from mine."

"You're so into her."

Shelby blushed. "I don't know. These things are always just in my head."

"That kiss looked real enough."

"Our shadows kissed. It's not the same thing."

Sam shook her head. "I don't believe this bullshit 'shadows' theory. Those people are a part of us. Julia talks to me in my dreams, all the time. I remember things about her life. About her mother, and the cramped insula where she grew up, and how she used to brush her hair with a cracked tortoiseshell comb. Whoever we are beyond the park—it's not as simple as putting on a costume. I can't tell where I end and the artifex begins."

"They're like middle names," Carl said.

Sam gave him an odd look. "Explain."

"We've all got middle names. Mine's Lazarillo. I never think about it, unless I'm filling out a customs card or talking to my mom. It's this part of me that I didn't choose. But it's also a connection to my past." He smiled. "And what if, one day, I just started going by Lazarillo, instead of Carl? I'd feel like a different person, even if nothing had really changed. Maybe Lazarillo prefers tea to coffee, or likes the crusts of his sandwich cut off. Maybe he's got it all figured out, or he's even more broken than I am. We all carry around these pieces from another life—names that our parents gave us. They're shadows too. Babieca may be some slanted version of me, but he's still in there, ready to be declared."

"Psychiatrists would make a fortune if they knew about the park," Shelby said.

"I'm sure that some of them do. Oliver said that everyone was basically in on it—from the police department to the mayor's office."

"Did you just quote Oliver?"

Carl shrugged. "What can I say? The guy gets my back up sometimes, but what's the world coming to if you can't trust a librarian?"

Sam was staring at her coffee. Finally, she looked up. "We should meet with Ingrid tonight. We have to figure out our next move."

"Big cheese lady is obviously on to us," Carl added. "It's not like that silenus was going for a brisk jog, and we happened to cross paths. Patty Lapona must have sent her."

Sam laughed. "God, Shelby, that was the worst lie I've ever heard."

"I was trying to be creative. I didn't exactly have a lot to work with"

"What if Andrew starts asking questions around the ed department? It won't take him long to realize that they didn't just hire a famous Broadway luminary."

"Ingrid will have to run some kind of interference."

"I don't think he's going to investigate," Carl said.

Shelby gave him a look. "Have you two met? The first time my mom invited him to dinner, he came over with a marked-up copy of her dissertation."

"He's preoccupied." Carl's voice was neutral, but his eyes told a different story.

"With what?"

"Nothing. Just weird dreams."

"Carl."

"What? I don't know much, okay? He barely said anything."

"Define *weird*."

"At this point, it would be easier to list the stuff in our lives that *wouldn't* qualify as the next Guillermo del Toro film."

"I dream about park things all the time," Sam said. "Even if he's technically cut off from that world, it stands to reason that he's still got memories. I mean, do they really just go *poof*? That doesn't even seem possible."

"He told me that salamanders were following him. In his dreams."

Shelby reached for her tumbler but found it already empty. "That can't be a sign for the good."

"Why not?" Carl's look of hope was slightly devastating. "Wouldn't that mean some small part of Roldan had survived?"

"No. It means that the lares don't want to let go of him."

"They could lead him back to the park."

"Or drive him insane."

"He saw an undina in Ingrid's bathroom," Shelby said.

Sam blinked. "How is that possible?"

"We don't know, but there's some kind of deep shit happening. Latona said it herself. The walls between the worlds are thinning. Stuff is getting through."

"Unless it was always here to begin with."

Carl glanced at his phone. "I have to go to campus. I've got an appointment with one of the student counselors."

"Are salamanders chasing you, as well?"

"No. I just figured out that you can request an emergency loan, which they take out of your student loan before it arrives. I need new pants."

"That seems financially sound."

"Pants are expensive."

"It's fine. I have to meet with my supervisor. I'll take the bus with you."

"I'm staying in," Sam said. "After hitting a silenus with my truck, I'd rather not leave the apartment for a while. Text me later tonight, though."

"Will do." Shelby grabbed her clothes. "Hey, check us out. Sounding like a company."

"I haven't decided yet if we're a real company or just a bunch of idiots."

"We applied to graduate studies." Carl grinned. "Who says we can't be both?"

They made their way downstairs. Sam's apartment was on Rose Street, in a respectable brick building with its own courtyard. Shelby was reminded, not for the first time, that she lived above a vegetarian restaurant. Access to falafel was nice, but she would have preferred a more adult living arrangement.

"How do you think she affords that rent?"

Carl kicked a stone. "Trust fund? Second job?"

"Maybe she figured out your emergency loan trick."

"It's only five hundred dollars."

"That's an awfully expensive pair of pants."

"It's going toward groceries, as well. I'm not a monster."

"Do you think she's acting funny?"

"Sam?"

"Yeah. Before, she was all, *I'm not in this, we're not a company.* She didn't trust us. Now she's talking about strategy meetings."

"Last I checked, we're all in the same shitstorm."

"But she had an out. She could have bailed, and she didn't."

"You're shocked that she's acting human?"

"No. Never mind. Now I'm the monster."

"You're skeptical. That's not the same thing."

She sighed. "It always turns into Donna Green."

"What?"

"Nothing. That's our bus—come on."

The university bus was only half full, since most of the city drove. In a place where nothing was more than ten minutes away, Shelby couldn't figure out why everyone had to clog the roads. Her students found it inconceivable that she used public transit, but parking her truck at school cost a small fortune. She'd seen people crying in front of Parking

Services because they'd been assigned to Z-lot, which was practically in the bush. Their bus idled outside the Rehabilitation Centre. Carl played Brick Breaker on his phone.

Shelby tried to go over her notes for the meeting with her supervisor, but they no longer made any sense. She'd written *Good research*, with *Good* underlined twice, and then in the corner, she'd added, *Find that article from JSTOR about female husbands*. Above that, she'd scrawled, *Search terms for EEBO*, but the only term that she could make out was *women*. What women? Women what? Obviously, she'd had more context at four in the morning, just before falling asleep. She'd just have to wing it. Dr. Marsden could be stern, but she had a soft spot for her graduate students. People who studied the eighteenth century had to stick together, because they knew that it was secretly the best period.

"How's that article coming along?" Shelby asked, desperate to escape the black hole of her own imposter syndrome.

"Huh?" Carl tilted his phone. "What article?"

"The one you've been working on all year."

"Oh. It's done."

"Really?"

"Of course not. It's awful, and I hate everything about it, even the font."

"You could always change that. I hear Comic Sans is making a comeback."

"Thanks. I'm sure that'll make the difference."

"Maybe you need to simplify. That's what Marsden is always telling me. 'Just simplify, Shelby. You're trying to make too many connections.'"

"I thought we were supposed to make connections."

"As it turns out, they were all made in 2007."

"I keep using the word *gesture* in my argument. Like, *allow me to gesture toward this point, without actually saying dick about it*." He made a waving motion with his free hand. "Look, Shel, this is me gesturing. What do you think?"

"Impressive."

The bus pulled up in front of the Innovation Centre, and everyone filed off slowly, still texting as they blindly groped for the door. Carl was invested in beating his high score and nearly stepped into the path of an oncoming car; Shelby managed to steer him away, just in time. The air-conditioning flooded over her as she stepped through the doors. People queued in front of Tim Horton's, quietly losing their minds as they waited for pastry. Athena's was already full, and she could hear fragments of neurotic conversation emerging from the bar. Keywords included *funding* and *fracking mid-terms*. A beer would have been nice, but she was afraid that Dr. Marsden might smell it on her and be disappointed. There was nothing worse than being pitied by someone who dressed like an adult.

"I'm off to the Student Success Centre," Carl said. "Do I look like a mess? I find it always goes better if I'm puffy and unshaven."

"You look sufficiently desperate."

"Great. Text me when you're done getting yelled at."

Unexpectedly, he squeezed her hand.

She smiled. "Thanks."

The Department of Literature and Cultural Studies was quiet today. Most of the professors had their doors only slightly ajar, which translated into: *Don't knock unless it involves an emergency reference letter.* She imagined them all sitting at their computers, fingers dancing across the keyboard as they produced something real, with footnotes and a two-part title separated by an ironic colon. Or perhaps they were sweating like her, unable to come up with anything that seemed useful. She couldn't imagine her supervisor glaring at the screen in frustration or squeezing a stress ball. Her mother never seemed stressed, either. She was always listening to her headphones, or autographing a stack of green forms. Her signature was elegant. Shelby's looked childish, as if she'd only just learned how to spell her own name.

Someone had put up an oversized poster of Audre Lorde. Hers was the only black face in a sea of white academics, blown up to frightening proportions. Beneath her was a quotation: *The master's tools will never dismantle the master's house.* But how could one avoid using the preassigned tool belts? Where were the sonic screwdrivers? Her mother would know the answer. She had a bookshelf full of radical literature and was always ready for a fight.

Shelby had tried to be like her, but it never came out right. She knew that she was out of touch with her traditions, that she barely spoke a word of Plains Cree. Her grandmother was fluent, but her efforts to teach Shelby had been frustrating and short-lived. It wasn't that she didn't want to learn. It would have been nice to understand what they were saying behind her back. She always got frustrated. It was the same as learning to drive. She knew that what her mother was shouting made perfect sense, but in the heat of the moment, her instinct was to slam on the brakes and get out of the car.

She took a deep breath and approached Dr. Marsden's door. Her notes were in order, even if they happened to be indecipherable. Her tiredness could be mistaken for late-night cramming rather than a poor sleep on someone's couch. As long as she asked random questions that circumnavigated her own lack of experience, she'd at least appear curious. That was better than staring blankly at her supervisor.

There was a note affixed to the door, announcing that Dr. Marsden was sick. There was no indication of when she might return. Shelby's relief was so intense, she nearly pumped her fist in the air. Then she felt terrible about feeling good and resolved to purchase a suitable get-well-soon card from the bookstore. Something with a nature scene, but no animals.

"Saved by the sign."

She turned in surprise. Andrew was standing in the hallway. He offered her a half-smile.

"Hey. I didn't see you there."

"I was sidling."

"Good job."

"It was a tricky throw, but I managed it."

She thought of her own die—or Morgan's, rather—and what she'd done with it. The fan of green blood as the silenus collapsed in a heap. Pulcheria's screams. The power of a roll to change everyone's fate. And she remembered what she'd wagered. How she'd bet their lives. For Andrew, it must have seemed like a dream, fading every day. He was losing his old life without alarm, in the same way that you let go of a nightmare, until it was nothing but the memory of some ancient, irrecoverable panic. The same thing you'd felt in the first grade when you were the only person who didn't know how to use the trampoline. But Carl remembered. He understood the choice that she'd made. He wouldn't be surprised if she made the same choice again. Every day, they rolled with their lives. That was magic's price.

It would be so much easier if rolling worked outside the park. If she could somehow offset those sacred numbers that, like some combination of stars, had shaped her since birth. Fortuna's double-edged gifts. Her thick hair, which never did anything that she wanted. Her chest. Her tuneless voice. Her impatience, which must have come from her father, because her mother was so serene that it hurt. If only she could toss the dice and change it all. Smudge out the stats on the character sheet and start over.

"What are you up to?" Shelby asked.

"Printing. I'm done now."

She glanced at her meaningless notes. "I have to type something up that makes sense. Otherwise, my supervisor will probably never speak to me again."

"There's nobody in the TA office."

"Want to keep me company?"

He nodded. "I'll get us coffee."

The office smelled like smoke, with traces of anxiety. Someone had left a pair of shoes in one corner. The ficus was near death but hadn't yet given up. Shelby moved it toward the light and gave it some water. Andrew returned with two travel mugs.

"Thanks," she said, taking one.

"You haven't tasted it yet."

"The goal is to stay conscious. This should do the trick."

He pulled out a copy of *Sweet's Anglo-Saxon Reader*. "I can amuse myself until you're done on the computer."

"How's Wulf doing? Still cryptic?"

"That's his best quality."

"It baffles me that English used to sound that way. All thorns and yoghs."

"Every poem has its thorns."

She rolled her eyes. "I walked right into that."

Shelby booted up the old computer, which muttered its disapproval. Like an aging cat, it just wanted to sleep. The keyboard was stained with sweat and nicotine. The Internet connection was dial-up, but it didn't annoy her. Something about it made her nostalgic. She remembered having to wait this long for everything. Watching a progress bar with growing frustration. Waiting for the moment when she'd be told to insert the next disc.

She fleshed out the notes into a brief report. It didn't say all that much, but it was better than nothing. She added several declarative statements that used the verb *intend*. Maybe the report knew something that she didn't. Andrew looked it over once she was done.

"You seem confident."

"Good. That's what I was going for."

"Are you really going to read John Evelyn's diary? I think it's pretty long."

"She'll see right through that, won't she?"

"Not necessarily."

"I really don't know what I'm doing."

"Well, what's your question? That's what we're always asking our students, right? What question are you asking about Restoration drama?"

"Why . . . is it so awesome?"

"I'm not sure that's going to attract funding."

"It's all I've got."

He smiled. "I think she'll like it."

Shelby looked out the window to the narrow patio beyond. "Remember when we first met? We ate Swedish meatballs out there, and Nanaimo bars."

"We did clean up after that candidate's interview."

"Were we so different, then?"

He looked at her oddly. "What do you mean?"

"I don't know. Have we changed? Are we wiser?"

"We're further in debt."

She sighed. "Are you coming to Ingrid's tonight?"

"I think I'll just stay in."

"Are you sure?"

He wasn't looking at her. "Yeah. I've got some reading. I don't really feel like playing Carl's RPG. It's fun and all, but sometimes I just want to get away from the fantasy."

"You love fantasy."

He shrugged. "I can't live there forever."

"Is everything okay?"

"Of course." He stood up. "Are you taking the bus home?"

She blinked. "Yeah. Carl's coming too. I just have to drop off this report, and then I'll text him. Be right back."

"Sounds good." He opened up *Sweet's*. "I'll decline while I wait."

"I don't think the chair is that fancy."

"I meant nouns."

Shelby walked out of the TA office. Her stomach was churning from the coffee. A part of her kept saying, *Go back, tell him everything, lay it all bare*. It was impossible, though. The park had its rules, messed up as they were. He couldn't know. Carl had managed to stay quiet this long, which was a miracle. Shelby had never thought she'd be the one to crack. But she could feel herself mouthing the words, rehearsing the conversation that would bring it all crashing down on them. *Your shadow died. The one who spoke to salamanders. Now we need you to come back. We need your peripheral vision, and your sense of hearing, and that beautiful knife that you never had the chance to use. We don't know what we're doing.*

What really dug at her, though, was the possibility that they might be okay. That they actually didn't need him. The auditor was gone, but their company had survived. They'd come this far without the help of invisible spirits. Their shadows were alive and well, and nobody was looking back to see if he'd followed them. All she could think of was how pale he'd been, floating like a bleached bone in the water. The moonlight silvering his hair, and the strange look of relief on his empty face. He'd made a deal with the waves. Perhaps he'd always wanted it this way. It was his decision, and they had no right to drag him back into the game.

Shelby walked into the main office. A row of mail cubes stood against the far wall. She slipped the report into Dr. Marsden's cube, which was already overflowing.

"You might want to give that to me."

Tom, the departmental advisor, was peering at her from his desk. Normally, he didn't look up from the computer. His full attention made Shelby feel awkward, as if she'd just wandered naked into someone else's classroom.

"What's up?"

"Dr. Marsden might be away for a while."

Shelby handed him the report. "Did she come down with something serious?"

"You haven't heard?"

"Obviously not. Is she okay?"

"She was hit by a car. It happened while she was walking through the park last night. Someone hit her, right in front of the parliament building. Then they just drove off."

Shelby heard a ringing in her ears. "Is . . . she going to be all right?"

"Yeah. She was quite lucky, I guess. But she may be in the hospital for a week. The department head is taking over her classes."

"And—" She swallowed. "Nobody saw the car?"

"The driver was long gone before they found her." Tom shook his head and returned his attention to the screen. "People are monsters."

2

MORGAN STOOD AT THE ENTRANCE TO THE black basia, watching people come and go. Some looked nervous, while others were too drunk to care. A few women circled the steps, uncertain as to whether they should take the plunge. They wore head scarves and exchanged quick, calibrating glances with each other. *Do I know her? Didn't I see her at the tower, yesterday morning? Does she recognize me?* Their soft sandals and cork-heeled shoes kicked up dust as they worried their way along the cobblestones. Morgan watched their spirals with interest. There was no rule against women visiting the basiorum. Fortuna's wheel touched all manner of pleasures, and desire was what kept it spinning.

Nevertheless, the meretrices had a predominantly male clientele. Most women, she imagined, sought pleasures more difficult to quantify. They met in networks at the baths or in shaded gardens. The idea of paying for sex was logical but it seldom occurred to her. It wasn't every day that she woke up and thought: *I'm going to exchange these coins for sweet little death in a stranger's arms.* Most of the time, she was content with imaginary pleasures. They never disappointed, spilled wine on you, or frowned at your stomach.

Still, it was diverting to watch the sheer variety of those who followed their desire. Curly-haired boys with their bula necklaces, trying to look stern, while their mouths trembled. Women who stared decorously at the ground or boldly at each other, trying to gauge how close they might come to the flame. Men whose hands were stained amethyst with dye or blackened by soot. Careful spadones who greeted each other with a nod while concealing weapons beneath their soft green tunicae. A fur testing the weight of her own purse while keeping an eye on the others that dangled nearby, like low-hanging fruit. Two old women with canes who made the sign of the wheel as they spoke of a lost friend. *She left me these earrings. How they sparkle.*

"You got here quickly."

She turned and smiled at Fel. "Old habit. I like to make a nest before anyone else arrives, so that I can secure a proper view."

"Babieca's waiting by the clepsydra. I saw him on my way."

"Did you stop him?"

"No. He was losing at stones, and I didn't want to embarrass him."

Morgan sighed. "He doesn't have the money for that."

"I gather that he has coins in places we've never seen—nor would we want to."

"He has no head for gambling."

"I always thought singers were supposed to be good at games."

"We found the exception."

Fel laughed kindly. "He has his uses."

"He can be charming, when he isn't stepping in it."

The miles gave her a long look. "Why them?"

"What do you mean?"

"Why did you choose them for your company—a singer who's shit at gambling, and a shy auditor without a gens?"

Morgan remembered the day when she'd almost lost her

bow. A companion—someone she'd trusted—had stolen it to wager in a game of Hazard. Roldan and Babieca had seen the whole thing happen and rescued her weapon. They were strangers, and yet they'd taken a considerable risk to help her.

"They wagered on me," she replied. "I'm not yet sure if it was the right move, but we seem to fit together, in our way."

"I think you're a safe bet."

"Oh?" Morgan smiled uncertainly. "I have my uses as well?"

"You're certainly worth the wager."

They stood still for a moment. The fountain rippled next to them. The old women stepped through the entrance to the basia, their canes tapping the marble. Before she could stop herself, Morgan took Fel's hand. Even if it was a tablet beyond her reach, she was willing to leave a mark. The miles had scarred knuckles, and she touched them lightly, as if she could follow the lines of the stylus that had formed them in wax. Fel didn't quite smile, but her eyes danced. In the warrior's mind, she could see that they were gliding across an impossible surface. They reeled to the music, turning faster and faster, until the floor dissolved and they were a brilliant wheel in the sky. The towers formed dark pips below them. The sun fired their spokes, and they were glass, ecstasy, rhythm.

Love is the wild roll, Fortuna said, as she turned them.

Morgan let go of her hand. She could see Babieca approaching, and she didn't want him to smirk. Fel looked at her, then at the ground, as if the sharp stones were a fascinating mosaic. Morgan was still in the clouds, and her stomach gave a lurch as she came back down.

"I was waiting at the clepsydra," Babieca said.

"I think you mean gambling," Fel replied.

"Waiting. Gambling. They're so close to each other, aren't they?"

"Not really."

"How much did you lose?" Morgan asked.

"Don't worry about it."

"We have no money. Pendelia hasn't hired us in a week,

and most of our time is spent running away from things that want to eat us. So I worry, Babieca."

"The loss was negligible."

"Sweet Fortuna—how can you be so bad at gaming?"

"It's not a talent that you're born with."

"But a singer who can't gamble is like—"

"I think the word you're looking for is *pointless*," Fel added.

He glared at them both. "You aren't exactly raking in the coin."

"But we're not losing it," Morgan said. "Do you see the distinction?"

"Let's just go inside. Drauca's waiting for us."

Fel surveyed the entrance to the basia. "I'm not sure I like this plan. What if the girl doesn't show up? What if she's followed?"

"I'd be more concerned with how we're going to convince her to help us," Morgan said. "She barely knows that I'm alive. The last time she saw me, I was being hauled to the Tower of Sagittarii for a bit of light torture. I'm not exactly a good influence."

"She was spying on her mother in the necropolis," Babieca replied. "She isn't looking for a good influence. She's flirting with danger. That might work for us."

"She's a child. We can't put her in harm's way."

"Septimus was hunting her. I'd say she's already tempting the wheel."

"It feels strange, though. Turning her against her mother. Isn't there some terrible afterlife designed for people who sow familial discord?"

"Every basilissa turns against her mother," Fel said. "That's the rhythm of the matriarchy. The trick will be making sure that Eumachia turns in our direction, rather than against us."

Morgan gave her an odd look. "I thought you shared my misgivings."

"I do. But as much as it pains me to say it, the singer isn't wrong. We're at a very dangerous curve, and if we don't brace ourselves properly, the wheel's going to crush us all. The girl may be the key."

Babieca smiled. "Allow me a moment to glory in not being wrong."

"You've got three seconds," Fel said. "Glory in silence."

They made their way through the sunlit atrium, whose black-and-white marble resembled a game of latrinculi. The veins in the marble seemed to dance, like clouds, while cithara music trembled in the air. A woman in a tall blue wig stood in the light of the impluvium, reading poetry. Nearby, two men drunkenly chased each other, spilling their cups in the process. An auditor was talking to a meretrix with close-cropped hair. Garnets gleamed in her mask. For a moment, Morgan was certain that she recognized the auditor. It was rare to see one of them in a basia. Their pleasures tended to be more esoteric. She tried to recall where she'd seen him before, but the memory was indistinct, like the mottled surface of the pillars. One of the drunken men crashed into him, nearly knocking them both to the ground. The auditor swore and roughly pushed him away. Then he turned his attention back to the meretrix, whose expression now revealed a shadow of disinterest. The auditor didn't seem to notice.

"I'm going to get a drink," Babieca said. "All of this will make more sense."

"Fine," Morgan said. "Bring me a cup of hippocrene."

He made a face. "That's like sucking on a honeycomb. And it smells—"

She handed him a coin. "Just get it."

Babieca nodded and disappeared into the crowd.

Morgan turned to Fel. "I have a favor to ask of you."

"Oh?"

"Keep him occupied."

She frowned. "I thought we were meeting Felix."

"I'm meeting Felix. I think your presence might just muddy the waters."

"You're not going to the undercroft alone."

"Eumachia doesn't trust any of us. If we show up as a group, she's going to bolt. I think she might listen to me, though."

"Morgan, she's royalty. To her, you're just another archer."

"It's more complicated than that."

"Truly? Because it sounds as if you're just being stubborn."

She almost took Fel's hand but stopped herself. "We were on that balcony together. She saw me kill the silenus—and she realized what her mother was trying to do. I could see the betrayal flash across her eyes."

Morgan felt a distant ache. How could she explain to Fel the enormity of that reversal? The knowledge that your own family might not be on your side? She could barely articulate the sensation, but it was like falling in a dream. The ground rushing toward you, and the prayer spinning in your head, *Wake up, wake up.* Only you didn't, and the impact was your whole life. The pain wasn't entirely hers. It belonged to her shadow. But Morgan could still feel it, and she knew that it was the same for Eumachia. A mother was supposed to catch you, to weave a transparent net beneath you, so that you were never afraid to fall. She wasn't supposed to forget about you while you roamed the halls of a palace that you scarcely understood.

Fel looked at her for a moment. Then she squared her shoulders. "If you want me to distract him, I'd best go now."

"Thank you."

"I expect to be repaid in full."

Morgan smiled. "That I can most certainly promise."

Fel scanned the crowd. Then she sighed. "Someone's given him a torch."

"You'd better hurry."

"I hope you roll true. We'll be waiting for you outside."

"Keep him away from all of the elements."

"I'll try."

Fel went after Babieca. She removed the torch from his grasp and began gesturing, like a mother explaining how dangerous the world was. Babieca nodded but kept one eye on a group of women in the corner who were dressed like undinae. Fel had her work cut out for her.

Morgan left the atrium. The music and laughter receded.

She imagined Fel trying to keep Babieca out of trouble, and the thought made her smile. That used to be Roldan's job, though he was never good at it. The two of them shared a certain boyish curiosity, and the auditor could usually be convinced that the singer's latest plan was sterling. Fel, she knew, was a mother in a different life and had the resolve to deal with Babieca's enthusiasm. Her shadow was softer but no less convincing. Morgan tried to remember what she looked like, that other Fel. She could almost smell something in the air—roasted and slightly bitter, yet inviting, like spiced wine. She saw another bright atrium, with an assortment of queer machinae crowding the corners. The shadow had been there, moments before. Morgan could almost perceive her footprints in the strange, blank tapestry that covered the floor.

She walked down the narrow hallway that led to Felix's tabularium. The fresco on the wall danced beneath uncertain lamplight. Morgan tilted her head, trying to imagine the balancing act that it depicted. It reminded her of how precipitous desire could be. It was always a rope dance, high above a void. She could almost feel the rope digging into her bare feet. At least the lovers in the fresco had something to hold on to. She was alone, dancing on the edge. Death sunned itself beneath her, waiting for a misstep. It was thrilling to realize that someone might want her, but then there was the fall. In her dreams, she was always falling.

The tabularium had an orange cast to it, lit by a half-dozen oil lamps that hung from chains. Long shadows moved along the walls, making the geometric designs appear to shiver and take on a life of their own. Wheels flickered, and Fortuna's many guises stalked across the margins, climbing out of their frames and beckoning to her. Morgan felt her sense of perspective shifting, like that fragile rope. For a moment, she was inside the various landscapes, the gardens of ocher and coral red, the metallic blue waves that sheltered whispering undinae. The artwork spun around her, until she didn't know what legend she properly belonged to. She heard a child's voice, from far away.

What square is this?

Morgan blinked to clear the shadows. Felix was looking at her curiously. Smoke from the lamps framed his silver mask. She felt as if she were looking at something fashioned. Only his eyes were real, but they also might have been polished crystal, turning in the dark for ages until they'd taken on some form of human transparency.

"You seem lost."

Morgan laughed softly. "That describes a lot of people here."

"Where's the rest of your company?"

"I thought I might have more luck if I spoke with her alone."

The edge of his mouth quirked. "You may be right. It's been a while since you've made such a bold decision—for the good of the company, that is."

She sat down in the uncomfortable chair across from him. "Stop worrying the edges of whatever you want to say, and just say it."

"It's nothing. Just that Fel seems to be leading you, as of late."

"She can move unseen. It makes sense for her to serve as our public face."

"When we first met, you were the public face. The only die-carrier among them. Now you're following the miles who guards my front door."

Morgan frowned. "Is this your attempt to drive a wedge between us? Normally, you're much more subtle at this sort of thing."

Felix set down the wax tablet that he'd been studying. "All I meant was that this is an interesting development. You're here, alone. I didn't see this spin coming."

She shifted in the hard chair. "The others are close by. It's not as if I did away with them or chained them to a wall."

"Babieca wouldn't have agreed to this. Not unless he was being diverted."

Morgan felt a bit of anger uncoiling within her. "You

think you know him? Because you had a few turns in the dark? You don't know the first thing about him—or us."

His expression hardened. The mask seemed to take him over, until he was nothing but chill surface. "I don't presume to be an expert on his character. I do know that he wouldn't allow you to proceed alone in this. He has a queer affection for you."

"We depend upon each other. Don't bother trying to understand that."

"Have I offended you, sagittarius?"

Morgan leaned across the desk. "You know precisely what I'm talking about. You've acted beneath your office."

"What do you know of my office?"

"You're a trained meretrix—a house father. You could have had anyone, but you chose a penniless singer."

"How do you know that he didn't choose me?"

"Because this is your house, and you make the rules." She shook her head. "You know better, Felix. You rolled when you should have walked away."

She could see that he was getting angry. The polish of his training was beginning to dissolve around the edges. "It meant nothing. What did you call it—a few turns in the dark? I was bored, and he was there. Our actions hurt no one."

"No one? Not a single soul?" Morgan shook her head. "You told me that you cared for him. That night at the arx, before the basilissa's ball—I saw it in your eyes. You said that you weren't boxing Fortuna, but that was a lie. You felt something."

Felix stood. "I was trained—as you so kindly put it—to feel nothing. My task is to make others feel things. Desire. Comfort. Pain. The mask does the work. We're everything and nothing. The boy who was rough. The girl who ignored you. Whatever sweet nightmare they've been living. That's why they can never see our face. They feel everything for us, but we feel nothing. We cannot. The spell depends on it."

"But you broke the spell. You let him see your face—if only for a moment."

"A moment," he said simply. "It doesn't matter now."

"If he finds out—"

"He's dead, Morgan. He can't feel or know anything. He's gone."

"Babieca isn't so sure."

"I've played this game far longer than he has. Trust me."

As he stood there, Morgan couldn't help but think of another man, standing nearly naked before her. Babieca's shadow, coming apart like a leaky ship. Her anger softened. She could see how pain had etched beautiful lines into his mask.

"What was it about, then?" Her voice had lost its edge. "Desire? Comfort?"

He sighed. "I don't know. I liked to hear him laugh. Sometimes, afterward—when everything was still—I could see the moonlight through the shutters. All the little love-cells in the basia were asleep, or so it seemed. And I remembered what it felt like when I was a child, to know that the world belonged to me. That I wasn't alone. Then I saw him, silvered by the light, snoring, and knew that I was."

Felix poured her a drink. She took the silver cup, and they drank in silence for a moment. The wine was sweet, like summer. *Boxing Fortuna*. Which poet had come up with that? It was precise. You faced her in the arena, with nothing but your bare hands. Then she pummeled you, until you were bloody and covered in sand.

"Is she down there?" Morgan asked.

He nodded. "She often visits. They play acedrex together, and Drauca lets her try on clothes. Latona allows it, so long as they don't appear publicly."

"They're truly sisters?"

"It's a long story, and I'm not the one to tell it." He gestured to the door behind the tapestry. "It's open. You might as well go down."

Morgan set her empty cup on the desk. "Are we doing the right thing? Or is this just another mistake that will get us all killed?"

"Hard to tell those things apart, sometimes."

"You're about as helpful as an inscription."

He saluted her with his cup. "I do try."

Morgan took one of the lamps and walked down the flight of stairs. Twice she nearly lost her purchase but managed to steady herself against the wall. The rich earth smell and cold air made her feel as if she were walking into an open grave. Lamplight caught veins of old quartz in the wall, making them shine forth. She allowed the staircase to lead her in a dance, turning and turning, until her feet touched the flagstones and the descent was done.

The girl and her aunt were sitting on the floor, playing acedrex. Eumachia was winning. She'd just captured one of Drauca's elephants. The woman's left hand trembled slightly, as always, but her expression remained still.

"That's a . . . bold move."

"You said that I should be bold."

"But not overbold, magpie."

"Is that even a word?"

Drauca moved her vizier. "The poets seem to think so."

"I hate poetry."

"You're too young to hate anything."

"I'm too young to be in the undercroft of a basia."

Drauca smiled. "You're safer here than upstairs."

Eumachia moved her miles three squares. "I heard groaning on the way here. It sounded like someone was dying."

"They probably were."

"Then we should call for a medicus."

"It wasn't . . . that kind of dying." She took the girl's miles with her remaining elephant. "You might as well announce yourself, sagittarius. Watching is . . . e-encouraged upstairs . . . but down here, it won't avail you."

Eumachia looked up. She wore a pearl diadem and a red stola with golden sleeves. Hummingbirds played across its surface. Her earrings, carved from rock crystal, twinkled as she turned her head.

"What is she doing here?"

"You'll have to ask here that."

"She's interrupted our game."

"It's already finished. Your b-basilissa is surrounded."

"What?" Eumachia glared at the board. "How did that happen?"

"You weren't thinking far enough ahead."

"I suppose you're proud of yourself," she muttered. "Beating a little girl."

"You aren't so little anymore." She gestured to Morgan. "The sagittarius has come to ask you a question."

Eumachia rose and dusted off her gown. "If I spent my days answering questions, I'd have no time to lose at acedrex."

"Don't be pert. Just talk to her."

She sighed and glanced at Morgan. "Fine. What is it?"

Morgan had been thinking all day of how to phrase the question. How might she expertly fashion it, so that Eumachia wouldn't simply dance away, or throw it back in her face? Drauca was right about the girl. She was young enough to be foolish, still, but not so young that she couldn't perceive the outlines of the truth. Noble children grew up fast. They were forced to learn the rules of the game in order to survive.

"Does Your Eminence remember me?"

She looked Morgan up and down. "I see a lot of archers, and miles, and people hiding in the ceiling with sharp things. You're all alike."

"Are you certain?"

Her gaze narrowed. "You were the one on the balcony."

"Yes. I shot the silenus. The one that was going to kill Basilissa Pulcheria."

"You were supposed to be imprisoned."

"That didn't quite work out."

Eumachia withdrew a bone whistle from her gown. "If I blow on this, a swarm of angry miles will come running down those stairs. They'll throw you in the carcer."

"That is within your power."

"Why shouldn't I do it?"

"Only Your Eminence can answer that question. But perhaps you don't think I belong in a cell beneath the arx."

"Don't tell me what I think."

"You'd best ask your true question," Drauca said, putting away the board. "She's a real . . . sauce box when she gets cranky."

Eumachia glared at her aunt. "I should have both of you put in the carcer."

"Then you would have to play against yourself, magpie."

She sighed and turned back to Morgan. "What do you really want?"

Morgan squared her shoulders. "I've come to ask Your Eminence—respectfully—what she was doing in the necropolis, dressed as a boy."

Eumachia seemed to deflate slightly. "You saw me."

"We tried to protect you."

Her eyes widened. "That light."

"A device of sorts. It distracted the silenus."

She looked at Drauca. "You set this up. Why? Am I being punished?"

"I rather think," Drauca replied, "that you are being tested. What you decide . . . shall determine your fate. But the s-spin belongs to you, dear."

"I'm tired of all this talk about spinning, and fates, and bloody wheels. I can't see Fortuna. I can't touch her. What has she ever done for me? How do I even know that she's real, and not just some story that everyone made up?"

"Hand me my cane."

Eumachia gave her aunt the ivory cane, helping her to stand. Drauca dusted herself off with a trembling hand.

"When I was born," she said, "the medicus told my mother to strangle me. Or to drown me in the r-river, like a cat. That was what they called . . . compassion. My mother went to each of the towers, asking for advice. Day and night, she went, and each gens agreed with the medicus. Except for the meretrices. Do you know what they said?"

Eumachia stared at the ground. "No."

"The house mother said . . . that Fortuna sometimes makes a defenseless flower. Something that cannot survive on its own. It requires endless care and will not bloom for ages. But when it does . . . everyone is astonished. For b-beauty often resides in a crooked form. And some flowers, which thrive in the dark, are the loveliest under creation . . . though they cannot be seen. It is the c-care that we give them, that makes them flawless . . . in their imperfection."

"She said all of that?"

"And more. But I can't tell you the rest . . . until you're older."

Eumachia was silent for a time. Then she said: "I thought Grandmother didn't want me to see you. That's what my mother said."

"That's . . . a simplification. The reality is more difficult to explain."

"I feel like she's been lying to me."

"Is that why you were at the necropolis?" Morgan asked.

Eumachia stared at her hands. It was an odd little gesture, and Morgan wanted to say something that would comfort her. But she couldn't think of anything.

"I don't trust her," the girl said finally. "She's plotting with that goat."

"Septimus."

Eumachia nodded. "He looked like he wanted to eat me."

"I don't think—" Morgan shook her head. "Never mind. The point is, Latona has arranged for some kind of meeting with the silenoi. Do you know anything about it?"

She gave Drauca a questioning look.

"You don't have to answer."

"Am I in danger?"

"If the sagittarius is right . . . we may all be."

Eumachia looked at the glass pieces, which Drauca had replaced in a bag.

"That's us," she murmured. "Maybe there's nothing we can do."

"I think you will find . . . that there's always an un-unexpected move." Drauca smiled. "You might have won . . . if you'd only seen the path."

"You always say that."

"I've played long enough to know   that the game is never truly over."

Eumachia's eyes narrowed. Then she suddenly smiled in surprise. "The nemo! She was so close. If I'd only moved her to the left—"

"Now you see it."

She turned to Morgan. Her expression hardened in resolve. "If I tell you," she said, "can you promise that my family won't be harmed?"

"I can promise to protect them," Morgan said. "On my honor."

Eumachia reached into her stola and withdrew a scrap of parchment. It was yellowed from smoke and had been folded numerous times.

"Read this," she said simply.

3

SHELBY HATED PARALLEL PARKING.

She'd failed her test twice because she couldn't manage to squeeze the car into a tiny spot, attended by a symphony of honking and profanity from the queue of drivers that were waiting. Now she drove a truck and wasn't entirely sure why. Now, at least, she could filter out the annoyed looks from those behind her. It wouldn't kill them to wait a single minute while she maneuvered the beast into place. It was the same attitude she assumed while hogging the library's self-checkout kiosk in order to scan a pile of books on Restoration theater. The screen would keep asking her to reposition the bar code, and she'd ignore the simmering rage that she could feel as the lineup behind her increased. They could go talk to a human if they wanted to sign out their precious reserve materials. She'd gotten here first, and the kiosk was hers.

She had to crawl out the passenger side. Traffic on Dewdney was precarious, and she always remembered her mother's story about the time a truck had sheared off her driver's-side door. It may have been a family legend, but Shelby could picture her mother standing in the middle of

Broad Street, looking in fascination at the place where her door had just been. *Almost fell out while I was driving home. I had a death grip on the dashboard.* The story always devolved after that, as her mother described what she'd used to replace the door. A beaded curtain, a tarp, a Hefty garbage bag, an old picnic blanket—it changed whenever she told the story. Back then, she'd been riding the poverty line, and Shelby wasn't surprised that it had taken her a while to replace the door. But she was pretty sure that the beaded curtain was made up.

Pasqua Hospital reminded Shelby of her *nicâpân*. Her great-grandmother had maintained an aura of fierce dignity, even near the end. In spite of the machines with their cold monitors, the room had seemed warm and full of life. She would hide the wires and tubes beneath a woven blanket, and they all pretended that the hospital was her parlor. Shelby could remember *nohkô* and her mother drinking bitter chamomile out of foam cups, as they laughed and told stories. It seemed more like a sweet parenthesis than an ending.

She stopped by the Robin's Donuts, with its cheerful neon façade, and bought a questionable breakfast sandwich. The surrounding tables were mostly empty. People occupied small islands, stirring their coffee, politely wiping crumbs. Many of them stared into space, their drinks rapidly cooling. The elevator chimed in the distance. Shelby wondered what miracle or catastrophe had brought them here. In the face of unimaginable chaos, the café was predictable, with its green trays and combos. Everything within its protected bubble seemed to make sense. A different world lay beyond the elevator, a world of breakdown and exception. She stared for a moment at the plastic wrapping of her sandwich. A film of cheese stuck to it, covering the message, so that it read: *joy our heal options.*

Shelby threw the remains in the trash and headed for the elevator. It was a broad, echoing space, with enormous buttons. For a moment, she didn't want to get on by herself. But she boarded the ship anyhow, pressing the button for the third floor. She followed the arrows on the polished linoleum

floor, which smelled freshly of antiseptic. Everything reminded her of a house that had been cleaned so well that all
of the paint and handprints and breath had been stripped
from its surface. You could prepare a meal on that floor. It
was probably safer than her kitchen counter, which sometimes had traces of jam stuck to it. Two paramedics were
pushing a stretcher down the hallway. A young girl lay on
it, covered in a thick gray blanket. She looked slightly bored,
as if this were a routine part of her morning commute.

She went to the desk and asked for Dr. Marsden's room
number. It suddenly reminded her of a story that Trish had
told her about being interviewed at the Modern Languages
Conference. The interview had been conducted in a small
hotel room, but applicants weren't given the room number.
The receptionist had to call them, Trish had said. *Then they'd
hand the phone to you, and someone would tell you the
number. Like you were an international spy, and this was a
clandestine exchange of information.* Apparently, she'd
known that the interview wasn't going well after lunch
arrived, and the committee ate in front of her, maintaining
complete and awkward silence. In the end, the job went to a
specialist in composition.

A tired nurse wearing a cheerful blouse gave her the
room number. She paused outside the door. There was
always the pressure to look optimistic whenever you visited
someone in the hospital. You weren't allowed to talk about
your first-world problems, or betray the fact that you might
be worrying about something exquisitely pointless. You had
to glow with satiety. She couldn't quite master the look and
was worried that her smile would seem cartoonish. In the
end, she went with her regular expression.

Trish was reading a Broadview edition of *The London Jilt.*
It was weird to see the remains of her lunch on a tray, next to
the bed. Shelby had never seen the woman eat, and part of
her had always assumed that her supervisor absorbed nutrients
from text alone. The little curtained square had a lived-in feel
to it. There was a stack of books and exams in the corner, and
some clothes folded on the chair. Trish had a Moleskine journal

next to her, in which she was recording notes with a fountain pen. The ink pot was beside the food tray. Shelby hoped that a nurse didn't take it away by accident.

"Hello, Shelby." She didn't look up from the book. "It's kind of you to visit. Have you brought me anything from the outside world?"

Shelby tried not to look at the dark bruises on her face, or her left eye, which was swollen and pinpricked with spots of blood. Her leg was in a cast. In her mind, all Shelby could see was the car hitting her, over and over. The lump of fur on the asphalt, which could have been a wild animal, if only you hadn't seen its eyes.

How had she survived? Was it something to do with the park?

Your supervisor is a monster.

She pushed the thought out of her mind, but it kept popping up, like something evil in water wings. There must be some clause about this in the Plains University Act. If your supervisor tried to eat you, at the very least, a term-long extension should be in order. Carl would know. He was probably lying to the school counselor right now, telling her that he had seasonal affective disorder, whatever it took to get that emergency loan.

"I brought you—" Shelby rifled through her bag. "Star-burst?"

"Which flavor?"

"Watermelon."

"I'll take it."

Shelby popped the remaining piece in her mouth, and they both chewed in silence for what felt like an age. She could hear someone behind another curtain, singing quietly to themselves. Or maybe it was the radio. It suddenly bothered her that she couldn't distinguish a human voice from something Auto-Tuned. She wanted to pull back the curtain, with its faded floral pattern, but was afraid of what she might find. Perhaps another silenus in human form, whistling a killing tune.

"I've read your proposal."

Shelby swallowed. How was it possible that her supervisor could look so composed? Even the green hospital socks gave her an air of imperial majesty. On Andrew, they'd seemed like elf boots. It took Shelby a moment to parse what she'd just said. Then her eyes narrowed.

"I just dropped it in your mailbox yesterday."

"Tom put all of my documents together and had them sent to the hospital."

Of course he did.

Shelby wasn't sure how to respond. Trish wasn't asking her a question so much as making a neutral statement. She might just as easily have said: *I watched an episode of* Regency House Party *last night.* What was she expecting? Confidence? Contrition? Some form of ritual sacrifice to the Old Ones of Academe?

"Was it okay?"

"Did you think that it was?"

"I was pretty confident about—" She stared at her hands. "The bibliography."

"It was certainly ambitious."

"I'm not going to read all of those diaries. I'll probably just skim them. Fuck. I don't mean that. I'm sorry that I just said *fuck.* And that I said it again. I'm going to stop talking, and just let you tell me what you hated about it." She stared miserably at the pile of books. They were all covered in sticky tabs. It looked as if she'd annotated every page.

Trish started to laugh.

Shelby looked up. She'd never heard her supervisor laugh before. It was high and clear, like a church bell. The sound of it filled the room.

"What is it?" Shelby asked, smiling uncertainly.

She wiped her eyes. "I was just remembering a conversation that I had with my supervisor, years ago. Dr. Fiona Tuttle. She'd published a definitive collection of eighteenth-century letters, and I was terrified of her."

"I've seen her book in your office."

"She gave me a signed copy. I've never quite known what to do with it." Trish smiled distantly. "Fiona was small—nearly frail—and she barely spoke above a whisper. But when she swept into a conference, the crowds parted. She could reduce a graduate student to tears simply by clearing her throat. Once, I had to ask her for an extension. I was writing a terrible paper—it had something to do with clock imagery in the work of Samuel Richardson. I wanted to set fire to that bloody thing. Fiona asked me why I needed the extension. I suppose she thought I was going to offer some thin excuse. A death in the family, a collapsed relationship—one of those climactic events that barely cause a ripple in the academic world."

Shelby felt as if she should be writing this down. Trish was about to give her something like the Key of Solomon. A way to face down your supervisor and survive.

She leaned forward. "What did you say?"

Dr. Marsden's smile widened. "I had an excuse that was ready to go. I'd even practiced it in front of the mirror. But then I looked at her desk, and there it was. A copy of Richardson's *Pamela*. All five hundred pages of it." She shook her head. "I lost control. In a moment of temporary insanity, I picked up the book and threw it against the wall. I screamed: '*Bloody Pamela! What is wrong with you? Mr. B holds you captive for two hundred pages, and you* marry *the sadistic bastard? I hate you! Richardson can go straight to hell!*'"

"You actually threw it?"

"It sailed past her. And it was so heavy that it dented the wall."

"Oh wow."

"I thought she was going to call the police. For a moment, all she could do was stare at me. Then she *snorted*. It was the most delightful sound I'd ever heard in my life. Both of us laughed for five minutes. Afterward, she told me to write about something else. That was when I discovered Sarah Fielding, whose work has enchanted me ever since."

"Are you saying that I have to change my thesis topic?"

"Of course not. I'm saying that you shouldn't be frightened of your topic. Nor should you be frightened of me. I'm here to help you, Shelby. I'm no monster."

Aren't you?

Shelby pushed away the image of the silenus. "I guess I just don't know what I'm doing anymore. I've lost my question."

"Go back to the texts. Try to remember what drew you to Margaret Cavendish in the first place. What do you share in common?"

"Unfortunately, quite a lot. We're both neurotic, anti-social misfits who fall down in public and refuse to answer the doorbell."

"You've just described a lot of academics."

"She wore ribbons around her wrists. I'm developing a pretty fierce footnote about that. She called herself a princess, but when someone came over unexpectedly, she'd make inarticulate sounds and sort of just back out of the room, like she was playing herself offstage."

"You're looking at her through the eyes of the public. Try to see her in the literature. It's a different kind of mirror."

"Dr. Marsden—can I ask you something personal?"

"Shelby, look at my socks."

"I'm kind of trying not to."

"The point is that you don't have to be so formal. This isn't a meeting."

"I'm just wondering . . . how you knew. That it was the right choice. That everything was going to work out in the end."

"Have you been reading the *Chronicle* again?"

"I just—" She looked away. "All of this reading. All of the crippling self-doubt, and the coffee gut, and the days when I forget my own name. Sometimes it seems like the search is pointless. But it has to work out in the end, right? It has to mean something."

"What works out in the end," Trish said, "what nobody can take away, is the fact that books are magic. They're necessary, and sacred, and they can change the world. They provide us with endless wonder, and they don't ever run out of power, or require a software update. When you open a book, you walk in the skin of the lion. You see beyond your own margins. But there are people who haven't figured that out, and it's your job to teach them."

"Does that mean I'm going to find a job?"

"Concentrate on the wonder."

She nodded. "All right. Thank you."

"Keep hammering away at the proposal. I want to see a revised copy in the next few weeks. And don't think I didn't notice that you kept using the word *intend*. Just figure out what your question is, and present it as plainly as possible."

My question. Shelby almost laughed at the thought. *My real question. What are you? What am I?*

"I'll work on it," she said.

Trish looked up, her expression changing slightly. Shelby turned around. Dr. Victor Laclos was standing in the doorway, holding a coffee tray.

"Oh. Hello, Shelby."

She blinked. "Hi, Dr. Laclos. I—was just leaving."

"It's nice to see you." He walked over to the bed. "I've smuggled you in a mocha. There's also a macaroon in my pocket."

She smiled. "That's the greatest thing I've heard all day."

Shelby waved to them both, unsure of what else to do. Then she awkwardly played herself out, as she imagined Margaret Cavendish would have done. All she lacked were the ribbons.

She'd never seen the two of them together. Perhaps they were just friends. All she could think of was the fact that they taught in different fields, as if that must render them eternally separate. Plus, she'd never seen either of them outside the university. It was always jarring to encounter a professor in the wild. Laclos had been wearing a T-shirt. For some reason, she'd assumed that he wore blazers at home. Now she suddenly imagined him in pajamas, and the thought made her uneasy.

As she was leaving the hospital, Shelby glanced at her phone. Two messages: one from Carl, the other from Andrew. She didn't want to read either of them. Carl was full of questions, and Andrew would only remind her of the work that she wasn't doing. She got into the truck and squeezed her way out of the tight spot. It involved a lot of second-guessing while traffic streamed past her, a blur of metallic paint, half-heard radios, motions frosted under glass. Eventually she worked her way free, like a loose tooth. She turned on *A Tribe Called Red* and merged onto Dewdney. Before she knew it, she was driving home.

Her mother's house always looked sun-touched and welcoming. It was the opposite of her own apartment, which resembled a postapocalyptic library. Shelby parked and rang the bell. When nobody answered, she let herself in with the spare key. As soon as she closed the door, Shelby could feel herself reverting back to early adolescence. She draped her jacket over the chair, then peeled off her shoes and socks. The kitchen was spotless and still smelled of fresh baking. She grabbed a piece of bannock from the plate on the counter. Her grandmother had also made Saskatoon berry jam. When she was done, she rewrapped the plate and washed the knife. It was still obvious that she'd struck like a natural disaster, but she could at least minimize the damage by cleaning up. She rummaged through the kitchen cupboards. The variety of their food astounded her. When she pulled out a box of cereal, there was another, identical one behind it, like a store shelf. For a moment, she wondered if the cupboard was infinite.

Shelby returned to the living room. Her own eyes looked back at her from various portraits. A toddler with chubby Michelin Man arms; a teenager with tragic bangs, frozen in her Northern Reflections sweater; a university student, looking slightly dazed with her diploma. The wall proved her existence. It should have been comforting. There was also a picture of her mother sitting at a picnic table. Her hair was long, and she squinted at the camera, half smiling as the light haloed around her. In the background you could see Wascana Lake, so bright that it resembled a curtain of sparks. Her mother's expression was difficult to translate. Was she the one who'd turned the lake molten? Anything seemed possible. She was young and wild with possibilities, her bare leg a paintbrush swirl in the corner. Beside her was a thin man wearing a striped shirt and cowboy boots. He stared at the curve of her ankle. Part of him had been cropped out of the photo.

She took down the photo and placed it on the coffee table. If she concentrated, she could almost hear what they were thinking. There was a woven blanket on the couch, and she wrapped it around her. The stillness grew, until everything was sharp and hazy at the same time. Her life seemed to move in the shadows along the wall. She heard the scrape of the blinds in the upstairs hallway, and some animal twittering on the other side of the window. Then sleep crept in on paws of smoke, and she was in the photo, watching all of her mother's secrets unfold. The tall grass covered her. The sun turned green, and she went back to the beginning of it all.

When she opened her eyes, the shadows had changed. Her grandmother sat across from her, knitting. Shelby could almost feel the crosshatch patterns of the couch on her cheek. She rubbed her face and tried to sit up gracefully.

"How long was I out for, *nohkô*?"

"Not too long." She didn't look up from her needles. "You were dreaming deep, though. I could feel it. Something was watching you."

Shelby felt herself grow cold. "What kind of something?"

"Not sure." *Click. Click.* "Something big."

"Big and friendly—like the BFG?"

She shrugged. "Just big. It had no boundaries—like smoke. Wasn't good or evil. Just very interested in you."

"The last thing I need is an immaterial stalker."

"Ghosts don't mean you any harm. You've got to share with them."

"Share what?"

"Everything."

"Did you take a cryptic pill this morning?"

"Don't sass me, Shelby Mae."

"Sorry, *nohkô*." She reached for the picture on the table. Her grandmother saw her looking at it but didn't say anything. "What was he like?"

"Who?"

"The man in the cowboy boots."

She set down her needlework. "What has your mother told you about him?"

"You're being evasive."

Her grandmother stared to say something. Then her expression went oddly distant. She seemed to be considering some old equation, never properly balanced. She was silent for a moment. Shelby ran her thumb along the grooves in the picture frame.

"He had his moments," her grandmother said finally.

"That's it?"

"He also had a temper. But so did your mother."

"How did they meet?"

"I forget."

"No, you don't."

"Fine. They met at a bowling alley."

"Seriously?"

"Your mother had a part-time job there. He was with some friends. Ball in the gutter, every time, but that didn't seem to matter."

"I can't imagine her spraying rented shoes."

"She had to pay for college. Sometimes she even worked with me at the cannery, but I didn't want her there. I'd rather she deal with stinky feet than lose a hand."

Shelby set the picture down. "Were they in love?"

"You'd have to ask her."

"She won't tell me anything."

"Maybe you're just asking the wrong questions."

"Don't I have the right to know?"

Her grandmother looked at her. The light played along her braid, iron-gray but still soft. She remembered touching it when she was little, trying to work the silvery hairs loose. They reminded her of a paintbrush.

"When he drove you home from the hospital," she said, "his hands were shaking. I remember that."

Shelby thought of saying something else, but her grandmother's look told her that it wasn't the right time. Instead, she rose and kissed her lightly on the cheek.

"I'm going to go. Love you."

"Wait." She rose stiffly. "I'll pack you something for the road."

The Tupperware container slid across the seat while she drove. She'd have to hide it from Carl. He could stress-eat like a garburator. She'd slipped the photo out of its frame while her grandmother was wrapping the bannock. Her mother probably wouldn't notice. She never dusted that part of the mantel.

She met Carl at the Green Spot Café. He was demolishing a steamed bun. Ingrid and Sam were sitting on either side of him, watching the carnage with polite fascination. She hadn't expected to see all of them. Carl must have sent out a hysterical mass text.

"Finally." He looked up from his plate. "Dodge my calls much?"

"I fell asleep at my mother's house. You know how comfortable her couch is."

"I completely understand that," Sam said. "My mom's house always smells like vanilla. I'm out like a light as soon as I sit down."

Shelby turned to Ingrid. "How's your car?"

She sighed. "It was a write-off. I had to invent a pretty creative story, involving a coyote and some loose gravel. Paul chewed me out for an hour, but he was more than happy to lease a new red hatchback. I may have bribed him with extra trunk space for his hockey equipment."

"He's probably just glad that you're okay."

"He doubts my ability to drive around the corner and insists on picking up Neil from day care. He keeps referring to my 'fugue state,' like I had some kind of dissociative event. Other than that, things are more or less normal."

"My truck is far from normal," Sam added. "It needs a new paint job, and I had a hard time explaining to the mechanic why there was fur stuck to the headlights."

"I thought you were going with the deer story," Carl said.

"The fur is crazy long. It looks like I hit Snuffleupagus. All I could do was distract him by talking about Darian Durant's completion percentage."

"Well," Carl said, "he does have a truck named after him, so that's a connection."

Shelby looked around the café. People were chatting over bowls of hot and sour soup or tapping away at laptops. Their screens glowed with promise. Nobody realized that Ingrid's car had been totaled by something out of a Greco-Roman nightmare.

She grabbed Carl's steamed bun and took a bite out of it.

He stared at her. "You know, they have them behind the counter."

"I'm sorry. I'm having a really weird day."

"You do have a bit of a caged-animal look."

"I—" She stared at the wreckage on his plate. The smear of hot sauce reminded her of blood on asphalt. "May have found something out. But I don't know what it means, or even if I'm completely right about it."

"Oh God," Sam said. "Did I really hit Snuffleupagus?"

"No. You hit my supervisor."

She blanched. "What?"

"It was Trish Marsden. I just visited her in the hospital, and she looks like—well, like she was in a car accident. Dr. Laclos was there too, for some weird reason."

"Wait a minute." Ingrid looked at Shelby. "You're saying that the silenus wasn't just human—she was a prof?"

"So it would seem."

"Holy shit," Carl murmured. "I really need to get my revisions in on time."

"Maybe they're all professors," Sam said. "That would explain so much."

"So—" Carl gave her a long look. "Exactly how long have you been sitting on this information? Or didn't you think it was relevant."

"I only figured it out yesterday. Our DA mentioned that she was in the hospital, and as soon as I saw her—I knew.

She's healing fast. Too fast for a—" Shelby looked around the café again, though it was clear that nobody was paying attention. "I mean, a human couldn't possibly recover that quickly."

"I hit an award-winning scholar with my car," Ingrid murmured.

"You're not the only one," Sam said. "I've still got scholar fur on my bumper."

Carl shook his head. "Don't say *scholar fur.*"

Shelby didn't want to think about what they'd done. Ingrid was the only one who'd hesitated. She'd suspected all along that the silenoi might be human, but after Carl was nearly harpooned in the backseat, their ethics had narrowed considerably. It was all screaming darkness, and glass in their hair, and the silent hunter closing the space between them. They'd had no choice. Like the silenus, they'd acted on instinct. It was her—

"—or us," Shelby said, mostly to herself.

Carl looked at her. "What?"

"I don't know. I shouldn't even be forming words right now."

"We can't think about last night. We need to focus on that note. If it's correct, then there's going to be a homicidal fur pile at the Arx of Violets, and we need to be there."

"Fur pile." Shelby giggled.

"Hey." Carl waved at her. "Keep your head in the game. We need you."

"It's not a game!" The people at the nearest table glanced at her. Shelby lowered her voice. "That was our mistake— thinking that it was just a game. *Oh, look at me, I'm a magical hero, la la, I think I'll hunt for some treasure.* But then people started dying. The park took control. I mean—God—have we even asked ourselves how the magic works? How it's possible? We don't care. We just believe in it, like gravity, or finals. Because we're so desperate to escape who we really are."

"Whoa, whoa. Rein it in, Susan Lucci. You're spiraling."

Shelby put her head in her hands. "I feel like I don't know how to be a person."

She felt a pressure on her wrist. She thought it was Carl, but when she looked up, it was Ingrid, touching her lightly. She could feel the cool metal of her ring.

"Let's just agree that we're all works in progress," Ingrid said. "I nearly burned down my house last week because I forgot to put water in the electric kettle. I was trying to get Neil to use the toilet, and he just kept screaming, 'I'm a herbivore!' But he wouldn't let me take his pants off. I didn't even smell the smoke until it was drifting down the hallway. There were no batteries in the smoke alarm. We all could have died in our sleep—because I'd swapped out the batteries and stuck them in the karaoke machine."

Carl's eyes brightened. "You've had a karaoke machine this whole time?"

"It's Paul's."

"This changes everything."

Ingrid turned back to Shelby. "The point is that we're all just hanging on. You have to let yourself off the hook. Just a little bit."

Shelby sighed. "This does feel like an epic spiral."

"We need an epic distraction, then," Carl said. "I say we go to the club."

"Right," Sam replied. "The silenoi can't get us if we're clubbing."

"I'm serious. We've got another day until this meeting goes down. Let's be human."

Ingrid looked uncertain. "Paul's got hockey practice. I could try to find a sitter."

"I'm sure the Sovereign Court would watch Neil," Carl said.

Ingrid pulled out her phone. "I'd prefer that he not learn the lyrics to 'Edge of Seventeen' just yet. I'm going outside to make a call."

She stood up and left the café. Shelby watched her go. If Ingrid was willing to do this, then maybe Carl was right. Maybe dancing was the appropriate response to fear.

"Sam?" Carl asked. "You're in, right?"

"Will there be straight men at this club?"

"Maybe a few bi guys. But they've got half-price drink specials."

"Then I'm in."

They went back to Ingrid's place to strategize, but the session dissolved when it was discovered that Paul had vodka in the fridge.

"He hides it behind the soy milk," Ingrid said. "But he keeps forgetting that it's there, so he probably won't notice if you have some. All we've got to mix it with is . . . ginger ale."

"Not a problem," Carl replied.

By the time Paul got home from work, they were all debating which was the better show: *Breaking Bad* or *Orange Is the New Black*. Sam said that she couldn't watch Bryan Cranston in his underwear, but Carl argued that it was high art. They could all agree that Laura Prepon was the person they'd most like to go dancing with. Paul instantly forgave them for stealing his vodka. Sam convinced him to skip practice and join them at the club. It took very little effort. Ingrid remained sober and played dinosaur games with Neil until the sitter arrived.

Andrew met them at the club. He looked slightly dazed to see them all, like a nature photographer whose subjects had climbed out of the wild. Shelby kissed him on the cheek.

"I miss you something fierce," she whispered in his ear.

"Likewise," he said, smiling oddly.

She took his right hand, while Carl took his left. Then they walked into the club. A string of lights guided them upstairs, where the music was already whumping. Carl ordered them shots. Ingrid abstained. She had a slightly faraway look, and Shelby could tell that she was thinking about Neil. But then Paul whispered something in her ear.

"Challenge accepted," she said, and reached for a shot.

"What did you say?" Sam asked.

"It's a sibling thing," Paul replied. "Involving blackmail."

"You got your wish," Ingrid said, clinking the shot against the bar. "Don't push it."

The dance floor was glowing like a hot-pink forge. Several ladies had put down their purses and were dancing around them, almost ritualistically. The DJ had wings. Paul and Sam danced together. She was taller than him, but his boots helped to make up the difference. Carl danced with Andrew. There was barely a breath between them. Every time Shelby turned around, Carl was ordering something blue or green. He was in his element. She danced with Ingrid. At first, they kept a respectable distance from each other. Then the distance grew friendly. The song changed tempo, and her arms were twined around Ingrid's neck. She was weightless.

The music stopped, and a beautiful drag queen in a Balenciaga gown ascended the stage. She was the Empress of Regina, and the entire Sovereign Court was gathered at the edges of the dance floor. They couldn't bend a knee, but they did lower their fans in a sign of reverence. The DJ handed her the microphone.

"And now, as they say, for something completely different," she purred. "One of you would like to read a little something. Come up here, baby."

A small shadow climbed onto the stage. At first, Shelby didn't register who it was. Then she realized that Carl was standing next to the empress. She handed him the microphone and glided back down to the parquet floor. Carl looked out at the crowd. For a second, she thought he might fall off the stage. Then his expression changed, and she saw that he was in teaching mode. This was just another classroom. He cleared his throat.

"These words," he said, "belong to that fabulous reprobate, John Wilmot, the Earl of Rochester. And to us."

He was silent for a moment.

Then he closed his eyes, and spoke:

So, when my days of impotence approach,
And I'm by pox and wine's unlucky chance
Forced from the pleasing billows of debauch
On the dull shore of lazy temperance,

My pains at least some respite shall afford
While I behold the battles you maintain
When fleets of glasses sail about the board,
From whose broadsides volleys of wit shall rain.

Shelby couldn't quite look at him. Light blossomed on all sides, twinkling, like spectral Christmas trees. His eyes were still closed. Both Paul and Ingrid were smiling in disbelief. Sam's expression was a mixture of mild horror and sympathy. Shelby looked at Andrew. His face, as usual, was impossible to read. A few people continued to stir, but most of them had stopped completely and were listening. They were children caught in the middle of a story, unable to turn away. Carl shifted from one foot to the other, but his voice remained steady. The poem was somewhere deep in his memory, rising up in bright waves.

I'll tell of whores attacked, their lords at home;
Bawds' quarters beaten up, and fortress won;
Windows demolished, watches overcome;
And handsome ills by my contrivance done.

Nor shall our love-fits, Chloris, be forgot,
When each the well-looked linkboy strove t' enjoy,
And the best kiss was the deciding lot
Whether the boy fucked you, or I the boy.

He leaned forward, until she thought he might fall. But something held him. The soft glow of the lights, the hiss of the speakers, the spell of indrawn breath. It held him as he drew the words to a close. And she could see him, careworn, looking back at this moment, at its fading fire. Looking far back, and realizing that he'd done his very best to ruin them as they deserved.

Thus, statesmanlike, I'll saucily impose,
And safe from action, valiantly advise;
Sheltered in impotence, urge you to blows,
And being good for nothing else, be wise.

Everyone applauded. He handed back the microphone to the DJ, and the music resumed. Carl rejoined them, looking as if he'd just climbed out of another dimension.

"Where did that come from?" Shelby asked.

He shrugged. "I guess I was just feeling metrical."

Andrew took his hand. "Let's dance."

Paul and Sam were heading toward the patio. For a moment, Ingrid and Shelby found themselves staring at each other, smiling awkwardly.

"I think . . . I have to pee." It wasn't what she'd been planning to say.

"Okay," Ingrid replied. "I'm going to get a soda. I'll wait for you at the bar."

Shelby headed downstairs. She was thinking about all of the other things that she could have said. They were all better than *I have to pee*. She turned a corner and walked through the open doorway. But it wasn't the bathroom. It was a small office, with a desk covered in folders and computer equipment. A man with red hair looked up as she entered.

"You're not supposed to be here," he said, though he was smiling slightly.

Ingrid appeared behind her. "I saw you turn right and instead of left, and wanted to make sure you didn't—" She looked at the man behind the desk and trailed off.

"This clearly isn't the bathroom," Shelby said.

"No." The man folded his hands. "It isn't."

"I feel like I know you."

"Shelby," Ingrid said, "we have to go."

"No." He rose. "Stay. We have some things to discuss."

"What are you doing here?" Ingrid whispered.

Shelby stared at her. "You know him too?"

"Look closely," she said.

Shelby squinted. He had a wispy orange beard and eyes that were dark but strangely kind. He was wearing a light green shirt, and his hands were pale and slightly freckled. There was something about his voice. It had a kind of trill to it.

"Narses?" She felt herself grow cold.

"I see the others are with you—including the artifex. There's one that I don't recognize."

"Leave him out of this," Ingrid said sharply. "Forget that you saw him."

"You know that's not possible."

"Please. Just let him go home."

"I can't do that, miles."

"I'm *not* a miles here. I'm a mother."

"You've always been both. Now, you'd best bring the others. We have some things to discuss, and it's already getting late. There's a meeting room downstairs. We'll be afforded some measure of privacy there."

"No." There was panic in her voice—Shelby could hear it. "You have to let him go. He's got nothing to do with this."

"Perhaps that was once the case, but not anymore." His voice softened. "He was going to find out sooner or later."

"Not tonight. Do you hear me? It's not going to happen."

Narses looked at her for a moment. Then he sighed. "Fine. He and the other one—Andrew—they can go. But the rest of you are staying."

"Can we wait one second here?" Shelby demanded. "I thought you were dead."

"A lot of people thought that."

"What are you doing at our club?"

"I should think that's obvious." He smiled. "I own it."

4

SHELBY STARED AT HERSELF IN THE BATHROOM mirror.

The fluorescent lights made her look as if she'd been caught in a camera's flash. Milky pale and washed out, with bruised shadows at the edges of her life. Mirrors were supposed to capture your soul, but this one seemed disinterested, offering up her reflection only to be polite. Someone had scrawled a phone number in black marker across the glass. It struck her as being strangely out of time. Did people really phone random numbers? With the exception of talking to Andrew on speakerphone, most of her conversations occurred in a stichomythia of text messaging. It was hard enough to dial up SaskTel, knowing that she'd have to talk to a stranger about her fiscal irresponsibility. She couldn't imagine dialing a completely random number. It was like opening a treasure chest that you'd found in a dungeon. You might get a handful of coins, a priceless artifact, or a poison dart.

Next to her, a member of the Sovereign Court was applying a touch-up. Shelby was impressed by her diaphanous eyelashes. Her hair was streaked blue at the tips, and she wore a strapless black gown that exposed the tattoo on her back.

Still looking in the mirror, she observed: "Judging from your expression, your cat just died, or you lost a bet."

Shelby reddened slightly. "I'm just having a very strange night."

"I've been having one of those for the last twenty years."

"Really? You seem very well adjusted."

"You don't know me, pumpkin."

"Sorry."

She put away her compact and looked at Shelby. "Obviously, you've watched too many movies—you know the kind, where the drag queen has mystical powers and gives you advice about your love life, renews your faith in humanity—" She rummaged around her purse. "That kind of shit. Am I right?"

Shelby felt her expectations falling. "Possibly."

"You know how you've got that undo button on your keyboard? Control-Z, or whatever? You just press it, and the mistake's gone, like magic."

It wasn't quite a question. "I'm familiar with control-Z," she said finally.

"Well, they should make one of those fucking buttons for life. Bad decision? Just undo it. The real shit-kicker is that the bad decisions are the good ones."

"Is that your advice?"

She smiled. "I'm not your therapist. You seem sweet, though. Have a good night, and remember what John Waters says. *If you go home with someone, and they don't have any books—don't fuck them.*"

She walked out of the bathroom.

Shelby listened to the song of her heels as she climbed the stairs. Then there was only the buzz of the overhead lights and the sound of her own breath, which seemed to belong to someone else. If she stayed in this little bathroom, this white-chocolate space egg, then nothing would change. She could just control-Z the last fifteen minutes. Turn in the right direction. Maybe drag Ingrid into the bathroom with her. Or they could run straight out of the club, hand in hand down Broad Street, ignoring the horns and curious stares of people on their way to Shoppers Drug Mart. They would blaze through the summer dark, a trans-Neptunian object made of irony and fire. Nothing could touch them. It would be like *Bridge to Terabithia*, if you stopped on page 130 and refused to read any further.

In a small, overheated office, full of humming computer equipment and the sweet trace of smoke, Carl and Ingrid were being interviewed by a eunuch. Or maybe he wasn't a eunuch on this side of the park. Maybe he never had been. Maybe he'd always lived in two worlds, trading his sword for a smartphone. Stepping over the park's line of beauty to take control of their club on Broad Street. The lubricated end to so many crooked pilgrimages. How many times had she crouched in a graffitied stall, trying to work up the courage to be real, and there he'd been, wreathed by smoke in that little room? The park had begun to annihilate her personal geography. She could no longer perceive its borders. Like any true game, it was taking over her life from the inside. Perhaps her bones would be added to the pile, sooner than she realized. The thought was almost comforting. She could pay her debt to the clay and the vigilant grasshoppers. All she had to do was leave the bathroom.

She used to have a thing for sinks. In grade school, she would hide in the brown-tiled bathroom and turn on all of the faucets. This was before they'd introduced the ones that shut off after a few minutes. Water arced into the blood-flecked porcelain, stained by some child's nosebleed. She watched it with great fascination, while the sounds of the school rumbled beyond the big door. Once, she'd peed herself because a substitute teacher wouldn't let her leave the classroom until she finished her math test. She remembered the feeling of her damp underwear, the biting odor, the silence of the empty stall, which offered no solutions. If only it could have transported her somewhere.

Shelby glanced at the mirror again. The phone number was written across her face. Should she call? It seemed as

safe as anything else in her life, at the moment. It was the
nakedness of the number that drew her in. No preliminaries.
No promises of a good time, or misspelled accusations. Did
it simply mean *I was here*? Or was it an invitation? Finally,
she turned away, exiting the bathroom. Music pulsed along
the floor. A man sat on the stairs, nodding off, one hand
curled protectively around his drink. She carefully stepped
around him.

She walked past the ATM, where someone was staring
blankly at the screen. Their balance flickered at them.

"That can't be right," she heard. "It *can't* be."

Shelby passed a long bench where people reclined and
collapsed into each other, like strange particles. Their con
versations blended into a chain of riddles:

so done PowerPoint couldn't
pay going to ex construction *every*where
all over me what the hell ladybugs
once torrents jumper cables not without
socks in trees lost the form
where's my where's oh
hold
just for one
winter

A boy looked at her, with hair the color of a prairie sunset, wine-bright and borderless. He was lit by the glow of
his phone. For a moment, she couldn't tell if he was really
there. He didn't smile. Just glanced at her with mild curiosity. How did she look to him, standing in the corridor with
people buzzing around her? Was she like a piece of furniture? Did he have any idea that she spent half of her life in
another world, framed by rival queens and offerings to
chance? Perhaps he knew that the dice were loaded. He was
old enough to be here, after all, surrounded by this glorious
accident of dance and rumor.

They all should have known better, yet still, they threw.
Rattling around like fireworks in a cup, they waited for their

grand entrance, the chance to roll across the green felt table. The kiss good night, or the turned cheek. Kneading in the dark, or walking home, one step ahead of the dawn. You threw because it felt like a choice, and last call was a distant storm. You could see it, but you had a while yet—there was still the possibility of shelter.

She stepped into the eunuch's office. Carl was sucking down a rum and Coke, while Ingrid stood with her arms crossed. Shelby tried to catch her eye, but she was staring at the overhead light, which flickered imperceptibly. What could she divine within its decay? She was so still, except for one curl of hair, which trembled beneath the air-conditioning. Neil was probably fast asleep, dreaming of their next adventure. A real adventure, involving dogs and comets and sunlight.

"Where's Sam?"

"Paul drove her home," Carl said.

"Andrew?"

Carl drained the last of his drink. For a moment, the office was filled with the sucking sound of his straw. Then he pushed the glass away.

"Gone."

"What did you tell him?"

"Does it even matter? I hope he goes home with someone. A hookup will distract him from the fact that we're all just messing with his head." He turned to the club owner. "So, you must get a lot of trim. And free drinks. Why did you ever leave? Was it ennui, or do you just have a fetish for sandals?"

"You might as well pretend that you're in a comedy," Narses said. "It's a good instinct. If your logic follows, we'll all be married by the end of this."

Carl nodded. "You've got to admit—all this story lacks is fairy juice."

"Hush." Shelby sat down next to him. "I need to think."

"I need to drink."

"Stop it! You need to help. You can't just sit there like a useless harlequin, and then puke on the floor as soon as things get dangerous."

She hadn't intended the words to be quite so acrid. Carl just stared at her. Then he pushed the glass farther away.

"I didn't mean—"

"It's fine. I get it."

Shelby didn't know what to say. She turned to Ingrid. "Is Paul okay?"

Ingrid didn't answer at first. Then she blinked and looked at Shelby, as if seeing her for the first time. "I told him—" She laughed, suddenly. "I don't even remember. Isn't that great? I just spun the wheel of lies, and who knows where it landed? Sam helped. My sweet brother. He never sees it coming."

"Deception drives the engine of this game," Narses said.

Shelby stared at him. "You sound like a character from a cheesy RPG. *I am the Dark Savant, and I get to be cryptic, because of my giant bubble helmet.* Is this really all you have to offer us? Because your clichés stink—"

"Like an evil fart," Carl added.

"Right. No. Ignore him. What are you even doing here?"

"I used to live here," Narses replied. "A lifetime ago. The only way to outdistance Latona was to come back."

"Is it parking when he does it?" Carl asked.

Ingrid stepped forward. "Are we in danger? Here, in this world?"

"The worlds are running into each other, like paint," Narses said. "That's what she wants. If you stand in her way, she'll devour you."

"That's not an answer. Why do you people insist on talking this way?"

"It's strange," Narses observed. "You've been on the other side of the park longer than they have. But you still think of us as different species."

"We're nothing alike. I have a life here. A family."

"So did I."

Shelby couldn't stand it anymore. She was so tired of feeling stupid. It was like being part of an infernal pyramid scheme. You could never quite see the apex, so you kept trying to pull your own weight, hoping that you'd rise. But they always wanted more, and nobody could ever explain what it was all for. How did the park even work? Was it magic? Was it a curse? She'd grown up reading C. S. Lewis and wanted so badly to be Lucy. She'd scoured every shitty duplex and subsidized apartment for a magical wardrobe. But she could never find the room with the dead bluebottle on the windowsill.

And, like most people, she'd given up on deeper magic from before the dawn of time. Until the night that she'd vanished into the park. Then she'd discovered that real magic was dangerous and volatile, a match hovering over celluloid, a look in the dark that might be the death of you. She hadn't even hesitated. But what was it turning into? Bleeding and running and riddles in the club, the one place where she'd felt safe.

She stood up. "Let's go."

Carl stared at her. "This is the exposition scene."

"He doesn't really know anything. He's in the dark—just like us."

"Trust me," Narses said. "You need my help. When she begins—"

"We'll call you," Shelby replied. "It's late, and I'm tired of being played with."

Narses leaned forward. "You have to be careful. They have your scent."

"She can send as many monsters as she likes. This is Saskatchewan. We'll just get a bigger truck."

Shelby walked out of the club with Carl and Ingrid trailing behind. Broad Street was humming with late-night activity. Students on bar crawls were headed toward O'Hanlon's downtown, or Bushwakker on the strip. Their nights had just begun. A few exhausted souls were carrying home TV dinners and pet food. The moon kept a yellow eye on them. A group of kids were smoking in the alley. Their braying laughter carried across the street.

"So—" Carl was half smiling, as if to reassure her. "We just walked out on the one person who might have been able to tell us what was going on. Any thoughts on that?"

"We already know what's happening. It was all in the

letter that Eumachia stole. Her batshit-crazy mom is meeting with the chieftain of the silenoi to give him some kind of relic. Of course, relics are always safe and never cause destruction, so we have no reason to worry."

"Shel, are you coming undone?"

They both looked at her kindly. She jammed her hands in her pockets, as if that might keep her from throttling someone.

"I'm just so tired of gambling," Shelby said. "That's all we do. We rattle around like dice in a cup, waiting for someone to tell us something. But we still don't know a thing about what the park is, or how it works, or if it's going to eventually kill us. Narses helped us—I'll admit that—but right now, he just seems like one more cryptic asshole." She shook her head. "This was our night, Carl. Our night to be normal. And we came so close. Andrew was here, and Paul, and everyone was dancing, and having fun. It was the first time that I didn't want the magic anymore. I just wanted everything to be like this, always."

But even as she said it, Shelby knew that it was a lie. Fantasy novels had taught her that it was useless to complain about wonder. She didn't want to be one of those vampires who whined about their immortality, or the child of prophecy who just wanted to be normal. Superheroes, wizards, monsters—they all just want to be us.

Nobody chose normal, if they could help it. The park was a bloody gift that tore her every night in its jaws, and she loved it, she welcomed it, because the pain meant that she was alive. She'd wept over Gandalf's death, over the Red Wedding, over the pile of bones that fantasy left behind. For years, she'd tried to explain it to everyone, but so few understood what it was like to ride a luck dragon, to lose yourself in the sacrifice of a brave white hole, to chase Tenar through the dust-choked halls of Atuan, searching for your name.

The park was real magic, and that was about pain. It left marks. It wasn't all in her head, because these people understood. That was what made it so seductive. It made more sense than all of her favorite authors, more sense than grad school, more sense than the desire that she'd felt in fits and starts for one person, then another. Those midnight collisions, fueled by alcohol and the sting of hope that so quickly dissolved beneath the sunlight. Those diurnal mistakes that you were supposed to make, over and over, not because you'd one day get it right, but because life was all digressions and apostrophes. You ventured out onto the edge of the dash, staring at that blank space beneath you, not knowing if you were going to make it. Everything you'd learned was supposed to guide you, but it only left you with a knapsack full of bullshit transitions and sadly glimmering footnotes. There was no forward. Only sideways.

She looked at Carl. He used to burn with confidence, but lately he'd been more like a long-suffering bulb that needed changing. There were dark circles under his eyes, and if she squinted, she could almost see a single white hair in his beard. What had the park shown him? Why did he keep coming back? She was beginning to doubt that she really knew anything about her friends, these stations of grace, who followed her around with their thin arms outstretched.

Ingrid was watching her. *Tell us what to do,* she thought. *You're the only real adult among us.* But her mortgage and the toys that littered her house, like baroque pearls, didn't make her any wiser. She was equally disoriented.

But there was also something curious in her expression. That shock of amity that drew you to someone, reaching across the gap to pull you in, so unexpectedly. It might be as simple as a shared sin, or as complicated as a fear that you both honored, when you were alone and the veil dropped. That moment when someone undressed before you. It wasn't just about the primeval thrill of attraction, which made a cuckold of your brain and all its plans. It was the voice that cut through the fog, the ordinary little way in which you realized that you were sharing the world. You weren't the only confused one, dragging your groceries and loves and dark thoughts behind you.

Maybe this digression would lead her somewhere. All she had to do was stay alive long enough, and avoid the black page.

"We should call Sam," she said. "Maybe she wants to meet us."

"Not if she's smart," Carl replied. "This night has gone postal. I wouldn't blame her if she finally bailed on us."

She dialed Sam's number. It rang, but there was no answer. Maybe she'd turned the ringer off. Maybe she and Paul were hooking up. Either way, it seemed as if their strategy night was over. Sam was the only member of their company who didn't seem entirely bound up in the world of the park. In spite of her mother's position as a known artifex, she treated it as a kind of part-time job. What was her secret? How did she keep herself from thinking about it, day and night, like they did? It was like going to a party and meeting that group of students who were unnaturally well adjusted. They talked about their families, their dream vacations, the renovations to their bathrooms. They didn't pass out in the library after eating nothing but a bag of Wheat Thins for six hours.

The park ran in her family, but what did that mean? Perhaps its closeness was what made it possible to avoid, like a surreal Thanksgiving dinner. It wasn't like heroin to her, because she'd grown up with it. Was that common? Had Naucrate always been a citizen, or did she find a way to smuggle her daughter in? Thinking about it made Shelby realize that they knew almost nothing about Sam, or her shadow. Andrew had been a tablet under lamplight, his script easy to read, but Sam's life had a pumiced cover.

Shelby realized that she'd been standing with her phone in her hand, saying nothing, for what must have been a full minute. Carl was frowning at her, while Ingrid looked away, as you did when you wanted to avoid an uncomfortable reality.

"I don't know what to do," Shelby admitted. "Tomorrow, Latona is going to make some kind of sketchy pact with the silenoi. Who knows—maybe my supervisor will be there. We've got no real plan, aside from running in and yelling, *Hey, feel like killing us?* Even with the help of Felix and Drauca, we don't stand much of a chance. And we don't even know if Sam's with us or just humoring us."

Carl nodded. "Good summary."

"Don't you have anything useful to add?"

"Not really. However—" He patted his bag. "I do have three cans of pilsner left in here. It used to be a six-pack, but things got real back at the club."

"You've been carrying those around the whole time?"

"I always have contingency beverages."

Ingrid put an arm around her. "This night—like my car— is officially a write-off. Let's take a walk and then go to bed."

Together?

The word very nearly escaped her lips. But she managed to just grin and nod, without embarrassing herself. Real heroes probably wouldn't have ended the night with three cans of pilsner, but they weren't real heroes, after all. They were students following their most basic instinct: to ramble while drinking.

Carl distributed the beer, and they walked down Broad Street. All the brightly colored stores and restaurants were asleep for the night. A few lights gleamed in the second-story apartments, but most people were dreaming, or absent. The shawarma restaurant by the bus depot was still open. Carl couldn't resist the spinning tower of meat, so they waited outside while he ordered them food. Shelby realized that beer and falafel weren't a charming couple, but she had a weakness for the pickled radish. Carl observed that if hobbits had embraced nightclub culture, they would have called this meal "second supper." Ingrid chortled at that. Shelby liked the rough texture of her laugh. She was beginning to see what Ingrid shared with Fel—the slender thread that linked their shadows. A laugh, a wink, a flash of temper. They weren't the same, of course, but they might have shared a family tree.

They walked through the ghostly downtown core. The bank buildings were glass mausoleums, their sharp angles chipping the moonlight. The windows of the SGI tower burned like gold damascene: something risen from an age-old hoard. Night buses made their pilgrimage toward the loop on Twelfth Street. A man played the saxophone on the corner of Scarth, and his sweet notes followed them as they crossed at the light. A few people were smoking by the flowerpots, and farther down the street, they could hear laughter and shouting from the patio at O'Hanlon's. The Canada Life building soared above it all, casting its neon glow over the length of Victoria Park. They strolled past the light sabers, watching them shift from green to electric purple, until they'd cycled through every Jedi possibility.

There was a stage across from the park where intrepid couples took salsa lessons. On alternate days, a collective yoga group met to practice stretching on the green. It all seemed terribly active. Shelby figured that climbing the stairs in the library was enough to get her blood moving. Any type of yoga made her feel as if she were revisiting the Canada Fitness Test, which had taught her that she had the flexibility of a bronze statue. *Take the participation card and run.* That had always been her motto.

Carl climbed onto the stage and lit a roach. It took a few tries, because he kept swearing and burning his fingers. Ingrid had to lend him a bobby pin, but finally he got it going. They passed it around, a pug-nosed little joint that threatened to go out at any moment. Ingrid took a discreet puff and then gave it to Shelby.

She coughed. "This smells like the inside of your bug."

"It's all I've got."

They sat with their legs dangling off the stage. Red, blue, green. The light sabers flickered through the spectrum, until they suddenly flashed bone-white. A metallic sculpture loomed above them, but nobody could figure out what it was supposed to be. Shelby thought it might be the giant fart living under the bed in *Good Families Don't.* Carl said it looked more like an imperial star destroyer. Ingrid declared it abstract, which prompted a long sigh from the others.

"That's like calling it a text," Carl said. "You lose."

"Isn't everything a text?" Shelby asked. "At least that's what Derrida says. Every text has an edge, and we're supposed to, like—I don't know—live on it, or something?"

"How do we fit?"

"We make ourselves really small, like *The Borrowers*."
He cackled. "What if it's an e-book? Where's the edge?"

"Up your ass."

Carl spread his arms. "Quick. What's everyone's favorite bullshit, made-up academic word that doesn't mean anything?"

They all considered the question for a moment. Then they answered in one voice:

"Problematize!"

"Criticality!"

"Chronotrigger!"

Shelby laughed. "That's a video game."

"Shit," Carl said. "I meant *chronotope*."

"I think I may have used *problematize* when I was at the bank," Shelby replied. "So I'm not blameless in this scenario."

"Do you think other people make fun of their calling?" Ingrid asked.

Carl made a face. "You're such an education student."

"What's that supposed to mean?"

"I hate it when people describe teaching as a calling, like someone handed them a stone tablet or Excalibur or something. It's a profession, sure, and it's not for everyone—but the fact that you can put a syllabus together isn't some kind of miracle. We're all just hanging on by the skin of our teeth."

"That's deeply motivating," Ingrid said.

"You're welcome." Carl stood up. "Besides. We need more dancing. There are studies, you know, about teaching and movement. Something called a kinesphere. I don't know what the fuck that is, but it sounds like something wicked from *Dune*."

He turned the volume up on his phone and set it on the stage. A moment later, they were waltzing to Leonard Cohen. Carl swayed on his own, while Shelby and Ingrid danced together, skirting the edge of the platform. When the song changed to "Everybody Knows," they all sang in unison, crying out that the dice were loaded. *The basilissa wins all.* Fate moves as it must. Even *Beowulf* was right about that. It didn't matter what world you were in. There was what you wanted, and then there was the din of the wheel.

They changed partners. Ingrid laughed in surprise as Carl spun her around. Then he fell off the stage, and everyone knew that it was time to go.

The moon invited them to take the long way home. They walked back down Broad Street and dropped off Carl at his apartment. Love Selection was humming with activity. There was always a sale going on. Ingrid was bemused by the fact that they played classical music. There was something oddly inviting about the well-lit store, where you could browse for silicone toys while listening to a Naxos sampler. It reminded her of that woodcut image of women shopping for dildos in the seventeenth century.

"We should meet first thing tomorrow morning," Shelby said. "We don't have much time to go over this plan."

"I thought we didn't have a plan," Carl said.

"I'm calling it a proto-plan."

"How about Frodo-plan? Those always end with volcanoes."

"Go to bed."

He hugged both of them good night and then made his way upstairs. Shelby waited until she saw the light in his apartment turn on. Then she looked at Ingrid.

"So."

Ingrid smiled. "Should I problematize your *so*?"

"I'm not sure that it has an argument."

"I think the Dodger might still be open," Ingrid said. "Want to grab a tea?"

"They sell tea?"

"Not happily. But it's on the menu. We could get it to go."

They walked down Osler Street. The old fire station cast a peeling shadow over them. People were crowded onto the Dodger's small patio, smoking and drinking martinis. A band was playing inside, but nobody seemed to be paying attention. They were all huddled around tables, yelling into each other's ears. Ingrid made her way past the crush of people. The bartender actually seemed relieved by her request. All she had to do was add hot water. Shelby watched Ingrid making small talk. She couldn't hear anything, but she could read their expressions. The bartender smiled. They weren't flirting, exactly. It was more like two frayed wires, connecting momentarily. A small flash of kindness in a place where most people were intent on self-fashioning.

Ingrid handed her the tea. "I hope peppermint is okay. It's all they had."

Shelby hated peppermint. "It's great," she said. "Thank you."

They crossed the street. There was a small park on the other side. You couldn't even really call it a park. The city had built it to memorialize a fire, but now it was overgrown, surrendering to its own wildness. Grass and weeds poked through a strange metal structure, and purple flowers made a kind of margin around the dust and gravel.

Shelby sat on a chunk of stone. She held her cup in both hands, absorbing the warmth. Ingrid sat down next to her. Grasshoppers leapt like popcorn at their feet. The sounds of the bar were fuzzy across the street. She couldn't quite look at Ingrid, so she looked at the moon, instead. Pollution had turned it amber. The sky had no limits, and she felt as if she could see forever, along the whole length of starless black prairie. Somewhere, there might be a galaxy in which she had the courage to take what she wanted.

"How do you think it works?" Shelby asked finally.

"How does what work?"

"Magic."

Ingrid shrugged. "I've never known for sure. When I first discovered the park, it felt like some wild spell that had been building inside me, ever since I was a little girl. Then I had Neil, and that was a different kind of magic. But I have no idea how it all functions."

Shelby gestured to the micropark around them. "Do you think Anfractus is *here*? I mean, is it like a transparency, laid over this world?"

"Maybe Regina *is* Anfractus. Or it used to be, or will be."

"Oliver seems to think it's some kind of conspiracy. That

Wascana Park was built to hide the bridge between worlds. But maybe he's just a shell-shocked librarian."

"He's a lot of things."

"How do you two really know each other?"

Something softened in her eyes. "I don't want to talk about that right now."

Ingrid leaned forward and kissed her. The grasshoppers danced. The weeds continued their impassive crusade. Shelby heard a low white humming in her ears. It was the sound of every word she'd ever known breaking free. Ingrid's hand slid down her back. Night dropped a curtain across the stage, which had already begun to spin. They pulled back for a moment. Then Shelby rallied and stopped caring about anything. She ran her hands through Ingrid's hair, which was soft from her conditioner and smelled of apples. For a moment, she thought they might strip off their clothes in the poor excuse for a park. But suddenly Ingrid stopped moving.

"Shelby," she murmured. "Look."

She turned, still holding on to Ingrid. Two figures were standing by the wall of a nearby building. At first, she didn't recognize them. But then one of them gestured slightly, in the middle of a sentence, and the movement jogged her memory.

It was Andrew.

Shelby squinted, trying to make out the other figure. He had an arm on Andrew's shoulder. She listened closely but couldn't make out anything that he was saying. He turned slightly, and the moonlight yellowed his face.

It was Oliver.

"What's he doing here?" Shelby whispered.

Ingrid's expression had darkened. "I have no idea."

That was when she remembered Carl's offhand comment, back at the club.

I hope he goes home with someone.

Her mind was racing. Had Oliver been there the whole time? Had he simply been waiting for them to leave Andrew alone? This was her fault. She should have called him. She should have stayed with Narses. Why did she think that she could lead this company? Her anger had brought her to this moment, wasting time in a false park, trying to get up on a single mother while her friend was possibly being grifted by a librarian. Could they really trust Oliver? What did they know about him, in the end?

The librarian took him by the hand. They walked into the undergrowth, beyond the sodium flicker of the streetlamps.

Shelby felt a kind of tug. It was sickeningly familiar. The weedy lacuna seemed suddenly more real than it had ever been. Visible darkness fired every blade of grass, every dandelion about to give itself to the passing breeze.

"Andrew!" She broke free and ran toward the deepest shadows.

But he was already gone.

PART FOUR

OCULUS

1

YELLOW MOSS FLUTTERED ABOVE HIM. At
first, he thought it was feathers. He could hear a distant
clanging, iron against iron, and the smell of fish was thick
in the air. He blinked. The moss clung to a brick wall, shimmering slightly beneath the heat. The ground bit into his
shoulder and other soft parts. He looked down and realized
that he was naked. He sat up, wrapping his thin arms around
his knees. His instinct was to cover himself, but there was
nobody around. This was an alley. Cries and hammering
and other vague noises floated down its mouth, but he
couldn't quite put them together. They sailed past him on
warm currents. The sun seemed too large, a sinister apple
that glared at him. The sky was the same color as the brick.

IIe tried to remember his name, but there was only white
space. The word had been scraped clean. He stared at his
hands, which were streaked with grime. They might have
belonged to anyone. He wiggled his fingers experimentally,
as if to prove that they were actually under his control. Little
flares of pain coursed along his muscles. He tried to stand up.
Everything tilted, and then he was on his knees, retching. He

wiped the strands of bile from his mouth and tried to stand again, this time more slowly. He used the wall for support.

Had he been here before? Something about the bricks, the maleficent sun, the plump black flies buzzing overhead—it seemed familiar. But the memory was wreathed in smoke. Like pain that you'd felt as a child, so immediate at the time, but now impossible to conjure up in detail. Had the hurt belonged to him, or someone else? Perhaps it was just a story that he'd heard, a bright fishhook dipping in, then vanishing just as quickly. He laid his hand against the dazed bricks.

These are mine.

He wasn't sure where this thought came from, but he trusted it. The bricks, the alley, this little cell that sheltered him. It felt like an extension of his body, a rib that he'd given up. Something had reached into him, unlocked the bone chamber while he was dreaming. He touched his side, but there was no mark.

Sweat beaded on the bridge of his nose, and he wiped it away. The alley may have been a part of him, but it wasn't offering anything. He needed clothes. He looked down at his bare feet. They wouldn't survive the hungry cobblestones. He would have to steal something, but that meant leaving the embrace of the alley. Should he cover himself and hobble along, or try to move quickly with his soft parts exposed? His third option was to stay here, until the heat and the hammer-song lulled him to sleep. He knew, however, that this would be no quick death. Better to risk the city than die of thirst and nightmares in his open cell.

He should be panicking. He was naked and alone in a strange place. He had no name. But something about the blank tablet was oddly comforting. He was nobody.

He said the word aloud.

Nobody.

Only, it sounded different when he said it.

Nemo.

The syllables were familiar. They meant "nobody." As he spoke them, he could hear different words uncoiling in the back of his mind. They didn't quite make sense but hovered just on the edge of his understanding. They were the motions of a dance that his body remembered. He said the word again. Maybe that was his name. Nobody.

He heard something. Leaves crunching, but there were no trees. A delicate shadow moved along the wall. He drew closer to the corner of the alley. There was nothing there. Not at first. Then, as he continued to stare, the light shifted.

At first, he thought that he was seeing a mirage. But the image slowly resolved itself, and he realized it was a lizard. Its scales were the color of fired clay, speckled with gold. All the heat in the alley seemed to gather around its compact form, which was roughly the size of his hand. A shy pink tongue tasted the air. Its eyes were perfect forges, ready to smelt a world of iron. He could feel the animal's heat. As he drew closer, it singed the hairs on his arm.

It didn't seem dangerous, precisely. But neither was it harmless. Those eyes held possibilities, and none of them were entirely without risk.

He dropped to one knee, a mixture of caution and fealty. Then he slowly extended his right hand, palm up. Maybe lizards were like cats. He lacked a ball of string (where would he have put it?), but at least he could appear friendly. He wasn't sure if you were supposed to look a lizard in the eyes. It seemed the polite thing to do.

The lizard's eyes grew. He felt that he could step into them. The pupils were shaped like hourglasses. Then it drew closer. Its tongue flicked the tips of his fingers. The pink underside was rough and had the texture of a comb. Startled, he watched as a perfect drop of blood coalesced on his index finger. He looked at it for a long moment, then carefully put the finger in his mouth. The lizard watched him. Its tail moved in slow circles against the ground.

"I'd tell you my name," he said, "but I've lost it."

The hourglasses turned. He watched the smoke as it pooled inside them. The lizard opened its mouth, revealing a row of needle-sharp teeth. For a moment, he thought it might leap at him. But it didn't move. Something about its eyes told him that it was smiling.

Then it turned and made its way toward the mouth of the alley. He watched it go. When it was halfway to the entrance, it stopped and craned its neck to look back at him. That was when he realized that it wanted him to follow.

A naked man with a lizard would probably attract the wrong kind of attention. But he didn't have a lot of options. Maybe it would lead him to some clothing, or a nest—did lizards have nests? At any rate, it was better than baking in the alley.

He paused at the mouth of the alley. He could hear the city now, a cloud of murmuring. Light settled in sharp planes along his body. The lizard gave him another indecipherable look and then kept walking. He followed. There was no other choice.

The street was busy. Wagons made their way along deep ruts, while people of every shape and color hurried past. They waited at white stones for the traffic to clear, then stormed forward in a decisive cloud, kicking up dust. Most of them wore plain clothing, weathered from constant use. Some were dressed in brighter colors, and a few wore masks of silver, gold, and polished ivory. He noticed that smaller, less-human things were following them, skittering along at their own odd pace. A closer investigation revealed that they were automata. He saw mechanical spiders; birds that hopped along, their gears chirping; and little dolls that sighed as they made their way across the broad street. They looked at him with dark, unfeeling eyes, and he couldn't tell if they were thinking or simply moving on instinct.

He followed the lizard. It seemed to know where it was going, and nobody paid it the slightest bit of attention. It kept to the long shadows beneath the buildings. A few people glanced at him, but for the most part, his nudity wasn't an issue. They saw him briefly, then looked away. He might have been a window, or a pebble on the ground, for all they cared. After the first few moments, the cut of shame was gone, and he stopped trying to cover himself. The lizard gave him what might have been an approving glance.

They walked through some kind of market. He saw

bizarre items for sale. Mechanical fruit with blades for leaves. Books with purple-pumiced covers whose pages expanded like giant accordions. A stylus that could write on any surface (the vendor was demonstrating on a piece of hardened leather). Clockwork dragonflies that circled a pond of geared frogs, all croaking in unison. There was a pile of cloaks with rampant tigers stitched into their linings, discarded on a table, as if tigers were too generic. Flies buzzed around them, drawn by the pyramid of oranges and star-shaped fruit in a bin next to the cloaks. He wanted to grab one of the oranges, but a vendor was watching him. In fact, the vendors, in their stained tunics, were the only ones who seemed to see him. Their sharp eyes followed him, issuing a subtle challenge. Obviously, he wasn't the first nude exile who'd had the idea of stealing fruit.

"I hope you know where you're going," he said to the lizard. "I'm getting a pretty thorough sunburn following you around."

He looked up and saw the stone skyways for the first time. They were artfully crafted bridges that connected the taller buildings. People made their way along them, not even bothering to look down, as if treading air were a perfectly ordinary part of their daily commute. What struck him were the colors of the stone. Pink, sea-green, slate, and spotted white that reminded him of a chess board. Only, when he thought of chess, his mind supplied a different word. *Acedrex*. He said it beneath his breath. It had more angles. Like everything, it felt oddly familiar.

The lizard had outpaced him while he was transfixed by the many-colored paths. He had to hurry to close the distance between them. He couldn't run—even if nobody was really paying attention, the thought of what he might look like was enough. It was also harder to avoid the sharper stones. The soles of his feet were already burning, and he could feel small cuts, leaving faint prints of blood in the dust. The lizard glanced at him once more, then made its way between two tall buildings. *Insulae*. They had balconies and gabled windows. Close to the ground, they were whitewashed and well tended, sporting small gardens. But as he looked upward, he saw that the higher levels were crumbling. Pigeons nested in the windows, and smoke settled in a heavy cloud at the apex of the buildings. The rich people must be living on the ground floors.

There were stores on the street level, as well as a restaurant of some kind. It had an L-shaped counter, with clay jugs stacked behind it. He smelled burning chickpeas. His mouth watered, but the woman behind the counter gave him a knowing look. She wouldn't stand for any kind of thievery. Feeling more than slightly defeated, he followed the lizard into the narrow space between the soaring insulae. There was something on the ground—it looked like a collapsed wooden umbrella and smelled slightly acrid. The lizard paused in front of it.

"What's that? Can I eat it?"

He looked closer and realized that there were clothes drying inside the funny umbrella. Quickly, he reached in and grabbed a blue tunic. The dye stuck to his fingers. They must have been absorbing their new colors—the "umbrella" was a drying rack. He sniffed the fabric. It smelled faintly of piss. He had no idea why, but neither was he in a position to be choosy. After all, it was fairly subtle. Nobody would notice, unless they drew close to him. And it was far better than the sunburned alternative. He slipped on the tunic. It felt strange not to be wearing anything underneath, but the breeze was also nice. It helped to dry some of the sweat that was building in uncomfortable places. He worried about chafing, but in the broad scheme of things, it was probably the least of his problems.

"Thanks," he said to the lizard. "It was very thoughtful of you to lead me—"

"Hey!" a voice shouted from a second-story window. "Just what the fuck do you think you're doing, nemo? Those don't belong to you!"

He looked up. A woman leaned out the window, holding a blade and glaring at him.

"I'm sorry," he called. "Do you mind if I borrow them?

I'm kind of in a bad situation right now, and I promise that I'll return them."

"Get out of here, before I carve you a new hole."

The lizard was already scampering away. He gave a quick wave to the woman, but she had disappeared from the window. Fearing that she might be on her way down, he hurried after his guide, who was heading back onto the street. He was still barefoot, but at least he had something to cover himself. It was best not to think too closely about the smell.

He walked downhill, keeping the lizard's tail in sight. Luckily, the slope was gradual. He really needed to find some sandals. He kept staring at the feet of passersby and thinking sullenly that they didn't deserve to be protected from sharp stones. The sun was making him tired and queasy, but as the buildings grew more densely packed, the shadows lengthened. He was grateful to walk beneath the edifices, until a pile of something awful landed next to his feet, and he realized that people were regularly tossing things out of windows. After that, he made sure to look up periodically, in order to avoid an unpleasant rain.

There was a roaring in the distance. He entered a kind of piazza, where people were gathered around fountains or playing games in the dust. Something towered over the space, but at first, he couldn't tell exactly what it was. It looked like a giant piece of scaffolding. There was a ceramic tank behind it, fed by a series of lead pipes. At the top, a giant wheel revolved, driven by water. That was the source of the roar. Each spoke of the wheel had a woman's face carved into its surface. Her watched her guises turn. Sometimes she was young, sometimes old, sometimes angry, joyous, skeptical. One face in particular seemed to be looking directly at him, partially in shadow. He watched it make a slow circle. Suddenly, there was a thunderous chime, and the people looked up, shaken from their games and dreams. He realized, finally, that the machine was a clepsydra: a water clock. He didn't understand the meaning of the faces, but the wheel chimed the hour.

He'd nearly lost sight of the lizard. It was making its way

toward the edge of the piazza, no longer looking back to ensure that he was following. He walked as quickly as he could, weaving his way among the fountains, where people cooled their feet, diced, and played a game involving tables. The lizard was a gold fleck in the distance. By the time he caught up, he had more cuts, and his feet were burning like mad.

"Could you find me some sandals next?" he asked.

It ignored him and kept walking. He followed, limping along, trying not to think about what his feet must look like. A great shadow fell across them both. He looked up and saw a giant aqueduct made of sand-colored stone. It cut across the horizon, seeming to undulate in the shimmering air, like a dragon with sunburned scales. People gathered beneath it in lively clusters, drinking, gaming, and pawing at each other. A few crafty vendors had set up tables, while figures in black wound their way among the granite bows. One man was getting his hair cut by a female barber, who sharpened her razor against a strip of leather. It seemed like an odd place for personal grooming, but he also suspected that there was more on offer than just a shave.

The street's decline grew more pronounced, in every sense. Taverns crowded the margins. A masked woman distributed wreaths and cups of wine. As he grew closer, she favored him with a kind look and placed a wreath on his head. She had moved on before he could thank her. The smell of smoke and sour wine was thick in the air. People danced in the streets or collapsed against the paving stones, unable to continue. Love cries echoed from above. Naked shadows moved in the open windows, and cursing issued from tangled alleys. Sometimes, a person would beckon him, but he feared the denser shadows. The street was precarious enough.

They passed a high building made of black stone, with smaller satellites gathered around it. A steady stream of people climbed the steps (a few could barely walk). He noticed a silver coin discarded on the ground and bent to pick it up. Upon studying the coin, he couldn't help but blush. It depicted two men engaged in acrobatic sex. At least, he thought it was two men, but their faces had been rubbed away by use. It was hard to tell. He searched his weeping blue tunic for something resembling a pocket but found nothing. He decided to hold on to the salacious coin. Perhaps it would buy him something diverting.

He looked up and saw a masked woman sitting on a balcony. Her left hand trembled slightly, as if due to a palsy. Her long hair was tied in a braid. She was looking directly at him, and her mask reminded him of a sheet of ice. Should he wave, or smile? He wasn't sure what kind of etiquette was involved. Plus, he was still holding the silver coin and didn't want to give her the wrong idea. He simply nodded. She continued to watch him, and he finally had to look away. He didn't want to lose sight of his guide. Luckily for him, the lizard had stopped by a roadside shrine, where it was helping itself to oil-soaked bread crumbs and some orange peels.

The flies were no bother. A man passed by and tossed a scrap of meat into the shrine's shallow bowl. The lizard devoured it.

He watched the crowd. A few people glanced at him, then looked away. Most simply ignored him, registering his presence just long enough to get out of the way. But nobody seemed to see the lizard. He took an orange peel and laid it on his palm. The lizard sniffed it, then ate the peel in one bite. A man walking by gave him an odd look, as if to say, *What do you think you're doing?* But the child that he was dragging behind him looked directly at where the peel had once been, wide-eyed, as if he'd just seen something delicious and impossible.

He realized for the first time that only he could see the lizard. Children may have suspected its presence, but adults ignored it completely. He looked once again into those amber eyes, with their hourglass pupils. He was worried that he might be following a hallucination, but if it was one, it seemed to know exactly where it was going. There were probably worse things than trailing after a figment of your imagination. At least he'd found some clothes.

Having satisfied its hunger, the lizard, or shadow—whatever it was—hopped off the shrine and continued down the narrowing street. He followed it past shops and squat buildings, where armored soldiers stood by the entrances. It felt as if he'd never walked this far in his life, but since he couldn't remember his life, the pain and exhaustion were somehow irrelevant. Just as he thought that his feet might actually crumble to dust, the lizard paused outside a small house. The neighborhood had grown strangely quiet. A wall with sharp barbicans stood behind the house, and he wondered if this was the boundary of the city proper. The house had been built flush against the wall, so that it seemed to emerge from the boundary itself. The front door, painted once, was now the same color as the dust.

The lizard gave him a long look. Then it curled into a golden ball and promptly fell asleep in a patch of sunlight.

"This is it?" He looked skeptically at the peeling door. "This is where you've been leading me, all this time?"

The lizard opened one eye, briefly. Then, realizing that he had nothing of significance to say, it fell back asleep. Within seconds, it was snoring. The sound reminded him of two pieces of flint being rubbed together.

"I suppose I ought to thank you." He considered scratching the lizard behind its ears, but something told him that this wouldn't end well. "At any rate—if I find any more orange peels inside, I'll be sure to give you some."

His stomach was making desperate noises. He should have grabbed a few of those oil-soaked bread crumbs, but it hadn't felt right to steal from the shrine. Maybe there was food in the house, and a fountain to soak his feet in, and somewhere to lie down. The possibilities multiplied in his mind, each seeming less likely. What if the house belonged to one of the armored soldiers? What if it was simply abandoned? There'd be no food, in that case. But at least he could get out of the sun for a bit and try to devise a plan. He trusted his guide, for some reason. If not for the lizard, he might have died in the alley.

Carefully, he stepped over the snoring ball and opened the door.

The house was dark, save for two lanterns suspended by chains. Their light made everything appear tremulous. He saw paintings on the walls but could only make out their edges. A blue smudge that might have been a dolphin, arcing out of its frame. Shapes that were either dancing or tearing each other apart—he couldn't tell. The floor was made of packed earth, rather than the stone that he'd been expecting. It felt cool and soft against his bleeding soles.

"Close the door," a voice said.

As his vision adjusted, he saw three figures, seated on stools around a trestle table. A fourth figure stood nearby, his chain-mail shirt gleaming beneath the lamps. He closed the door, and the sliver of light from the outside world vanished. He was left with the orange lamplight, which made him feel as if he might be dreaming.

"Come closer," the same voice said.

He approached the table. As he drew closer, he saw that one of the figures was a woman. Her gown was dyed purple, and its embroidered hem touched the ground, hiding her feet. Her hair was swept up into a tower by a series of gleaming pins and combs.

"You're back," she said, raising her wine cup. "I feared it might not work."

"It was a gamble," said the figure next to her—the one who'd said to close the door. He was wearing a mask, like the woman he'd seen on the balcony. His yellow tunic was made of silk, and dragonflies of vermilion thread played along the sleeves. There was an amethyst ring on his finger, carved into the shape of a wheel. It reminded him of the clepsydra in miniature.

"Everything is a gamble here," the woman said. "It worked. That's all that matters."

The third figure was silent. He was farthest from the lamplight, and his features remained indistinct. All he could see was a flash of green tunic, and a jeweled pin, winking.

He was heavier than the other two and shifted on the stool with some measure of discomfort. But he didn't say anything. His hands were still.

"Nice wreath," the woman said. "I see you've been through the Subura."

"What's that?" he asked finally.

"A diversion. Like most of this great city."

He took a step forward. "Have you been waiting for me?"

She smiled and took another sip of wine.

"You must be thirsty." The masked man held out a cup. "Here."

He snatched it without asking questions, just as the lizard had snatched the orange peel. The water tasted like a miracle. It dribbled down his chin, but he didn't care.

"There's food as well," the man said. "Cakes, a bit of roast boar, and dormice rolled in honey. The latter is a bit of an acquired taste."

He noticed the food for the first time, on a nearby table. The smell was so intoxicating that, for a moment, he thought that he was going to pass out.

"You might as well have some," the woman said, "before your friend wakes up and realizes what he's missing. Salamanders have voracious appetites."

"I thought only I could see it."

"We know that it led you here."

"Is that what it is? A salamander?"

She exchanged a curious look with the masked man but said nothing.

Before he could lose his resolve, he stumbled over to the table and began heaping food onto a gilt plate. He ate with his fingers, tearing into the cold slices of boar and swallowing dormouse whole. It tasted like candy. There was a small bowl filled with water, and he washed his hands in that when he was done. The three figures at the table watched his every move, as if he were a mosaic that had come to life. The woman with the vertical hair was smiling, but there was also something else behind her expression that he couldn't quite place. The masked man watched him dry his hands on the tunic. They came away tinged blue.

He placed the silver coin on the table. "I found this on the ground. I'm not sure what to do with it, and I don't have any pockets."

The woman smirked when she saw the coin. "I didn't realize that you still offered this service, Felix. It seems very—athletic."

"We offer anything that the mind can conjure."

"That's a dangerous promise. You'll have to design a lot more coins."

"Spintriae," he corrected. "You can't exchange them for bread, after all."

"The lupo who came up with that system was a genius." She saw his jaw tighten. "Apologies. I forgot that we no longer use that term. How about love engineer?"

He raised his hand, uncertain of what else to do. "I don't mean to interrupt, but I don't really know what you're talking about. I woke up naked in an alley. I can't remember anything—not even my own name. I followed a salamander across sharp cobblestones, and my head feels like it's going to explode. Can someone please tell me where I am, at least?"

There was a chuckle from the far end of the table. It was the figure still in shadow.

"I'm always impressed," he said, "by the consistency of magic. It never fails. He truly doesn't remember a thing." The man's voice was high, like a soft timbrel.

He drew closer. "Do we know each other?"

The figure leaned forward. He had gray eyes and a pale, wispy beard. The skin on his left cheek was mottled. His close-cropped hair revealed little islands of scar tissue, extending a burned coastline down to his neck. His left hand was also scarred.

"See anything you recognize?"

He shook his head slowly. "No. I'm sorry."

The man grabbed his wrist. Before he could pull away,

he touched his palm to his ruined cheek. It felt like the surface of a frayed rope.

"Your salamander did this to me," he said. "You ran and left me to burn in that library. Not even a glance backward at what you'd done."

"Mardian." The woman's voice held a touch of annoyance. "Leave him be. You can't scare him into remembering."

But he did remember something. The library. It was hazy and distorted, as if someone had dimmed the lights. But he could recall the smoke and the near-kiss of the flames. Someone grabbing his hand, dragging him outside. A scream following him. Was it Mardian's?

He traced the scars with his fingertips. "I did this?"

"No." Felix stood. "A lar did it. You were only defending yourself."

Mardian laughed bitterly. "Of course. Why hold him responsible for anything?"

"He's paid for it," Felix snapped. "Or can't you see that, spado?"

Mardian looked him up and down. He took in the weeping blue tunic, his bare bloody feet, the grime on his face.

"Some debts cannot be settled." He leaned back, until the left side of his face was in shadow again. "But it's a start."

Felix approached him. "We can tell you more. About this place, and what it means. About what brought you here. But it may be easier to show you."

"Show me?"

"Take it off."

At first, he didn't know what the man was talking about. The tunic? What was the use in being naked again, unless they were planning something awful for him? But then he realized what Felix meant. Gently, he touched the mask. It was graven with leaves and other things that flickered in the dim light. He hesitated for a moment. Then he lifted the mask. It was surprisingly heavy and left a faint imprint. Felix was sweating underneath. His cheeks were slightly flushed.

For a moment, he wasn't sure where Felix ended and the mask began. He looked at the mask as if he were holding a part of him in his hands. Then the man smiled, and he was struck by another memory. Felix standing in a park, leading him into the dark undergrowth. No. Not Felix. Someone else. A shadow.

"I know you," he murmured. "Or—some version of you."

"We all have two lives," he said. "One is lived here, in this city of infinite alleys, which we call Anfractus. The other is lived beyond the city walls, in that other place. Some of us choose to live both lives, while others settle upon one. Twice the life means twice the danger, after all."

"Are we friends? In that other place?"

"Felix has no friends," the woman said. "No permanent ones, at any rate."

He turned to her. "Do we also know each other?"

"I knew your shadow, some time ago. There's a family resemblance, but you're different. I can see that." She inclined her head. "You knew me as Domina Pendelia."

He frowned. "I don't understand. My shadow? Is that like—my other life?"

"This isn't your first time in Anfractus," Felix said. "You've already met all of us. Even Tylo, who's standing guard, over there."

He'd completely forgotten about the soldier. He wasn't quite scowling, but neither did he look impressed. He winced, and shifted position. There seemed to be something wrong with his left leg. He favored it slightly. He also kept flexing his hand, as if it pained him.

"Are you all right?" he asked.

"Just a little stiff," he muttered.

"I wish I could remember who you were."

"No, you don't." The guard returned his attention to the door.

"So—" He turned back to Felix. "You say I had this shadow. This other life. What happened to him?"

Something flickered across Felix's face. Then he put the mask back on.

"You died," he said. "Well—not you, precisely. The shadow died."

"What was his name?"

He looked slightly uncomfortable. "We aren't allowed to say. When someone's shadow dies, their name dies with them. It's no longer spoken aloud."

"Then how am I supposed to figure out who I am?" For the first time since waking in the alley, he felt anger. "I don't even have a name. When I try to remember, it's just flashes, voices, and words that I barely recognize. Nothing you've told me sounds even remotely plausible."

"Call the salamander," Pendelia said.

"What?"

Mardian seemed to flinch at the mention of the lizard.

"Call him," she repeated. "If anyone knows your name, it's him. We certainly don't. And we won't be able to continue this conversation until you know who you are."

"What am I supposed to do—whistle? Pat my knee?"

"He's not a cat. Just ask him to come inside, like a civilized person would."

For a moment, he remained still. All of this was too much. Everyone was staring at him. Even the guard was curious to see what he'd do next.

There seemed to be no other choice. He opened the door and found the salamander on the step, asleep.

"Ah. Excuse me."

The lizard opened a single eye. Then it yawned a puff of smoke and looked at him.

"Would you mind coming inside, for a moment?"

It rose and followed him into the house, as if it had been waiting for an invitation. He closed the door behind it. He half expected Mardian to recoil from the salamander, but then he remembered that none of them could see it.

"All right—" He gestured to a spot on the floor, feeling a bit foolish, like a child introducing his imaginary friend. "It's sitting right here."

"Go ahead," Pendelia said. "Ask what your name is."

"This lizard really knows my name?"

"You won't know until you ask."

He knelt down beside the salamander. "Can you tell me—" He swallowed. "Do you know what my name is?"

The salamander gave him a long look. The hourglasses turned. Then it flashed forward and bit his hand. Its teeth left half-moon imprints, which quickly welled up with blood. He snatched his hand away. At first, there was just a sting. Then it started to burn. Fire moved along the length of his hand. He cried out and ran across the room. He plunged his burning hand into the bowl of water, but the pain didn't stop. His blood was on fire. It sang through his veins until it reached his heart.

Aleo.

He saw a polished wooden stave with a jade pommel, winking death beneath the sun. A black tunic with scarlet swans, whose outline reminded him of settling blood. A basalt tower that cut the horizon, where all manner of creatures gathered and fought among the steps: wizened-looking children with long claws, drowned beings with hair of seaweed and smashed shells, giant spotted salamanders who clustered like moths near the light. And at the top of the tower, a cloud of eyes that filled him with unspeakable dread.

He gripped the table, still trembling slightly. The salamander, now satisfied, curled up beneath the nearest lantern and went back to sleep.

"Well?" Pendelia asked. "What did you see?"

Aleo stared at the mark on his hand. He might have been imagining it, but there seemed to be flecks of gold within the blood.

"I think I know who I am," he said, "but not what I am."

"An oculus," Felix said. "You can see lares. It allows you to communicate with them on an instinctual level, through dreams and visions. There are others—called auditors—who can hear the spirits, but can't see them."

"Was I an auditor, once?"

"Yes."

"But this is different."

He glanced at the sleeping salamander. "Very much so."

Aleo looked around the room. "Why am I here?"

Pendelia leaned forward. "That depends. How would you feel about fomenting a little revolution?"

2

When he woke up, his hand was still on fire. He flexed it experimentally. His knuckles felt as if they'd been dragged across broken glass, although the flesh was unmarked. He walked to the bathroom and stood with his hand under cold water. It made little difference. The burn was on the inside, and no ice pack was going to help. Still, the action made him feel better. He looked for some cream to put on it, but all he could find was Vaseline with aloe. He absently rubbed his knuckles, staring at the water-flecked mirror. The bathroom was a misstep from the seventies, with a looking glass framed in wicker and two pendulous lamps hanging from a chain. The odd lamps reminded him of something, but he couldn't quite say what. They tended to sway when a truck passed too close to the house.

When you were just a little thing, his father had told him, *you used to scream every time the train passed by.* The house is evaporating! *You meant to say "vibrating," but I couldn't bear to correct you.*

He pressed *Brew* on the coffeemaker. Lights flashed, and for a moment, he thought it might blast off. But then it started to burble, as usual. He ate a banana, waiting for the travel mug to fill up. He tried to remember his name. It took a moment, as if the world's software were slowly coming to life around him. The drive whirred. He stood astride a synaptic gap. Myelin spread like frost, and when he touched it, some silver clung to his hands. He waited for a spark. Waited for the light to change. Then the machine beeped, and he remembered.

He got dressed. All of his shirts were primary colors. He chose the cleanest one. The bedroom resembled a garage sale. There were books and clothes everywhere, along with a broken set of speakers, a plastic tote filled with dusty miscellany, and scattered DVDs. He shouldered the knapsack with the broken zipper, his holy relic, which had been with him since undergrad. Threads of anxiety and desire and slender hope were woven into it. The interior pocket was always sticky, but he couldn't remember what he'd spilled there, or when.

His phone chimed. It was a text from Shelby.

Are you coming to school?

He started to reply, then closed the phone. It was a simple question, but he couldn't quite bring himself to answer. Carl would soon text him, and then Shelby again. For the past several months, they'd been treating him with kid gloves. All the kind smiles and hapless questions about what he got up to all day, how he was doing. It had seemed so odd. For a long time, he'd felt the loop closing. They cared about him, but they'd also changed the locks. And it hadn't made sense, until now.

Some people valued honesty. This was something that they announced upon meeting you, as if to properly calibrate the conversation. And then they proceeded to tenderize you with their honesty, leaving you slightly concussed. He didn't value honesty, but he was a terrible liar. Whenever he tried to dissimulate, his tongue stopped working. He couldn't keep the dark detours of the story straight. It all came unraveled in the end. So, in a way, he was slightly impressed by what they'd done. He never would have been able to fuel a piece of deception for so long. But they had committed to the lie. They'd made it into something durable, something that you could lean against without falling down. It had brought them together.

It was an Anglo-Saxon riddle. It could have been a butter churn, or sex, or some inscrutable act whose significance had faded with the parchment. The truth was in the margins, but it didn't make sense. Just a smooth surface of gold leaf, trapped under egg yolk that a monk had applied centuries ago. If he tapped it with a fingernail, it would remain inviolate. Unlike an e-book, a scroll didn't run out of energy, or require a software update. It persisted, curiously, painfully, long after its world had vanished. Someday this brilliant, harried age would pass into shadow as well, and someone like him would survey its ruins, comparing them to giant's work.

He waited for the bus to come. The sky was uncomfortably blue, and traffic roared down Albert Street. The wastebasket next to him was overflowing with plastic cups, a feast for the wasps that droned in circles around it. Light cut through the glass of the bus shelter. People glanced at him as they walked by. All he needed was an artist's statement, with an audio recording to go along with it. *Feed me. Ask me my name. Flash photography is encouraged.*

The wrong bus drove by, then the next wrong bus. The #4 was a miracle of inconsistency. It rattled along like entropy on wheels, only appearing when your back was turned. Plains University had recently purchased advertising space on buses, vans, electronic billboards, and any other conceivable surface. *This is your [insert season]. It starts with you.* They should have included the price of tuition in the advertisement.

A woman with a cane walked by him. "Beautiful day," she observed.

"It is."

He tried to smile convincingly. She smiled back. Success.

If he ever saw the woman with the cane again, he could resurrect that hazy, well-meaning smile, which signaled that, yes, the day was beautiful. She kept walking. A student's face drove by, smiling hugely. It looked almost painful. He wasn't sure that he could display that kind of enthusiasm, not even for metronomes, book-binding glue, or yoghs. It was exhausting to react to things, all day long. People claimed that frowning required more effort than smiling. But wasn't it easier to take the path of least resistance, and avoid reacting at all?

For most of his childhood, it had felt as if people were speaking a foreign language. Their drives were a mystery. What they cared about, what they fought for, remained a blurry watercolor whose flecks of color might have been anything, or nothing. When a boy would say, *Look at my new truck,* he would reply: *Bats communicate through echolocation.* When someone pushed him into the sand, he would stare at the hand in puzzlement. What had he missed? Why was there grit and cat smell in his hair? There was a mysterious choreography at work, but nobody had given him the notes. He tried to hear it. He listened so hard. But all he could hear was microwave background radiation, the white noise of everything settling into heavy matter.

I am a baby bat, he told his father. *But my echolocation is broken.*

He slid into the blue vinyl seat of the bus. Two men across from him were speaking in Farsi, while a woman yelled into her earpiece. Most of the students were manipulating their screens, tapping or stretching or thumbing from one picture to the next. They chatted without making eye contact, nodding absently, spinning empty morphemes while they texted. The bus turned a corner sharply, and he watched them slide across their seats, still typing. He was the only person looking out the window. He felt suddenly self-conscious and tried to load a social media site on his phone, but the screen froze. A blue wheel turned and turned, refusing to deliver the page. He stared at the wheel, and his stomach did a roller-coaster flip. He remembered the shrieking clepsydra, the amethyst ring that Felix wore, the salamander's kiss. Fortuna had struck his life in the sweet spot, and now he was whirling through space.

Felix needed him. They all did. And he couldn't remember the last time that someone had asked for his help. It didn't count that Shelby needed him to update her antivirus software, or that Carl sometimes faltered while preparing his taxes and couldn't remember how to declare his education credit. This was different. He'd longed for it while sitting in the sawdust at the foot of the Adventure Playground—the name that his school gave to a dangerous play structure full of splinters and sharp edges. Diving between crooked trees, watching for dragons in the vegetable patch, drawing runes while everyone else was crumpling paper for spitballs. All of it, surely, had led to this moment. The longing that had seemed unbearable, the days spent on the roof, listening for stardust, had actually meant something.

But what was he supposed to do now? What could he do with this spark in his pocket, this hungry secret, that the people he trusted had kept from him? Carl distracting him, leading him on false adventures meant to conceal the true ones, like Virgil in reverse. Shelby managing him, while something frayed beneath her kindness. Ingrid refilling his coffee, telling him not to worry, even as she waited for him to leave the room. Sam was the only one who'd hesitated. She didn't quite understand their rhythms, and he could see it in her eyes. A blip of something that might have been pity, there and gone. But he'd caught it, once or twice.

The shadow died. Felix adjusting his mask. *You. The shadow.*

What was his name? Who had he been? He touched his chest lightly, as if he could feel some ruined heart, silent alongside the other. A shadow sinus rhythm. But only a flutter of ashes remained. How did you mourn for something without a name?

He tried to remember, but the bus turned again, knocking his mind off track. A pebble came through the open window, landing on his knee. If he stayed absolutely still, it might remain on his knee. Some scrap of augury that would lead him to somewhere. But he shifted, and it fell beneath the seat.

He thought of the wanderer, who had buried his gold-friend, now remembering the warmth of the hall. How he had held and kissed his lord, his head an insensible pebble on the man's knee. Life, the medieval poets said, was a sparrow's flight through a well-lit hall. Outside was darkness and the promise of winter. Aeschere's head waited at the foot of the mere; dragons would poison you before giving up their hoard. The flight was short and erring, but what more could we do? Fate moves as it must.

The bus pulled up to the Innovation Centre. People stood beneath the shadows of the young trees, rooting through backpacks, collating, applying sticky tabs like bandages. Music was thumping from the campus green. Midterms were still a distant threat. A few choice parking spots remained, and it was still possible to drop a class without having *Withdrawn* marked on your record in burning script. Life was good.

His phone buzzed. It was Carl, as he'd predicted. They were tracking him like a stray neutrino, but the downside of closing ranks was that they no longer knew his routine. The lie was actually a beautiful thing. Like a constellation of Tinkertoys. It must have been difficult to maintain. The ridiculous idea that Carl had been playing hockey. Shelby's late-night study sessions. Even the game that Carl had invented. So close to the fire. But they were growing frustrated. They couldn't avoid the topic every time he wandered into a room, as if they were trapped in a Restoration comedy. So they'd found ways to let off steam, to let fall a crumb of knowledge here and there.

And that was how he'd begun to suspect that he wasn't crazy. That they really were keeping something from him. All the bullshit about last semester. The crazy fight in the library that they'd explained away. *It was just a LARP that got out of hand. The fire was an effect. Those hospital drugs made it look real.* The hours of therapy that he'd endured, sitting across from a man in slacks who made him practice acceptable eye contact.

How would you characterize your relationships with others?
Sketchy.

How does it make you feel when a stranger looks at you?
Like I just put my head in a bucket of scorpions.

Did you leave the house yesterday?
Yes.

Where did you go?
Lankhmar.

I'm not familiar with that neighborhood.
It's in Nehwon, between the Great Salt Marsh and the
    River Hlal.

That doesn't sound real.
You've obviously never been there.

Going to made-up places doesn't count.
Why not?

*Because they aren't real. You can't experience
    meaningful interactions.*
My interactions there are quite meaningful.

But they aren't real.
Fafhrd and the Gray Mouser would probably argue that
    fact.

Those aren't people.
Tell that to the Lankhmarese authorities.

    Social interaction, apparently, did not include books.
Which was news to him, because he'd been socially interact-
ing with books for as long as he could remember. His discipline was based on the idea that books could change your

life, that the people living inside them had a voice that you could hear. Their lives mattered, not simply because they might echo your own, but because they offered a thousand plateaus of joy and radical difference. He had followed Conan as he scaled the Tower of the Elephant. He had held his breath when Goodman Durnik presented the sorceress Polgara with a rose made of iron. He had wept bitter tears over the death of Atreyu's horse, Artax, who could not resist the Swamps of Sadness. Weren't they real? Didn't their battles, their love-turns, their outrageous mistakes, leap off the page? The whole point of reading was to live in another form, to encounter a shadow that had been following you all along.

His friends understood that. Carl and Shelby had their share of lives, reading furiously as the light changed and various essays came due. Reading as an emergency exit, reading to feel alive, reading themselves into corners, down alleys, through forests, across bridges that shuddered beneath them. They knew what it was all for. They would have been just as baffled by the psychiatrist, even if they managed to go through the motions a tad more convincingly than he could.

They knew what it meant, and what it could do. The serrated pleasure of an alliterative line, the shock of two words coming together, assuming the crash position, then suddenly flowering into a kenning that cut you deep. A riddle that would never give you up. They knew, and they made him believe that he was out of his mind.

Systems decline. Patterns unravel. It's how the universe works. A little heat escapes, and suddenly, the void isn't friendly anymore. The constant is anything but. Heraclitus dipped his toe in the river and drew it back, shocked by the change. He knew that Carl was lying to him about hockey practice but couldn't figure out why. Carl had never lied to him about anything before, save for his claim that he appreciated *Babylon 5* (in fact, he'd only watched it because he had a weird thing for Bruce Boxleitner). The lie was new, and rather than pressing, he chose to let it grow roots in the dark. Then they visited that pretty little lie of a park, across from the Dodger, whose outlines had softened to dandelion felt. And he knew that Carl's lie went deeper, because his hands were sweating and he couldn't stop looking at the broken stones.

After that, he'd run into Paul, who was on his way to Canadian Tire. Ingrid had totaled their car. *She was off-roading through the park, or something,* he'd said. *I don't get it. The car was just sitting at the foot of the legislature, and it looked like some monster had stepped on it.*

That was in the morning. He waited all day to hear more about this disaster, but there were no texts, no e-mails. He ran into Shelby at school, but when he asked her about Ingrid, she seemed confused. It was as if she'd forgotten that they knew each other. No mention of the crash. Surely, Ingrid would have said something. Even someone as distracted as he was could tell that the two of them were getting closer. That left 2.5 possibilities. (1) Shelby didn't want him to worry. (2) Shelby didn't want him to know about the accident. (2.5) The accident wasn't at all what it seemed. The fractional possibility was what made up his mind.

The next day, he followed her to the hospital. He stood behind the curtain on the other side of the room, where there was an empty bed and a radio playing. The conversation wasn't particularly illuminating, but he lived in the margins. If there was anyone who knew how to furnish a radical interpretation of the text, it was a grad student who studied Anglo-Saxon fragments that were literally crumbling. He listened. And what he heard was a different lie, something that Shelby was fashioning on the spot. It had something to do with Dr. Marsden, Ingrid's car, and the park. He had the feeling—however terrible it might be—that Trish Marsden was admitted to the hospital soon after Ingrid's car was destroyed. *It looked like some monster had stepped on it.* Perhaps the car had struck something. A big something. But what could that mean?

When they all met at the club, it felt as if they might have reached the fifth act. Someone was finally going to tell him something. Shelby and Carl seemed visibly relieved to see him there, and everyone was having such a good time. Carl's poem was both a challenge and an apology. For a moment, he thought that they might simply dance their way to some kind of truth. But then Paul was driving him home, and he could feel the vibrations of the lie, struggling to cover a surface that was now impossibly vast.

Sometimes, Paul said, staring straight ahead as they drove down Broad Street, *I think that she's keeping something from me. But I can never tell. Maybe I'm just paranoid.*

His knuckles were white as he gripped the wheel. He knew, then, that Ingrid was managing Paul in exactly the same way. Paul was too busy, or perhaps too good-natured, to tease out the threads of the lie. Paul would relieve the babysitter, put Neil to bed, and then fall asleep before his DVD had even loaded.

Ungelich is us. It's different with us.

That was the refrain of *Wulf and Eadwacer,* one of his favorite poems. Wulf brings a bundle to the woods, for no purpose that we can fathom. What's wrapped in cloth? The word *hwelp* could mean "child" or "pup." The narrator is a shadow with no name, but whatever Wulf bears to the woods belongs to her. It is their *giedd,* their riddle. *None can sunder what was never whole.* The cloth conceals a poem itself, a fragment of vellum and bone. The refrain—*it's different with us*—has been torn from all context. What could it mean? To him, it had always referred not only to those enigmatic characters, but to future readers. *It's different with us, the kind of people who find themselves in a* wyndleas *grove, or reading a poem with no beginning or end. It will always be different with us.*

Because he had one foot in the grove already, it was different. There was no trampoline leap into dreamless space. No comfort of sleep. All he could do was retrace his steps, walking back down Broad Street, toward the club. He would unwrap the riddle. Now there was a loose thread, and if he pulled—

But he didn't know what would fall out. A *hwelp*? A shadow? A word-hoard? Monsters came in all shapes and sizes. They didn't just step on your car. They could be small enough to hold to your chest as you carried them deeper into the woods. He feared that he might be the pup, wrapped in a bag and left to the elements.

Then he saw the librarian, standing in the lamplight behind the club.

And everything shifted sideways.

A memory dangled in front of him. Fire and bloody paws.

I'm Oliver.

I think I know you.

Yes. You do.

The thread was there. It had practically snagged on his thumbnail. But it was Oliver who tugged on it, pulling him out of the light and back to the park.

He walked past the frozen clock in Campus West (it had never struck him as being a "westerly" building, and none of the other wings of campus were described using the compass rose). For the first time, he realized that the clock wasn't completely dead. The second hand was mortally wounded but still struggling to move. Time shivered but couldn't bring itself to go forward. Decaying posters surrounded the clock, layer upon layer that had been stapled over each other, announcing fossilized events. The bookstore was advertising a sale on maple fudge. Students rushed by him as he stared at the clock. He could fix it. He could be a Time Lord. But it seemed best not to meddle with cosmic forces, and so he kept walking.

The department was quiet. The oversized posters of theorists watched him like Gothic paintings as he made his way down the hall. Foucault was blurry and purple. Kenneth Burke looked devilish, wearing just one glove. The faculty offices were compact, with frosted glass windows. Various articles, conference fliers, and comic strips were taped to each door.

The shared TA office was bare. He opened the door, and the smell of coffee flew out, along with a patina of stale cigarettes. He watered the ficus and turned on the computer, waiting for its sleepy parts to wake up. He wasn't even sure what he was looking for. It was just reflex. The computer yawned and struggled to pull itself together. He stared out the window. A colony of spiders was having some kind of meeting on the balcony. Students were sunning themselves below. In the office next door, he could hear strains of hip-hop.

When the computer had sufficiently roused itself, he logged onto the EBSCO database and tried a few search terms. *Wascana Park. Coyotes. Disappearances.* He had a faint memory of going through the same motions before, as if he were following his own research tracks. He read. He poured himself a coffee from the communal machine. He read some more and refilled his cup.

When he was done, he printed off a few more articles. The general office was empty, and the whine of the printer split the silence. He retrieved the warm stack of paper from the tray, then turned out the lights and locked the door behind him. If he went back to the shared TA space, someone would find him. Grad students were always dropping in and out of that snug closet as they feverishly graded exams or worked on conference papers.

Instead, he went to a classroom across the hall. It had fallen into disuse, but he had a special affection for it. Decades ago, the room had been designed for experiments involving LSD. The walls were covered in beige carpet, which reminded him of a pelt. There were no angles—the room had a peculiar ovoid shape, which he found strangely comforting.

There was a chalkboard on the far wall. Many of the other classrooms had been outfitted with space-age whiteboards that you could draw on with laser pens, transferring your ideas to a larger screen. But he liked the older technology of chalk. It broke, and you reached for another. The dust settled over everything, leaving its trace. The smudges on his sleeves reminded him that something had happened. The tutorial hadn't been written in light.

He began writing notes on the board. Like his tutorial notes, they were curlicued and mostly illegible, a mess of arrows and words that ran into each other. The result was a single stem with fantastic roots, the type of word that linguists called *agglutinative*, because it was really a small core with modifiers glued onto each end. The notes unscrolled in all directions. They became an array that made no sense.

"Coyotes can't destroy a car," he murmured.

"Clearly, you haven't watched enough Road Runner cartoons."

He looked up. Carl was standing in the doorway.

"How did you find me?"

"I heard the blizzard of chalk." Carl stepped into the room. "Plus, you always talk to yourself when you're making notes. I just had to listen for the disembodied conversation."

"I guess you know me pretty well." He returned his attention to the board. "Maybe you can clear something up. What was Ingrid's car doing in front of the legislature?"

Carl closed the door softly. Then he walked down the aisle of desks. He took a piece of chalk and drew a crude picture of a box, which he labeled *TNT.*

"There's your answer," he said.

"Stop joking."

"Andrew—"

"No. Just stop. Late-night study sessions? Hockey practice? An RPG set in ancient Rome?"

Carl took a deep breath. "Okay. I can see that you're pissed. But let's stop this merry-go-round of blame for a second, and just slow down. The situation is—unstable."

"Unstable?" Andrew put down the chalk and really looked at him—not at the safe point above Carl's shoulder but straight into his eyes. The connection jolted him. The intimacy was sharp and unexpected, but he didn't look away. "I'm a terrible liar. We both know that. What I didn't know, until this moment, is that you're an even worse one. Nothing that comes out of your mouth contains an ounce of plausibility or sense."

Carl stepped forward. "That's not completely fair. Like I said—"

"It's complicated? Life isn't a status update. Life is brutal and full of exceptions. I just never thought you would be one of them."

He looked stung. "Andrew, please. You have to give me a chance to explain."

"No need. I get it now." He returned his attention to the notes. "It doesn't make any sense, but I get it."

"There's a lot that you don't understand."

"I used to know all of this. I was part of the equation. Then—" Andrew wiped the notes clean with an eraser. "This happened. Whose fault was that, exactly?"

Carl took the eraser from his hand. "It was the park. There are rules."

"You used your emergency student loan to buy new pants. You're telling me that you couldn't bend the rules? Not even a little?"

"It's not that simple. If we'd told you anything—if we'd let something slip—"

"You made a choice."

Carl blinked in confusion. Then he leaned closer. Andrew felt the proximity run through him in currents of silver. He could smell Carl's deodorant and the faded dryer sheet that he must have fished out of someone else's machine. There was a daub of soy sauce on his jeans, like a lost island. He wanted to step back, to reestablish his personal Fortress of Solitude, but the room was beginning to shrink. He couldn't remember which direction was safest, which point on the compass promised escape.

"No," Carl said. "It was never a choice. I wanted to tell you. So many times, I nearly broke down and told you everything. But the magic doesn't work that way."

"You don't know how it works. Oliver says—"

Carl's expression hardened. "Oliver is playing with you. He's playing with all of us. I never trusted him. But Ingrid couldn't see it, and of course, nobody listens to me."

"That night at the club—" Andrew managed to take a

step back, although now his shoulder was awkwardly pressed against the board. "I was going to ask you. We were dancing, and I could see that you wanted to tell me something. I went to grab us drinks, but then I saw Ingrid talking to Paul. She told him that the babysitter had to leave early."

"She was trying to protect him."

"Why did you need to get rid of us?"

He looked uncomfortable. Andrew could see that he was weighing his options. "We met with Narses," he said finally. "Do you remember him?"

"No."

"He's a spado. Like Mardian, but with a conscience."

"Mardian." He felt his chest tighten. "It was my fault."

Carl touched his shoulder. "It wasn't. You were scared and confused. You couldn't control the salamander. It lashed out."

"I knew what I was doing. The fire and blood. It felt right."

"Andrew, you were out of your mind."

He pushed Carl away. "Do you know how many times I've wondered if I was crazy? How many times I've nearly asked for a prescription that would just make it all go away? It turns out they don't make a cocktail for that. I get to feel this every day. But you and Shelby—even Ingrid—you were the only ones who didn't make me feel broken. When I was with you, I wasn't out of my mind. I was home. I was safe. And then you started fiddling with the dial, until I couldn't tell what was real anymore."

Carl took his hand. "You're still home. Still safe. Nothing's going to happen to you. And now that you understand— now that you remember—"

"Everything can be like it was?" Andrew shook his head. "What's done is done. That person—that shadow—whatever it was, it's gone. I didn't find my way back, Carl. I came through the side door. And the view is entirely different. I'm different."

"You're still Roldan." Carl's voice broke slightly as he said the name. "Some little part of him survived."

"It's just a word. It doesn't mean anything to me."

"That's not how it's supposed to work! You must remember something—" Carl's hand was like ice. "The foxes? The frayed tapestry? You told me that we were breathing stolen air, and that was when I realized how much every day mattered."

Andrew took his hand away. "I don't know what you're talking about."

"I almost told you that night. About the crack in the lute."

"You're not making any sense."

"The crack is what makes the music. My mother taught me that. I threw the lute across the room, because I was afraid that I had no music in me. When I picked it up, the lute had a scar. But it wasn't ugly. It was a crook where love had settled. It reminded me that the instrument was alive. I touched the scar, and then I played my first song."

"You can't even play a recorder."

Carl took Andrew's hand and laid it against his chest. "Feel that. You want crazy? I look at you, and my heart sings like a tomcat. I can't make it shut up."

Andrew looked at him uncertainly. The rhythm was a match for his own. The carpeted walls were closing in again, and all he could hear was Carl's *lub-dub*, the only true thing. The equation was crumbling. He drew back.

"I have to go," he said.

"Where?"

"I could tell you—but it would be a lie."

"Andrew."

"Make it stop," he said.

Then he walked out of the room, ignoring the sound in his ears.

3

HE STARED AT THE BLUE SMUDGE IN THE fresco. It could have been anything. Outside, the light was changing. It trickled through the window slats, red-tinted, as if the day were drowning in cheap wine. The salamander was asleep on the front step, dreaming no doubt of volcanic glass, or a bed of coals to lie in. Anyone passing by would have seen a heat shimmer against the flagstones, a trick of the sun, but nothing more. Its tail left ashy whorls. It remembered the older, world-destroying fire, untamed, rushing through underground cells, warming the roots of mountains. In dreams, it basked on the edge of magma lakes, purring a threnody with its brothers and sisters. Fire, now chained to braziers and singing kettles, would not remain captive forever. One day, the blinding estuaries would rush their banks and spray hoarse pain through rocky vents. The salamander was patient, because it knew that all things were flammable.

"Is it a dolphin?"

Felix secured his mask, then looked at him. "What?"

He pointed. "The blue mark. What do you think it is?"

The mask squinted. "Maybe an undina. Or a sapphire."

"Or an eye."

"Time doesn't spare frescoes."

"Fate moves as it must."

Felix looked at him oddly. "Where did you hear that?"

"I can't remember."

"Most people say *the wheel*, not *fate*."

"What's the difference?"

"Fortuna leans her shoulder to the wheel. Fate is just—" He shrugged. "I don't know. I picture it as the winter that waits outside, knocking, always knocking."

"It sounds like we're all in this tapestry together." He returned his attention to the knife sitting on the table. "Is that part of it too? Just another thread?"

"A sharp one."

"What am I supposed to do with it?"

"Try it out. Test its balance."

"It doesn't seem to have anything to do with balance."

"Then think of it as a tool for unraveling."

He picked up the knife. Wrought animals played along the surface of its hilt, joined beak and claw. Lapidary winked in the failing light, forming spiderweb trails that danced before his eyes. It was light and heavy at the same time. The blade, serrated, reminded him of a dangerous comb that would part you, ghost from bone-house, as ivory teeth parted strands of hair.

"There used to be blades that were sharp enough to cut day and night," Felix said. "The artifices gave them impossible edges. They could cut a thought from your head. One knife could cut love out of your heart, just like paring a fish. But that risky craft is gone."

His hand moved the blade, while he watched from a distance.

"What do you expect me to do with this?"

"You'll know, when the time comes."

He looked at Felix. His tunica was slightly rumpled, his feet stained with clay. Like the mosaic, he seemed to flicker, his shadow prowling along the frame. Those parts of him smudged by ash and dirt, the parts that time hadn't spared, were the most interesting. They were already weighted with a regret, words that had outlived their story. He had made up his mind to do something—that much was visible in the settling. He had his own shoulder to the wheel, but it was yet too dark to catch a glimpse of the outcome. The spokes sang out. He felt his hoard opening, every precious thing rising to the surface.

> *currite ducentes subtegmina,*
> *currite, fusi*

The words broke into a run. They had slept beneath the dragon, beneath his vast, bejeweled softness, warmed into insensibility. Now they were on the move, and he saw their meaning in a flash as they passed by him. Spindles running in the deep dark, running toward something that was smoke, enormity, spreading end. There was a path through the smoke, but he couldn't quite see it. Maybe the smoke itself was the path. Something breathed nearby, and he knew that there wasn't much time.

"What are you thinking?"

He looked again at Felix. "Your name means luck."

"That's one interpretation."

"Will this work? If I believe in you, in your name—is there a chance?"

Felix fingered the die around his neck. "Always."

"I've never killed anything."

"Are you so sure of that?"

He blinked. "I suppose not. My shadow—did he—"

"There's no sense looking back. Everything changes tonight."

He placed the knife in a brass sheath, which he belted to his new tunica. The weight was oddly comforting, which surprised him.

"I think I'm ready. I just have to follow the smoke."

Felix frowned. "Does that mean what I think?"

"I'm not sure. But it's all I can see, for the moment." He looked once more at the blue smudge on the fresco. Then he laughed. "*That's* what it was. The whole time."

"What do you see?"

"Never mind. Let's go."

They left the house. Felix shut the door and locked it with an L-shaped key. Its layer of gold had flaked off, but it was still a formidable device in his hands. The house seemed to shrink as they stepped away from it. Pressed so close to the curtain wall, it was hard to say whether it belonged to the city at all. Felix had told him that it was a tricky place, a kind of crossroads—that he must never take its magic for granted. The salamander looked up. Its eyes were old, but not kind. He knelt down and carefully scratched its head, just with the tips of his fingers. He thought it might bite him again, but instead it began to purr.

"Can the lares speak?"

"Only the auditores hear them," Felix said. "And only the oculi see them. If you could do both, you'd probably go mad."

"I wonder what they sound like."

"I'm told it's like reading a book, all at once. Their thoughts press the wax of your senses. The conversation isn't strictly consensual."

"If you could speak," he said to the salamander, "you might tell me what to do. Although, I suppose you did lead me here. That didn't require words."

Felix chuckled. "It's funny—listening to you converse with the air. Before, there were pauses, while you waited for a reply."

"Before?"

Felix smiled. "You fed him apple peels. I watched them vanish. I suppose it was the first real piece of magic I'd seen, close up."

He looked at the salamander again. "*This* one? We've met before?"

"I've no idea. I can't see it, remember?"

The sense of recognition was faint. He couldn't tell if it meant anything or if it was just a trick of the creature's gaze. For a moment, he felt as if every salamander watched him, staring curiously through those speckled eyes. But he couldn't say for sure. The more he looked at it, the blurrier it grew, until it was a mirage at his feet.

They walked uphill. This time, the Subura was different. He no longer noticed the riot of people, the gleaming cups and wreaths. The snores that rose from behind paving stones, the puddles of wine and fouler fare, didn't capture his attention. What he saw, for the first time, were the lares. They were everywhere. Dark geniuses of the city, crawling and floating and making their inarticulate way through the dust. Salamanders slept in piles by the roadside shrines. A few intrepid ones had crawled into the basin and were lapping up the oil with pink tongues. But most of them snored at the base of the altar, rumbling as loud as the wagons that passed by. It was strange that he could hear their noises but not their speech. Perhaps the auditores, of which Felix spoke, could also see hints of them without perceiving the whole.

The salamanders weren't alone. Semitransparent things peeked over the rims of fountains, watching him with eyes like sallow green lamps. They were covered in bits of shell and long strands of kelp. Some of them had beards, where ghost crabs slept, claws twitching as they dreamed of underwater cloisters. The undinae swam in slow circles or crouched in the spray, following his progress silently. He looked up and realized that they were also a current of shadow, moving along the top of the great aqueduct. They bobbed and leapt in the channel of water, occasionally scurrying along the sides of the basin. Somehow they could cling to the stone without falling. It might have had something to do with their webbed hands.

He saw a child standing in the mouth of an alley. He started to draw closer, but the salamander growled and stepped in front of him. The child's face contorted, and he realized that it wasn't human. It was made of some hard, striated substance, like petrified wood. It hissed at the salamander, then ran back down the alley, dragging its claws along the brick wall. He could hear their din, shrill at first, then receding, until the creature had vanished.

Felix touched his shoulder. It startled him. The mask looked concerned.

"You nearly wandered into the path of a litter. If you don't keep your eyes on the road, you'll be trampled."

"Sorry." He swallowed. "I'm distracted."

"You can see them."

He nodded. "They're all over the place. Why doesn't anyone notice?"

"People see what's in front of them. The road. The bottegha with half-priced goods. They aren't trained to notice spirits."

"It's hard not to trip over them." He glanced down another alley. "Some don't appear to be friendly. Even the salamander is wary."

"Lares are territorial."

"Are they older than the city?"

"Nobody knows their age. The ones you're seeing might have been here since the beginning, when Anfractus was a collection of huts and fire pits. Or you could be looking at the grandchildren of those old ones. There's no way to tell for sure."

"We could check their teeth. Doesn't that work with horses?"

Felix grinned. "You first."

As he watched, he realized that the lares had burrowed their way into human affairs. The salamanders gathered by forges, braziers, and the public baths. Where they slept, the fires burned hotter and brighter. The undinae crowded the fountains and slithered along the aqueduct. Their fins stirred up the water, keeping it clear of debris, encouraging the pipes to flow. He couldn't quite tell what the petrified wood children were doing, but he imagined that it had something to do with the upkeep of the alleys. If Anfractus was the city of infinite alleys, then perhaps their task was the most essential of all. Not that he wanted to meet one up close. Their claws could crack bone as easily as brick.

He saw the smoke as it moved on gray paws, high above the insulae. The pigeons watched as well from their aeries, fluttering nervously at the massing clouds. There was something inside the smoke. A glimmering piece of network, a cluster of red-rimmed eyes that saw him, not just as he was, but as he might be.

Don't look, the pigeons said. *Tend your own nest.*

But he had to look. And the smoke grew darker, until it was a dragon, yawning oblivion as it watched him from above. Its scales were filth and torpor, rubbing against blackened chimneys, gleaming with night soil. And yet there was something beautiful about it, the glide of its disaster, the tail of ash and lucre. The eyes flamed, every scale an eye, until the mist was all that he had ever known. He heard something, but whether it was a word or an old spark coming to life in the heart of the cumulus, he couldn't say.

"What are you looking at?"

He realized that Felix was staring at him, along with a few strangers. He was standing dangerously close to the middle of the road. He shook his head, as if to clear it. Then he stepped back onto the curb.

"Ghosts," he said. "I think."

"You can see *them*?"

For the first time, he heard real fear. It wasn't the mask talking. Felix himself was looking out from the plane of silver. His eyes were slightly wide. For a moment, he was a child, asking whether dragons slept under the bed.

"I'm not sure," he said. "Nothing is clear. I feel as if I'm learning to see for the first time. Maybe it's like building a muscle. The salamanders are bright. The swimmers and the children with knives for fingernails—they're less distinct."

"And what of—" He looked up, wordlessly.

"Smoke. The breath of the city. That's all it is."

"You're certain."

"No," he murmured. "I wish that I were."

"Some people think that they never left—the lares of the air. That they've merely been biding their time, watching us from above."

He looked up again, but the dragon's shadow was gone.

All he could see was the ashen halo, a black curtain brushing the tallest buildings. The salamander had paused next to him. It also watched the sky, and its expression remained impossible to read. It seemed to be looking back through time, to a much older skyline. Beginnings and endings collided within its gold irises, half-lines of verse that were balanced by a cut, so neither could devour the other. Sadness rose from the bitter, burned caesura. Somewhere along that cruel staff, which had witnessed suns of a different color, the lizard saw its own end. Just another pause in this pale yard, where they all waited for the smoke to make its move.

"And she wants to bring them back?"

Felix nodded. "She aims to make a deal. She's forgotten that you can't bargain with something that hates you."

"What about the giant goats?"

"The silenoi? They're hungry and impatient. They don't realize it yet, but she's backed them into a corner."

Violets were blooming around them. The path sloped sharply upward as they approached the arx. He expected a steady stream of wagon traffic and opulent carriages, but the road was deserted. Figures in armor patrolled the margins. One of them noticed Felix and nodded. The meretrix raised his hand in greeting.

"They haven't yet figured out that they can't trust me," he said. "It's the mask. It plays tricks on the best of them."

"How do I know it isn't working on me?"

"I suppose you can't ever know for sure."

He frowned. "Maybe your intention is to betray us all—including Pendelia and Mardian. They don't seem to trust you either."

"They trust my connections. All I am to them is a key." He smiled. "If I bubbled them, I'd die horribly. Something long and imaginative. Spadones have a knack for torture."

"You could always escape. Through the house, or one of the alleys."

"All the alleys are connected. Mardian would find me, just as he found you, once. Besides. I'm not just protecting myself."

Before he had the chance to ask what this meant, they reached the entrance. Miles stood by the painted doors, their bronze armor gleaming in the half-light. Red-and-white horseshoe arches supported the gate, forming an ingenious vault that was carved with braided designs. The geometric shapes made him dizzy for a moment, but he recovered. The trick was not to stare at them directly. Like the smoke, they had to be met with a kind of deference. Salamanders lazed at the foot of the arches, watching him absently. One of them was practically touching the sandal of a nearby miles. What was it like, standing adjacent to wonder, not seeing its pink tongue hovering next to your toenail?

Beyond the miles, he saw a snaking corridor that seemed to end in sharp angles. He could hear nothing beyond it. Just the hiss of the lamps, swaying on their chains, and the rustling of brass scales whenever a guard moved. The doors were painted with hexagons, interlocking to form strange patterns that might have been animals or human faces.

A woman in a plumed helmet stepped forward. Her hand rested on the pommel of her blade, which was carved with undinae. The likeness, he realized, was cheap.

"Who's this?"

"Entertainment," Felix said. "An oculus was requested."

"Not to my knowledge."

Felix stiffened slightly. "The girl wants fireworks. Do you want to tell her that you've barred the oculus? Because she likes me, but she'll feed you to the lampreys if you spoil this evening for her."

The miles looked uncertain. "I thought the lampreys died with her grandmother."

"They keep them in the carcer, in a lightless room. I've seen them." Felix shivered. "It's no way to meet the wheel, I can tell you that."

She looked again at him. "You can really do fireworks?"

"Yes." He tried to make it a statement, rather than a question.

"Fine. Let's see them."

"Right here?"

"Good a place as any."

He stared at Felix. The mask said: *I've done my job. This is on you.*

His salamander had wandered off. The one sleeping by her sandal was starting to rouse itself, though. It looked at him with one eye. He knelt down beside it. He drew an orange peel out of his tunica. Some of the fragrance, no doubt, would cleave to the blade. The salamander brightened when it saw the peel. He laid it on the ground. It sniffed the treat, then devoured it in a single bite. The miles swore softly. Although she couldn't see the salamander, she'd definitely seen the peel vanish, as if the dust had swallowed it.

"I'm not completely sure how this works," he whispered, "but I'd be grateful if you could breathe a bit of fire. Just a little bit. I don't want you to burn anything down. Even a smoke ring or two would—"

The salamander belched.

Flame scoured the spot directly in front of the miles, and she jumped back to avoid it. He smelled sulfur, and something that might have been undigested meat. Then the salamander, pleased with itself, curled into a burnished ball and went back to sleep. Its full stomach would no doubt bring pleasant dreams.

"Fortuna's cunny! That nearly singed me!"

"They love oranges." It was all he could think to say.

"Satisfied?" Felix asked.

The miles stepped aside. "Go ahead. But if the spado holds you up, don't mention me. I've no desire to cross that mean little spider."

They walked past the gates and down the corridor. He looked up and saw archers poised in landings above. At every blind corner, a sagittarius waited, bow trained. They crouched in front of murder holes, and all he could see were the gleaming points of arrows, a cloud that might break open at any moment.

"Was she talking about Mardian?" He tried to keep his voice down.

"We're well positioned. As long as nobody sounds the alarm, this could work."

"You don't sound certain."

"Now I'm the one who's distracted," he murmured, glancing at the archers. "There are a million ways to die here."

"We got in too easily. That can't be good."

"It's not just the inside that I'm worried about. There are other dice in the cup."

"You mean—" He felt something in the pit of his stomach. "My old company."

Felix looked at him closely. "They're strangers to you, now. It may not feel that way, but trust me. You've paid your debt to them."

Felix led him deeper into the arx. He marveled at the stalactite ceilings, where eyes both painted and real watched him from dizzying panels. Tapestries depicted Fortuna in all of her guises: masked, armed, locked in an embrace, reflecting bone. In the last image, she was a ragged fur, alone, clutching a bronze dagger. He looked down and realized that the salamander was still following them. It studied the tapestries, exhaling two thin plumes of smoke as it pondered the dance of Fortuna. There were no lares woven in the background, and he couldn't tell if the lizard was slightly offended or not.

Now he could hear voices. It might have been a party or a war council. He couldn't make out what anyone was saying. They climbed a flight of stairs, which ended in a dirty clerestory, full of disused fountains with lion's heads. There was a pile of frayed textiles in one corner, and something unidentifiable in the other, which smelled awful. He thought he could make out a few animal bones and small shadows moving in the margins, which were probably rats.

"It's not much," Felix said, "but it offers a splendid view."

He looked down and realized that he could see into a grand chamber below. There was a throne in the center, attached to a metal cylinder that was currently raised about five feet off the ground. A woman sat on the pneumatic throne, and everyone was watching her while trying to appear as if they were occupied with other things. She wore a pearl diadem and a gold collar that caught the light of a hundred swinging lamps. Her expression was distant. Before he could examine her more closely, Felix pulled him toward the ruined fountain.

"If she sees us," he whispered, "we're not getting out of here alive."

He knelt by the ledge. The chamber was crawling with miles and sagittarii. They were looking unsteadily at a group of creatures that gathered some distance away from the throne. Parts of them were vaguely human, although he couldn't stop himself from staring at their cloven feet. One of them wore a heavy gold chain, and he was watching the woman with the pearl earrings, suspended in space. He felt as if he'd seen this monster—this *silenus*—before, but the details were only a faint impression. A memory of some other life. He knew that he should be frightened. They were surrounded, not just by blades and arrows, but by creatures who had stepped out of an ominous frieze. This was not his world, however much Felix told him otherwise. He had no idea what to do.

But it wasn't fear that he felt. It was a dark sense of excitement. He looked down at the salamander and saw that it too, was waiting. Its tail dusted the ground. Something was about to happen, and it was larger than him, larger than this gilded palace surrounded by violets and knives. He was a stone in someone else's game, but for the first time, he could see the board clearly. The next move would change everything. He might not survive the glide across that dark space, but wasn't it worth the risk? To be part of something primeval. To step into those tapestries, where even Fortuna herself was alone. Some part of him had always wanted this. He'd just never expected that it would happen next to a pile of bones and mouse droppings.

"What's he doing here?"

A girl in a violet dress was standing at the foot of the stairs. Her soft shoes had holes in them, and her hair was in disarray. Only half of it was swept up in glittering pins, while the other half sagged, like a deflated cake. She must have been about ten years old, though her expression had a shrewdness that he wouldn't have associated with a child. She had the eyes of a royal daughter, expectant, freighted with a thin sadness. It wasn't ultimately the girl that drew his attention, though. It was the two mechanical foxes that crouched on either side of her.

He took a step forward. The foxes whirred as they regarded him, their black eyes swiveling in delicate brass cases. One was slightly smaller than the other. He heard a faint growl and realized that it was the salamander. It approached them warily. The foxes didn't move. It was clear that they could see the lizard, but they weren't about to offer a salutation.

"Quickly," Felix said, "come over here, before she catches sight of you."

The girl joined them in the shadows. "What are you doing here? And who is—" She frowned, looking at him. "Wait. I think I know you."

"Not exactly," Felix replied. "It's hard to explain. You shouldn't be here, Eumachia. It's not safe." He turned to the larger fox. "Propertius, can you take her somewhere less exposed? I have a key to one of the hidden cells."

"We merely advise," the fox answered. His voice was low and had an odd, mechanical purr to it. "We can't drag her down the stairs."

Felix sighed. "This is about to get ugly."

"Are they alive?" He couldn't stop looking at the foxes. "Or is it some trick?"

"You have a short memory," the smaller fox said. "When last we met, you knew the measure of us. Even after you'd just—"

Felix raised his hand to cut her off. "I don't mean to be rude, Sulpicia, but now isn't the best time to revisit that night. The shadow that you remember is no more."

"I can see that." She inclined her head. "My condolences."

Eumachia stared at him again. "*Oh*. The auditor's dead."

"That's what they tell me," he said.

"I'm sorry," she added. "I didn't mind him." Before he could respond, she returned her attention to Felix. "I don't understand, though. Why aren't you with the others? Wasn't that why I gave you the note?"

He frowned. "What note?"

Felix didn't answer. Instead, he approached the edge. Something was happening. The foxes drew closer, silencing their gears. Eumachia followed. Below, he saw a round figure in a green tunic approach the raised throne. It was Mardian. He held something bulky, wrapped in embroidered silk. It was long enough to be a sword. He heard a *thrum* as the chair lowered itself on the metal cylinder, until she was at ground level. Then the basilissa rose, and all eyes were on her as she received the gift. Mardian didn't look up. He bowed slightly, and stepped back.

We're well positioned, Felix had said.

But what was the note? Why did the girl seem confused?

Something wasn't right. It occurred to him that he couldn't see the entirety of Felix's plan. Only the mask saw everything, while the others remained in the dark. Even the foxes might have been uncertain, though their flawless eyes registered no emotion.

He couldn't say why he chose to look away from the scene below. Everyone was waiting for her to unwrap the silk. But for some reason, he stared across the room, at the mirror image of the clerestory where they were hiding. There was another staircase, joined to another landing, with its own ruined fountains and pile of bones. He could barely make out four figures, leaning over their own shadow edge. Watching.

Most of them, anyhow.

Their gaze was fixed on the strange tableau: monsters on one side, armed guards on the other, and in the middle, a woman holding something in her hands that might have been a weapon, or a body, some secret that had lain in an undercroft for centuries. A riddle that someone had borne to the woods, rain-soaked, never whole to begin with.

He felt a shock of recognition move through him. This was his company. Or it had been, in some dark before. There was a sagittarius in a rust-colored cloak, leaning against her bow. She had dark, tangled hair, and her eyes were fixed on the throne. Beside her, a miles stood, one hand resting on her sword. The lamplight caught her lone greave, making it shine like quicksilver. She was studying the guards. Next to her, an artifex was fiddling with something—he couldn't be sure, but it looked almost like a frog. Her hair was tied back, and she seemed entirely distracted by the device in her hand. She had no clue that across the gap of smoke and wavering light, two mechanical foxes were examining her workmanship.

But the fourth member of the company was looking at him. A trovador in a torn cloak, embroidered with what might have been dancing tigers. He held a lute, ridiculously, as if it were the closest thing he could find to a sword. They saw each other, he on one island, the trovador on another, fen-fast, worn down by pitiless tides. The smoke was all that joined them, parting momentarily so that they could gaze across these margins, which neither had chosen. The singer looked as if he might say something.

Then the basilissa raised her voice.

"This treasure was separated from its rightful home. It brings me great satisfaction to return it. Let this exchange mark a new age of cooperation for our people."

She held a horn, which looked as if it had been carved from a mammoth's tusk. It was gilded with silver bands, and carved figures moved along its surface, engaged in some secret colloquy whose details remained elusive. If he squinted, the forms might have been lares, dancing to the edge of the horn's gilded tip. Mardian was staring at it with undisguised hunger.

The silenus in the gold chain approached. For the first time, he saw streaks of green in the creature's fur and gemstones in his long hair. The basilissa displayed the horn but didn't quite give it up. She was still in control.

"We share this world with wonders," she said. "Spirits that emerged from the void, long before we built our cities. They are Fortuna's children—the lares." She wore a wry smile. "Of course, I have never seen them. I was never touched by that dark gift. But I am told that we all have our chaos. The air that we breathe is not ours alone. It once belonged to those exiled spirits of the air: the caela."

The silenoi looked uneasy when she spoke the word, if monsters could be said to look uneasy. All except for the one with the gold chain. His eyes never left the ivory horn. Even the singer was watching it, now. The night seemed to pivot upon it, a salvaged star from another world, slowly burning the edges of their own.

Latona raised the horn. "I am the daughter of imperium. Some say that rule has fallen, that our cities stand ruined, like the work of giants. But imperium cannot die. It has only slept, waiting for the return of its heralds."

"She means to do it," Felix whispered. "We must act now."

"I don't know what to do."

"Look around. There are no auditores, no oculi. The gens aren't here. This meeting was never sanctioned. It's just us, and her. That means you have a chance."

He looked across the throne room. "Why aren't we with them?"

Before Felix could answer, he heard a murmuring below. Latona was passing the horn to the silenus. The guards held themselves absolutely still. Mardian stood behind the throne. Suddenly, he realized that Pendelia should have been there. Nothing was right. The tapestry was fraying at the edges, and he didn't know where to leap.

The lares had begun to creep into the chamber. Salamanders were drawn to the lamps, while undinae dipped their webbed hands in the finger bowls. Gnomoi crawled along the ground, leaving claw marks on the flagstones. All of them were staring at the horn. They hissed in unison, and the sound made him feel as if the world were ending. It cleaved every part of him, a vibration that threatened to shake the walls of the arx. But nobody else seemed to hear it.

Shadows moved beyond the high, tempered windows. No. Not shadows. Clouds. A storm that had quite suddenly taken notice.

"When the horn sounds," Latona said, "all our ghosts are mended. The lares of the air will return, and with their power, we shall heal imperium. A new age begins tonight."

"What do I do?" He stared at Felix. "Tell me what to do!"

But even as he said the words, he felt everything slow to a crawl. Thunder shook the glass. Lightning flashed them all into startling relief, and for a single moment, he saw the pattern. From edge to edge, he saw it, and knew what came next.

The silenus put the horn to his lips and blew a single note.

The glass broke, showering the throne room in colored shards. They skittered in drifts across the marble floor. The smoke poured in, blacking out the lanterns, spreading across the chamber until everything was in shadow.

He saw the dragon open its jaws. His death was beneath its tongue. He saw the miles raise something into the air, an impossible glitter. It was a die.

He reached out and tore the die from Felix's neck.

Then he was shouting

Then he was flying.

4

A ROLL ON A STOLEN DIE.

He stood on the edge of the stone landing, arms out for balance. The chaos revolved below him, little fireworks that were people with weapons, a woman in pearls, a rain of glass fragments swept up in dark clouds. Bows aimed at shadows, blades grim under lamplight, whispering out of bronze scabbards. Every pommel a head of Fortuna, chipped or worn smooth by hands, greening now with age. The heads moved in a bizarre puppet show. He saw her down there, watching, even as she spoke to him from above:

A double roll, no less. When was the last time such a thing happened? I can't remember, which is strange, because I remember everything.

One of his sandals fell, striking the floor. *Boom!* It was a thunderclap, landing on the black-and-white mosaic. Latona looked up, her pearls a net of fire beneath the lamps. At first, she couldn't quite see him. But then she was able to make him out, a stick of a thing with one bare foot, waving his arms. Her eyes narrowed, and he could feel her opening a small, inlaid box that contained extraordinary deaths.

He expected her to shout, but she didn't. She was waiting to see if he would fall.

Impudence is what I call it. A nemo's roll. What could be more dangerous? And now three are involved. Oculus, meretrix, and miles. Let the smoke sort it out. Let the twilight rider take them all. Why not?

Time moved slowly, trapped in amber. Latona was forever looking up at him. Felix was frozen in his surprise. Where the black die had hung, there was only his bare throat. Eumachia was a child's statue in purple slippers. In the mirror clerestory, his old company was reflected, unable to move. The singer looked sad. His fingers hovered over the lute strings. The smoke shimmered below, a curtain of black scales. He could feel himself begin to slip, but the descent would last forever. They were all caught in Fortuna's blink. He knew, without being able to turn, that the eyes of the lion-head fountain were upon him. The stone mouth twisted into a smile as the rats looked up from their nest of bones, and the foxes watched the rats in turn.

What do you really want? In the settling dark, in the moment just before sleep, when the words fall—what is it? Do you even know? All I see is a child with a missing sandal.

Now he was leaning, about to fall. And his body would make no sound. It would surrender to the mosaic, until he was just another tessera. How could he be more than a tile in this story? By what right did he ask for something different? The stone was slippery. It bit into his left foot, a salamander's kiss. Was the creature still behind him? There was no way to look. The others were coiled in golden hoards. The lares would tear him apart. No reasoning with something older than language. Smoke would devour what was left.

They're ghosts, you know. It's their world too, and you've got to share.

"Share what?" he asked. But he already knew the answer. The mosaic waited. It was growing larger in anticipation. Smoke strained against the roof. The die in his hand was sucking in all of the light. It was a piece of the night gens. Though it didn't belong to him, it still knew him, responding to his touch with frost. On the other side, the second die radiated heat. They were stars meeting for the first time, circling each other warily.

Are you ready?

"I don't know!" He clutched the die with its freezing white pips. "What if this isn't the answer? What if I'm wrong?"

There was no response.

He couldn't tell the difference between flying and falling. The stone lion was silent. He knew nothing. Then Fortuna blinked. The smoke rushed up. The lute sounded a note that made the whole arx tremble.

He leaned into the song. He may have only been a tile, but he would not shatter. He was volcanic glass, euphony, stardust. Life was a swallow's flight through a well-lit hall, surrounded on all sides by measureless dark. But he was more than a tessera. They all were. They contained mosaics, defiant in their color. Not one story. A dazzling floor of possibilities, where pale marble touched aquamarine. Fate moved as it must, but you could still leap. And your doom would lift you on wings of cinder and smoke.

The mosaic turned, black on white on black, his tumulus. He closed his eyes. But the impact never came. The smoke was holding him, curiously, almost carefully. Hundreds of eyes watched him from within the cloud of ash. Eyes and wings and tongues, moving roughly down his body, as a lioness might wash her cub into shape. He hung in the dark, unable to move or speak, while bright eyes took the measure of him. Beyond that hungry curtain, he could make out the outlines of the throne room, pinpoints of lamplight, shadows, all gauzy and indistinct. It was getting harder to breathe. His eyes watered, and he thought he might sneeze. It seemed rude to sneeze in front of all those eyes. The lares were currently holding him over empty space, and any sudden movement might cause them to let go.

The eyes flickered, staring first at him, then at each other. Some of them watched the ivory horn, which the chief of the silenoi was holding. The silenus was trying to gather his brethren, most of whom were scattered across the room, snarling at miles who had drawn their green-headed blades. Others advanced upon the ring of sagittarii, who struggled to keep everyone in sight of their bows. The horn was the clearest thing in the room, beyond the veil of smoke. It shone like a quartz filament. The chieftain almost seemed to have forgotten what he was holding. He was too busy growling commands across the wide mosaic.

He strained to see the landing, where the other company waited. They were gone. He could just make out four shapes, running down the stairs.

This was the gift of the stolen roll. This blink of a moment, riding on wings of smoke. The chance would never come again.

He returned the gaze of the cacla. He looked into the ruby window of eyes, all of which were attempting to translate his position. What was this fly, dangling before them? Should they hold on, or let go?

What do you really want?

Fortuna's question applied to them both, oculus and ancient cloud. He still wasn't sure that he could answer for himself, but he knew what they wanted. It was in their grasp, and they only hesitated because of what he was. A seer with one sandal, twirling in the wind. A nemo whose greatest trick had been stealing a wolf's die.

He pointed to the horn. "Take me to it," he said, "and you'll have what you want. More than this city of alleys. More than you've dreamed of, locked in cells of smoke for a thousand years. It's your world too. And I'll give it to you. I swear it."

The eyes regarded him for a long moment. They blinked in unison. He heard thunder in his ears, but he couldn't tell if it was a storm or his own heart struggling to beat.

Then he was racing downward. The smoke no longer held him in its core. He was riding the black dragon, its catastrophic wings unfurling around him, beating the air. The lamps blew out. All was dark, save for the moss-colored eyes of the silenoi, and the gleaming horn.

The caela shrieked, and the hammer of their voice broke Latona's chair. It burst into sparks and deadly metal snowflakes that spun across the room. He realized that it was also his scream, but the sound was pierced with joy. He raised both of his arms, forgetting to hold on to the insubstantial dragon as it swooped down, laughing as the throne burst asunder.

The princeps of the silenoi looked up. Who knows what he must have thought as he saw a transparent dragon rushing toward him, with a pale, whooping creature on its back? They skimmed close to the black-and-white floor. The tesserae rushed past, and he reached out, so far that he nearly fell. The horn was a flash of moonlight that didn't belong. It froze the air, just as the die had, after Fortuna breathed on it. For a moment, they were both touching ivory. His hand brushed the silenus, and the dark hair—which seemed coarse from a distance—was surprisingly soft. He had only a second to marvel at this.

Then the horn was in his grasp, and he pulled with all of his strength. He couldn't say what made the creature let go. Simple astonishment, perhaps. Those green eyes fixed on him, and he was terrified. But there was no time to hesitate. The horn froze his fingers as he lifted it, and the wings carried him away. He couldn't believe his luck. The patterns in the ivory had been carved by some unearthly stylus. They formed the very dragon that he rode upon, breaking free of a dawn-forged chain. Fortuna watched the wings as they unfurled, her expression impossible to read.

Bright pain raked across his arm. He cried out and saw that the chief of the silenoi was directly below him, claws outstretched. He was screaming something, most likely an imprecation, but the dark vowels were meaningless. He reached for his spear, just as the pillar of smoke leapt upward and away. The spear was a line of barbed beauty. Then it was receding.

He looked down, trembling from the pain. His tunica was shredded, and there were crooked lines beneath it, welling up with blood. It dripped down his arm and pooled within the smoke, wine blooming at the bottom of a dark vessel. The caela paid no attention. They swirled across the oecus, heading for the vaulted exit.

Miles and sagittarii ran toward the opening. Arrows tore through the smoke, narrowly missing him. Swords flashed like bright threads against the underbelly of the creature. He wasn't sure if it was possible to hurt something made of vapor, but he didn't want to take the chance. The smoke was his only means of escape. He looked down and saw the salamanders, still outraged by the darkening of the lamps. They were moving toward the overturned braziers, which had scattered hot coals across the floor.

"Lares of fire!" he called.

The salamanders looked up. Their golden eyes were coins in the dim light, wobbling between heads and tails. They were torn between his voice and the lure of embers.

"Give me a wall of flame," he shouted, "and I promise to keep all of your shrines lit, from now until the end of days! I'll show you the way to the heart of the arx, where a great hypocaust warms every bath and chamber. You'll have more coals than you could ever dream of!"

The salamanders hesitated. They were slow to decide on anything, when the heat was so far away. Then, his lizard the one who'd bitten him and shown him the way—opened its mouth and yawned a tongue of flame. The others exchanged a look.

He heard them inhale: the low whistle of a bellows.

Then fire arced in every direction, a font of light that turned the oecus into a forge. The miles raised their gilded shields, only to drop them as they glowed cherry-red. Arrows burned in midflight, until the room was alive with falling stars. Yew bows cracked and melted. At last, fire followed smoke as the dragon roared past. He had to duck to avoid the stalactite ceiling beyond the double doors. He didn't know what he was holding on to. There was only the smell of ashes, the soaring pain in his arm, and the cries receding behind them.

The passages of the arx were a blur of color. Painted

horseshoe arches, embossed golden panels, tapestries that looked more like ribbons as they flew past. He could hear shouting and the clamor of caligae on flagstones, nails scraping the floor. He had lost his salamander, and through the dull pain, that realization made him nervous. Funny how diving into space couldn't equal that feeling in the pit of his stomach. He craned his neck, half expecting to see the lizard keeping pace behind him, or a skulk of mechanical foxes. But there was nothing. Felix had disappeared. No company followed him. The smoke advanced in all directions.

They burst into the night, and he smelled violets. The two miles on duty stared at his mount, then at him, and their faces went white. One advanced, raising his weapon, but the smoke whirled past him before he could swing.

It suddenly occurred to him that he didn't know how to steer the dragon.

He raised the horn with his good hand. "Stop!"

The caela obeyed.

The red curtain of eyes looked at him. The cinder wings fluttered. If a dragon could be said to look expectant, that was what the uncanny gaze felt like.

Had he even thought beyond this moment? He was holding a relic and riding a nightmare, but what came next? In a few moments, every archer and guardian and hired sword in Anfractus would be chasing him.

He didn't know how its particular magic worked. Did the lares of air submit to its power? Surely, they didn't obey him simply because he was an oculus. If that were the case, then anyone could influence them. It had to be the horn. The chieftain of the silenus had sounded the note that released them, but where had they been? Languishing in some kind of unseen captivity? He had the feeling, which grew stronger with every moment, that the caela had never left.

Whatever the nature of the horn, it was too volatile. It needed to stay lost.

"Take me to the house by the wall," he said. "You should be able to smell it. The border between worlds there is—"

But they were already on the move. They passed tall

insulae where the wealthy organized tabularia while the poor fed pigeons. Cauponae that glowed from the inside, fluttering with drunken laughter. Sleeping botteghi that were shuttered for the night, their windows offering hoards of necessary things: lamps with self-trimming wicks, rainproof tunicae, personalized rock crystal charms, and weapons for every occasion. A hair salon was still open, and the tonstrix watched him soar past, her eyes widening as she was about to shave a customer.

They flew through the Subura, and drunken celebrants scattered before them, dropping their wine cups. He was high enough to see various couples and triads, their shutters thrown open to the warm night, sweating against threadbare sheets. Two women kissed on a balcony, so absorbed that they didn't think to look up. All around him, love carved its deep ruts into the road, wheels singing. It did not stop to admire the dragon.

As they neared the wall, he saw flickering light. At first, he thought it was merely the lamps. But then he saw that the house was on fire.

"No!"

The caela trembled. There was no rhyme or reason to his exclamation—they couldn't decipher it. But it sounded like *stop.* The dragon wheeled about, and he fell, rolling across the sharp stones. He landed on his good side, but the impact still tore through his wounded arm, making him cry out. His mouth was dry, and everything felt too hard and brilliant. The pain was threading him through its eye. Soon, he would be flat and senseless, a scream stitched into an unremarkable tapestry.

The roof of the house was ablaze. Smoke poured through the windows, and a clutch of salamanders had arrived to take in the beauty of the flames. Their brass-button eyes followed the progress of the disaster, while a few basked near the ruined entrance.

His arm was throbbing. He looked around, wincing from the heat. Aside from the lares, this corner of the street was empty. Surely, this was Latona's work. She was blocking his escape. But how had she known? Had someone warned her? Perhaps burning down the house was simply hedging her bets. This dark miracle by the wall was too dangerous. She couldn't allow people to bypass the alleys. This was her city, and she controlled the exits.

Someone called out a name that he didn't recognize. He turned, holding his arm. It was starting to go numb. A man in a torn cloak stood in the street. The flames threw his shadow against the ground. It was the singer. His eyes were strangely familiar, but the rest of him remained opaque. He said the name again.

"That's not me."

"I'm not convinced," Babieca said.

"You'd better go. She's coming for me."

"She's coming for all of us. I'm not going anywhere."

He pointed to the dragon, which hovered nearby. "Are you blind? This is a monster. And not the kind that we've domesticated. It will devour you."

"Doesn't seem to be doing much devouring at the moment."

He had a point. The caela were no longer watching them. Instead, the eyes were fixed on the crowd of lares, which had gathered near the margins of the fire. They observed each other from a politic distance. It was a kind of family reunion, without the food. Unless he and the singer were to be the food. That remained a possibility.

"You have to go," he said again. This time, he wasn't as convinced. The pain was making everything narrow. It was getting harder to concentrate.

"We've been over this."

"What's wrong with you? Do you think you can just crash through life and fix everything with a few songs? Life isn't music. This doesn't end well."

"Life," Babieca said, "is absolutely music. I know that, because otherwise, I'm just hearing things. Like a crazy person. I may be drunk, and selfish, and wrong most of the time, but I'm not crazy. Neither are you."

He stared at the horn. Beneath the light of the flames, he

could see every figure carved along its length. The chain, he saw, was broken in half. The links were separated by the line that divided two panels. The space between them was polished to a sheen. A lovely blank that could have been anything. He stared at the strange gutter between panels. It was a chance. A leap in the dark, much like his own. Fortuna watched it as well. In the dimness of the arx, he'd thought that she was looking at the rising smoke, but it was the gap that she stared at. The smooth emptiness where one story ended and another began.

"I have to take this beyond the city," he said. "It can't stay here. But she was thinking ahead. She lit our egress on fire."

"Maybe it's not about the house," Babieca replied.

"What do you mean?"

"We don't know why the alleys work, or why the house works. But maybe it has nothing to do with the mortar and stone, after all. She can burn that down. But she can't burn the place. The magic should still be there."

He watched the house begin to collapse. "You're saying that it still works. All we have to do is walk in there."

"Simple, right? Except for the part where we die."

He looked down and saw that his salamander had returned. He recognized the spots on the creature's back. Like the others, it was watching the blaze.

"That part might be negotiable," he said.

Babieca's expression tightened. "I don't like the sound of that."

He knelt down beside the lizard. "I need a favor. I know I've already asked a lot of your people, but this is just between us. We need to walk into that building. Is there a way that you can—I don't know—bend the fire away from us? Can you tell it not to harm us?"

The salamander looked skeptical.

"I wish there were some way for you to answer back. I guess, though, if I could see you and hear you at the same time, I'd go mad. Not that I don't feel as if I'm going mad already."

"I don't mean to interrupt this conversation with yourself," Babieca said, "but I can hear someone coming. I imagine we don't want to be here when they arrive."

"You can do this," he continued. "I trust you."

He held out his hand.

The lizard sniffed his outstretched palm. For a second, he thought it might bite him again. Instead, it dragged its rough tongue across his skin. The tongue left a dark smudge.

"I think this might work," he said.

"What are you talking about? You haven't done anything."

He took Babieca's hand. "Do you trust me?"

"I trust that the fire will be quick. Unlike whatever Latona has planned." Babieca seemed to notice his arm for the first time. "You're hurt."

"It's only a life-threatening scratch. Are you ready?"

Fortuna had asked the same thing. The pillar of smoke revolved above him. Eyes in the dark, waiting for his next move.

"How are we going to survive this, again?"

"A lizard licked me."

"Oh. Well, that's something."

Hand in hand, they entered the burning house.

Flame had destroyed what little furniture there was. The old tapestries had gone up quickly, and the trestle tables were a pile of kindling. The fresco was obscured by ash, but he knew that the blue mark was there, even if he couldn't see it. The fire was all around him. It whispered in his ears. It was frustrated because it couldn't seem to reach him. The salamander's touch had granted them a kind of immunity, which would not last for long.

This was where his life had changed. He'd been standing right here when the salamander revealed his name. Or perhaps he'd always known it, and the creature's bite had simply reminded him of that old word. Here was where Felix had taken off his mask, where Mardian had shown his scars. Now his epiphany was in flames.

"My toes are getting hot," Babieca said. He was sweating profusely. "That's not a good sign, is it?"

"If you're right about the magic, then you must be able to get us out."

"It's a little hard to concentrate with my boots on fire."

"This is all new to me, but you've been here before. You know how it works."

Babieca looked at him. "I have to think of home."

"I don't know where that is."

"I do."

The singer kissed him. The roof collapsed. For a moment, they were inside a bright disaster, with smoke rushing in through the broken windows.

Then they were in a clearing, with stars above them.

Andrew stepped back. Carl was giving him a funny look. Then his eyes widened.

"Your arm."

He looked down. He was naked, and the claw marks were ragged, as if he'd been mauled by a bear. The pain was extraordinary. But there was also something oddly distant about it. The wound had come from another world. It didn't have quite the same power here. It had already stopped bleeding, for the most part.

Suddenly, he remembered. "The horn! Where is it?"

How could he have been so stupid? Nothing survived the transit: not clothes, not weapons, and certainly not relics. He'd been so intent on dragging the horn away from Anfractus, he'd forgotten that such a thing wasn't possible. But where was it now? Blackening in the heat of the fire? What if it was immune to flame, like the salamanders? He'd simply left it there, a treasure in the ashes.

"Andrew. Look." Carl knelt in the grass and held something up.

It took him a moment to realize what it was. Then Andrew laughed. He laughed so hard that he curled into a ball, trembling.

A piano key.

Carl helped him up. They were both shivering violently.

"I think I hid some clothes around here. Just give me a second."

Andrew stared at the piano key. So relics could survive after all, but not unchanged. This was the aftermath. The horn that summoned the caela was now an ivory to be tickled, just one key that might have belonged to a baby grand.

"Found them!" Carl dragged a sack behind him. "I doubt there's anything fashionable in here, but it'll keep us from freezing to death."

They dressed quickly. Andrew pulled on a worn pair of jeans and some runners that didn't quite fit. When he got to the shirt, he sucked in his breath, trying to get his arm through the sleeve. Carl helped him. The shirt, he realized, was from the university bookstore.

"Plains U Guarantee," he read. "What exactly is that?"

"If you're not satisfied with your courses, they let you take more."

"That sounds like—" He looked up. "*Oh.* Carl? Do you see that?"

"You mean the giant smoke dragon?"

"Uh-huh."

"Unfortunately, yes."

The caela were spreading across the sky, blacking out even the suggestion of dawn. Their eyes gazed impassively at the green cloister of Wascana Park. They didn't seem surprised. For them, perhaps, all worlds were connected. The geese hissed at the smoke, outraged by this intrusion within their territory.

Then he heard growling.

"Maybe it's a dog," Carl whispered.

"You know it's not."

"Couldn't it be, though? Just this once? A nice, fluffy—" His face fell. "Pack of silenoi, heading this way."

He saw them burst from the treeline. And behind them, Latona was riding a metal horse. It was, he realized, the mount that belonged to Queen Elizabeth II.

Andrew stared at the piano key. His only weapon. The

plan had seemed so noble, so excellent, until the point when it had completely stopped making sense. He'd left out several variables with teeth and hooves.

"We don't have a truck this time," Carl said.

"No." He looked at the smoke. "This time, we've got something better."

"Are you shitting me?"

"Just hold on!"

They rode the dragon across Wascana Park. Carl screamed the whole way. Andrew struggled to hold on to the piano key, which might have been the only thing keeping them alive, at this point. Behind them, he caught glimpses of Latona on her shrieking metal horse, following the pack of silenoi. They trampled the manicured gardens and smashed the decorative lights along the footpaths, rendering Wascana Lake a plane of shadow.

Two police cars drove up, sirens flashing. The metal horse reared up and shattered the windshield of the first car. Silenoi encircled the second, and the police officers made frantic motions inside, yelling something into their radio. Andrew thought he should help them, but there wasn't time. Hopefully, the RCMP knew how to deal with monsters.

They flew over the legislature. He heard more sirens in the distance.

"If only we had a mechanical bee," Carl said. He looked green.

"What are you talking about?"

"Oh, right. You don't remember that."

"I really don't. I guess magic cuts both ways."

"Where are we going?"

"To the university. I may have an idea."

"I hope it's a good one. She's going to destroy the city."

He shook his head. "She won't. She'd much rather colonize it."

As they soared over the lake, he noticed a familiar truck barreling across the Albert Street bridge. It was small and indistinct in the dark, but he saw it, all the same. The headlights cut through ragged bits of smoke that were falling from the sky, like unearthly snow. Latona and her pack were close behind. Not for the first time, he wished that the bridge were a bit longer. Just enough to offer a slight delay.

They reached the university. The doors would be locked, but he had the feeling that glass was no impediment to the caela. He pointed the piano key in the direction of the entrance and cried out: "Storm the Innovation Centre!"

As the entrance rushed up to meet them, he thought for a moment that this could be a terrible mistake. It wouldn't be the first misstep of the evening. He grabbed Carl and tried to shield his face. Then they were crashing through the doors. The smoke accrued a wild, impossible pressure, which burst the glass. The eyes and wings carried them forward, through the wreckage and into the silent cafeteria. The pizza parlor was asleep. The vending machines glowed in the half-light, casting their chocolate bar shadows across the tiles.

They hurtled past the bookstore. A student had just emerged from the elevator, wearing House Targaryen pajamas. When he saw the dragon made of cinder and smoke, his eyes grew very wide, and he dropped his phone.

"Go back to the residence!" Carl yelled. "Now isn't a great time for a midnight snack!"

They nearly overshot their destination. When Andrew saw it, he made a desperate motion with the piano key, as if performing a U-turn. The caela wheeled about. Red eyes gazed at him. Carl looked as if he might be sick.

"Upstairs!" Andrew pointed with the key. "That is, if you can—"

Before he could finish the sentence, they were climbing, like a demonic roller coaster. Their mount swirled up the stairs that led to the second floor. When they reached the Department of Music, he cried: "Stop!"

The dragon dumped them on the ground. He landed on top of Carl, which softened the impact somewhat.

"What's the plan here?" His voice was muffled. "Are we going to dazzle Latona with an amateur production of *Rocky Horror*? If so, dibs on Frank."

Andrew got up, trying to ignore the pain in his arm. "Stay here. I saw Shelby's truck, which means that they're not far behind. If this doesn't work, get them out."

"What about you?"

He almost smiled. "I never said the plan was perfect."

"Andrew—I'm sorry."

"There's a pack of silenoi running through Campus West. I think we've moved past the 'I'm sorry' portion of the evening."

"I don't know what Oliver told you, but it wasn't all lies. We had no choice."

"It doesn't matter anymore. Just—try not to get mauled."

He ran down the hallway before Carl could reply. The smoke followed him, clinging to the walls and making his eyes water. He didn't know the Fine Arts floor very well. He was in the business of analyzing verse, not creating music. But he did remember the storage room, where they kept a wealth of instruments. He'd stumbled upon it once, while looking for a fabled "healthy" vending machine that dispensed vegan candy. It was supposed to be on this level, hidden away in some corner. Instead, he'd discovered the pianos.

They were covered in cloth and pushed against the walls. Quickly, he threw off the covers, revealing Steinways and Forsters and even a harpsichord. Smoke poured into the room. He could hear shouting and pounding. There wasn't much time. He chose one of the pianos and ran his fingers lightly along its keys. The middle C was loose. The two keys matched. He grabbed a screwdriver from a plastic bin full of tools and used it to pry off the key. Then he replaced it with the horn key. It was indistinguishable. Just another piece of ivory.

Latona rode into the room. She wore jeans and a university sweatshirt. Her horse left dented prints in the floor. Behind her, the chieftain of the silenoi emerged. His green eyes found Andrew. He may have been smiling, but it was hard to tell.

He heard footsteps on the other side of the room. Carl emerged from the other entrance, followed by Shelby, Ingrid, and Sam. They all froze when they saw Latona with the chieftain. Another silenus appeared, and Carl's expression changed. He seemed to recognize the creature, although Andrew had never seen him before. The smoke hung above them. For the first time, the red eyes were uncertain. They glanced at the pianos, then at Andrew. They couldn't see where the relic had gone.

"You've cornered yourself in a room full of instruments," Latona said. "Splendid plan. Why don't you play us something?"

"I would," Andrew said, "but I can't seem to find my horn."

Her eyes narrowed. "What have you done?"

"It's over. The lares of the air won't serve you. They won't serve anybody."

"Where is it?"

"You're welcome to look for it."

"I'll tear this place apart."

"It doesn't matter. You still won't find it. Besides—I'm sure the people who built this school have connections to the park. You're in their neighborhood now, and they won't be impressed if you burn it to the ground."

She looked around, as if slowly beginning to recognize her surroundings. "There are a million reasons why I left this place. And now you've dragged me back here. I ought to kill you for that indignity."

"You won't."

"Oh?" She glanced at the chieftain. "One word from me, and his pack will slaughter your friends. They'll let you watch. They love that sort of thing."

He struggled to keep his voice steady. "No. You aren't going to hurt them. If you do, I won't be able to help you."

Her expression darkened. "Help me? What do you know about the park? What makes you think that you can fumble and fuck about with my plans? I was on the verge of changing both worlds. This treaty would have altered the whole playing field, and that—" She pointed at the pillar of smoke above him. "Those—whatever you want to call them—were the key."

"Treaties are rarely honored," Shelby said.

"They won't serve you," Andrew repeated, though he wasn't sure if he believed it.

"Cinder and smoke." She shook her head. "More powerful than you could imagine. My mother could never have arranged this meeting. She made sure that the horn stayed buried. I was the one who found it. I was the one who risked my life to form this alliance. You're a nemo. A nobody who's already died once, if I remember correctly. What can you possibly offer?"

"I was sent to kill you."

Maybe it wasn't quite true. Felix had never told him what the knife was for, and now the weapon lay in a bed of cinders. It could have happened, though. Better that she believed it.

She laughed. "You'd be riddled with arrows before you got close."

"I flew into your chamber and stole your weapon. Riddle-free. I rode away on wings of smoke."

She looked slightly less certain. "Who trained you?"

A liar in a mask. A burned spado. A woman with tall hair who keeps disappearing. A lizard that can see the end of everything.

"That's no longer important." He locked eyes with the princeps. "Call them off. Leave my friends alone. Go back to your world, and in return, I'll talk to the lares. They won't follow you blindly. But they will march for you, if you make it worth their while. Even the caela. I can't unsound the note that freed them. Now they're just another dangerous thing. The question is: what will you do with them?"

"Andrew." Shelby was staring at him. "You can't."

They were all he had. These beautiful, lopsided people. He loved them awkwardly, imperfectly. He couldn't imagine a world without them.

He looked steadily at Latona, who was beginning to realize that he meant it.

"There's no other choice," he said.

Latona smiled. "You'll help me forge an army?"

"Yes."

She glanced at his former company. "And what of them? What if they decide to get in our way?"

They will. That's what they do best.

"Fate," he said, "moves as it must."

"So it does." She watched him beneath the red glow of all those eyes. "Not even Fortuna could have seen this coming."

Andrew looked at Shelby and the old harpsichord that stood next to her.

Then he stepped forward and offered his wounded arm to the basilissa.

GLOSSARY OF TERMS

Aditus: An intersecting avenue.

Anfractus: A city controlled by Basilissa Latona.

Artifex: A member of the Gens of Artifices. They build machines, which they can occasionally infuse with life.

Arx: The palace of the basilissa and the seat of the court.

Auditor: A member of the Gens of Auditores. They are able to speak with lares (though they cannot see them).

Baculum: A ceremonial staff carried by some auditores and oculi.

Basia: A brothel that serves a diverse clientele.

Basilissa: A hereditary position and a vestige of the former empire. City-states such as Anfractus and Egressus are governed by a basilissa. The position is matrilineal.

Caelum: A lar whose natural habitat is smoke.

Caupona: An inn that offers food and entertainment.

Chlamys: A ceremonial robe fashioned of leather and worn by the basilissa.

Cloaca: The sewer, which contains a system of tunnels.

Domina/us: A wealthy landowner who administers a large house (domus).

Egressus: A city controlled by Basilissa Pulcheria.

Fortuna: The goddess of chance, whose wheel determines fate.

Fur: A member of the Gens of Furs. They are thieves or peddlers who serve the Fur Queen.

Gens: A guild or "family" of members devoted to a particular mastery. There are six gens devoted to the day (miles, sagittarii, auditores, trovadores, medica, and artifices) and six gens devoted to the night (spadones, meretrices, sicarii, furs, oculi, and silenoi, the last constituting a wild gens).

Gladius: A short sword generally carried by a miles.

Gnomo: A lar whose natural habitat is earth. They are rarely seen.

Hippodrome: A complex that features chariot racing, duels between miles, and performances.

Hypocaust: A furnace designed to heat a domus (larger versions heat public baths).

Impluvium: A basin in a house designed to catch rainwater.

Insula: A block of apartments, often with shops on the ground floor.

Lar: An elemental spirit.

Lararium: A roadside or indoor shrine to lares.

Lupo: A slang term for meretrices, meaning "wolf."

Machina: An automaton built by an artifex.

Medicus: A member of the Gens of Medica. They are surgeons and chemists.

Meretrix: A member of the Gens of Meretrices. They are courtesans and sex workers who offer their services at the basiorum.

Miles: A member of the Gens of Miles. They are soldiers and law keepers who also guard the grounds of the palace.

Nemo: An individual who does not belong to a gens.

Oculus: A member of the Gens of Oculi. They can see lares (though they cannot hear them).

Oscana: The territory covered by Wascana Park.

Pedes: A servant under the protection of a wealthy dominus or domina.

Popina: A street-side bar that offers food.

Sagittarius: A member of the Gens of Sagittarii. They are archers who patrol the battlements of the arx and are considered the first defense against intruders.

Salamander: A lar whose natural habitat is fire. They are generally amenable.

Sicarius: A member of the Gens of Sicarii. They are assassins who sell their services.

Silenus: A satyr (half humanoid, half hircine) who hunts at night. They comprise the Gens of Silenoi, though they do not respect the tradition.

Spado: A member of the Gens of Spadones. They are eunuchs who serve as palace officials in addition to supervising archives and libraries.

Subura: The entertainment district of Anfractus.

Tabularium: A room for storing books and parchments.

Triclinium: A formal dining room, which is named after a style of slanted couch upon which guests can recline while eating.

Trovador: A member of the Gens of Trovadores. They are musicians, entertainers, and poets.

Undina: A lar whose natural habitat is water. They are natural tricksters.

Via: A main road

Vici: A neighborhood.

Learn more about the work of Bailey Cunningham
by visiting his website: cunningbailey.com.